The Forever Sky

The Forever Sky

Montana Gold Series

By
Janalyn Voigt

The Forever Sky
Published by Mountain Brook Ink
White Salmon, WA U.S.A.

The website addresses shown in this book are not intended in any way to be or imply an endorsement on the part of Mountain Brook Ink, nor do we vouch for their content.

This story is a work of fiction. All characters and events are the product of the author's imagination other than those stated in the author notes as based on historical characters. Any other resemblance to any person, living or dead, is coincidental.

Scripture quotations are taken from the King James Version of the Bible. Public domain.

The Author is represented by and this book is published in association with the literary agency of WordServe Literary Group, Ltd, www.wordserveliterary.com.

ISBN 9781-943959-72-3

The Team: Miralee Ferrell, Nikki Wright, Cindy Jackson
Cover Design: Indie Cover Design, Lynnette Bonner Designer

Mountain Brook Ink is an inspirational publisher offering fiction you can believe in.
Printed in the United States of America

Reader Bonuses

Read the stories behind the story, try recipes from the pages of the Montana Gold series, and learn more about the author here: www.janalynvoigt.com/the-forever-sky-readers.

Dedication

This book is dedicated to my son, Jeremy Main.
May you live a full and happy life. Love, Mom

Acknowledgments

I am humbled by the dedication and devotion of the publishing team at Mountain Brook Ink. I am especially grateful to Miralee Ferrell for her excellent editing and guidance during every stage of this book. I appreciate her more than I can say.

My agent, Sarah Joy Freese, was instrumental in landing a contract for this fourth book in the Montana Gold series. I'm thankful for her faith in me.

Nikki Wright, MBI's gifted publicist, has served as a wonderful help and encouragement as I've stepped out in new ways to tell readers about the Montana Gold books.

Those who proofread the manuscript have no doubt saved me from embarrassing myself.

Hats off to Just Read Book Tours for helping me put the word out about this series. Thanks also to the book reviewers and tour hosts who told readers about this book.

My family has, as usual, supported me in many ways while I worked to complete this book. I am grateful.

I must also thank the God who inspired and guided these stories during the writing process. Without His touch, I and they are nothing.

CHAPTER ONE

Liberty, Montana Territory, July 1870

"I SHOULDN'T LINGER, THERE'S SO MUCH to do." Maisey Wilcox sipped the last of her tea but made no move to leave. It was much more pleasant to visit with her friend.

"I'll make another pot of tea." America Hayes smiled, correctly discerning that Maisey wasn't going anywhere.

Maisey knew she ought to go home and bake bread before the day warmed. She should also see to her neglected mending. And she needed to put together lessons for the local tribe's children. They should be ready when the Salish children came to the Indian school on Saturday. Maisey sank against the backrest of her chair. Those tasks could wait a little longer.

War whoops pierced the air outside the open window. Seth and Liam, the Hayes's young boys, were embroiled in imaginary adventures. High-pitched chatter interspersed with giggling drifted in from the parlor. At eight, Maisey's daughter Phoebe was two years older than America's Liberty, but the girls played well together. Phoebe's mischievousness contrasted against Liberty's serious nature sometimes made her seem the younger of the two. Maisey's lips curved in a soft smile. She wouldn't change a thing about her lively, mischievous, adorable daughter.

The door to the hallway opened silently, and a shadow fell across the floorboards. America's husband Shane filled the open doorway. He grinned at Maisey and put a finger to his lips before sneaking up on his wife. America stood unsuspectingly at the counter measuring tea into a blue willow pot. She lifted her head as if she'd heard something. America started to turn just as her husband reached her. Shane slipped his arms around his wife and landed a triumphant kiss on her cheek.

"I'm surprised at you, Reverend Hayes, ambushing an unsuspecting woman." America's dancing eyes belied her protest. Shane pulled her more tightly into his arms.

Glancing away from the loving couple, Maisey tried not to mind that she sat alone at the table. She didn't begrudge Shane and America their happiness, but at times it keenly reminded her of all she'd lost. It had been five years since her husband drowned while fording the Laramie River. The memories of her life with Avery were fading. Maisey sighed. One day she might forget how it felt to be cherished by a man who adored her.

"'Tis a fair day, and no mistake." Shane caught hold of his wife's hand and twirled her gently about. "What do you say to a picnic, Mrs. Hayes?"

America fetched against him, laughing breathlessly. "It's cheating to use your Irish charm against me. You're after fried chicken and apple pie, no doubt."

"How you wrong me. It's the cook I want, and I'll eat beans to prove it." His hands slid to her thickened waist. "Come away into the sunshine. We can't have you working too hard with a new babe on the way."

America's face blushed pink. "All right, you rogue. Only take your distracting self out of here or I'll never get ready."

He gave her a peck on the lips. "The children will be pleased."

Maisey stood. "I should be going." They wouldn't want

her and Phoebe underfoot while they prepared for their picnic.

"There's no need." Shane glanced back from the doorway. "You and Phoebe are welcome to join us."

America's eyes lit. "Yes, please do."

"I'd like to go." Maisey hesitated. She would rather return home to lament her losses in private, but that wouldn't be fair to her daughter.

"Good." Shane bestowed a beatific smile on Maisey. "Then it's all settled."

"Don't rush the woman, Shane." America frowned at her husband but chided him in a gentle voice. She poured hot water from the cast iron kettle into the teapot. "You will come, won't you, Maisey? It won't be as much fun without you."

Maisey's reluctance melted in the warmth of America's sincere invitation. "All right."

"I'm glad you can come." America beamed.

"I'll let the children know." Shane sauntered from the room.

"What shall I bring?" Maisey frowned in concentration, trying to picture the contents of her larder. The shelves were sparse at the moment. She needed to take a trip to town for supplies before she did the week's baking.

"Not a thing. There's enough food left over from yesterday to feed five families."

Maisey knew that members of the congregation often gave food left over from the potluck after Sunday meeting to the preacher's family. "I'd still like to contribute something."

"You can if you'd like." America carried the tea tray to the table.

"You should have let me lift that."

America's lips tightened into a firm smile. "I'm capable of carrying a tray of tea. Speaking of which, would you like some more?"

"Maybe a drop." Maisey picked up her cup after America filled it. "I know what I can add to the picnic. I saved part of the saltwater taffy Emma gave me for my birthday. Shall I bring it for a treat?" The other schoolteacher had warmed a wintry day by leaving the small gift in the desk she and Maisey traded off using in the schoolroom.

"The children would love that, I'm sure. Only, don't let on or they won't eat anything else." America's forehead puckered. "I have half a mind to invite Emma. Do you think she's up to it?"

"Not really." Maisey shook her head. "That was a nasty cold that she caught. I took over a pot of soup for her last night. Emma's color looked better, but it's clear that she needs rest."

"I'm glad she's on the mend."

"I should look in on her before we leave." Maisey found her tea at the perfect temperature for warming her stomach without scalding her mouth.

"That would ease my mind. I'll ask Shane to let the neighbors know we'll be away from home. I doubt we'll go very far, but I'd feel better knowing the Buckthorns are looking out for Emma."

America poured tea into her own cup but didn't sit down again. She stood on tiptoe below the shelves lining the wall and reached upward. Her fingers brushed the wicker picnic basket above her but failed to dislodge it. The basket wobbled and seemed ready to fall, but then settled into place once more.

"You shouldn't be doing that." Maisey pushed back her chair. "Let me try."

America shifted out of the way. "I almost reached it."

Maisey stood on tiptoe and retrieved the basket easily.

"I'd like to know how you did that." America glared at

her, but a smile settled on her lips.

Maisey laughed. "Don't blame me because God made me taller than you. I'd better go get that taffy. Is there anything else I can fetch for you before I leave?"

"I'll manage, thanks." America spoke with quiet dignity.

Maisey pulled the back door shut behind her. After long months spent enduring the cold of winter, the sunshine that bathed the path felt like a touch from heaven. A few tattered clouds scurried across the pale sky, and the wind searched her face. Bitterroot flowers threaded the grass, their purple faces gay. Maisey rounded a corner of the barn but stopped short as the clopping of hooves reached her. She backed into the shadow beside the building. Traffic on the road beyond wasn't unusual, but using caution never hurt.

A man on horseback turned into the barnyard. The sunlight picked out features Maisey knew all too well. Rob Walsh sat tall in the saddle and held himself with an air of confidence he'd once lacked.

Maisey swallowed against the lump that formed in her throat as tears pricked her eyes. She drew a shaky breath. She had known this moment would come when she'd decided to stay on in Liberty. That didn't make it any easier to bear, however. She hadn't seen Rob Walsh since he'd left her with a kiss on her lips three years ago. She'd convinced herself that their futures lay apart, but she couldn't stop herself from yearning for the impossible.

It wasn't fair that the old feelings should come rushing back simply from the sight of him. The sun picked out the ginger hair below Rob's hat, his clean jawline, and the blue of his eyes. He didn't appear to have seen her. The shade must be hiding her from view. If she stood quite still and made no sound, he might not notice her at all. Should she speak or risk being caught out by him?

If only she'd started for home a little earlier or waited longer to leave, she wouldn't be in this situation. Maybe she should wait for him to go into the barn, and then cut behind the building. She could go home by the roundabout route through the stand of cottonwoods between the Hayes's house and the schoolteachers' cabins.

Running away, while tempting, didn't sit well with her. What if Rob spotted her through one of the barn windows? She would hate for him to see her slinking off like a coward when she wasn't one.

Maisey stepped out of the shadow beside the barn and into the sunlight. She knew when he saw her by the stiffening of his spine.

She lifted her chin. "Hello, Rob."

Rob tensed at the sound of Maisey's voice, his gut twisting. He reined in his horse. Questions reeled through his mind. Why was Maisey still living on his cousin Shane's land after saying she was moving away? What had caused her to stay? Why had he ever let her go?

The years since he'd last seen her had treated Maisey well. Her brown eyes lacked the haunted look they'd held so often before. She wore a dress of gold calico and a shawl woven in brown hues. Her chestnut hair swept from her forehead in gleaming wings and was caught somehow behind her head. Despite her simple clothing and plain hairstyle, desire kicked through Rob like a stubborn mule that refused to be tamed. The impulse to leap from his horse, pull her into his arms, and kiss away the pucker between her brows took his breath away.

He tipped his hat instead. "Good morning, Maisey."

"You've come back." She curved her lips into a smile that didn't include her eyes. Those remained wary.

Rob couldn't blame her. Perhaps she wondered, as he did, how they would make it through this encounter. A sudden urge to shelter her swarmed over him. "Only for a little while." Perhaps knowing she wouldn't have to endure his nearness very long would comfort her.

"Oh." Her smile faltered. "I hear you've made your fortune in gold."

"I've done well for myself, but it's time for a new adventure."

Surprise swept across her face, but she frowned and gave no reply. Rob suspected her silence was not for a lack of opinions. She must feel she no longer had the right to speak. He dismounted to hide his confusion and give himself time to think. Had she believed he would continue to mine his brother's claim and never strike out on his own? Surely, she knew him better than that. But then, he shouldn't expect her to understand his reasoning any more than he did himself.

She'd been right to accuse him of pretending they were family when it wasn't true. He hadn't been willing to settle down back then. Hurting Maisey and disappointing Phoebe still haunted him. He'd wanted to offer the woman he married more of a life than he could afford. Asking Maisey to wait for him when he didn't know whether he would succeed had been out of the question. Now that he could properly care for a wife and Maisey was standing before him, she seemed to want nothing to do with him. Judging by the scowl on her face, she would roundly reject any overture he made.

Rob's horse stomped and snorted, making it plain that stopping short of the barn was less than satisfactory. Maisey stood poised, as if ready to flee. For his part, Rob would like to end this painful meeting. He should go into the barn and put them all out of their misery. "Why didn't you leave Liberty township?" Rob asked the question against his better judgment. He didn't want to wonder, ever after, what she might have said.

Her face lit. "Some of the Salish parents asked me to continue teaching their children. I couldn't refuse."

"Of course not." He'd been a fool to hope that she'd waited for his return without him asking her to do so. Their bridges were most thoroughly burned. All that remained was for him to accept that fact.

Rob revised his decision to visit Shane and America for several weeks. He would spend the night, and in the morning remove himself to his brother's ranch. Situated a day's hard ride to the south, it bordered the Bitterroot River with the mountains beyond. He'd wanted to purchase a spread of his own nearby, and then search for Maisey. Those plans might need to change, although it broke his heart to contemplate the idea. While staying at his cousin Shane's house, avoiding Maisey seemed best. The uneasy expression on her face betrayed her discomfort at being near him. Rob touched the brim of his hat. "Don't let me keep you."

She flinched, ever so slightly.

Rob frowned. Maybe he shouldn't have dismissed her like that. He always seemed to wound Maisey while trying to spare her. It was too late to fix his gaffe, even if he knew how. He strode to the barn but paused with his hand on the door.

Maisey was walking down the path toward the schoolhouse and the cabins that housed the teachers. She never looked back. Otherwise, she'd have caught him watching her. Rob didn't care if she did. This might be his last sight of the woman he loved, and he wanted to commit it to memory.

Maisey shut the door rather firmly behind her. She cast herself into the wingback chair by the fire, her mind racing. It would be impossible to cope with the picnic if Rob came along, and he probably would. Shane and America were bound to invite him. What could she do but go anyway? Shane had already told Phoebe, and Maisey couldn't disappoint her child. That held true in another matter as well. Phoebe had been down with measles and unable to say goodbye to Rob before he'd ridden away. She'd asked about him ever since. Phoebe had made Rob into something of a father figure, and Maisey couldn't deprive her of the chance to finally say goodbye. Maisey pressed a hand to her temple, where a headache throbbed. She would manage to survive the outing somehow, for Phoebe's sake.

Even in the sanctuary of her home, Rob's presence surrounded Maisey. He'd helped Shane build her cabin. Maisey had looked forward to Rob's reports on their progress for more than one reason. After she'd moved into the finished cabin, Rob had continued to spend a lot of time under its roof.

Maisey could picture him sitting in the chair he favored, across from her in the front room. He'd enjoyed entertaining Phoebe with songs and stories. The three of them had shared many suppers and much laughter around the oak table. She could remember too, Rob kissing her in the kitchen before riding out of her life.

Maybe she should send Phoebe on the picnic without her. The idea held merit. If Maisey explained that she had a headache, it wouldn't even be lying.

Maisey sagged in her chair. She couldn't do it. Even if Shane and America didn't mind, Phoebe might. Liberty would have her brothers and parents near on the outing, but Phoebe would be without a family. Maisey refused to let that happen. She worked hard and sacrificed as a widowed parent to give Phoebe all she needed. She wasn't about to sell her daughter short in order to spare herself discomfort.

Maisey rose from her chair reluctantly. In the kitchen, she climbed on a stool and retrieved the box of saltwater taffy from the shelf where she'd hidden it, away from Phoebe's notice. She snatched up an old quilt to sit on with Phoebe, then hurried toward the door to let herself out. She would check on Emma, who was confined to her cabin by sickness, but knock lightly to avoid disturbing the other teacher if she was asleep.

Maisey's cabin door burst open from the outside before she reached it. A tall Indian Maisey unfortunately recognized loomed in the doorway, his dark eyes fixed on her. Fur wraps secured Spukani's long braids. Round shells hung from his ear lobes and laddered in ropes across his chest. Behind him stood two other Indians in similar garb. One gazed at her from bright eyes above a long nose. The other wore twin braids on either side of his fleshy face.

Maisey gasped, but after the initial shock of being intruded upon, held her ground. The absence of war paint on their faces would have sparked hope within her, except for the scowl on the leader's face. Maisey braced herself to confront him. "Spukani, why have you come?" After failing to steal Phoebe, he'd stayed away for years. Maisey had let herself believe he'd given up on punishing her for his daughter's death from measles while under her care. What purpose had returned him to Maisey's cabin?

Spukani thrust out his chin. "You come with us, Teacher."

Maisey hauled in a breath. "I can't today." He was only asking, not forcing her to go. She found the distinction hard to remember while pinned under his glare. If she didn't come up with a reason for not accompanying him, he might insist. "The other teacher is sick and needs my help." She rushed out the words, then realized her mistake. Spukani would not want to picture her caring for a sick person, as she had his daughter. Maisey deeply regretted his daughter's death. It had not been her fault, no matter what he believed.

The cords of Spukani's neck stood out, and his face splotched with red. "You bad medicine!" he asserted so forcefully that his spittle flew. He tensed, as if ready to reach for her.

Maisey's thoughts raced. "I must tell the preacher and his wife where I'm going."

His nostrils flared. "You come!"

Against the force of his anger, Maisey felt like a small leaf blasted by an angry gale. "They will want to know where to find me."

He blinked, clearly taken aback by the calm tone she'd mustered. "The new chief asks for you."

"I have heard of Chief Charlo." Maisey paused for effect, all the while quaking inside. "I understand that he seeks peace, like his father before him."

Spukani gritted his teeth but did not speak. He stepped back from the doorway. Behind him, a breeze rattled the cottonwoods above a group of ponies, their manes tied with feathers.

With a glittering glance, Spukani turned away from Maisey. "Bring her."

CHAPTER TWO

EMMA'S NIGHTMARE FADED INTO THE MIST-shrouded landscape between wakefulness and sleep. Her aching body and the pain in her chest from coughing brought her fully awake. She opened her eyes, but winced at the brightness that met them. She'd forgotten to close the bedroom curtains, and light slanted through the panes in fitful bursts. Clouds scuttled across the sky, like rafts caught by a strong current. Even so, only a faint breeze stirred the trees in the wildlands beyond the window.

Emma shifted, ready to rise, but subsided at once. She would have to wait until she gathered more strength for the attempt. Emma pressed one hand to her forehead. She found it clammy, an indication that she had a fever. Her dry throat was another sign. Swallowing provided little relief, and at last the need for water drove Emma to her feet. She steadied herself with a hand to the wall. The water bucket gleamed on the kitchen counter, but it might as well be miles rather than feet away. Determination carried her forward. The dipper shook in her hand, spattering droplets to darken the floorboards. Emma gulped the tepid water and lowered the ladle for more. Her thirst slaked at last, she sagged against the counter and wished for the energy to stay out of bed.

Maybe tomorrow.

Emma knew she ought to eat something, and Maisey's dried-apple pie waited on the counter mere inches away. *No.* Lying down seemed more appealing. She turned to go back to bed.

The stamp of a hoof carried to her from outside the cabin. A flicker of movement beyond the kitchen window caught her side vision.

What was going on?

Emma peered out the window. She sucked in a breath.

A group of Indians stood on Maisey's porch.

Emma fought the urge to panic. There might be good reason for what she saw. Maisey did teach the Salish children, after all. If only Emma wasn't so feverish, she might think of a reason the Indians would disturb Maisey at home.

A tall Indian backed away from the open cabin door while the others pushed forward. A cry, quickly cut off, shattered the peace. A moment later, the Indians pulled Maisey through the doorway. A bright bandana covered her mouth.

Emma clutched her throat, where her pulse beat rapidly.

The tall Indian grabbed Maisey by the upper arms and dragged her down the steps.

Emma cast a glance at her Pa's rifle, supported by pegs above her door. She wasn't certain she had the strength to take the rifle down, let alone shoot it. She had to try. Emma lurched toward the weapon, but dizziness swarmed over her. She caught the back of a chair and closed her eyes until the world stopped spinning.

Please, God, help me. I can't let Maisey down.

Emma's head cleared. She let go of the chair and propelled herself to the door. Her heart thumped as she lowered the firearm. If she was too weak to fire, Maisey's kidnappers might take her too.

Emma scolded herself. Letting fear stop her was no way to live. She jerked the door open and stepped onto her porch. Maisey was seated on the back of a pony, flanked by captors. The band of Indians slipped into tree shadows on the path to the road and carried Maisey out of sight.

Emma blinked at tears. *I'm too late.* Her knees went weak, and she gripped the porch rail. After a moment, she lowered herself down the porch steps. Somewhat restored by the fresh air, she covered the small distance to the Hayes house more easily. Emma climbed the back steps and raised her fist to the door, which quivered beneath her assault. "America? It's me, Emma!" Giving up on waiting for an answer, she turned the handle and hurtled inside.

Strong arms caught her in a firm grip. "Woah, there! Where's the fire?"

Emma, rendered speechless, gazed into Rob Walsh's blue eyes. It had been years since she'd set eyes on this man. He'd broken her heart when he went away, but she'd kept that secret for the sake of her pride.

"Hello, Miss Duncan." Rob smiled. He tilted his head questioningly. "Where were you going in such a rush?"

Emma started. How could she have forgotten her errand? "It's Maisey! The Indians took her." She didn't know what was responsible for her shaking—the fever, reaction to Maisey's capture, or the shock of seeing Rob again.

He gripped her arms. "When did this happen?"

"I came right after it happened. Fever slowed me down a bit, but it's probably only fifteen minutes since they took her. Please, you're hurting my arm."

"Stop manhandling the teacher, Rob, and let her come inside." Shane spoke from behind him.

"Sorry." Rob released her and backed out of the doorway.

Emma followed him into the kitchen.

Shane came forward, frowning. "What did you say is wrong?"

"A band of Indians rode off with Maisey." Emma swayed

on her feet.

"You look ready to drop. Let's sit you down." Shane guided Emma to a chair. "Now tell us exactly what you saw."

"Drink this first." America interposed herself in front of Shane. She gave Emma a glass of water and touched her forehead. "You're burning up."

"Sorry to bring my sickness into your house." Emma gulped the cooling liquid.

"Never mind about that." America studied her gravely. "You need looking after."

"In a moment, if you don't mind." Shane gently shifted his wife aside. "Miss Duncan, do you have any idea which tribe Maisey's abductors belong to?"

Emma cast backward in memory. "The markings on the horses and clothing looked familiar. I think they were Salish."

Shane glanced at Rob. "We'd better follow them right away."

"My thought exactly." Rob strode to the back doorway, where he took his hat down from the rack beside it.

Shane returned his attention to Emma. "Any idea which way they went?"

Emma thought hard but had to shake her head. "They took the path toward the road. That's all I know."

"Which way did they turn?" Rob came back to her.

"I can't see that far from my cabin." Emma's voice shook, and she felt perilously close to tears.

"Stop badgering the poor woman," America protested. "Can't you tell that she's muddled from fever?"

Shane's hand came down on Rob's shoulder. "Stand back, Cousin. She's told us all she can."

Rob contented himself with pacing at the edges of the room while Shane threw together supplies for their trip.

America looked after Emma. Rob could barely tolerate the delay. Every minute they waited, Maisey moved farther from him. He couldn't imagine what she was going through. He fisted his hands. It was too cruel for her to suffer as an Indian captive a second time. The memory of her sorrow after she and Bry had escaped the Cheyenne returned to haunt him. Maisey's husband had died in that raid. The depth of her mourning had made Rob wonder if she would ever recover.

He took a step toward Shane, intent on helping so they could hit the road sooner. The door from the hallway burst open, and Phoebe Wilcox swept into the kitchen. Excitement radiated from her slight frame. She'd grown taller since he'd last seen her, but her blond hair swept into the same ringlets as before. Her face lit. "I thought I heard you, Papa Bear, but I couldn't believe it."

"I'm really here, Goldilocks." Rob smiled, The silly pet names they'd given one another in a lighthearted moment returned him to a long-ago game of tag with this golden-haired child. Phoebe's delighted screams might thrum his ear drum, but that was all part of the experience. Maisey would look on, and her eyes warmed whenever his gaze touched hers.

Rob held out his arms to Phoebe, and she plowed into him. He caught her up, and for a blissful moment breathed in the scent of lavender in her hair.

"I hate to interrupt such a sweet reunion, but we should ride out." Shane stepped into Rob's line of sight.

Rob held Phoebe at arm's length. "I'm sorry, darling, but I have to go."

"No! You can't leave me again." Phoebe's eyes shone with tears.

Rob swallowed hard. He hadn't seen until now how deeply his going away had affected her. When he'd stopped by to say goodbye, she'd been both feverish and sleeping. He could comfort her in this moment, however, if he could only find the words.

He hauled in a breath. "I plan to come back this time." The reckless promise slipped out against his better judgment. He'd decided to move on, hadn't he? He should help rescue Maisey, then keep going until he reached his brother's ranch. And yet, he couldn't forsake Phoebe. He'd known for a while that he needed to mend fences with his brother, Con. The stricken look on Phoebe's face revealed that he had more of them to repair than he'd realized.

"Wait and talk to Ma before you go." Her voice rose on a note of panic.

Rob glanced at Shane questioningly and received a nod. Rob took Phoebe by the shoulders. "I have to help your ma."

Phoebe shook her head. "You won't help her by leaving. She'll want you to stay. I'm sure of it. Ma cried hard when you went away."

"It grieves me to hear that." Rob gazed into her frightened eyes. "I have to help your ma come home."

Phoebe's forehead puckered. "But she's already at our cabin."

"No, Phoebe, she's not."

Her eyes widened. "Where's my ma?"

Rob swallowed an acid taste. "She went on a trip with some of the Indians."

"But, we were about to go on a picnic—" Understanding dawned on her face. "They stole her, didn't they?"

He could barely answer past the lump in his throat. "I'm sorry, Phoebe."

"*Please…*" She gripped his arms. "You have to bring Ma back."

Rob kissed her forehead. "That's what we aim to do."

Shane's wool jacket scratched against America's cheek, but she didn't pull away. The sweetness of hay mingling in the air with musty barn odors would forever recall saying goodbye to her husband. Shane traveled from home more than either of them would like, but such were a preacher's duties. A hoof thudded and a bridle jingled, reminders of how fleeting their embrace must be. If only she could hold on longer, but it was already time to step away. She released her husband with the full knowledge that he was about to ride into danger. He had done so before and no doubt would again. Only through her faith in God could she withstand her fears.

"Pray that the Lord keeps us both while we're apart." Shane swept her into his arms for a long kiss. He let go before she could blink away her tears.

America never grew used to parting from her husband, and she didn't like it this time any better than the last. She normally weathered their separations with more grace, but this time felt different. Being with child made her more sensitive, but this seemed more than emotion. "Be careful!" she burst out, ignoring her own desire to keep their parting harmonious. "I wish you'd wait for the men Mr. Buckthorn is rounding up."

Shane shook his head. "That would take too long. Silas is a good man, mind you, but too meticulous for such a task. The tracks will go cold before he is ready to depart."

"But you and Rob shouldn't go after Maisey alone." America hated the pleading note in her voice.

Shane gave her a direct look. "What choice do we have?"

America subsided. What was the point in objecting? She knew the hard-headed man she'd married and his rash cousin well. She would never persuade either of them to err on the side of caution. Much as she hated to admit it, Shane was probably right.

Shane kissed her forehead. "Don't frown so, my love, or I can never leave you."

America summoned the words he needed to hear. "You must, for Maisey's sake."

He gave a swift nod. "And also for Phoebe."

"Yes."

Phoebe had positioned herself in the chair beside Liberty's bedroom window, poised as if watching for her mother to return at any moment.

Shane gazed at America with love shining from his blue eyes. "I must trust God to look after you."

"And I, you." Her voice caught, and she looked away to hide fresh tears.

Shane gathered his children. He rumpled Seth and Liam's hair and caressed Liberty's cheek. "Be good for your mother." He swung into the saddle and took up the reins. After a final glance at his family, he joined Rob, waiting outside the open barn door with an impatient look on his face. The two men turned their horses toward the road.

America rushed to the doorway and watched her husband ride away. She heaved a sigh and brushed away her tears, then instructed her children to go inside. Household duties waited for no one. It was time to start supper.

She took two-year-old Liam's hand and let him toddle beside her. Seth ran ahead, but Liberty held back. She clasped America's free hand and tilted her face upward, sending golden waves cascading down her back. America noted absently that her daughter was growing into a beauty. "Don't be sad, Ma." Liberty's deep blue eyes, so like her father's, lit. "I can do Da's chores."

America smiled. She doubted a child of six could manage everything Shane did, but Liberty's intention could not be faulted. "Thank you for your willingness to help. Of course, it wouldn't be fair to leave everything to you with Phoebe as our guest. She looks to you for company."

"She seems so sad." Liberty's forehead furrowed. "Is her ma going to be all right?"

"I hope so, darling. Meanwhile, we must be especially kind to Phoebe."

Liberty fell silent, but tugged America's hand before they went inside their house. "How long will Da stay away this time?"

America sighed. Past experience had taught her that Liberty would repeat this question daily. She rarely could answer it with any precision, and especially not today. "As long as God allows."

Maisey kept her pony in line with her captors, certain any attempt to break away would not fare well. She had ridden with Indians against her wishes once before when she'd been carried off after witnessing Avery's murder. She would rather not revive that memory, and yet it traveled within her. With every jostling step, her pony carried her back to the terrible time after Avery's death. Blinded by grief for her husband, she was unable to do more than cling to the saddle and weep. Captivity had almost broken her spirit.

Today she possessed more grit. Maisey straightened her spine and let indignation sharpen her mind. That she should be kidnapped again felt an unbearable insult. She would call upon her rightful anger to strengthen her until this ordeal was over.

That it would not come to an end was something she refused to imagine. Rescuers would ride out from Liberty township, at the very least. If soldiers came, it would take longer, but eventually she would return home to Phoebe.

Their journey north seemed to go on endlessly. Maisey was unused to riding and ached to stretch her cramped legs. At last they stopped in a glade beside the river. Rapids ran here, but rocks trapped water into placid pools by the banks. Maisey dismounted with the others, emboldened when no one noticed her. Her hands were tied in front of her and a bandana gagged her mouth, but her unbound feet allowed her to move about.

Spukani stood on the bank, watching the horses drink. He was speaking with a hook-nosed Indian who wore a quill vest. Eager to avoid contact with the pair, Maisey led her pony to water a short way downstream. The two men's voices followed her. They spoke in their native tongue, a language she could decipher fairly well after years of working with a translator from the tribe. She'd made the effort in order to teach her students in their own dialect, never realizing that she would one day need to follow it for her own sake.

"I don't understand why Chief Charlo sent for her." The hook-nosed Indian tossed a stone, which plopped into the pool at his feet and radiated circles across the quiet surface of a shallow pool.

Spukani shrugged. "I don't know his reason, Little Elk, or why he chose me to bring her."

"Maybe he guessed that you would not let her escape, after what happened to Rain."

"She is bad medicine." Spukani's glittering gaze searched her out.

Maisey glanced away quickly. If Spukani didn't already know how well she grasped his language, she didn't want her reaction to inform him.

"It doesn't make sense that he would want us to bring her to him." Little Elk's voice followed Maisey downstream, where she plucked at a huckleberry bush to ease her thirst. Her throat felt dry, even after swallowing cooling handfuls from one of the pools. While her pony grazed the bank, Maisey clawed the gag from her mouth with her hands bound before her. She moistened her mouth with the deep blue berries. She could hear only snatches of the conversation between Spukani and Little Elk. That might be best, given Spukani's fondness for spewing vile remarks about her. She noticed some of the tribesmen gnawing on jerky, but none was offered to her. Maisey doubted she could eat anyway. Solid food would probably gag her, then afterwards form a lump in her stomach.

The sun shone high in the sky, radiating heat, but the swishing of the river through stones brought an illusion of coolness. She squatted at the edge of the bank and bathed her face and neck. A shadow fell over Maisey, and she looked over her shoulder. She gasped and rose quickly.

Spukani towered over her. "You come." He pointed to her pony wandering nearby, then turned away.

"Wait!" Maisey called after him.

Spukani stopped and pierced her with his glare. "What do you wish to say?"

"Why are you taking me to Chief Charlo against my will?" Maisey tensed her jaw. "Explain this to me."

Spukani glared at her. "You have no right to ask and no need to know."

"Don't talk to me in that manner," Maisey snapped. Cords in his neck stood out, and she wondered if she'd gone too far.

He smirked. "I should cover your mouth again."

Maisey pulled in a sharp breath. "Mistreat me, and you

will suffer. My people will come after me, you can count on it. They'll send soldiers too." She'd exaggerated the threat, but he couldn't know that. Rescuers from Liberty township would ride out right away, but someone would have to carry word to Fort Benton. If no other duties engaged them, the soldiers might decide to search for her. However, they wouldn't arrive for weeks.

"Let them." He lifted his head higher. "I am not afraid."

"Your words are not wise." Spukani, like others within his tribe, did not understand how vastly the soldiers and settlers outnumbered them.

He cut his hand sideways through the air. "Speak no more."

Maisey held her tongue. A man could be driven past control, and Spukani had a hair-trigger. The bitterness that darkened his mind made trying to reason with him a waste of breath. He would not listen to her now any more than when she'd explained that his daughter Rain had died despite her care, not because of it.

Maisey left off trying to figure out Spukani's motives. That task was far too difficult and might even be impossible. She started toward her pony, but the creature shied away.

"You come!" Spukani spat. A glance behind her revealed that he and the others were climbing onto their horses. They might have little patience for her, or else view her struggle as amusing.

Maisey crept toward her pony, whispering comforts. Ears twitching, the creature watched her with a dark eye. As she neared, it shied and retreated.

Maisey resigned herself to a hard journey.

CHAPTER THREE

AMERICA PAUSED WITH HER HANDS IN the bread dough and glanced out the kitchen window. She'd opened it upon rising to let in the coolness before the day's heat. A sky touched by gold and primrose glowed above the outlines of trees. Morning would harden into full day eventually, but right now the landscape was soft at the edges. It almost seemed to America that she could listen closely and hear angels sing.

She smiled at her fanciful thoughts and went back to kneading. The children would clamor for their breakfast before long. She swayed at the rhythmic task, and strands of hair fell into her eyes. Blowing at them didn't help. It never failed. She always needed the use of her hands when they were covered in flour.

Early in their marriage, Shane had embraced her from behind while she was doing the kneading. Unused to his ambushes, she'd started and spun around to face him, showering them both with flour. He'd kissed her so thoroughly she'd forgotten all about the bread. The memory still brought a smile. Where was her husband right now? She wished she knew. It wasn't hard to guess that he and Rob were on the trail, unless they'd already caught up to Maisey and those who had taken her. When that event arrived, and she had no doubt it would, she hoped that the trust Shane had built with the local tribe would weigh in their favor.

America formed the dough into loaves and set them to rise in the warming oven. Giving attention to the morning meal, she carved slices of bacon from the slab in the larder, then reached for a mixing bowl. The children would delight in warm flapjacks drizzled with molasses. She saved this recipe to make for a special treat, and today they all needed a lift.

Voices, the jingle of tack, and the thump of hooves sounded outside the window. America looked out and stopped stirring. A dozen or so men rode past on the way from the Buckthorn property to the road. *Finally!* Silas Buckthorn's group was riding out to search for Maisey.

America hurried out the back door and ran onto the path in time to see the last of the riders vanish around the barn. Running while pregnant was not easy, and she rounded the corner breathing deeply. America braced herself against the side of the barn until the stitch in her side let up. By the time she reached the road, dust was hovering in the air. The riders were gone.

Speed their journey, please God, and bring everyone safely home again.

America started toward home more slowly than she'd left it. Emma approached on the path, looking pale and shaky. America quickened her step. "Goodness! What are you doing out of bed?"

"I heard the horses." Emma craned to look past her. "Was that Mr. Buckthorn and those riding with him on the way to search for Maisey?"

America nodded. "May God watch over them."

"I'm sure He will." Emma patted her disheveled hair but failed to tidy it. "I should have better attended my grooming, but I was in a rush."

"You look fine but too pale. Won't you come in? I'll give you a cup of tea, and I'm about to fix flapjacks."

"I wish I could." Emma held back. "I might still be

contagious, but thanks all the same."

"Shall I bring over a plate for you?"

Emma's face lit. "I'd welcome that, thank you. I've reached the stage where I'm hungry but too tired to prepare food."

America gave a swift nod, then smiled. "I'm glad you're showing signs of improvement."

"Me too." Emma grinned. "I haven't been that sick in quite a while."

"Good morning, ladies!" Gideon Buckthorn strode toward them. A handsome young man with soulful dark eyes and black hair, he wasn't much older than Emma's eighteen years.

"Hello, Gideon. I thought you'd ridden out with the men." America regretted her remark at once. Gideon Buckthorn was at such a tender age.

Gideon's face went red. "I stayed behind for an important reason."

"I never doubted that." America assured him, doing her best to repair any damage from her thoughtless remark.

"Pa wanted me to look after Ma and my younger brothers while he's gone."

"He placed a lot of trust in you." America listened for her children. All the commotion, and then voices outside the house would likely wake them.

"Ma sent me to find out how you are doing." Gideon glanced at them both, but his gaze lingered on Emma. He returned his attention to America. "Do you need anything?"

"Why thank you for being so neighborly." America hid her amusement. Gideon's preference for the young school teacher could not be more evident, but Emma gave every appearance of being oblivious to his interest. "I don't need anything."

"Be sure to let me know when you do." Gideon turned to Emma. "What about you? Ma said to look after you especially, since you're so sick."

Emma's cheeks pinkened. "You must express my gratitude to your mother for her kindness in sending you."

America had noticed that Emma resorted to a kind of forced formality in awkward situations. The result was strange and unnatural, coming from such a vivacious person.

Gideon's forehead puckered, and she thought he looked puzzled. "Can I do anything to help while you recover?"

"I'll be fine, thanks." Emma answered with predictable independence. It was her defining quality, but one America wished she would reconsider.

"I'd feel better if you'd see Emma to her cabin." America spoke quickly, before Emma could refuse. Especially after what had happened to Maisey, she didn't like Emma living alone at the edge of town in a cabin separated from view by a stand of cottonwood trees. She would rather have Emma stay with her until Maisey returned. It was doubtful, however, that the young schoolteacher would accept an invitation until the risk of infecting the children passed.

"I'd be happy to walk you home." Gideon offered his arm to Emma in a formal gesture that was as out of place as it was adorable. "If I may say so without offense, you look like a stiff wind would blow you down."

Emma frowned, but then smiled. "Well, if you can spare the time—"

"It's no trouble, I promise." They moved off together, but their voices carried to America. "It bothers me to think you have no one to look after you."

"That's not quite true. Mrs. Hayes is an angel."

Gideon's head bent toward hers. "What if those Indians come back?"

"I have my Pa's rifle to protect me, should I need it."

America returned home with a lighter step. She wouldn't worry quite so much about Emma with Gideon watching out for her.

Birds chattered in the trees and sunrise tinted the sky as Emma walked beside Gideon on the path toward her cabin. On such a fine morning, troubles seemed distant. Even the awful sickness that gripped her seemed to loosen its hold. She found that it ebbed and flowed as her body struggled to cast it off.

"A sweet girl like you shouldn't need to use a rifle." Gideon had been sunk in thought but roused and spoke beside her.

Emma smiled. "You've never met my pa."

"That's true." He sent her a sideways glance, as if aware that he trod on dangerous ground.

"He made sure I knew how to defend myself, if called upon."

"That's a mite"–Gideon fell silent several minutes–"careful of him."

"Living in the West requires caution." She huffed a little, weary from matching her stride to his.

He frowned. "Am I going too fast?"

She smiled as gratitude flooded her. "Could we slow down a little?"

"Of course." He shortened his stride. "Sorry about that. I'm used to covering ground while working outdoors."

Emma had often seen him out and about on the Buckthorn property. "Have you always farmed?"

"Pretty much. We owned a farm in Michigan before heading West." Gideon's expression grew remote, as if he was thinking about his former home.

"Is that where you were born?"

"I was indeed." He glanced at her. "How about you? From what you said, it sounded like you grew up in the West."

"Yes, at Fort Laramie. Pa served as an officer at the fort until his death."

"I'm sorry you lost your father."

"That was over three years ago, but I still miss him, and Ma too." She blinked away tears, fighting for composure. It had been months since she'd cried over Pa, but being sick made her miss both her parents more.

"Careful there." Gideon pointed out a tree root that lay across the path. "What brought you to Liberty?"

"It was a chance to start over somewhere else." The invitation to teach had seemed a godsend at the time. And now, years later, Emma couldn't deny its fortuity. Upon arriving in Liberty, she'd promptly withdrawn. It had taken time and the encouragement of others to help her past her grief.

Her cabin came into view around a turn. Emma could almost wish it wasn't so near. She enjoyed walking beside Gideon and engaging him in conversation. By unspoken consent, they each slowed their steps. Emma sighed. "I wish summer would last all year."

Gideon laughed. "If only it could. The cold doesn't suit me much."

"Maybe you should go somewhere warmer. I hear they don't see much of winter in Texas."

"What, and move far away from my family?" He shook his head. "That's not likely to happen."

Emma admitted to a certain relief at his pronouncement. She could understand his desire to stay near, especially because her own family was gone. "Do you plan to live in Liberty?"

"No doubt." Gideon held a branch aside for her. "How about you?"

"I'm here for the present." She spoke lightheartedly to hide the ache in her chest. It felt strange to have nowhere to really belong. After Ma's death, Pa had followed her to the grave within a year. Pneumonia proved the culprit in Ma's case, but Emma suspected that she'd died of a broken heart. She shuddered and pulled her thoughts from their course. "Thank you for seeing me home."

"My pleasure." Gideon's blue eyes met hers for a heart-stopping second. "Mind if I take a gander inside? After everything that's happened, I'd prefer to know that you are safe."

She would rather that he didn't see the disarray in her cabin. She'd been sick for more than a week, and it looked pretty bad. What could she say that wouldn't sound fussy? "Don't mind the mess."

"Of course not." His boots rang hollowly on the porch steps.

Emma hung back and allowed him to invade her home. She wasn't comfortable with being looked after in this way. It struck her as impractical. The wilderness started not far from where she stood waiting. Really, what was to stop all manner of perils from overtaking her while he ensured it was safe to go inside? Unnerved by her reflections, she darted glances about her.

Emma banished such thoughts. Why worry about something that probably wouldn't happen? She'd seen plenty of wildlife from the cabin, but even the bears slunk into shadow when they caught wind of a human presence.

There was a lot to be said for Pa's way of doing things.

He'd never expect her to depend on a man's protection when she had a perfectly good aim herself.

On the other hand, she couldn't deny that it felt nice that Gideon cared to look after her.

He appeared in the doorway. "All's clear." Gideon held the door open wider.

"Thank you." Emma walked past him into the kitchen.

Gideon turned to her. "Why don't you sit down and rest? I'll make tea, if you like."

"I'd appreciate that." She didn't want tea particularly, but she could tell he wanted to make it for her. She slid into a kitchen chair and tried to compose her thoughts, which wasn't easy with Gideon around. Dark-haired and lean featured, he was entirely too fascinating for her peace of mind. Pa had taught her to protect herself against intruders, but he'd given her no advice on what to do when a man came knocking at her heart.

Emma watched in bemusement as Gideon located and filled the kettle, then lit a fire with minimal fuss. "You've done that before."

"A time or two." He sank down across from her. "I try to make myself useful."

"Your ma must appreciate your help."

"She does when I try to keep up with her." The corners of Gideon's mouth ticked upward. "Ma is a force to be reckoned with in her own right."

Emma thought back to the few times she'd met Mrs. Buckthorn. The brown-haired, strong-faced woman had seemed slight but sturdy. "I think I know what you mean."

Gideon laughed outright. "She'd have liked your pa." The tea kettle whistled, and he jumped to his feet.

Emma had noticed Gideon doing chores on his family's property. It was hard to reconcile the strong man she'd seen sweating behind the plow and chopping wood with the softer one spooning tea leaves into Grandma Rose's flowered teapot.

He glanced up and caught her looking. "Seems like you have something to say."

"Not really." She glanced away, her face flaming. Watching Gideon occupied her mind wonderfully, but she'd rather keep that information to herself.

She put a hand to her head, which ached, all of a sudden.

Gideon's smile faded. "Are you all right? You were starting to show some color, but you've gone pale again."

"I'm thirsty."

He filled a glass from the water pail. "Here, drink this."

Emma tipped the glass to her mouth and drank deeply. The tepid liquid soothed her dry throat.

Gideon studied her. "Better?"

Emma took a quick inventory. Her head throbbed, her throat felt scratchy, and her chest hurt. "I think so."

He reached toward her forehead but paused before touching her. "May I?"

Emma nodded.

His eyes widened. "You're burning up."

"Am I?" She'd suspected as much.

Gideon frowned. "How do you feel?"

"A bit dizzy."

"That's not surprising. You'd better lie down." He glanced toward her bedroom door, which stood ajar. "Do you want me to help you?"

Emma's face heated. "I can manage." She stood up but had to clutch the back of the ladderback chair for support. "Thank you for making tea, but I shouldn't drink anything warm."

"Probably not.." Gideon stood up.

"Sorry, but I'd better not see you to the door."

He smiled. "I can't believe that you're burning up with fever but worried about manners. Don't give it another thought, Miss Duncan. I can let myself out once I'm sure you're safe."

Emma wanted to insist there was no need for him to watch over her, but she couldn't quite convince herself of that. After taking several wobbly steps, she was thankful when Gideon offered his arm for her to lean on.

He halted in her bedroom doorway. "Can you make it the rest of the way alone?" He nodded toward her rumpled bed.

"I'm fine, really." She took several steps, but the room swung alarmingly.

Gideon caught her before she fell. He lifted her into his arms.

"How annoying to be so weak," Emma murmured.

He took a couple of steps, then lowered her gently. The feathered tick gave beneath her.

Gideon pulled the covers over her, then stepped back. "I'll bathe your forehead, and then fetch Doc Bailey to have a look at you."

"I'm sure it's nothing to trouble him over."

"That may be, but I'd feel better if you'd let him see you."

Emma hadn't realized how bad she felt until he'd started fussing over her. "All right."

"I'm sure my mother will come over and look after you until he arrives."

The urge to cry swamped Emma. "Why is this happening? I was improving."

He turned in the doorway. "Going out this morning must have set you back."

Emma felt she was floating, an illusion heightened by the splashing of water in the other room. Gideon appeared, holding her wash basin in one hand and a washcloth in the other. The washcloth settled soothingly over her forehead. Emma let her eyelids drift shut. Pa had raised her to be an independent woman, and she would follow his advice. Except, of course, when relying on another person's strength made sense.

CHAPTER FOUR

ROB SHIFTED IN THE SADDLE, CRANING to spot marks of passage in the grass. Tracking was no easy job, and he was by no means an expert. The hoofprints he believed belonged to Maisey's captors had become harder to find after heading off the road. Bry's half-Cheyenne husband, Nick, had taught him what to watch for, though. The trail traversed a meadow dotted with bitterroot flowers and cut to the river bank. A patch of flattened, dampened grass drew his attention. Rob reined in and waited for Shane to draw up, then pointed to a mark in the mud near the water's edge. "See that hoofprint? They watered their horses here."

"That's not a bad idea." Shane lifted his hat and wiped his brow. "I suggest we do the same."

Everything in Rob protested the delay, but Shane was right. They couldn't neglect the horses. Caring for their mounts would save more time than pushing them. Rob swung a leg over the saddle and dismounted. He bent over the hoofprint "We're not far behind."

Shane joined him. "How long, would you say?"

Rob shrugged. "An hour? Two? The question is which way they went when they left this place."

"You'll figure that out, I'm certain." Shane watched over the horses, which stood fetlock-deep in the water.

Rob normally found Shane's composure calming, but today it grated. He doubted his cousin was unfeeling. Shane and America set a lot of store by Maisey and wouldn't take well to anyone troubling her. No. This had to be his cousin's faith speaking. Rob wondered how Shane held onto it so well. He himself never put blind trust in God nor man, although he admired his cousin's ability to do so.

Having a practical bent had helped Rob survive his childhood in the slums of Manhattan. Both Shane and Con seemed to have shed the effects of growing up in the Five Point slum better than he ever could. After departing three years ago to prove himself, Rob had learned the impossibility of that feat. He'd acquired wealth and its trappings but felt less than worthy of his success.

He'd done right by leaving. Otherwise, he'd have built a life based on his brother's charity and not his own abilities. A man wanted to hold his head up and feel beholden to no one. Con hadn't taken his decision well, and Maisey less so. Rob could admit that he ought to have managed the manner of his going better. He and Con had reached common ground—well, mostly. Rob's attempt to say goodbye to Maisey had failed badly. He shouldn't have kissed her, for his own sake as much as hers. The memory of it sought him at odd moments ever after, a tormenting taste of love that would never be his.

What Maisey's captors wanted with her Rob couldn't say for certain, but his imagination filled in horrifying possibilities. He chafed, wanting to continue searching for Maisey. She had suffered enough. She spoke little about her time among the Cheyenne, but he'd heard stories of the treatment meted out to captives. Rob shook his head. Her every trial in captivity must pale in comparison to seeing her husband murdered in front of her by a band of warriors. Maisey never talked about what had happened during the wagon train journey to Montana Territory, but he could always tell when the memories haunted her.

"Eat." Shane passed him a strip of jerky.

Rob dutifully bit into the salty morsel, then uncorked his canteen and drank. Taking off his hat, he let the breeze off the water ruffle his hair while he crouched beside the water. Even the small wait to refill his canteen stretched his nerves. Shane rummaged in his saddlebags and pulled out a packet of hardtack. Rob eyed it skeptically. "I won't break a tooth on that, will I?"

"Count your blessings, Cousin." Shane grinned. "I've decided not to pass that remark on to America."

"She made it?" Rob accepted a piece.

"My wife is a marvel of self-sufficiency. Lord knows, she's had to be. Has no one ever shown you how to eat hardtack?"

Rob lifted an eyebrow. "There's a right and wrong way?"

Shane laughed. "'Tis a wonder what a person misses in life. Soak it a bit first, and you'll like it better."

"I'll wait until our next stop."

Shane searched his face, his gaze probing. "Waiting to find Maisey is trying, I know."

Rob ran a hand over his face. "Well, yes."

Shane lifted an eyebrow. "Maybe it's time to tell that woman how you feel."

"I doubt she'd want to hear."

"You never know. She might surprise you."

Rob looked toward the river, squinting against the sun. "We'd have to find her first."

"Right." Shane turned toward their horses.

Rob strode into the glade, scanning the flower-tangled grass with every step. A barely-noticeable trail set off westward. "They went this way."

Shane joined him, leading the horses. He stared at the 'path' Rob indicated and shook his head. "I'd have never guessed."

"Thank goodness for Nick's instruction." Rob grimaced. "Without it, we'd both be lost."

Several hours later, Rob reined in his horse. "It will be dark soon."

Shane pulled abreast of him. "We might as well make camp."

"I'd rather go on, but I know that's best."

Shane nodded. "I can't imagine tracking at night, and I doubt you are that skilled. We'd have to use our lantern once dark fell, anyway. That would give us away to any interested parties. We'd arrive exhausted, and then have to deal with freeing Maisey."

"You make a good point." This was why Rob needed Shane along. If left to himself, he would lead with his heart instead of his logic. Rob found it impossible to be neutral where Maisey was concerned.

Shane smiled. "Let's rest up and start again at first light, shall we?"

They watered the horses, then set up camp on a grassy bank above the river. Rob joined Shane, who was perched on a boulder eating jerky, and plunked down beside him. He took out the hardtack from earlier, then poured water from his canteen into his tin cup. He sent Shane a doubtful look. "How do you soak this?"

"Just like you'd think." Shane smiled. "Give it a little time, but watch so it doesn't turn soggy on you."

Rob dropped the hardtack in the cup and set it beside him on the boulder. "I've been wondering why that Salish band captured Maisey. It's been two years since Red Cloud's War upset everyone. I thought the area would have settled down by now."

"The Marias massacre in January did nothing to improve relations with the tribes."

Rob considered that idea. "I wouldn't think that General Sheridan going after the Blackfeet would upset the Salish."

"Even bitter enemies can find common ground against a new invader." Shane bit into another piece of jerky.

"Whatever the cause, Maisey is the last person who should suffer." Rob shook his head. "She pours out her heart and soul to teach the Salish children. What stirred up the Salish people in the first place?" A frog started croaking beside the water, a homey sound that in other circumstances might have cheered Rob.

"From what I've heard, it began with the Hell Gate Treaty."

"That was quite a few years ago." Rob poked at his hardtack.

"Fifteen, if I recall correctly." Shane swigged from his canteen. "The government negotiated the agreement for three tribes, only two of which spoke the Salish language. That didn't matter to Governor Stevens, nor did he care that the Kootenai and Salish tribes are hostile to one another."

Rob tested a bite of hardtack. "Say, this isn't bad."

"That's a backhanded compliment, if I ever heard one." Shane grinned. "Should I pass it along to the cook?"

"Not if you value my safety." Rob took a larger bite. "So, what happened at the treaty council?"

"Nothing good. Chief Victor was appointed head over the three tribes, and he signed the agreement, under the impression that it limited settlement in the Bitterroot Valley. His tribe retained the right to hunt and gather food, so the chief believed they still owned their land."

"And they didn't?"

"The government considered that he'd ceded ownership."

Rob blew out his breath. "That's quite a difference of opinion. I don't have to ask how the three tribes feel about that."

"They aren't happy, that's certain. With more people settling in the valley, problems are bound to crop up."

They finished their supper, such as it was, before night fell. Taking the first watch made sense for Rob. With Maisey on his mind, he doubted sleep would come easily. It would be better to wear himself out before trying to sleep.

Rob sat alone on the boulder while Shane settled in his bedroll. Stars scattered across the heavens above him, so dense they shed a light all their own. The river gleamed in the moonlight, rippling like dark silk. Wind rustled in the grasses and touched his face. The keening wail of a fox calling for a mate pierced the night.

Rob would never grow tired of this valley. Staying away from it hadn't been easy. How could he bear turning his back on it? It was more than a place where his family lived. He'd come to think of it as home. Living on lonely mining claims had taught him the value of all he'd left behind.

How was Maisey doing? If only he could comfort her right now. He hated picturing her tied up and afraid. *If they harmed her —*

He pulled his thoughts up sharply. Continuing along those lines would guarantee a sleepless night. When it was his turn to sleep, he must rest. Tomorrow would tax his strength.

Maisey sucked in a breath to keep from crying out as she rolled onto her back. Her muscles protested too many hours in the saddle. Also, the cords binding her wrists and ankles rubbed them painfully. She was thankful that her captors hadn't gagged her again, nor had they staked her to the ground like the Cheyenne.

The star-swept sky stretched above her, so vast her mind couldn't fathom its size. How far away, in all that space, God in His heaven felt. A distant lament carried to her. She'd often heard foxes in the forest beyond her cabin. Safe and snug in her bed, she'd welcomed the wild cries. Tonight, they raised the hair on the back of her neck.

Where was Rob? Was he sleeping in his cousin's household or under these same stars in the open? She would have once believed he would ride after her in this situation, but she didn't know what to think anymore. When they'd met earlier, he'd seemed ready to say something soft, but for some reason changed his mind.

She sighed. That was probably just as well. If only she could drive him from her heart and mind, her sorrow would go away. During his absence, she'd managed to stop thinking of him so much, but she'd never known when memories would flood her. Something always triggered them—drinking coffee from a cup he'd favored, sitting in his place beside the fire, walking around a turn in the path and picturing him carrying Phoebe on his shoulders. She'd wept a lot at first, usually behind her bedroom door to avoid upsetting Phoebe. Time had dulled the pain, but her sorrow never quite went away. Maybe it would always be with her.

Maisey didn't want to believe that Rob had only pretended to care about her, but why else would he stay away all that time? If he'd missed her as much as she had him, he'd have come back to visit.

God, where are you? She'd thought He cared about her too. If so, why was she in this situation?

Maisey closed her eyes to shut out the starlight, no longer pleased to see it.

Rob reined in, hidden by the long shadow cast by the granite boulder beside him. The sun still glared even as it sank, and heat shimmered the air like a banshee's locks. How long ago it was since he'd heard the myths of the wailing fairy women in his homeland. His family had left when he was a lad. No one spoke of banshees in America, which he supposed was just as well. Being in this wild place with night lowering raised goosebumps on his arms without such tales.

Uneasiness crept up his spine, and he peered through the dusty pines. The nearer trunks shone in the last rays of the setting sun. Farther back, the trees lifted their branches in deep shadow. All manner of creatures could be lurking in the dense forest.

Nothing moved.

Shane pulled his horse up beside Rob. "Did you hear something?"

Rob gestured to the southwest. "Stones clattering, I think, over there." He strained his ears and caught the faint thud of a hoof. He laid his hand over his holstered pistol.

Shane straightened in the saddle, a vigilant look on his face. He nodded to Rob's gun hand. "We may not need that."

Rob opened his mouth to counter his cousin, but Shane moved off before he could speak. He followed his cousin as he threaded between the trees in silence. The ground lifted into foothills that climbed toward snow-clad mountains in the Bitterroot range. The clouds went pink in the first flush of sunset. A flock of mallards arced overhead, batting their wings and quacking. Nearly full, the moon shone through the gathering darkness, putting the stars to shame.

Shane halted on the crest of a hill in the deep shadow beneath a lodgepole pine. Rob stopped beside him. In the small valley below, a dark line of perhaps a dozen riders climbed toward the next rise. The feathers in their hair and attached to their bridles gave away their identity, as did the woman in their midst. With her brown hair tumbled about her shoulders, she slumped on her pony in a posture of utter exhaustion. Rob pulled in a painful breath. How he yearned to lift her into his arms and carry her to safety. He could do neither.

"Maisey is alive anyway." Shane murmured. "We can take comfort from that fact."

Rob peered into the near distance. "She appears unharmed."

"Let's make sure she remains so, shall we?" Shane's voice held a hint of steel. "No hasty actions."

"Maybe we won't need to use force." Rob offered an olive branch to his preacher cousin. "If they make camp, we might be able to sneak in and free her."

"Try that and we'll probably get ourselves and Maisey killed."

Rob sighed. "Do you have any other ideas?"

"Possibly, but it depends on who we find with Maisey. I'm on friendly terms with certain members of the tribe. If any are included in this band, they might help me gain Maisey's release."

Rob restrained his initial reaction to Shane's idea. "You're a good preacher, but I don't think even you can do that."

"That's true, but God is able to accomplish the task despite me."

Maybe throwing up obstacles would dissuade Shane. "You'd need daylight to recognize anyone."

"Or firelight, assuming they make camp. Otherwise, we'll wait to trail them until morning."

"Yesterday you said you were against tracking at night." Rob wasn't finding fault by pointing out his cousin's inconsistencies but rather doing Shane a service.

Shane sighed. "I would be today as well, but these are special circumstances."

Rob had no recourse but to speak the truth. "I don't like trusting Maisey's safety, or our own for that matter, to your gift of blarney,"

"It's a bit more than that, as I've explained. God has a way of stepping in."

There it was again, Shane's unflagging faith. It was like a boulder in Rob's way, so big there was no getting around it. "There's no time for preaching, if that's where this conversation is headed."

"Granted, but we can pray." Shane sounded beleaguered. "Or do you plan to forbid that too?"

"Perish the thought, preacher. You're more than welcome to consult the Almighty on our behalf. Only do it on the hoof, will you?"

"When did you become so jaded?"

Regret lanced Rob. He'd spoken hasty words out of frustration. "If we survive, I'll tell you."

"In case we don't, Cousin, I suggest making your peace with God now."

For once, Rob could think of no reply.

"I'll touch my hat if I recognize anyone likely to help." Shane's saddle creaked as he shifted. "You'll know by that to let me talk and leave your gun in its holster."

Rob took Shane's point. "All right. We'll do it your way—to start." Despite what Rob had said, if anyone could succeed at diplomacy, Shane would. How he made it work so often, Rob never knew. He himself lacked the skill. Maybe Shane was right about God intervening. Whether or not that was true, Rob planned to keep his gun handy. You never knew when God might need a little help. "What happens if you don't recognize anyone?"

"We're better off waiting for reinforcements from Liberty to join us."

Rob frowned. "I don't like that idea."

"No, I didn't suppose you would." Shane's voice held a trace of humor.

"Silas might lose our trail." Rob introduced another set of obstacles.

"I don't see how that can happen. We left clear waymarks."

"If we delay, we'll risk losing their tracks. Also, we might not be able to intervene before the band reaches the main camp."

"I've never known you to be such a worrier, Cousin. Don't you think we have enough trouble in this moment without imagining more?" The sardonic note in Shane's voice informed Rob that he'd guessed his tactics.

"Right." Recognizing that the discussion was at an end, Rob clucked to his horse and started into the valley. Shane kept pace beside him. Every so often, Rob glimpsed the band moving ahead of them. Keeping to cover became more difficult as the trees thinned. Rob pulled aside to wait in the shadow of a lone pine at the edge of a grassy meadow. They held back until the line of riders crested the next hill and vanished out of sight.

The journey continued in this manner until the moon sailed behind the clouds gathering across the sky. The moon remained hidden, and the thickening clouds further obscured its light. Rob chafed to follow Maisey, but they couldn't risk lighting a lantern so close to her captors.

Flames pierced the darkness ahead of them. The band must have made camp. This late, the fire was probably for warmth and not cooking. Night at this elevation held a chill. Maisey's captors must not fear pursuit or they wouldn't have lit a fire. That meant that he and Shane could gain the advantage of surprise.

Leaving their horses grazing, they crept toward the Indian camp. In the darkness, this proved treacherous. Rob made forceful contact with a stump, but managed to bite off his cry. A thud and a grunt came from nearby. Rob felt his way toward his cousin. "Are you all right?" he whispered.

"This time, yes, but I'd as soon not break my neck blundering about in the dark. Maybe we should wait for the moon to come out again." Shane's rueful tone gave Rob a pretty good idea of the expression on his face.

Rob half-expected Shane to tell him he'd prayed for the moon to light their way again. "Who knows when or if that will happen?" he snapped.

The clouds shifted and moonbeams spilled from the sky, limning the mountains in blue light and thrusting the landscape into eerie relief.

Shane chuckled softly. "You were saying?"

"Never mind."

Seeing well enough to avoid treacherous hurdles made a difference, and they covered the distance rapidly. Without trees to cast long shadows, the clearing shone brightly. Voices murmured close at hand. Rob and Shane halted. They stood at the edge of the undergrowth surrounding the Salish camp. Proceeding any further would give away their presence.

Rob scanned the clearing and located Maisey. She was at the river watering the horses. His jaw tightened. Seeing her forced to work while stumbling with weariness didn't sit well with him. One of her captors kept watch over her while the rest lounged about, talking.

Shane turned toward Rob and touched his hat.

Rob gestured for his cousin to go forward. He would watch over Shane from cover.

Shane nodded and started forward.

Rob moved to a new spot and drew his pistol. He would give his cousin enough time to prove himself, but then he'd go in with his gun.

CHAPTER FIVE

AMERICA GASPED AWAKE AND SAT UP in bed, breathing heavily. A shiver ran up her spine. The night shadows in her room seemed to reach toward her. The nightmare clutching her loosened its grip and fell away, but its horror remained. She'd seen them all—Shane, Rob, and Maisey–staked out in the sun, dying of thirst.

She groped on the bedside table, and her fingers brushed the hard edges of the match safe. America fumbled to open the tin with clumsy fingers. By the faint moonlight penetrating the curtains, she rasped a match against the striker. A tiny flame flared, and she promptly carried it to her candle. The wick caught, and a circle of light pushed back the darkness.

America released her breath on a sigh. The dream had seemed so real, but she shouldn't fear. Time and again, God had protected her husband, herself, and their children. He'd delivered Bry and Maisey from captivity, provided Bry a husband, and given Maisey a purpose to live. He'd brought first Con, then Rob, home.

America pulled the shawl she kept behind her pillow up around her shoulders. She left the comfort of her bed and lowered herself to the padded kneeler in the corner. The Lord's faithfulness was all the more reason to beseech Him in the dark of night.

She whispered prayers for them all. How much time passed, she didn't know. She opened her eyes to a guttering candle. The room had grown dim, but shadows no longer crouched in her mind.

Rob recognized the Indian facing Shane as the man who had once tried to kidnap Phoebe. He'd seemed unstable on that occasion and wild-eyed tonight. Members of his band moved in behind their leader as he stalked toward Shane.

Rob leveled his pistol, ready to assist his cousin.

"Why have you barged into our camp, Preacher?" Spukani challenged Shane in English.

The leader assumed a fighting stance Rob knew well from his childhood. How interesting to find it in use far west of Manhattan's slums. Some things were common to all men, he supposed, the urge to fight being one of them.

"You must know why I've come, Spukani—to return the schoolteacher home." Shane didn't turn his head to look at Maisey but kept his attention on the men before him. This was the only sign Rob could detect of his cousin's vigilance. Otherwise, Shane maintained a relaxed posture, for all the world as if engaged in an enjoyable conversation.

Spukani tensed and knotted his hands into fists. "You waste your time."

Rob eased his grip, despite the urge to shoot the feather from Spukani's hair. Shane would commend his restraint, he felt certain. Besides, clasping his gun so tightly would ruin his aim.

Maisey watched the confrontation from the river bank. A lump formed in Rob's throat. In bedraggled clothing and with her dark hair tangled, she looked utterly bereft. Her guard edged toward the gathered men, craning to see.

A rash idea presented itself to Rob.

"Why have you taken Maisey?" Shane's tone carried more

interest than heat, as if he was only mildly curious.

"That is not your concern," Spukani growled.

Rob crept closer to Maisey and her inattentive guard. He couldn't keep his gun trained on Spukani much longer if he continued going this direction. Shane seemed to be holding his own at the moment, but Rob doubted he would much longer. The temptation to dash out and claim Maisey tugged at Rob.

Shane would pay the price of such an impulsive action. Rob couldn't do that to his cousin. It was unlikely to work anyway. Assuming that Rob succeeded at rescuing Maisey, the entire band would chase them to the ground afterwards. It wasn't hard to conclude that narrowing the odds against that happening was better than increasing them.

Maisey raised her head in a defiant gesture and looked toward Shane. "They're taking me to chief Charlo."

Rob exhaled on a long breath, glad he'd decided not to rush out to save her. He wouldn't have reached her before every pair of eyes swung her direction.

Repressing his urge to protect Maisey wasn't easy with the guard towering over her threateningly. The gun weighted Rob's hand and his thoughts, but firing might hurt more than it helped. Violence was apt to follow, and that would place him in an untenable position. With so many poised to attack, he wouldn't be able to protect both Maisey and Shane simultaneously. If Rob pulled the trigger, someone he loved would be hurt and possibly killed.

"Go back, Preacher." Spukani's voice rose in pitch. "If you refuse, I can't promise that you will be safe."

Shane displayed no signs of retreat, a fact that made Rob want to shake him. Couldn't he see that his tactics weren't working? Sometimes you had to cut your losses.

"Does your new chief understand that what you are doing

is wrong?" Shane's voice remained conversational.

"Silence!" Spukani jerked with anger.

Shane held the gaze of each man standing behind Spukani. "Do none of you question your leader's wisdom in taking the teacher?" he called in the Salish tongue. "Little Elk? Running Horse?" Rob understood most of the words, grateful that Maisey had taught him the language. He'd picked it up quickly, then learned more from the tribe he fell in with when traveling from Virginia City to the trading post in Deer Valley.

Rage convulsed Spukani's face. "Do not listen to him."

"I am told that in your tribe each man thinks for himself," Shane continued in the same even tone. "You follow no chief, even a good one, blindly."

"The preacher is right." An Indian wearing a quillwork vest and long braids murmured softly, but his voice carried.

"He wants to confuse you, Little Elk. Do not listen to his lies." Spukani paced in agitation, the eagle feather in his hair flying about.

"Is it lying to ask questions?" Shane stood his ground magnificently, in Rob's view.

Spukani halted his pacing and glared at Shane. "Take the preacher captive."

Several of his followers hesitated, but others took hold of Shane. Offering no resistance, he stood among them with quiet dignity. "By kidnapping me, you only make more trouble."

"No." Spukani shook his head. "It keeps you from telling the soldiers where to find us."

Rob restrained himself yet again from pulling the trigger. Acting in haste might get Shane killed, plus result in his own freedom being curtailed. His best bet would be to attempt to rescue Maisey and Shane after the camp slept. He would have to remain undetected until then. To ensure that outcome, he had better attend to a certain matter.

Moving as quietly as possible, he headed toward the place he and Shane had left their horses. If the Indians found Archibald alongside Rob's mare, they would guess Shane wasn't alone. Haste seemed in order, since Rob doubted it would take the Indians long to search for Shane's horse.

The moon ducked behind clouds, leaving Rob to plunge through the underbrush in wavering light. He kept his gun handy, but shooting it would be a last resort to save his life. He would do nothing willingly to bring down Spukani's wrath on Maisey and Shane.

From the sounds of snapping of wood and hushed voices behind him, several of Spukani's men had set out his direction. Tasked with the need to remain undetected, he was making slower progress than they were. He'd heard that Indians possessed an uncanny ability to see at night. Whether that was true or not, he couldn't say. He'd never been sufficiently curious on the topic to ask his Salish friends at the trading post. He did know they could move about stealthily. That fact made the noise they raised more telling. It meant that he hadn't given away his presence.

Shane traveled about on his own so often that those who knew him would logically assume he had ridden alone this time as well. They were unlikely to suspect Rob's presence, if he could reach the horses before they did. He picked up his pace, hurtling through the darkness with more speed than caution.

Something snagged his foot, and Rob crashed to the ground. Exclamations rang out behind him. He pushed to his hands and knees. No illusions of secrecy remained. Even if the approaching Indians took him for an animal, they were sure to investigate. He staggered onward, doing his best to ignore the pain in his leg. His was the haste of the hunted. He propelled himself toward the grove of pines where the horses waited. Even in faint moonlight, a white mane gleamed. He issued a silent apology to the mare he'd purchased in Virginia City. He couldn't allow Archibald, Shane's beloved horse, to fall into other hands. Rob whistled, low, in a close imitation of Shane's signal.

He couldn't pick out Archibald in the darkness, but hooves thudded his direction. He hurried toward the sound.

This time when he fell, his shoulder took the impact, and the gun flew from his hand. Rob lay stunned, staring up at the heavens.

Hoofbeats rang out, followed by shouts so close he knew he was lost.

Rob rolled slowly to his hands and knees. Struggling to breathe and without a weapon, he had no defense.

Phoebe turned sad eyes toward America from across the supper table. "Mrs. Hayes, may I be excused?"

America frowned. "You've hardly touched your food. Try to eat a little more."

Phoebe's shining curls wreathed her head in the lantern light as she hunched over her plate with a martyred air.

Liberty, seated next to Phoebe, gave her friend a bracing smile. "Ma made huckleberry pie for dessert."

Seth sat taller. "If Phoebe doesn't want her slice, can I have it?"

Liberty arched her eyebrows at her brother. "Finish those lima beans, young man, or you won't get your own slice."

"You're not the boss of me." Seth stuck out his tongue at his sister.

"Children! Where are your manners?" America fastened a disapproving look on Seth and Liberty in turn. Liam, for once, wasn't in trouble. "Need I remind you that you have company?"

"Sorry, Ma," Seth and Liberty chimed in unison.

Phoebe toyed with her food until America could stand it no longer. She removed the offending plate, and plunked a piece of pie in front of the girl. Phoebe needed nourishment, by any means possible. She'd eaten little since her mother's kidnapping two days ago.

"I want pie." Seth piped up instantly.

"Me too!" Liam echoed.

"Eat your beans first." America issued the command automatically.

"But Phoebe didn't have to eat hers," Seth pointed out with perfect logic.

"Quiet, this minute!" Liberty made a face at Seth. "Can't you tell that Phoebe's upset about her ma?"

Phoebe pushed the dessert plate away. "I'm sorry, Mrs. Hayes, but I'm not hungry."

A familiar knock shook the back door. The unexpected sound made America jump. She recovered quickly, trying not to show the children how on-edge she felt with Shane gone.

Gideon stood on the back porch, his hat in his hands. "Good evening, Mrs. Hayes. Sorry to disturb you at supper. Ma said you were baking a pie for Emma. She sent me to take it over to her."

"How thoughtful of you both to save me the trouble." America went to get the covered pie plate waiting on the counter.

"It sure looks good." A wistful note crept into Gideon's voice.

"Would you like a slice? I made a second one for tonight's dessert."

He held up his hands. "I don't want to trouble you."

"It's no bother." She waved him toward an empty dining chair. "Won't you take a seat?"

"Well, if you're sure." Gideon sat down, much to the children's delight.

America drew a relieved breath, happy that they had stopped quarreling.

"Of course, I am. You and your ma have taken a big responsibility from me by looking after Emma so well." America sliced a thick slab of pie, added a fork, and slid the dessert in front of him. "How is she doing? I hope she's well enough to eat the pie I made."

"Emma is improving." Gideon picked up the fork and dug in. "My, that's good."

"She gave us a scare yesterday." America poured a glass of water and set it on the table in front of him.

"I'm thankful the doctor didn't think it was serious." He reached for the glass.

"Not this time."

Gideon drew his brows together. "What do you mean?"

"Children, carry your plates to the counter and pick up your toys. If you're ready early, I'll read to you before bed."

Seth, who loved stories, jumped up at once. "*Robinson Crusoe*?"

"You always want that book." Liberty glared at her brother, then turned an angelic face toward her mother.

"Phoebe and I want *Thumbelina*."

Phoebe, waiting for Liberty beside the hallway door, had voiced no opinion, nor did she look the least concerned which book America chose.

"I'll decide what to read in a bit."

Once the children left, America sat down across from Gideon. "I'm worried about Emma."

Gideon put down his fork. "Oh?"

"She keeps to herself a lot."

"There's no harm in preferring your own company." He lifted his fork again. "I often do."

"Something is troubling her, and I suspect it's affecting her health."

Gideon frowned. "Any idea what might be wrong?"

America nodded. "Her father died several years ago, not long before she came to teach. He was the last living member of her family. I don't think she's recovered fully from her loss. A young girl should be full of energy and interested in life. Emma is pale and withdrawn much of the time. She sickens more easily than she should."

"It sounds like she could stand a bit of company." Gideon polished off his last bite. "I have an idea that might help. Thanks for dessert, Mrs. Hayes." He stood up and retrieved Emma's pie from the counter. "I hate to eat and run, but I should take this over soon. Emma hasn't been eating much, but it might tempt her."

America shut the back door behind Gideon and drove the bolt home, locking her children and herself in for the night. She wiped down the kitchen then while mulling which book to read. She decided on neither story requested by her children. They would revisit those old favorites again, but Shane read them best. Either tale might cause the children to miss their father. America was not immune, either. She lit the oil lamp in the parlor, ready to search the bookcase for something else to read. A rustling sound in the room claimed her attention, and America turned to see what had caused it.

Phoebe sat on the window seat with her knees drawn up, gazing out the living room window. With her bright ringlets tied back in a ribbon and her attention fixed on a point outside the window, she looked like a tragic heroine in one of the fairytales America was considering.

"What are you doing there?"

Phoebe glanced up, her blue eyes luminous. "Do you suppose Ma can see the same stars I can tonight?"

America crossed the room to stand behind her. "I'm sure she can."

"When I was young, I used to think the sky went on forever." Phoebe spoke with all the authority of an eight-year-old.

"It seems to, doesn't it?"

"Ma says that can't be true."

America sank onto the window seat beside her. "Did you know that the Bible calls the heavens God's throne and the Earth His footstool?"

Phoebe's eyes widened. "He's a giant."

America smiled. "God is larger than the sky, and He's bigger than any of our troubles."

Phoebe's forehead puckered. "Do you think He notices my Ma?"

"God sees every person, and He cares about us all."

"Will He bring Ma back home to me?" Phoebe's eyes pleaded for something impossible to promise.

America chose her words carefully. "It depends on what happens when we pray."

"Could we pray right now?"

"Of course."

Phoebe closed her eyes, and her lashes cast shadows on her cheek.

America nudged her shoulder. "You go first."

"All right." Phoebe frowned, as if considering what to say. "Dear God, I guess you know what happened with my Ma. I hope you'll look after her. Also, would you let her know I love her? Please bring her home right away."

America had to wait for her emotions to settle before she could speak. "Lord, please help everyone at home make it through this uncertain time. It's hard not knowing what's happening out there, but we trust you to look after us all."

Phoebe opened her eyes and gave America a faint smile. "I feel better."

"You know what? I do too." She held out her hand to Phoebe. "Want to help me pick out a story?"

"Yes, but—" A sheepish look stole over Phoebe's face. "May I have a piece of pie first?"

Emma plunked into one of the wingback chairs by the fireplace. She hadn't cleaned much of the cabin, but she already needed to rest. The fever was gone but not the muddled sensation that came with it. Striking a compromise between her wish to restore order and the reality of her need to recover seemed in order. Emma closed her eyes. She would allow herself to sit, but only for a moment. Emma drifted into gentle waters.

A knock at the door startled Emma awake. She opened her eyes, heart pounding. The knock came again, and this time she recognized Gideon's two light raps followed by two harder ones. She let out a sigh of relief. After seeing Maisey abducted, she couldn't help being on edge.

Emma hurried to the window and peered out at the edges of the gingham curtains.

Gideon had his back to the sun, so she couldn't see his expression, but the fading daylight picked out his dark head tilted inquiringly as he waited. Emma opened the door.

Gideon stood on the porch with a covered pie plate in his hands. The lantern she'd lit earlier shed warm light over him. He looked pensive in its illumination. What thoughts occupied his mind?

He cleared his throat. "Mrs. Hayes sent dessert for you."

Emma didn't answer, still taking in the sight of him. He must have been working outside. Wearing overalls and with his shirt sleeves rolled up, he looked capable and strong. Remembering herself, she stepped back. "Won't you come in?"

She took the plate and deposited it on the kitchen counter. "Would you like a slice?"

A lopsided smile lit his face. "Thank you, but no. Mrs. Hayes already gave me one. "

"Will you take tea?"

"Only if I can make it while you sit. You look fair to dropping."

Heat bloomed in Emma's cheeks. "I'm much better, actually. I haven't had a fever for two days."

"That's good news. However, I'm in full health and capable of boiling water. Have a seat and let me take care of you, please."

"All right, since you insist." Emma sank into a chair at the table.

Gideon glanced about. "You've been straightening, haven't you?"

"A little." How ridiculous to feel so pleased that he'd noticed her efforts. "Your mother is coming to clean in the morning, and I want to tidy up beforehand."

His gaze traveled over her face. "Ma wouldn't want you to wear yourself out on her account."

"My pa taught me to look after myself as much as possible."

"That's a good idea, if you don't carry it too far."

Emma frowned. "I'm not sure what you mean."

Gideon smiled. "You want to avoid becoming a hermit."

"I'm a teacher, so there's little danger of that. I'll keep your advice in mind if I ever feel the inkling." Emma answered politely, although his suggestion annoyed her. What was he implying?

"I hope you will." Gideon ladled water into the kettle. "Your water pail is getting low. I'll draw some more from the well before I go."

"Thank you. You and your mother have been a blessing. I must thank her properly." Emma warmed to her subject. "What is her favorite pie? Or does she prefer cake?"

Gideon looked up from measuring tea into her grandmother's teapot. "I'm glad you have the good sense to recognize that my mother is wonderful. Save the baking until you've recovered, though. She wouldn't want you to overdo it on her account."

"I told you that I'm almost well." Emma spoke precisely.

"How could I forget?" He arranged cups on the tea tray.

"There's something special you can do for Ma, if you've a mind to. Living with three sons and a husband makes a woman short on female company. I hope you'll want to remedy that for her."

"I'd welcome the chance to pay back her kindness." Emma mused with her chin on her hand. "I suppose that would be all right."

He grinned. "I'm glad to hear it."

Emma glanced at him in suspicion. Why did he look so smug, all of a sudden?

CHAPTER SIX

MAISEY CLUNG TO THE SADDLE AS her pony's hooves scattered fragments of scree on the slope they traversed, down a dizzying drop. She had never climbed this high into the Bitterroot Mountains. The sun beat down mercilessly, providing a clear view into the long valley below. Liberty township seemed so far away. No wonder her student's parents didn't bring their children to school when the tribe foraged in the mountains. The children might appear for a week or two, but then go away again. This made the continuity of lessons difficult, but she'd adapted to the children's needs. That they arrived at all spoke volumes. The tribe was willing to bridge the gap between their cultures. If only the same attitude could be returned to them. Attitudes varied among the settlers. Some feared the Indians. Others thought them wily or dirty. Only a few respected the local tribes and sympathized with their plight. Entire tribes had been wiped out in the East. Maisey hoped that wouldn't be repeated in the West.

She couldn't entirely blame Spukani for his animosity. His world had shifted drastically, and it must be hard to know who to trust. Keeping this in mind might allow her the ability to forgive him for his misdeeds.

Rob and Shane rode a little distance behind her. Seemingly unaffected by captivity, Shane sat tall in the saddle and broke into song upon occasion. This habit elicited both amusement and annoyance from his fellow travelers. Rob in particular scowled at him. While Shane presented a happy demeanor,

Rob's gaze met Maisey's darkly. He appeared sunk in gloom. She turned around and faced forward to cut off the strong emotions that seeing Rob in captivity sparked within her.

Maisey swallowed against a dry throat, but the action brought little relief. She licked her chapped lips and squinted to spare her eyes, which ached from too much sunshine. Spukani turned aside into the shade. The Indians dismounted at a pool fed by a spring that cascaded down the face of a rocky bluff. Maisey slid to the ground but held back while her captors slaked their thirst and allowed their horses to drink. When they moved off to pick huckleberries or lounge in the shade, it was Maisey's turn. She stood beneath the falling water and let it cool her, uncaring that her clothing would cling to her afterwards. The sun would go down before long, and that would bring some comfort. Hopefully, Spukani would not want to venture across the rough terrain in the dark. They had arrived at last night's camp quite late. She didn't want to endure so long in the saddle again.

She came out of the water to find Rob and Shane waiting. Maisey stepped away from the waterfall to allow them access. Shane doused his head and brought handfuls of water to his mouth with his bound hands.

Rob joined her where she stood, plucking huckleberries from a bush. "How are you holding up?"

"All right, but I'd rather be home." Tears started to her eyes, but she blinked them back.

"Maisey—" Rob's voice cracked.

"Steady, Cousin." Shane's arm clamped around Rob's shoulder. "You'd better drink while you may."

Rob turned back to Maisey. "I'll do everything in my power to free you."

Maisey nodded, moved beyond measure by his promise.

She watched Rob drink from the spring with a blend of feelings, not all of which she could identify. Shane picked huckleberries nearby. In this idle moment with none of their captors watching, strain showed in Shane's face.

Maisey made up her mind in a burst of outrage. She moved off to find Spukani.

Sitting a little apart from his men in the shade of a boulder, he stood at her approach. "What do you want?"

She clenched her fists. "You must not force these men to remain with you any longer."

Anger spasmed Spukani's face. "You do not tell me what to do."

Maisey refused to back down. "Chief Charlo wants to see me, not them. You have no reason to hold them."

"Silence!" Spukani slapped her with the speed of a striking snake. Maisey cried out, her head jerking sideways. She covered her stinging cheek with one hand while fighting to stop her tears. She wouldn't allow Spukani to break her spirit. That was one thing he could never touch.

"Leave her alone!" Rob lunged toward Spukani but was caught and held by several of his followers.

"Let him go!" Maisey bit back everything she wanted to say. No good would come of losing her temper and berating the man.

Spukani stalked to Rob. "You are nothing but trouble."

"Thank you." Rob's mouth twisted into a smile. "I'm glad to hear it."

Spukani let his fists fly. Rob doubled over.

"Stop it!" Maisey launched herself toward them.

Little Elk stepped in front of her.

She tried to run around him, but he encircled her upper arms, all the while blocking her from seeing Rob. The sick thud of another blow assaulted her ears.

"You don't want to do that, Spukani." Shane spoke quickly.

"Quiet, Preacher." Spukani spat out the words.

"Chief Charlo prefers to live in peace," Shane snapped out. "How many of you know this?"

Grunts came from among the Indians.

Maisey held her breath.

"Mount your horses. It's time to leave." Anger laced Spukani's voice.

Little Elk released Maisey and stepped aside. She bolted toward Rob, who was curled on the ground. Shane reached him first and propped him into a sitting position. Rob clutched his stomach, moaning. Maisey halted, uncertain what to do. Shane struggled to raise Rob to his feet, and she moved forward to help.

Little Elk arrived at Rob's side before she did. Together, he and Shane lifted Rob to his feet and helped him onto his pony.

"Thank you." Shane nodded to Little Elk. "I'm glad to know there is one member of this band who understands that harming a defenseless man and brutalizing a woman is not the Salish way."

The lowering darkness matched Rob's mood perfectly. His inability to rescue Maisey was something that put his back to the wall far more than the pain in his belly. Maisey was riding only slightly ahead of him, but she might as well be miles away. He wished that he could travel beside her, but he couldn't even do that much. Rob didn't want to speculate on what would happen to them when they reached the Indian camp. It was enough to endure this infernal journey.

His pony stumbled on a stone, jarring him. Rob gritted his teeth until the pain in his side passed. Judging by Spukani's wild blows, he wasn't as accomplished a fighter as he wanted them to think. Rob had come up against a boy like that in the slums while growing up. One encounter had been enough to convince him that he never wanted another. He was thankful that Spukani lacked the skill to inflict major harm, but Rob was still in no shape to try to escape. He would have to bide his time, an activity he never did well. He had to believe that an opportunity to free himself and those he loved would present itself sooner or later. With his strength gone, his determination to face the world in his own power without the help of God or man was proving futile. At this present pass, he had only God's intervention to call upon. Daring to believe that might happen brought him closer to thinking like his preacher cousin than felt comfortable. He curved his lips into a wry smile. Life had its ironies.

Behind him, Shane lifted his voice in church songs, his constant cheerfulness grating on Rob's nerves. How his cousin could find anything to rejoice about in captivity, Rob would never know.

The band of Indians entered a defile that widened from a narrow passageway into a high valley ringed by crags. Alpine grasses scantly stretched over the rocky soil deadened his horse's hooves. Every so often a stone pinged, deflected by a hoof. Dogs barked sharply, and smoke curled into the sky above clustering tepees. A group of children crouched at the edge of camp straightened and cast the bones and sticks they'd been playing with aside. The children ran toward them, but then hung back and stared with wide eyes.

Women rushed to greet the returning men, who jumped from their horses to embrace them. Excited chatter filled the camp. Maisey alighted from her pony, casting tentative glances about her.

Spukani took hold of her arm. "You come."

"Harm her, and you'll answer to me!" Rob issued what amounted to an empty threat. Spukani knew that he lacked the means to back up his challenge.

Spukani barked something, and guards moved in, partially blocking Rob's view. He glimpsed Spukani forcing Maisey toward one of the tepees. Rob clenched his jaw in frustration. He could not rescue the woman he loved any more than he could save himself.

"It's best not to keep them waiting." Shane's voice penetrated Rob's gloom.

"What?" Rob stared blankly at his cousin. Shane stood beside Rob's horse, looking up at him.

"Where has your mind gone? They instructed us to dismount."

Rob stepped out of the saddle, and guards immediately took hold of him. Speaking in their tongue so rapidly that Rob couldn't follow, they dragged their two captives away from camp.

Rob recalled, all of a sudden, Shane's suggestion that he make peace with the Almighty. The idea held merit, he decided. He had no idea where they were going, but he had a hunch it was somewhere unpleasant.

A woman with her braids wrapped in hide strips peered with undisguised interest through the circular opening in the tepee Spukani dragged Maisey toward. "Who is this?" the woman asked in the Salish tongue.

Spukani gripped Masiey's arm, as if he suspected she

would try to flee. "Let me speak with our chief."

"I will let him know what you want." The woman's dark gaze traveled over Spukani's face before swinging back to Maisey.

"Who is there, Margaret?" a deep voice asked from inside the tepee.

The woman turned her head. "Spukani is here with one of the settler women. He asks to see you."

"Invite them inside."

"Come in." Margaret stepped back.

Maisey blinked, adjusting to the softer light inside the tepee after the bright sunlight. Wood was stacked in the central pit. When lit, the fire would send smoke upward to exit through the opening at the top of the tepee. A man sat on one of several benches lining the walls. He wore a blue buttoned shirt and breeches but also a collar studded with bear claws. Maisey knew that the chief's name meant 'claw of the little grizzly.' That might have been the inspiration for his choice of ornamentation. The chief's stern face also matched his name.

"Make yourselves comfortable." The chief waved a hand, including Maisey in the gesture.

Spukani took the bench opposite Charlo. Maisey lowered herself onto the far end of the same bench. Margaret sank down between her and Spukani.

Charlo studied Maisey from bright eyes. "Why do you bring this woman among us?"

Maisey barely repressed her start. Wasn't the chief expecting her? She clearly remembered Spukani telling her that Charlo had asked for her, and he'd said as much to Little Elk.

"She is the teacher from the Indian school."

Charlo's frown etched crevices in his craggy face. "I am not sure why my father agreed to let our children go to the

Indian school. We have no need to learn the white man's ways."

"She teaches them the settlers' language. I brought her to teach it to you."

"A translator makes my words known and explains what is said to me. That is all I need."

Spukani's nostils flared, but he kept his tone civil. "Should a chief rely on another man's interpretation?"

The chief pinned Spukani with a glance. "Her hands are tied. She does not come with you willingly."

"What does that matter?" Spukani's smile did not reach his eyes. "She has come."

"All you do not say speaks for you." Charlo sat forward. "You are foolish to put our tribe in danger by capturing her."

"Does Charlo fear the soldiers?" A sly expression, quickly concealed, crossed Spukani's face. "Chief Victor did not."

"Do not reproach me with my father. He did everything for peace, as you well know. It was my father's boast that his hand had never in seventy years been bloodied with the white man's blood, and I am the son of my father."

"I am not against peace." Spukani's lips lifted in that insincere smile again. "That is why I brought the woman. Understanding what the white man says will help you protect our people."

Charlo's face tightened. "Let them learn *our* language."

Spukani jutted out his chin. "I ask the chief to reconsider."

"I am sorry, Spukani, but you have made a mistake." Charlo swept a glance over Maisey. "We cannot keep this woman. You must give the teacher back to her people."

Spukani stood, scowling. Any minute, he would reach for her.

"Chief Charlo, may I speak?" Maisey asked quickly in

Salish.

"Be quiet." Spukani latched onto her arm. "You have no voice here."

"Let her go." Charlo spoke quietly.

Spukani released Maisey but continued to glower at her.

Charlo turned to her. "I am listening."

"Please don't send me back with this man." Maisey rubbed the red spot Spukani had made on her arm. "He hates me."

"I can tell that he does." Charlo looked from her to Spukani. "Why is this?"

"She killed Rain." Spukani ground out the words.

"That's not true!" Maisey looked only at the chief, unable to tolerate Spukani's wrath. "It's true that his daughter died while under my care, but I did my best to save her." Tears pricked her eyes. "It wasn't enough."

Spukani leaped to his feet. "I should not have allowed my wife to bring her to you."

"I wish she never had." Maisey's sobs shook her frame.

The chief's forehead creased. "I wish I could agree to your request, Teacher, but I cannot. You would not be safe if you traveled alone, and no one but the man who stole you should risk returning you."

"If you freed the two men who were also captured, I could go home with them."

"They belong to me." Spukani paced toward her, scowling.

"Sit down, Spukani." The chief's frown furrowed his face. "When did you plan to tell me about these others?"

Spukani crouched on the edge of the bench. "Those men are not important."

Charlo's eyes gleamed. "Then you won't mind taking me to them."

"I'm warning you, Shane—" Rob struggled against the ties binding him. "If you belt out one more hymn—"

"It's good to sing the Lord's praises, wouldn't you say?" Shane grinned, despite being tied to a stake. They were secured to tall poles that overlooked the camp from a rise at its edge. The ropes tethering Rob to his stake allowed him enough leeway to sit or stand but otherwise restrained his movement. Two guards sat on a fallen log, watching them with bored postures. The moon already shone in the sky, which darkened to deep blue while the sun edged toward oblivion.

"Honestly, Cousin." Rob pulled at the cords around his wrists, which were bound together behind him. He succeeded only in rubbing his already-raw skin. Rob gritted his teeth until the pain subsided. "I hate to break it to you, but the kinder, gentler world you imagine doesn't exist."

"From that, may I assume you dislike my singing?"

Rob curled his lip. "In case you didn't notice, there's nothing to celebrate in our situation."

"Unless, of course, the men who rode out from Liberty have excellent hearing."

"What does that—" Rob turned his head to stare at his cousin. "So *that's* why you've been caterwauling."

"Careful, or you'll offend my sensibilities." Shane sniffed. "Caterwauling, indeed."

Rob restrained the urge to laugh. "It's a long shot that anyone would locate us from a song."

"Better slim chances than none. But please, if you have another idea, let me know."

"You have a point." Rob subsided against the stake behind

him. "I wish I'd never let you land us in this mess."

"How is this my fault, if I may ask?" Shane sounded a lot less cheerful than he had a few minutes ago.

"If I'd had any sense, I wouldn't have given you the chance to negotiate. I didn't like it from the beginning, nor did it work."

"It might have with someone other than Spukani," Shane shot back.

"I'll grant you that." Rob blew at a mosquito buzzing about his head.

"What else could we have done? Gone in firing?"

"That's one idea."

"Would you take lives so lightly?" Shane's tone dripped disapproval.

"Please allow me to clarify. I didn't say I'd welcome killing, but a man needs to protect those he loves."

"I can't fault that sentiment, having taken the long way around to reach that conclusion myself. Determining how much force is required and when to use it is where we differ."

"I doubt I'd have tried, anyway." Rob conceded the point for the sake of peace. "Although, I certainly wanted to shoot first and talk later."

"Maisey or I could have been hurt."

"That's why I didn't—well, and maybe a little of your compassion has rubbed off on me." Honesty compelled Rob to admit the truth. Shane's example grew on a person.

"Glad to hear it. I was wondering. I'll admit you don't seem the same man who left to seek his fortune."

Rob closed his eyes, but he couldn't shut out Daphne's remembered screams. An image of her face, shuttered in death, returned to haunt him. "Life has a way of changing a person."

"What happened to put that haunted look on your face?"

Rob frowned. "You see entirely too much, Cousin."

Shane smiled. "I'm a preacher, as you'll recall."

"There's Maisey coming out of a tepee." Thankful for both the interruption and a chance to assure himself of Maisey's wellbeing, Rob peered into the camp.

Shane sat taller against his pole. "That's Charlo with her and Spukani."

Rob glanced at him, intrigued. "How do you know the chief?"

"I met him here and there during my travels as a circuit preacher." Shane narrowed his eyes. "That was a long time ago, before I married America and settled in Liberty. I've seen him once in a while since then."

"They're headed this way." Rob struggled to his feet. Even trussed like a prized turkey, he would stand to face whatever fate dealt him. A glance sideways showed Shane doing the same.

The guards jumped to their feet also.

Maisey was standing straighter than before, but her face wore a guarded expression. Even with her face dirty and her hair tangled, Maisey's beauty shone through. She watched him out of sad eyes. As their gazes clung, the realization that he would lay his life down to free this woman shook him to the core.

Charlo and Spukani walked beside her, engaged in quiet conversation. After passing the guards, Charlo started toward Rob, who was nearest to him.

Tears glistened in Maisey's eyes as she looked up at Rob. The urge to kiss away her sorrow took possession of him. She stopped before him and pulled in a quick breath. "Chief

Charlo, I must object to these men being tied up like animals. They've done nothing to deserve it."

"Stop trying to deceive." Spukani rounded on Maisey, gripping her arm.

"Let go of her." Rob gritted out, chafing for more of a fight than words could provide.

Spukani released Maisey and sidled close to Rob, a smirk on his face. "This prisoner attacked me."

"That's not true." Maisey touched the red stain on her cheek. "He only tried to defend me after Spukani slapped me."

Charlo gave Spukani a stern look. "The Salish do not harm women." He issued the reprimand in a quiet voice.

Spukani glared at Maisey but said no more.

Charlo turned his head toward Shane. "Hello, Preacher. It's good to see you again."

"Good evening, Chief." Shane's eyes glowed as he smiled. "It's been a while since we've spoken. How are you keeping?"

"Well enough, but you seem to be having trouble." Charlo moved nearer to Shane. "Why were you taken captive?"

"I'm not entirely sure, except that I tried to persuade Spukani to let the teacher go." Shane nodded toward Spukani, pacing behind the chief. "He will have another opinion on the matter, I'm certain."

Charlo grunted. "It is mine that counts."

"Reverend Hayes is a good man." Maisey stepped into the opening the chief had provided by greeting Shane. "He is always kind to your people."

"That is one thing I do know." Charlo smiled. "Tell me, who is this other one?"

"Rob is my cousin."

Charlo turned to Maisey. "Would you say he is a good

man too?"

"Yes." Maisey answered without hesitation. She realized with a quiver of surprise that despite all the pain Rob had brought her, she still believed in him.

Charlo gave Spukani a firm glance. "It is better that you free them."

Spukani paced nearer. "I'll let the preacher go, but I claim the other man as my slave."

"No!" Maisey thrust herself in front of Rob. Spukani's scowling face filled her vision. She spoke without turning her head. "Please don't let him keep my betrothed."

CHAPTER SEVEN

MAISEY HEARD ROB'S BREATH GO IN on a hiss. She had only to lift her head to glimpse his expression, but she couldn't bring herself to do so. Neither could she look at Shane. What would they think of her? The urge to save Rob from the hardships he would suffer as Spukani's slave had gotten the best of her. Where had the untruth come from? It seemed to have entered her brain of its own accord. It must have arisen from the desire she'd hidden for so long.

"Don't believe her." Spukani glared at Maisey. "She does not speak the truth."

Maisey averted her gaze from Spukani. If only she could make him understand she was not his enemy.

"Preacher?" Charlo turned to Shane. "Do you know if this is true?"

Maisey trembled, waiting for Shane to expose her lie.

"Well—" Shane paused to clear his throat.

"I love Maisey with all my heart." Rob jumped into the breach.

Maisey jerked her head upward, snared at once by Rob's gaze.

"He has another reason to say that." Spukani scoffed.

"Even a blind fool can see that there's love between these two," Shane had apparently resolved the difficulty with his throat.

Charlo studied Maisey, and she forced herself to meet his gaze without flinching. He nodded, and apparently satisfied, turned his attention to Shane. "That may be true, but love alone is not enough to free a slave."

"Take our horses in exchange." Shane's voice held an edge.

Spukani smirked. "We already have their horses."

"You must return them." The chief rapped out the words. "They need to ride home. I will give you a horse in exchange for each captive. You must content yourself with that."

"Liars should not go free." With rage flaring his nostrils and the cords in his neck standing out, Spukani looked every inch a warrior.

"I'm ready to marry this woman, if she wants me." Rob spoke slowly and deliberately, his gaze never leaving Maisey's.

"I do." Maisey answered softly.

"Preacher," Charlo smiled at Shane, "you can perform the ceremony."

"This is my way of saying thanks for helping me when I was sick." Emma placed the cake she'd baked on the counter in America's kitchen.

"Goodness, you didn't need to trouble yourself." America beamed, clearly delighted that she had.

Emma surveyed her handiwork. The sweet confection consisted of two layers of white cake with homemade rose jam sandwiched between them. "I flavored the frosting with rosewater and used beet juice to color it pink."

"How did you know that I adore rosewater frosting?"

Emma shrugged. "You've mentioned it before."

"Remembering my preference shows how thoughtful you are."

"I'm glad you'll enjoy it."

America's face lit. "Why don't we have a slice with a cup

of tea? It's the perfect time during the lull after lunch."

Emma smiled. "All right. You've convinced me."

"Oh, good. Sweets are always better when eaten with someone else. I'll get the tea. Would you mind cutting the cake?"

Emma reached for a knife from the wooden tray set well back on the counter. "How many slices shall I cut?"

"Only two." America smiled conspiratorially. "The children are building forts in their bedrooms. I doubt they'll emerge. We can have a nice, peaceful visit, and I'll surprise them with dessert after supper."

She laughed. "They do sound busy." Excited chatter punctuated by squeals of joy had rung out since Emma entered the house.

"I'm thankful that Liberty has started joining in again." America gestured toward one of the ladderback chairs around the kitchen table. "Have a seat."

Emma sank down with a sigh. "I'm glad to rest, I must admit. I made a cake for Mrs. Buckthorn today too."

"Did you really?"

"I couldn't leave her out after all she's done for me."

"It's remarkable how quickly you're recovering, but then you have the vigor of youth on your side." America bustled about the kitchen, putting the kettle on to boil and setting up the tea tray.

"Have you heard any news of Maisey yet?" Emma couldn't resist asking the question.

"I'm afraid not." America laid teaspoons beside the cups on the tray.

"I sure hope she is all right, plus everyone who went with her."

"We'll have to trust the Lord to take care of them. That's

all we can do." America added a sugar bowl to the tray, a crystal dish Emma recognized as one she used on special occasions.

"I like Mrs. Buckthorn very much." America spooned tea into her blue willow pot. "I wish I could get over more often, but with the children it's hard to leave the house sometimes. I've invited her here, but she seldom comes over."

"I think she's busy around her place with a husband and three sons to feed. Now that I'm feeling better, I don't mind watching the children so you two can have a visit."

America smiled. "That's thoughtful of you. I'll take you up on the offer after Shane comes back, if you still feel up to it. Until then, the children need me near."

"That's understandable." Emma added a fork to one of the plates. "How are they weathering the separation?"

"Well enough, I suppose. My children are used to their father being away from home, but that doesn't make it easy. They don't cling to me, but if I went away also, it might unsettle them."

Emma shook her head. "I don't know how you keep your own spirits up, let alone your children's. You make motherhood seem simple."

America laughed. "It isn't, as you will no doubt learn one day. I'm glad you like Gideon's mother. I can't think of a nicer person to take care of you when you're sick."

"She's an angel. I see why Gideon adores her."

"The entire family is smitten with her." America carried the tea tray to the table and poured the steaming liquid into their cups. "You have to hand it to a woman like Felicity Buckthorn. Raising a pack of sons with no daughter is just plain hard."

"She seems the right person for the job."

America tilted her head questioningly. "What do you think of Gideon?"

"Oh, he's nice but awfully young." Emma took a cautious sip from her cup.

America's eyes gleamed. "I assume you speak from the vast experience of your many years."

Emma laughed self-consciously. "Well, no. I have a good idea of what I admire in a man, though."

The conversation ranged to other topics and it wasn't until they were on the porch saying goodbye that America brought the subject up again. "I hope you'll give Gideon a chance. I suspect he would like to court you."

Emma lifted her face to the breeze, considering the idea. She shook her head. "He should get over any such notion. I prefer an experienced man who knows how to make his way in the world. Someone like Rob, for instance. Compared to him, Gideon is a baby."

"You have an awfully good opinion of Rob."

"Between you and me, I suffered a broken heart after learning that Rob was sweet on Maisey." It felt strangely good to tell someone what she had endured.

"And yet, you befriended Maisey."

"It wasn't her fault, and I didn't blame Rob either."

"I suspect that's still the way things are between them." America leaned on the porch rail. "At some point, I expect they will get married."

Emma didn't want to discuss the possibility. "I'd better deliver the cake I made for Mrs. Buckthorn before it grows any later." She started. "What was that noise?"

"Do you mean that rustling sound? A rabbit must have made it. We've seen a lot of them lately."

Emma rubbed the goosebumps on her arms. "I wish I

could stop being on edge."

"You're not alone in that. I must say I'll be glad when Shane returns."

"I didn't realize how comforting it was with Maisey living in the cabin next door." Emma shuddered. "I can't get what happened to her out of my mind."

"That's not surprising, since you saw it take place. I can understand how unnerving it might be for the cabin next door to stand empty. We located those cabins to provide privacy, but I wish we'd built them within view of the house instead. Any time you want to spend the night at my place, you're welcome."

"I appreciate that." Emma wouldn't take her up on the offer, though.

"Please don't hesitate. I'm sure it would help me too."

A craven part of Emma wanted to head back over with her toothbrush before nightfall. She'd learned in recent days to depend on others sometimes. Being afraid of a rabbit in broad daylight wasn't one of them.

In the grooming stall, Gideon stroked the curry comb over Lady Gray's withers. He'd rather put himself to work than brood over what he'd overheard Emma say about him. Not that labor was doing much good. His mind refused to remain on the task at hand.

A shadow broke the late afternoon sunlight slanting through the open barn door. He glanced up in time to glimpse Emma hurrying past. She wore the same blue calico as when she'd called him a baby. He'd always liked seeing her in that dress, but not anymore. It would ever after bring back her unkind remark. He'd been on the footpath between his parents' house and the Hayes place, and had ducked out of sight. It would have been too humiliating for her to know he'd overheard. That had happened only a little while ago, and the shock wasn't anywhere near to wearing off. Emma's criticism had cut so deeply it would take time and effort for him to forgive her.

Meanwhile, he would focus on caring for the livestock. The barn stalls held an assortment of animals—swift horses for riding, draft horses to hitch to the wagon and for plowing, several beef cattle, an ox that had become more of a pet, and even a milk cow. Ma had insisted on bringing Daisy from their old home to provide milk, butter, and cream when they reached Liberty. Gideon suspected, also, that his mother had made a pet of the cow and couldn't bring herself to part with her.

His mother's gray mare snorted and tossed her mane.

"Sorry, girl." Gideon slowed the curry comb and pressed more softly. He hadn't meant to afflict the mare with his frustrations. Returning his attention to the task before him, he ran the comb over the mare's coat.

Emma sure expected a lot from a man. He was all of twenty, and it wasn't fair to compare him to someone who had a head start of seven years or more. Gideon might get around to traveling at some point, but it wasn't first on his list. That place belonged to being near his family.

Lady stomped a hoof and stared at him with a baleful eye.

Gideon massaged the gray mare's neck to apologize. Lady turned her head into his shoulder and whickered. He put down the curry comb in favor of a soft brush.

In a few years, he might be able to compete with someone like Rob for a woman's affections. He shouldn't even consider vying for Emma, though. She valued altogether different things than he did. Gideon shook his head. Why should he care that she obviously wanted Rob, and not him?

And yet, somehow, he did.

Sunset mantled the shoulders of the mountains and dyed the clouds vibrant hues. The sun hung low in the sky, as if eager to retire for the night. A dog barked in the Indian encampment, then fell silent. Maisey stood beside Rob on the small hill above the village. The shadows of the stakes reached toward them across the long grass stippled by flowers. Shane faced them, a prayer book and Bible in his hands. Spukani was nowhere in sight, having stomped off earlier. Maisey could not be sorry that he had removed his glowering presence from her wedding to Rob. His disbelief had brought them to this moment—well, and her own dishonesty. Chief Charlo waited with Margaret beside him a little apart from the guards.

Shane scanned her face, his forehead creased, but then gave her a reassuring smile. "Are you ready?"

Maisey couldn't imagine feeling less prepared. What had she gotten herself into? There was no question that she loved Rob. The riddle was whether he loved her in return. Today he'd said he did, but how much had the desire to escape slavery influenced him?

What else could she do but marry Rob after declaring herself so emphatically? Chief Charlo might allow her to go home, but if she resisted, it seemed certain Spukani would force Rob to remain. She could not abide leaving anyone to Spukani's tender mercies, especially Rob. She answered Shane with a swift nod, not quite trusting her voice.

Shane shifted his attention to his cousin and lifted a brow inquiringly. "How about you?"

"Just a minute." Rob plucked a handful of the Indian paintbrush and fireweed growing at his feet. He pressed the bouquet into Maisey's hands.

The wildflowers wavered behind a veil of tears. They seemed so delicate, as if they could be easily crushed.

Rob planted himself firmly beside her. "Get on with it."

"All right, then." Shane cleared his throat. "We'll dispense with formalities and go straight to the point, shall we?"

"That's best," Rob agreed.

Maisey nodded. Her elopement with Avery seemed a grand wedding compared to this strained affair. What was the point of dragging out such a disappointing ceremony?

"Repeat after me." Shane barely glanced at the text in his hands. "I, Robert Devin Walsh, take thee, Maisey Lucille Wilcox, to be my wedded wife…"

Rob, wearing a solemn expression, echoed the words. Maisey wanted very much to believe he meant them. "To have and to hold from this day forward…" Rob's voice rose and fell as he made his vows. "…and thereto I plight thee my troth."

Shane bolstered Maisey with an encouraging smile. "If the bride will repeat after me…"

Maisey pulled in a shaky breath and echoed the words that would bind her to Rob for better or worse, richer or poorer, and in sickness or health. She hoped it could be for a lifetime.

Shane looked up from his prayer book. "We've forgotten the ring."

Charlo stepped forward. "What is wrong, Preacher?"

"It is customary for the groom to seal the vows that have been spoken by placing a ring on the bride's finger." Shane frowned. "We need something. Even a short length of cord would work."

"You may have it." Charlo spoke to one of the guards in

rapid Salish.

The guard pulled his hunting knife and cut a length from the fringe on his belt, which he presented to Shane.

"Thank you." Shane accepted the gift and held up the thin strip of soft leather before Maisey. "Rob will have to tie this around your finger."

She nodded swiftly. "It will do."

Shane held out the scrap to Rob. "Whatever you do, don't drop it."

Maisey could see why he'd given the warning. If Rob fumbled while tying the strip on her finger, it would disappear into the flower-ridden grass waving at their feet.

Rob bowed over Maisey's finger and tied the cord with deft fingers. It felt strange and clumsy on her hand, as awkward as the wedding itself.

"All right, then." Shane let out a breath. "Speak the following words, Rob. With this ring I thee wed…"

Rob's face looked solemn as he gave the age-old promises of a husband to a wife. By all appearances, he meant every word.

"I now pronounce you man and wife." Shane's declaration penetrated Maisey's reeling mind. "You may kiss the bride."

Rob's mouth brushed hers, featherlight. Maisey caught her breath, captivated. He lifted his head, but his gaze clung to hers. She parted her lips. The expression on Rob's face intensified, ruining her composure. He pressed his mouth to hers in a deeper caress. Maisey gripped the front of his shirt, trying to steady herself as the world spun. She made a small sound in her throat, part desire and part fear. She had tasted Rob's lips once before, after which he'd turned his back on her.

Rob released her, and they stood apart.

"After witnessing that kiss, I'm certain I've done right to

join you in wedlock," Shane remarked dryly.

"If ever there was a more public courtship, I don't know of one." Rob tucked his arm around Maisey. "We seem to have weathered the lack of privacy, regardless."

Smiles wreathed Charlo's face as he stepped forward. "Little Elk and his wife want you to stay in their tepee tonight. They will sleep in our lodge."

In the rush of things, Maisey's thoughts hadn't yet carried her to the wedding night. How could she have forgotten it? She offered him a smile. "You must thank your sister and her husband for us."

"I will tell them you are grateful. Come. Margaret has prepared food for us. After we eat, I will take you to their tepee." Charlo led the way toward the village.

Rob gestured sweepingly. "After you, Mrs. Walsh."

CHAPTER EIGHT

EMMA BALANCED GRANDMA ROSE'S best cake plate in her hands and climbed the steps onto the Buckthorn porch. She had admired its rose pattern and gold edges since childhood. It belonged to her now that her family was gone. She considered it priceless but shared it with others on rare occasions. This was one of them. An apple cake dusted with cinnamon sugar sat on top of the plate, her gift to Mrs. Buckthorn, or Felicity as Gideon's mother had invited Emma to call her.

The front door opened and Felicity appeared in the doorway. Her face showed lines of strain, but she greeted Emma warmly. "Oh, my. What do you have there?"

"I baked an apple cake to express my gratitude for the way you looked after me while I was sick."

"It's for me? I'm honored. That wasn't necessary, but of course I'll enjoy it. Apple cake is my favorite."

"Gideon told me." Emma glanced about nervously, but the person she had just named was nowhere in sight. Whistling coming from the barn hinted at his location, unless that was one of his brothers. In case it happened to be Gideon, she would avoid the open barn doorway on her way home. Returning her attention to Felicity, she surprised a knowing look on the older woman's face. Emma's cheeks heated. Why did Gideon's mother think she was looking toward the barn? Of course, she couldn't ask.

The strain in Felicity's face vanished and humor lit her eyes. "Are you free to stay for supper?"

Emma drew a quick breath. "I wouldn't want to intrude, but I appreciate the offer."

"My dear, you are more than welcome to share our table tonight." Felicity pushed a strand of graying blond hair out of her eyes. "My younger boys were invited to eat at the Hayes's house, so there are extra portions in the pot and space to spare around the table. To be honest, I'm a little lonely with Mr. Buckthorn away from home. I could use company."

Emma bit her lip. She'd only meant to dash over to deliver the cake, and then return home, all without running into Gideon. If she hadn't lingered so long over tea at America's house she wouldn't be in this predicament.

It would be unkind of her not to provide the distraction Felicity so badly needed. The heavenly aroma wafting from the kitchen clenched the matter. Whatever Felicity was cooking would be a good sight better than the bit of bacon and cold plate of beans awaiting her at home. "All right, if you're sure I'm not intruding."

"Of course not." Felicity opened the door wider. "Why don't you come in and set the table while I make biscuits and finish up the smoked venison stew?"

Emma followed her into the kitchen and deposited her cake on the counter. She already regretted her rash decision. A combination of sympathy and hunger had prompted it. Neither would help her survive a supper that would surely include Gideon.

"Everything you need is on the shelf behind you." Felicity tossed the comment over her shoulder as she hurried to stir the steaming pot on her stove.

Emma laid out the plates, forks, knives, and spoons on the dining table. Moving through the familiar task felt good. She had done this often for her own mother.

"Would you mind filling the glasses?" Felicity thumped a pitcher of water onto the table. She swept a gaze over the table. "The place settings look lovely. Where did you learn to pleat napkins like that?"

"My mother taught me." Emma smiled softly. "She made it fun."

"What wonderful memories of her you must have." Felicity gave her shoulders a quick squeeze.

Emma didn't normally like others to touch her casually, but she didn't mind Felicity's touches. They reminded Emma of her mother's gentle expressions of love.

"Supper will be ready soon." Felicity peered out the window. "Would you be a dear and let Gideon know supper is ready? He's tending to the livestock in the barn."

Emma could think of no polite way to refuse, and Felicity did truly need her help. She found Gideon bending over one of the draft horse's hooves. "Your mother sent me to tell you that supper is ready."

"Thanks for the information." Gideon spoke without looking up.

Was it her imagination or did his tone sound clipped? She couldn't think why that should be so. With her duty discharged, Emma hurried back to the house.

Gideon entered while she was lighting the candles in twin silver candlesticks that graced the middle of the table.

"Are you staying to supper?" He sent her a surprised look, his face still damp from the scrubbing he must have given it.

She ignored the unaccountable urge to run her fingers through his hair, which was drying in loose waves. "Your mother invited me," Emma answered defensively. He must have thought she'd stopped by the barn on her way home.

"Oh." He looked away from her, a guarded expression on

his face.

Emma had the distinct impression that Gideon would have begged off if he'd known she would be a guest at their table. Although she'd been determined to avoid him, it piqued her to suspect that he felt the same in reverse. As they sat down to supper, Gideon held Emma's chair with stiff formality. Emma looked at him in puzzlement. Why was he acting this way?

Felicity leveled a stern glance on her son. "Aren't the napkins clever, Gideon? Emma folded them."

"I guessed as much." He shook his square of gingham out of its swan shape.

"Isn't it sweet?" Felicity smiled at Emma. "How many other ways can you fold napkins?"

"I know a lot of them." Emma sighed. "But I don't have much call for fancy table settings anymore. The life of a teacher doesn't allow for much gaiety."

"We should throw a party so you can show off your skill." Felicity's smile dimmed a little. "Once the men return, of course."

"They will, Ma." Gideon touched his mother's arm. "They will."

Emma stared at her plate, wishing he would speak to her in that warm voice. Sitting at the Bucthorn table reminded her of the meals she'd shared with her own family. It felt too cruel that she would never sit down to supper with them again.

Something had changed between her and Gideon. When had his tone for her become so disapproving? It matched the slightly lifted eyebrows above the cold eyes he turned her direction. "I doubt you'll find Liberty much of a place to practice your napkin folding."

It was all too much. Emma caught her breath on a sob.

Felicity aimed a faintly reproachful glance at her son, then turned to Emma. "What is it, dear?"

"I'm sorry." Emma dabbed her eyes with her napkin. "Sometimes I miss my family so badly I ache."

Felicity gave her a sympathetic look. "I understand. My mother passed away years ago, but it feels like only yesterday that I lost her."

Emma pulled in a breath. "I hope to feel that way about my family always. I'm afraid I'll forget them."

"I doubt you will." Felicity's eyes held warmth. "They must have been very special for you to miss them so deeply. You'll always have the memories to sustain you."

"Yes, you're right." Emma thumbed away a tear. "I have a great deal for which to be thankful."

Gideon offered her no words of comfort but afterwards watched her with a softer expression.

The conversation lagged after her outburst, but Felicity stepped in with well-mannered ease. "Tell me, Emma, are you already preparing for the start of school?"

"Yes, actually. I've reviewed the lessons I'll teach. I was going to turn out the schoolroom, but then I came down sick."

A crease formed between Felicity's eyes. "You've had several bouts with illness lately. I hope you'll get plenty of rest before September arrives."

"I will." Emma picked up her glass. "Once school starts, I'll move the children into a full schedule gradually. It's hard to capture their attention when it's nice outside, plus harvest time brings extra duties for them at home."

"Miss Duncan is thoughtful to consider such things, don't you think, Gideon?" A steely note entered Felicity's voice. Emma wanted to smile despite her embarrassment at the pointed question. Clearly, Gideon had better agree with his mother's assessment. He had called his mother a force to be reckoned with, and Emma began to see why.

Gideon's gaze rested on her, then shifted away. "I'm sure you are quite a treasure."

Emma put down her spoon, no longer relishing her food. She took sips from her water glass to cover the fact that she wasn't eating.

Felicity frowned. "Don't you like the stew?"

The sharp-eyed woman missed nothing, apparently. "It's delicious, but my appetite isn't fully restored yet." That fact would have to serve as her excuse, and it had the advantage of being true. Emma refused to go into the whole reason she'd lost the desire to eat, but it had a lot to do with Gideon's icy attitude.

The strained supper finally ended, much to Emma's relief. She should have followed her first inclination and gone home. Better a cold plate of beans than Gideon's hostility. Avoiding running into him while they cleared the table together was tricky, but she managed it.

Felicity refused Emma's help with the dishes. "I can take care of them later. Why don't we sit in the parlor for a while? Gideon can play the piano."

"Thank you, but I'd better make my way home." Emma couched her refusal in suitable tones of regret. "It's darkening outside."

"So it is." Felicity glanced out the window. "I wonder if winter will come early this year. The days seem to be growing shorter."

"I'll walk you home." Gideon spoke from the doorway that led into the hall, looking thoroughly annoyed at his own suggestion.

"I wouldn't dream of putting you to the trouble." Emma

spoke with withering politeness. He wasn't the only one who could adopt that tactic.

"I must insist." His smile did not reach his eyes. "What kind of *man* lets a woman walk home alone in the dark?"

Emma stared at him, trying to figure out the odd inflection he'd used.

"Do let my son accompany you." Felicity touched her arm lightly. "I'll rest easier knowing that you arrived home safely."

Emma wavered, then surrendered her pride. "All right." She couldn't imagine a more uncomfortable walk home. "Thank you," she added a moment later, for the sake of politeness.

"Think nothing of it." Gideon turned into the hallway, leaving her to follow.

The sweet fragrance of the night, made up of cottonwoods, evergreens, and wild grass wafted to Emma as she kept pace with Gideon. The last wash of blue was fading from the sky above the blackened treetops. A distant dog barked from the direction of town. In the wooded lands beyond the schoolhouse, a wild call reverberated. *Hoo hoo-hoo hoo-hoo…* The moon hovered above the eastern horizon, and a cooling breeze stirred. Emma filled her lungs with the living air and tilted her face toward the stars that winked in the heavens.

She caught up with Gideon, who hadn't waited while she lingered. Nor did he slow his pace or shorten his stride when she reached him. Pride forbade her to protest, which left only one other option. Emma did her best to match her gait to his. She had to give up, unfortunately. Breathing hard, she slowed down. Gideon continued on without even noticing she wasn't with him.

He traveled a good way down the path before glancing about. "Am I going too fast for you?" he called.

Emma waited until she reached him to answer. "I'm not quite over my illness."

Gideon studied her. "Sorry. You seem so much better that I forgot you're not all the way mended." Genuine warmth crept into his voice for the first time that night, and he offered her his arm.

Emma waged an inner battle then slid her hand into the crook of his arm. "I'm not contagious anymore, I don't think. I hated being unable to relieve America with her children. With her husband away, I'm sure she can use a break."

Gideon set off more slowly. "I know it's tempting, but don't tax yourself overmuch. You don't want another relapse."

"That's hard for me since I've always been strong. I'm not used to sickness holding me back."

Gideon bent his head toward her. "What happened to change that?"

"I'm not sure. I've struggled since coming to Liberty. I hope the area isn't bad for me."

"It might not be the place but the time that is at fault."

Emma tried to comprehend his meaning. "I don't understand."

"The strain of losing your family could be affecting you. Many people would find that a hardship."

She considered the idea. "It's possible."

The shadows of the trees closed over them as they entered into the grove of cottonwoods. Emma drew closer to Gideon, glad that he'd offered her his arm. In the dimness, it wouldn't be hard to trip.

"I should have brought a lantern." Gideon put his hand protectively over the one she'd placed on his arm.

"Be sure to take one of mine before you return through here." Emma clung to his arm. "Thank you for seeing me home, by the way. I don't like walking beneath these trees at sunset."

"Worried the Bogeyman will snatch you?"

Emma forgot to answer him. She was too busy darting glances about. It was all well and good to consider courage a virtue. She found it more of a survival tactic. "You shouldn't tease."

Gideon laughed. "Or you'll tell my ma on me?"

"Why are you acting so—"

"Immature?"

"You said that, not me."

"Yes, but it's what you meant."

Emma sighed. "All right, so I did. You're certainly not behaving like an adult at the moment."

He halted and turned her toward him. "I'm a man, Emma, fully grown."

"Gideon—"

"We'd better move on." He made no move to go.

Gideon had sounded rueful, and Emma thought she knew why. It didn't take much to figure out that he wanted to kiss her. The idea occupied her mind, driving away everything else. If he tried, how would she respond? She wasn't certain.

Something caught her ankle. Emma cried out as she fell.

Gideon caught her and pulled her against his chest in an awkward embrace. "What happened?"

It was hard to think with his heartbeat racing beneath her ear. "I believe a root snagged my foot."

"Can you stand?"

Emma sucked in a breath and made the attempt. "No. I twisted my ankle. Maybe I can after a minute."

"This is my fault, rushing out in a hurry without a lantern."

The reason for his impatience seemed obvious. Gideon had been annoyed with her for some reason only he knew, and he'd let the eagerness to be rid of her lead him astray. She wasn't sure whether being on the wrong side of Gideon's anger or exposed to his ardor endangered her equilibrium more.

While holding her close with his arms around her, the quality of his embrace shifted, becoming much friendlier than earlier. Unexpected emotions rushed through Emma, too many to name. Feeling completely off-balance, she clutched his shirt.

Gideon released a long sigh. "Emma—"

"I know," she whispered.

He lowered his head and captured her mouth in a tantalizing caress. Emma instinctively leaned into his embrace. He dragged her closer, tightening the contact between their mouths. Desire uncurled within her, and she ran her fingers along his neck and into his hair. Gideon responded by deepening their kiss.

Emma could barely collect her thoughts, let alone find her balance. She managed to pull away somehow. "We mustn't –"

"I'm sorry, Emma." Gideon's voice sounded ragged. "You are right, of course."

She put her weight on her twisted ankle and discovered it much improved. "It's high time you delivered me home, Mr. Buckthorn."

"Miss Duncan, I couldn't agree more."

The smell of sun-warmed hide permeated the air as the tepee's flap thumped into place, shutting Maisey in with Rob. She came to a standstill at once. Maisey held her eyes open wide but still couldn't penetrate the darkness inside the tepee. "I can't see a thing." Her whisper sounded loud in the stillness.

"Can you?"

"Nothing. We'll have to wait for our eyes to adjust."

By the faint moonlight falling through the central smoke hole, Maisey finally made out the circular fire ring and the gleaming edges of wooden sleeping benches. She lowered herself cautiously to one of the benches and discovered furs beneath her. Maisey ran a hand over their softness. It felt good to sit after so long on her feet. She longed to sleep, but it was her wedding night. Maisey sighed. In all her dreams of remarrying, she'd never pictured spending this night of all nights in such a location.

Rob loomed above her. If only she could see his face and gauge what he was thinking. She would soon find out if he had married her because he truly loved her. She hadn't ever considered that her wedding night would serve as a test.

Rob moved nearer. "Are you comfortable?"

"As much as can be expected under the circumstances."

"May I join you?" Rob sounded tentative.

"Yes." Maisey couldn't hide her surprise that he would ask so considerately. What had happened to the brash man she'd known? He seemed to have carried himself off, to be replaced by a stranger.

Rob sat a little apart from her. "We've come to quite a pass, haven't we?"

Not understanding what he meant by that, she gave no reply.

"Maisey, I want you to know—" He fell silent.

"Yes?"

"You don't have to worry— What I mean to say is—oh, hang it all." He heaved a sigh. "I'm trying to tell you that I won't expect anything from you."

Maisey's stomach clenched. Rob had declared his love for

her, given his vows, even kissed her with every appearance of enthusiasm. None of that changed the answer to her question. "Thank you." She forced the words past the constriction in her throat. Her conscience chided her for the lie. She could never summon gratitude that Rob didn't want her in the way she did him. He'd decided against their having a real marriage. If only she didn't know what they would miss. The short years she'd spent as Avery's bride had revealed to her the joy she would never have again.

She hauled in a breath and flicked away a tear. What more had she expected from a man who had abandoned her? Why had she let hope deceive her into thinking his heart would change? Rob had already made his feelings clear. He had never loved her, nor would he ever. She would have been better off to remain as Avery's widow.

How they would straighten out this mess, she had no idea. Tonight, all she wanted to do was weep.

Rob's efforts to comfort Maisey only made her cry harder. Everything he did seemed to have the opposite effect than the one he intended. If he'd needed proof of his incompetence in matters of the heart, he had it yet again. With no clear idea how to reach this woman he so loved, he waited in quiet sorrow until Maisey's muffled sobs faded into sleep.

He'd wanted to say so much to her on this, their wedding night. He could have taken her to wife, despite his weariness. He wanted Maisey to give herself to him from a willing heart though, not out of duty. He was painfully aware that she had married him to protect his freedom. Believing anything else would be deluding himself. Letting her marry him anyway had been a selfish act he might come to regret. He had no excuse, except perhaps that possessing the privilege of courting her had been irresistible. He could only hope that marrying her hadn't been a mistake that would ruin both their lives.

He rolled over on the sleeping bench, trying to shed his uncomfortable thoughts. They came with him anyway.

He'd never expected to have this chance to show Maisey his love for her over time. If he worked very hard to win his new wife's affections, she might fall in love with him. All he had to do was figure out what to do. The best thing would be to ask Shane for advice. His cousin's marriage was solid as a rock. Shane's faith annoyed him at times, but Rob was the first to admit it solved problems. At the least, it gave Shane the backbone to live with courage. Rob could use a bit of that himself. The challenge of proving his love to Maisey frightened the wits out of him. He'd already tried and failed several times over. Truth to tell, he would far rather confront a claim jumper than his own ineptitude where Maisey was concerned.

Rob shifted onto his side again. Receiving mercy instead of enslavement had unlocked the deep place within where doubts lurked. He had questioned his own competence since his unsettling childhood. After he and his family were crammed into the hull of a ship with barely anything to eat, they'd taken up residence in a tenement that failed to protect against the elements. His experiences in the Five Points slum had formed him in his youth. Living on a landfill over the polluted Collect Pond could only foster diseases. Those who survived sicknesses might succumb to the gangs that made mischief in the streets. He could picture the bully who had accosted him before he'd learned to fight. That lapse had occurred only once.

He'd received a new lease on life, and it was time to put the past to rest. He wasn't entirely sure how, but he was willing to try. Letting go of the effects of the slum would take effort. The drive to free himself for Maisey's sake as well as his own burned in his chest.

With no other recourse, Rob lowered himself to his knees.

All right, God. I guess I'd better follow Shane's advice and make peace with You. I've tried to look after myself without turning to You for help. That hasn't worked out very well. All I can say is I'm sorry. If I haven't offended You past redemption, I'd appreciate Your help figuring out this mess I've made.

CHAPTER NINE

AMERICA TWITCHED HER BEDROOM CURTAINS AGAINST the dark of night. She rubbed a kink at the back of her neck and released a deep breath. The clock in the hallway chimed in even strokes, repeated twelve times. Instead of going to bed at a decent hour, she'd rushed about trying to catch up on her chores. Tea and cake with Emma, although fun, had caused her to fall behind on her day.

America slipped between the sheets and blew out her candle. She pulled Shane's pillow into her embrace. If only her husband lay beside her instead of making his bed somewhere in the wilderness. His image rose behind her closed lids, smiling down at her from atop his beloved horse. The joy that lit his eyes swept her in its tide. How she loved this man.

Separation from Shane came more easily on some days, but this was not one of them. Unwelcome speculations had crept up on her at various times throughout the day. She'd pictured him injured, overwhelmed by sickness, forced into slavery, and with his eyes staring sightlessly toward the heavens. These mental images did nothing for her composure. She and Shane had grown together so completely over the years that she couldn't imagine life without him.

Lord, please bring my husband safely home to me.

America knew that God heard her every prayer, but she sometimes found that hard to believe while spilling words into empty air. She smoothed a hand over her husband's pillow. "Come home to me, my darling."

A faint cry echoed down the hallway. America threw aside her covers and stood wearily. She followed the soft sounds of weeping to Liberty's room.

"Don't take on so." Phoebe's murmur carried through the open doorway.

America paused before going in. Phoebe seemed to have the matter in hand. She stole close enough to peer inside. Moonlight filtered through the white cotton curtains at the window, revealing Liberty sitting up in bed. Phoebe was holding her while she vented her emotions.

"The Indians tomahawked my pa," Liberty gasped.

"No, they didn't." Phoebe stroked Liberty's hair. "That was only a nightmare."

Liberty shuddered. "It seemed so real."

"Well, it wasn't."

America smiled. Phoebe was mature beyond her years and possessed a practical bent that was precisely what imaginative Liberty needed.

"Well, it was horrible."

"Nightmares usually are, but go back to sleep." A bar of moonlight rippled over Phoebe as she stood up. "Things always look better in the morning."

Liberty laid her head on her pillow once more. "Do you suppose God is looking after my pa?"

"Of course." Phoebe slipped into the cot where she slept whenever she visited. "Same as He's taking care of my ma."

"Do you really believe that?" Liberty's question sounded so wistful America wanted to go in and comfort her. She held back to allow Phoebe to answer.

"Yes, but it's not always easy." Phoebe spoke with infinite weariness.

Liberty sighed. "God seems far away sometimes."

"That isn't true either."

"How do you know?"

"I just do. Go to sleep, Liberty. God is closer than you think."

A verse from the book of Psalms ran through America's head. *Out of the mouth of babies and infants, you have established strength because of your foes, to still the enemy and the avenger.*

She withdrew from the doorway and returned to her bedroom with a lighter step.

Rob stood beside Shane and Maisey on the small rise where he'd been staked. From this vantage point, he could easily scan the Indian camp. Women and children were already about, gathering firewood, filling water bags from the stream that tumbled a short distance behind the tepees, and attending other domestic duties. A few of the men were gathered in a knot, talking quietly. Rob released a pent breath. Spukani was nowhere in sight.

Charlo, with several men beside him, climbed to them. He stopped before Shane. "I am sorry this visit to our camp was not pleasant. You must return under better circumstances." The chief put his arms around Shane's neck, which Rob recognized as the Salish way of leave-taking.

"I will, my friend." Shane stepped back.

Charlo grinned at Maisey. "May your new husband hunt plenty of game for the winter."

Maisey smiled. "Thank you for your kind wish, and for giving us our horses to carry us home."

"You are welcome, Teacher." Charlo slanted a glance sideways to Rob. "I hope you live well the life that was returned to you."

"That is my intention." Rob made the promise not only to the chief, but to God also.

Yesterday's guards led their horses to them. Maisey accepted Rob's help into the saddle, letting him touch her in spite of last night's upset. Hope furled like a fragile blossom inside him. She did not speak, however, and averted her face from his gaze.

Shane divided a questioning glance between them. He furrowed his brow but remained silent. Rob could only feel grateful. Trouble with his new wife was hard enough without involving anyone else, especially another family member.

Rob's horse nickered in greeting. He rubbed its sleek neck, and then swung a leg over the saddle.

Shane turned Archibald's head away from the Salish camp.

Rob held back, allowing Maisey to ride in the middle.

Before long, the defile, a narrow channel between bluffs, closed about them. After emerging, they followed an animal trail that descended through forests of fir, spruce, and pine. The sky shone, softly blue. This high up, the temperature felt pleasant, but it climbed as they dropped toward the valley.

Perhaps an hour later Shane drew up ahead of them. "Well, if it isn't—"

Rob squinted to see past his cousin. A group of men wearing western clothing was heading toward them. The other riders pointed, and a whoop went up before they picked up their speed.

"That's Silas Buckthorn and the others from Liberty." Shane clicked to Archibald and started forward.

"Why are we meeting them head-on?" Rob shielded his eyes to see better. He counted about a dozen riders. "If they were tracking us, they'd be following behnd us."

"I don't know the answer to that, but we're about to find out." Shane picked up the pace.

A small wind swept over the peaks toward the valley, rippling the buffalo grass on the hillside they traversed. A golden eagle stretched its wings in a cloudless sky. The hills below them unfolded toward the valley in long swells. Streams fed into the river as it snaked through grassy meadows. At this distance, the trees lining its banks appeared little more than bushy clumps.

They met the other riders on the crest of a hill. Much celebration ensued before the riders brought their horses around to encircle them.

"Ma'am." Silas nodded to Maisey and scraped the hat from his head. The sun gleamed on his high forehead and in the gray threading his brown hair. "I'm glad to find you safe."

"Thank you, Mr. Buckthorn." Maisey awarded him a smile. "I appreciate all of you taking the time and trouble to search for me."

"By the way, Silas, what happened to you?" Shane waved a fly away. "We counted on seeing you sooner."

"That's a pitiful tale." Silas shook his head. "We lost your tracks, and then our way."

"At least you tried." Shane gave Rob a speaking glance.

"Yes, tracking is tough when you're not used to it." Rob chimed in, taking his cousin's unspoken cue. "Anyone can get turned around in these hills."

"Thanks for trying to make us feel better." Silas's slouching posture revealed that they hadn't succeeded. "We'd figured out our location and were about to go back when we spotted you."

"Where are we, then?" Shane straightened. "We're most interested."

"South of your cousin's ranch." Silas pointed. "Do you see it there?"

Rob squinted. "Yes, now that you mention it. Well, what do you know? I thought these hills seemed familiar. I must have ridden over them a time or two while looking after Con's ranch."

"I feel better about getting lost now." Silas grinned. "These hills are confusing. I'm sure you'd have sorted it out eventually."

"It's a relief to find ourselves so near family." Shane shifted in the saddle, making the leather creak. "I don't suppose Con will mind overnight guests. With so many, some might have to sleep in the bunk house, but that's a good sight better than out in the open with nothing to protect us should it rain."

"If it's all the same to you, we'll keep riding toward Liberty." Silas glanced around at his men, who all nodded. "We're more than ready to head home. Our families will be missing us."

"I understand." Shane's expression grew pensive. "Let Mrs. Hayes know we're safe, if you will."

"I'm happy to." Silas smiled ruefully. "At least I can be of that much use to you."

"Don't be hard on yourself, Silas." Shane gave him a sympathetic look. "Once they captured us, neither Rob nor I could leave waymarks to guide you."

"Is that what happened?" March Hill, a neighbor whose property bordered the Buckthorns', spoke up from beside Silas. "We wondered."

Silas wet his lips. "How'd you escape, anyhow?"

Rob waited for his cousin's explanation. Would it include his own wedding to Maisey?

"That's a longer story than we have time to discuss on this hillside." Shane glanced at Rob. "We should probably take a day or two at the ranch to recover, don't you think, Rob?"

"I agree." Rob studied Maisey, who sat silently. The drooping of her shoulders made her exhaustion plain. "Maisey should rest before riding any farther."

"We're thinking alike." Shane gathered Archibald's reins.

Rob braced himself mentally as they rode to the ford across the Bitterroot River. He'd meant to look up his brother, only not quite like this. He and Con had come to a sort of peace over his move to Virginia City. However, Rob was well aware that he'd disappointed his brother. At the rate they were traveling, they would reach the ranch before nightfall. How would Con react when they showed up unannounced on his doorstep?

"Here you go, Mrs. Hayes." Gideon hefted the sack of cornmeal onto the pantry shelf.

America hovered behind him in the doorway from the kitchen. "Thank you for picking that up for me."

He shrugged. "I'm glad to look after you while Reverend Hayes is away."

"You've been a big help. I can't tell you how grateful I am to be spared a trip to town with three children in tow."

Gideon grinned. "If there's anything else you need, let me know."

She laughed. "You may be sorry you said that."

Gideon went out the back door. His boots thumped across the porch boards and down the steps. Emma was next in line for a delivery. He strode to his wagon, newly parked in his family's barn, and lifted down the bushel of apples he'd bought for her.

About to turn away, he caught sight of the stack of papers he'd tossed onto the driving box. He'd fetched mail for the Hayes family along with his own. Gideon set down the apples and picked up the letter on top of the pile. The envelope felt substantial, was obviously made from high-quality paper, and bore the monogrammed letters 'MJD.' A bold scrawl in black ink addressed it to Maisey, care of Reverend Hayes.

Gideon took the porch steps two at a time and rapped on the back door.

America opened the door and looked out, her brow puckered.

"I almost forgot to give you your mail. There's a letter for Mrs. Wilcox."

She examined the letter on top of the stack. "I have to admit, I'm curious. Look at that stationery, and the postmark."

He turned his head to read it. "St. Louis, huh? I wonder who sent it."

"There's no return address, but I'm sure it's from her family. I wonder why they wrote to her? I remember her telling me that they aren't close." America glanced up. "Don't repeat that, please. I shouldn't have said it."

Gideon grinned. "Don't worry, Mrs. Hayes. It never occurs to me to gossip."

She smiled. "The world needs more people like you."

"Some might disagree with that idea." Gideon thought of Emma. He hadn't seen her since the fateful night he'd walked her home. Maybe the apples would help him make amends. He nodded at the letter. "Hopefully it's not bad news."

"Maisey isn't here to find out, if it is. I wonder if I should open it on her behalf." America inserted her finger under the flap, but then removed it without breaking the seal. "I won't. It might be extremely private."

He gave her a bracing smile. "I expect Mrs. Wilcox will be able to read it herself before long."

"Yes, of course. I mustn't lose faith that she will."

Gideon gave her an encouraging nod. "I doubt we'll have to wait much longer."

America lifted the letter and held it gingerly. "I'll put this somewhere safe until then." She went inside.

Gideon smiled at the shut door. He hoped one day to find a woman with as much character as America Hayes. Meanwhile, it was time to make amends with Emma. He returned to his wagon and hefted the apples. Their heady fragrance wafted to him as he strode through the cottonwood grove.

Emma answered the door on his first knock. "I saw you from the window."

Gideon nodded. "I guessed that."

Her gaze went to the basket of apples. "Those aren't mine."

"Yes, they are, if you want them." Gideon smiled, he hoped winningly.

"But—"

"Would you accept them as a gift?" He wished she would so he could put down the heavy bushel basket.

She looked at the apples, then at him. "Do you mean, a gift from you?"

He nodded. "I bought them for you."

She hesitated. "It wouldn't be proper for me to accept them."

Gideon felt a strong urge to kiss the pucker from her brow. "Are you going to stand by some antiquated rules? We're in the West, Emma, where we can decide what we do."

"Well…"

"They sure smell sweet."

"Yes, they do." She picked up an apple and held it to the light. "They're beautifully red."

Sensing victory, Gideon pressed the advantage. "Where would you like them?"

"I suppose it wouldn't hurt, this once." Emma backed out of the doorway and gestured toward an unoccupied corner in the kitchen. "Over there is fine."

Gideon stepped into the kitchen and plunked the basket down, glad to take the weight off his arms. He straightened, congratulating himself for initiating a truce between them.

She surveyed the apples with a bemused expression on her face. "I'll have to decide what to do with them all."

Gideon grinned. "I was hoping for apple pie."

Rob reined in his horse as an ache went through him. Rising two stories, the white clapboard ranch house shone in the sun near the end of a sweeping drive. Its roof was pitched steep to shed the heaviest snows in winter. Green shutters embraced the casement windows. Closed, they would shut out the heat in summer or trap the warmth in colder seasons. Columns ringed by carved leaves at their tops held up the small balcony that shaded the front porch.

Emotions flooded him, too many to name. He counted joy and pride but also regret and shame. He'd returned to this elegant building in his memory many times. Those visits had seemed more real to him than the dream-like sensation of actually being here in this moment. Running this ranch in Con's absence had claimed several years of his life. How green he'd been. Desiring everything Con owned was one reason to strike out on his own.

He no longer coveted his brother's ranch. He had the money to buy his own. If he could keep Maisey by his side, Rob stood a good chance of capturing his every dream. Would his brother celebrate his victory with him? They'd both risen above their upbringing in the slums. He liked to think Mam would be proud. He knew for certain his father would have been. It was too bad that life hadn't given Da the chance to see his sons' success.

Rob studied Maisey beside him. She and Shane had also stopped to look at the ranch house from the drive. Maisey's face held a certain softness. What thoughts lay claim to her? Did he dare hope she was remembering their first meeting? That had occurred here, after she and Bry had escaped being kidnapped by the Cheyenne. He'd been drawn to Maisey at once. As Bry's friend, he hadn't expected her to earn her keep, but she'd taken up a role in the kitchen out of gratitude. He smiled to himself. Completely smitten, he'd found every excuse to cross her path.

Rob pulled his thoughts back to the present. He glanced at Shane, and by unspoken consent they set off again. With shelter and feed in the offing, the horses picked up their pace.

The front door opened, and Rob's sister Bry stepped onto the porch beside Elsa, carrying a baby on her hip. Shane had informed Rob of Con's marriage to the beautiful German woman he'd rescued after unscrupulous people tried to exploit her. A mist blurred Rob's vision, and he swallowed hard. How could he have stayed away so long that Con had married and fathered a child while he was gone?

Rob wouldn't make the same mistake twice. He'd learned what he became without family—a stray soul wandering the earth. He never wanted to be that lonely again.

Bry hurried down the porch steps, beaming. "Is it really you, Rob? I thought my eyes might be deceiving me."

He grinned and hopped down from his horse. "Is that your way of telling me I've neglected you?"

"Perish the thought." She watched him with a guarded expression.

He could make no excuse. "I'm sorry, Sis. I should have come back sometimes."

"Mind you never stay away so long again." She frowned at him, but afterwards brought out a smile. "I'm thankful I came over to visit Elsa, or I'd have missed your arrival. We live in our own house that Nick built on the property. He manages the ranch for Con."

He swept her up in an embrace that became tearful. Rob recognized just how much he had to make up for. He'd sworn to himself not to return to the ranch until he'd made his fortune. He'd expected that to happen sooner than it had. Looking back, he could see that requiring that of himself had been a mistake. It had hurt not only those he loved, but himself.

Bry broke away and went to Maisey, who climbed down from her pony. "I'm so glad to find you with Shane and Rob. America sent word of your misadventure. I hope you've come to no harm."

Rob couldn't decipher Maisey's expression. "I'll recover," she said simply.

Bry caught her friend into a fierce hug. "I felt so badly that you were captured again. Let's hope it's the last time it ever happens."

"It will be if I have anything to say about it." Rob stressed in a hard tone. Bry's surprised glance revealed that he'd spoken more vehemently than she'd expected. He'd better watch himself or he'd reveal their marriage before Maisey was willing to acknowledge it.

Bry turned her smile on Shane. "I'm glad to see you again, Cousin."

"Hello, Bry." Shane engulfed her, then held her apart from him. "I hope you and all your household are well."

"We're at the peak of health except that our Katie wears us out while teething."

"You have my sympathy. Those times are hard for parents."

"We'll survive." Bry frowned. "I'm sorry for Katie, that's all."

"How old is your daughter?" Rob asked, trying to get his bearings.

"Katie is two." Bry held out a hand to Elsa, who stood a little apart from them. "Elsa, I'm sure you remember Rob."

"Yes, of course," Elsa said in her charming German accent. "Con will be especially happy to see you again."

"The privilege is mine." Rob extended his hand, which she took. "Tell me, who is that in your arms?"

"Fiona, this is your uncle." Elsa kissed the top of the baby's downy head.

Rob's breath caught, and he had to blink moisture away. "You've named her after our mother."

Elsa's face softened. "It was Con's idea."

"Speaking of which—" Shane glanced about. "Where, may I ask, are the men of the house?"

"I've been wondering that myself." Rob glanced about, hoping to spot Con within sight. He would rather not delay his reunion with his brother.

"Oh, they're around somewhere." Bry lifted a shoulder. "I think Nick said they were going to check the fish traps."

"I'll put the horses away and have a look for them." Shane reached for Archibald's reins, and then turned toward Maisey's pony.

Rob detached himself from Maisey's side. "I can tend our horses, but thanks all the same."

"Are you certain? You and Maisey have had a rough time for newly-marrieds."

Bry stared at him. "*What* did you say?"

"Sorry, but that slipped out." Shane cast a sheepish glance at Rob and Maisey. "I meant to let you tell the news yourself. Close your mouth, Bry, before a fly lands inside."

Maisey's cheeks flamed.

"Finally!" Bry bounced on her feet a little in her excitement. "If ever two people belong together, you do. I'm terribly happy that you've figured that out at last."

"I'm glad you're pleased," Maisey murmured.

"Pleased? I'm ecstatic. This means that the three of us are sisters." Bry's glance included Elsa.

Elsa smiled. "Why don't we ladies talk over tea and let Rob and Shane deal with the horses and finding our husbands?"

"That sounds lovely." Bry grinned. She put her arm around Maisey. "I'm anxious to hear all about you and Rob."

Maisey burst into tears.

"Oh, you poor darling." Bry gave her a squeeze. "You must be beside yourself with exhaustion." She led Maisey toward the door.

Rob watched Maisey vanish into the house. He wished that only weariness had made her cry, rather than regret over marrying him.

"Well, then." Shane's voice claimed Rob's attention. "We'd better see to the horses."

They groomed, stabled, and fed the horses before walking down to the banks of the Bitterroot. The river glistened like blue silk shot with green. A line of geese arrowed through the sky, and several ducks flapped low to the surface. The willows along the bank tossed their heads in the wind.

Nick, with Con beside him, was bent over a fish trap downstream. A gust lifted Nick's black hair in a smooth wing and ruffled Con's shaggier mane.

Shane cupped his hands to his mouth and shouted.

Nick looked up, and Con's head turned toward them. The two conversed briefly, then Nick picked up the bucket and climbed the bank. Con trailed behind, and Rob wondered if his brother felt reluctant to greet him.

Nick drew near to where they stood. He stopped before Rob. "You've come back."

"That I have." Rob watched him for a reaction.

"Welcome." Nick shook Rob's hand.

Some of the tension sloughed from Rob. "Thank you."

Nick turned to Shane. "It's good to see you."

"Likewise." Shane smiled, and they exchanged handshakes.

Nick looked at Shane. "I understand there's been a bit of trouble lately."

"Yes, well." Shane squinted against the sun. "Let's hope we've seen the last of it."

"We were ready to ride out after you in the morning." Nick fell into stride beside Shane. "We were out on the range when the news came or we'd have gone before."

Shane and Nick moved off together.

Con drew level with Rob. "Hello, Rob. It's good to see you

at last."

"And you." Rob swept his gaze over his brother's face. "I'm glad to find you unchanged."

"It's only been three years, Rob. I must say, though, that it seems like more."

"You went west for five."

"Maybe now I know how you felt about that."

"I wondered if I'd ever see you again." Rob shrugged. "You will recall that I stopped holding your feet to the fire over that."

"I'll afford you the same privilege." Con clapped an arm around his shoulder.

"Thank you." Rob let out his breath. "I feel like an utter wretch."

Con's eyes gleamed. "That's promising anyway. Let's go in."

They started for the house.

"Con?"

"Hmm?"

"I think I understand the reason you left."

Con nodded. "And I can guess why you returned."

Maisey sat on a stool at the kitchen counter while Bry put on the kettle and Elsa assembled the tea set one-handed. Fiona nestled close to Elsa and followed her movements with bright green eyes very like her father's.

"I'll put on water for washing." Bry carried a large pot to the tap, part of a makeshift system that piped in water from the river. "Would you like me to heat enough to fill the bath?"

"Yes, thank you." Maisey let out a sigh. "That would be

wonderful."

Elsa ran an assessing gaze over her. "I'll fix something for you to eat, ja?"

"To be honest, I barely feel hungry." All Maisey really wanted to do was sleep, but these moments with Bry and Elsa were too precious to miss. They felt so normal compared to what she had endured that she could hardly take it in.

"I see." Elsa's forehead puckered. "Maybe a little porridge?"

"That sounds best." Maisey smiled in gratitude. "Where is Katie?"

"I'd just put her down in the nursery when you arrived. She's fast asleep." Bry shook her head. "I couldn't keep her awake. She'll be up all night, more's the pity."

"That's too bad." Maisey wished she could offer to take a shift with the baby. That was out of the question when she could hardly keep her own eyes open.

"Nick likes to lend a hand with her. He thinks the sun rises and sets on our little girl." Bry winked. "For that matter, I do too."

"She has wonderful parents." Elsa tugged the pot of water to the stove. "Not everyone is so blessed."

The old sadness returned to Maisey. It was always the same whenever she thought of her parents' rejection after she'd married Avery. She pushed away the memories, having no defense in her tired state against the emotions they roused.

"Fiona has been up most of the night with colic the past couple of days." Elsa frowned. "I hope her crying doesn't wake you. I'll give you and Rob a room as far as possible from her nursery."

Maisey's face heated. Sleeping in the same room as Rob

would be expected, and Maisey couldn't bring herself to ask for separate rooms. After Bry's joyful reaction to the news, Maisey didn't want to disappoint her friend by revealing the false nature of her marriage. It was more than that, if she was honest. Being married to Rob gave her a family at last. That it was a dream-come-true made it hard to deny.

Sharing a room with Rob would put him in an awkward position after stating that he didn't intend to consummate their marriage. That was his problem to sort out, she decided a little testily. Her wounded feminine pride hoped that finding a solution would prove difficult for him.

Elsa showed Maisey to their room, as it happened, before Rob came up. Maisey stared into the wash table mirror, seeing herself for the first time since her captivity began. Scrubbed clean and with her damp hair falling in waves about her face, she must appear quite a different woman than when she'd arrived. After scrubbing her scalp, Bry had dunked her head under water, then brushed out the tangled mess with special care. She removed the blue watered-silk wrapper Elsa had loaned her and hung it on a hook in the wardrobe. She stood in a borrowed shift, her feet bare, and her head covered with one of Elsa's linen nightcaps. She tied the soft muslin confection shaped like a bonnet beneath her chin. She normally wouldn't bother with such fripperies except perhaps for warmth at night. However, wearing the cap might prevent her hair from drying into an unruly mop.

After cleaning her teeth with the toothbrush and paste Elsa had given her, she crawled beneath the covers, too weary to wonder where Rob would lay his head. Sleep claimed her at once but embraced her only lightly.

She woke to find Rob standing beside the bed in the

illumination of the candle he held. Did she imagine it, or was he gazing down at her with a tender expression? Weariness tugged her eyelids shut.

"Rest, darling." His whisper stirred the air so softly she almost thought she'd dreamed it. A creak roused her, and she opened her eyes to glimpse him bending over the chest beneath the window. He straightened with a folded blanket in his arms. She drifted away again.

Maisey stirred and lifted her head. The candle no longer shone, and a dark shape lay on the couch against the wall.

She rolled onto her side with her back to Rob, trying not to care where her husband slept.

CHAPTER TEN

MAISEY SAT UP IN BED, BLINKING in confusion. A glance about the room revealed a nest of bedding crumpled on the couch. Rob had slept there she remembered, although barely. Sunlight shone through a gap in the curtains. Judging by its strength, the day was well advanced. After the harshness of the trail, lingering in bed seemed shockingly luxurious.

They would not return home until tomorrow, Elsa had informed her, so that she could rest up for the journey. Knowing that Bry was missing so much sleep over her daughter's teething made taking it easy herself seem somehow wrong. On that thought, Maisey pushed back her covers, ready to step out of bed.

A light tapping came at the door.

"Who's there?" Maisey dove back into bed and pulled the covers over herself.

"It's me, Bry."

"Are you quite alone?"

"Sorry to worry you, but your modesty is safe." Humor crept into Bry's voice. "The men are all out fawning over Nick's new colt. Hard telling when they'll come back. May I come in? You'll be happy you let me."

"Yes." Maisey sat up in bed.

The door opened and Bry entered. "I've brought you nourishment." She lowered the footed tray in her hands over Maisey's lap. Fried eggs, bacon, buttered toast, and a cup of what looked like applesauce sent up a heavenly aroma. Maisey's appetite awakened, but she was most interested in the steaming cup perched on its saucer. "Have you brought me tea?"

"You sound like a little girl at Christmas." Bry grinned. "Yes, there's tea, and a little pot of honey to go with it."

"You'll have me completely spoiled." Maisey blinked away tears.

"You'll recall that I have an aversion to cooking. This is Elsa's doing, so blame her not me if your waist expands. Mine has." Bry smiled secretively. "Elsa isn't entirely responsible for that, I must admit. It's hard to keep your figure with a baby on the way."

"What?" Maisey's hand shook as she started, and the tea in her cup sloshed perilously close to the rim. "Are you certain?"

Bry's eyes shone. "The doctor tells me that I am."

"How wonderful." Maisey set her cup safely down. "It's unfair to tell me this when my lap is covered by a tray and I can't hug you."

Bry laughed. "I'll know that you meant to."

"Does Nick know yet?"

"Yes. He's taking it much better than when he learned we were expecting Katie. You'll recall that he worried about bringing a child of mixed blood into the world. He's recovered from that fairly well."

"Fatherhood seems to suit him."

"It makes him too tired to entertain his fears for long, anyway." Bry grinned.

"Congratulations on your new baby." Maisey beamed. "I couldn't be happier for you."

"Thank you." Bry perched on the chair beside the trunk at

the window. "I don't deliver breakfast in bed often. Enjoy it, will you?"

Maisey laughed. "Sorry, but you did distract me." She nibbled on a strip of bacon and swirled honey into her tea. "I never expected you to wait on me hand and foot."

"Don't be silly. I wanted to." She glanced at the curtains, which billowed in the fitful breeze. "It's going to be hot again today. Shall I close the window to trap the cool air inside?"

Maisey took a soothing sip from her cup. "I can do that."

"I don't mind." Bry jumped up. She pulled the curtains aside and turned the crank. The casement thunked into place, cutting off the rushing sound of the river, which had been a constant backdrop through the night. Bry turned around, and glanced past Maisey toward the couch, where the rumpled bedding betrayed that Rob had slept. "I can't help noticing—" She sat down, concern in her eyes. "It's none of my business, of course."

"Rob spent the night on the couch." Maisey's voice caught as she confirmed Bry's suspicions.

"Don't worry, Maisey. I'm sure you and Rob will patch things up. When two people first learn to live together, it doesn't always go smoothly." Bry shook her head. "I can remember a spat or two with Nick at the start of our marriage."

"You and Nick fought?" Maisey couldn't help being diverted. She'd never known the pair to so much as raise their voices to one another.

Bry lifted an eyebrow. "We're quite capable of disagreeing, I assure you."

Maisey chortled. "I feel much relieved to know that."

"Will you laugh when I speak of my pain?" Bry grinned, then stood and smoothed her skirts. "That's enough of me interfering, though. When you're ready, come down to the parlor. We ladies can visit there and wait for the men to get hungry. They'll remember to come back home then."

The colt's shadow flowed over the ground as the beautiful creature raced past Rob along the corral rail. Hiamovie meant 'whirlwind' in Cheyenne, a name he considered very suitable for the fleet-footed yearling. Rob grinned at Con beside him. "There are few pleasures quite like watching a fresh colt test his mettle against an accomplished trainer."

Con nodded. "I don't think he's figured out that he's met his match in Nick."

"I've never seen anyone handle horses better." Rob had witnessed Nick's soft touch and gentle manner calm an ornery horse in record time. Nick had won Bry over with similar tactics. She'd needed a man with finesse. That his brother-in-law was half-Cheyenne made no difference to Rob. Con had felt differently about the match, but he'd come around eventually.

"Does it make you miss ranching, Rob?" Shane asked from Con's other side.

Rob shrugged. "I already did."

"There's always a place for you here, if you want one." Con spoke without looking at Rob. "Now that Elsa and I have started our family, the ranch house has begun to shrink. But it's big enough to shelter our two families for a while. You could build a home on the property, the same as Nick."

Rob tried not to bristle at the suggestion. "I can pay my own way."

"Are you suggesting that Nick doesn't?" Con's voice held

an edge. "Because I can assure you, he earned his house and land."

"This has nothing to do with Nick." Rob responded in an even tone while he held onto his temper.

Shane, perhaps sensing a touchy moment, moved off toward Nick, who was vaulting over the corral fence.

"Honestly, you're as stubborn as Da ever was," Con ground out.

"Yes, well. That trait runs in the family." Rob chose his next words carefully. "I appreciate your offer, but I'm planning on buying a spread of my own."

Con glanced at him. "You have the mettle to succeed at ranching, and I can see why you want to settle down with Maisey on your own place."

"I'm glad you understand." Rob gave his brother a grateful smile. "Do you know of any ranches for sale nearby?"

Squinting, Con pulled his hat brim down to shade his eyes. "I'll ask around."

"Thank you."

"In case it doesn't work out, I'll repeat my offer."

Rob grinned. "Is that a warning?"

Con's eyes gleamed. "Take it as you will."

"Fair enough." Rob started toward Shane and Nick.

Con kept pace. "If it comes to that, I'll charge you for the land."

"I would expect no less, but surely I can find someone willing to sell around these parts. Folks have trouble staying in one place these days. The urge to move westward is like a fever in the blood."

"I've noticed that, but the Bitterroot Valley has a way of holding onto a person."

"That's partly why I want to live here." Rob cleared his throat to remove a certain huskiness.

"I'd like to think another reason might be living closer to your family."

"Of course."

Con smiled. "I'm glad to hear it."

"Probably no more than I am to say it." The sudden memory of Daphne begging him to give her money caught Rob by surprise. Would what had happened ever stop haunting him? He'd thought Daphne was only out to pick his pocket, never realizing that she really needed help. He should have been paying attention. Rob's gut twisted, and sudden moisture filled his eyes. He blinked and glanced away, gathering his composure. Refusing to help a woman in need hadn't been his finest moment.

Shane and Nick were engaged in a lively comparison of Hiamovie to his sire, Mo'kôhtavo'ha, or Tavo as Nick called his favorite horse. Both were sleek black steeds with fire in their veins, but Shane held that the colt possessed a smoother gait.

"He's like his dam, Kilkenny, in that respect." Nick conceded the point. "Ah, but Tavo is brighter."

"As he should be." Shane chuckled. "A father needs to keep ahead of his son."

"I can well imagine." Con smiled. "Maybe I'll find out next time Elsa and I add to our family."

Shane quirked an eyebrow. "Any news in the offing?"

"Give us time, man." Con laughed. "Fiona is only six-months old. A new baby is the last thing on Elsa's mind at the moment. Her mother and some of her siblings are about to immigrate from Germany. It took them a long time to agree to come, and Elsa wants everything to be perfect when they arrive."

Shane winced. "I'm sorry we've intruded at such a time."

Con gave him a startled look. "Don't be thick, Cousin. You couldn't possibly be in the way."

Despite Con's assurances, it was just as well that they planned to leave in the morning. Rob would like to give Maisey more time to recover before making the trip home, but they should move on. Maisey wouldn't want to delay the reunion with her daughter, anyway.

"What finally convinced Elsa's mother, if I may ask?" Shane asked.

"Her health is failing, and she needs the care we are in a position to give her. Otherwise, she might not have been willing since it means leaving several of her children behind."

"Her reluctance is understandable."

"We invited them all to come, but some of them don't want to part with their native land."

"I can't blame them for that." Shane's expression grew distant. "I still miss Éire."

Rob smiled. "I haven't heard the name of our homeland spoken in Irish for many a year."

Con grinned. "Erin go Bragh."

"Ah, yes. Ireland till the end of time." Rob shook his head but smiled. "You two are making me sentimental. Before you know it, I'll be misty-eyed."

"Elsa and I don't hold it against her siblings who want to stay put. We even promised to take Elsa's mother back for visits, but that depends on her health." Con blew out a breath. "It's become something of a mess."

"That's the trouble with moving about, isn't it?" Shane murmured. "People are more important than places, and families belong together."

Rob doubted the comment was aimed his direction, but he took his cousin's point all the same.

"Ma, Seth is looking at me." Liberty glared at her brother. "Make him stop."

"Seth, stop pestering your sister." America spoke absently while bending to swipe Liam's face with a damp cloth. Her youngest son's blue eyes gleamed, and he turned his head, avoiding her efforts.

"I have to look somewhere, don't I?" Seth spoke in a martyred voice.

From the corner of her eye, America glimpsed him pulling a face at Liberty.

"He did it again!" Liberty wailed.

America held onto her patience. Her children had been out-of-sorts all day, but she didn't have to join them in ill-temper. "Do it again, Seth Alexander Hayes, and I'll make you stand in the corner."

Liberty smiled and stuck her tongue out at Seth.

"Behave yourself, young lady. This kitchen has more than one corner. Liam, sit still." America renewed her efforts to cleanse mashed potatoes from her youngest child's face.

Liam tried to avoid the cloth again, but America followed his movement. He emerged looking so disgruntled that she wanted to laugh. What was it about Liam that reminded her so much of Shane? He had the same very blue eyes as his father, but his features resembled hers.

The sound of hooves and the creak of leather carried through the open window. America sucked in her breath.

Could it be? She jumped to her feet and hurried to the door. Liberty reached it first and yanked it open.

"Wait on the porch, children." America warned sharply before stepping into the worn path that ran past her house to the Buckthorns' property. She shielded her eyes from the sun, which hung low in the sky at this hour. Around the corner of the barn, Cyrus rode into view. He reined in when he reached her.

"Hello, Cyrus." She glanced past him, sagging a little when there was no sign of Shane.

"Evening, Mrs. Hayes." He touched his hat. "Your husband asked me to let you know he's safe. He and Rob rescued Mrs. Wilcox. They're all unharmed."

"Thank goodness." America let out a sigh. "Where are they?"

Cyrus smiled. "Shane thought it best to stop at Con's ranch for a rest. Mrs. Wilcox was plumb worn out."

"Yes, of course. Thank you for letting me know."

"I'm glad to bring you good news."

"I tried not to worry." America touched the corner of her eye with her apron and blew out a breath. "We're all in God's hands, after all."

"Ain't that the truth." Cyrus cleared his throat, his eyes suspiciously bright. "I'd better get home to Mrs. Buckthorn."

America stepped aside, allowing him to pass. She went back to her children and gathered them in her arms. "Pa's safe." Each word lifted a heavy load from her shoulders.

Washed, groomed, and clad in a blue, watered-silk dress with gold and white stripes over a corset and petticoat, Maisey felt like a new woman. She walked in her borrowed finery into the dining room alongside Rob, who was equally transformed. Maisey felt self-conscious and overdressed for a schoolteacher, but Rob's eyes gleamed whenever he looked at her. Small wonder that he was enjoying the improvement in her appearance. He'd been forced to look for days on end at the unkempt woman with wild hair that she had become during their captivity.

The large window in the outer wall framed a view of the river. Umber light tinged the sky and cast a sheen over the countryside. Clumps of trees along the river banks bent like gossips whispering secrets. The wind that usually followed the river channel plucked at their leaves and tossed the grasses along the bank in waves. When Maisey entered, Shane and Con rose with well-mannered grace from their chairs at the table. Elsa stood up also and came to meet them. She clasped Maisey's hand. "You look beautiful in that dress. It never looks right on me. I must send it home with you."

"That's kind of you." Maisey had no idea where she would wear such a fancy dress again, but she didn't want to refuse her new sister-in-law's gift.

Elsa turned to Rob. "I hope my husband hasn't worn you out with his love of horses." Her eyes twinkled, as if she well knew the opposite was true.

Rob laughed. "I've managed to survive it."

"Your places are there." Elsa gestured toward two ladderback chairs near Con, who sat talking to Shane at one end of the long oak table. In one arm, he held his sleeping daughter. Nick and Bry sat closer to Elsa's seat at the other end of the table. Between them, dark-haired Katie nibbled a fluffy roll. She watched them with bright eyes.

Rob slid out one of the chairs with a smile for Maisey. Her feet sank into the oriental carpet as she walked forward to slip into her seat. Rob rested his hand on her shoulder briefly before sitting beside her.

The gold and crystal oil chandelier dangling above the table cast a warm glow over them. Maisey had always loved the ceiling cove with its painted border of green and gold branches. She'd sat for long stretches gazing into the paintings in their gilded frames. Suspended from the picture rail encircling the room a foot below the ceiling, they depicted river scenes. A wooden folding screen hid the doorway into the kitchen from view. It lent a more intimate feeling to the dining area than would otherwise have been possible in the large room.

Maisey stole a glance at Rob. He was behaving very much like an attentive husband. She could admit that she was enjoying his interest in her, but an annoying question kept returning to her mind. *Would it last?* Rob had acted besotted before, but that hadn't stopped him from abandoning her.

Con shook out his napkin. "I must say that you all seem much improved."

Shane grinned. "I suppose we resembled part of the vagrant population before."

Con smiled. "I didn't mean it like that, as I'm sure you're aware."

"Maisey could never look anything less than lovely." Rob gazed at her adoringly.

"Flatterer!" Maisey chided him in mock-indignation.

Bry laughed. "Beware the trap of insincerity, brother of mine."

Maisey's light-hearted mood evaporated. Bry had meant

the remark in fun, but it brought back her suspicions. She kept her unhappiness to herself, trying not to spoil the others' enjoyment. Rob kept sending her questioning glances. Had he guessed what had upset her?

A white porcelain soup tureen decorated in blue and red flowers made the rounds. It was a Wedgewood, identical to one belonging to Maisey's mother. At least, her mother had once owned such a tureen. Maisey no longer knew what her mother used for china anymore. Her family was gone from her so completely it might never have existed. She tried not to dwell on her grief, but she never knew when something inconsequential—an idle comment, a glance between family members, or even a piece of china—would trigger it.

Maisey ladled bean soup into her bowl but passed the bread basket to Rob without taking a slice. Her appetite was better but not fully recovered. When the main dishes went around, Maisey was glad to have shown restraint. She helped herself to larger portions of chicken, rice, and vegetables but only a sliver of huckleberry pie.

Con sipped coffee from a gold-rimmed demitasse cup. "Do you still intend to leave in the morning?"

"We do," Rob and Shane chimed in unison.

"Are you sure?" Elsa looked at her husband, who nodded. "You're welcome to stay on."

Maisey turned to Rob and pitched her voice low. "I really should go home to Phoebe."

"That settles it. We should make an early start." Shane bit into a forkful of pie.

"I agree." Rob clinked his cup into its saucer.

Maisey didn't protest. Even thinking about rising early seemed hard with her eyelids so heavy. Seeing the children around the table reawakened the yearning for her own daughter. How was Phoebe faring? Maisey knew that her strong-minded daughter would weather what had happened, but that didn't mean she'd suffered any less.

"Well then, I guess it's settled." Con polished off the last of his huckleberry pie. "Would you like to borrow the wagon?"

"I'm sure Maisey would appreciate the chance to be out of the saddle." Shane picked up his cup.

"Don't trouble yourselves on my behalf. I've grown used to riding." Maisey would rather they didn't slow their journey with a wagon.

"I must insist." Con's smile contained a trace of steel. He reminded her, all at once, of Rob in a determined frame of mind.

"You should." Elsa added her own invitation. "We don't need to use the wagon right now, and it would make your journey more comfortable."

"Then it's settled." Shane winked at Maisey.

"Oh good." Elsa clapped her hands. "There will be room to send you some *Kirschenmichel*—"

"Pumpernickel bread," Con interpreted. "It's delicious."

"I'll put in some of the leftovers from supper." Elsa brightened. "And America would like a little gift too, ja? She won't want to cook much when Shane first arrives."

Shane smiled. "I'm sure America will appreciate whatever you send."

"My wife has a generous heart." Con beamed.

Elsa blushed a charming shade of pink.

That's how love should be. Maisey felt like a fraud. She and Rob were no more married than they'd been before they'd taken their vows. Reflecting on that fateful day, she could barely remember the ceremony. Exhaustion and emotional upset had conspired to dull the memory. By contrast, the recollection of her traumatic wedding night remained vivid in her mind. Maisey helped clear the table, then retired with the ladies to the parlor. Katie was contentedly flipping through a children's picture book. Fiona, fenced in by cushions, slumbered on a blanket in a dark corner of the room,

Whether caused by the amount of food she'd eaten or an early morning, Maisey was having trouble staying awake. The clock above the mantle revealed the dismal truth. "It's not yet six o'clock."

"What's the matter?" Elsa, seated on the sofa, glanced up from embroidering a dishtowel.

Bry peered at Maisey above the sock she was crocheting. "You look sleepy."

"It's true, I'm afraid." Maisey stifled a yawn.

"You're still exhausted from your ordeal." Bry looped yarn onto her hook.

Elsa glanced up from threading a needle in the light of the oil lamp beside her. "You do look tired."

"We won't fault you if you need to turn in." Bry smiled softly. "I'm planning to go home to bed early myself."

"I probably should say goodnight," Maisey admitted. Leaving Elsa and Bry to their needlework, she let herself into the entryway. She paused with a foot on the first stair. The door to Con's study stood ajar, and Maisey could hear men's voices engaged in a lively discussion about horse trading. She released her breath. Rob was unlikely to join her anytime soon.

The rattle of the door handle jerked Maisey from sleep. The

door opened, and light fell across the bed. Maisey squinted and made out Rob's face above the candle he held. He turned, and the door clicked shut. Light wavered along the wall then pooled on the bed. The flame glowed above the night table where Rob set the candlestick.

How late was the hour? From the utter silence, no other soul was stirring in the ranch house. She wasn't sure what to expect. Did he mean to sleep in the bed with her tonight? Maisey wasn't sure how she felt about that idea anymore. He'd behaved very differently tonight than when he'd rejected her in Little Elk's tepee. Did his attentiveness at supper signal a change of heart about their marriage? Then again, maybe it didn't. She never quite knew what Rob was thinking or feeling. His erratic behavior made her wonder whether *he* even did. If he wanted a real marriage after shunning her on their wedding night, she would need time to accept the idea.

Time wasn't something she had much of with Rob creeping around the bed toward her. Maisey went limp, feigning sleep. Her heartbeat pounded so loudly in her ears that she thought he must hear it.

Rob stopped beside her. He made no sound other than the gentle rush of his breathing. *What was he doing?* Maisey couldn't resist opening her eyelids a slit. Rob was watching her, a soft expression on his face. He leaned down, and his lips touched her forehead in a gentle caress.

Maisey opened her eyes wider. Rob was very near. The candlelight revealed every plane of Rob's face. She gazed into her husband's eyes and read unmistakable desire. Her breathing quickened, parting her lips.

Rob took possession of her mouth in a very different kiss from the one on their wedding day. That had been a tentative question followed by cautious exploration. This staked a claim.

Losing her inner battle, Maisey wound her arms around her husband's neck and returned his passion.

Rob pulled away, his breathing ragged. "I want you, and that's the truth." He pushed a hand through his hair. "But I can't take advantage of your weakness."

Tears gathered, but she turned her face to the wall. Why had she given him the opportunity to deny her again? She wouldn't do it again.

A few minutes later the sofa creaked, and the candle went out.

CHAPTER ELEVEN

R OB GAZED DOWN AT THE WIFE he couldn't claim. Relaxed in sleep, Maisey shed the weariness and strain she too often wore. She was facing the window, where the curtains lifted in a breeze. Their movement sent soft morning light back and forth across the bed. Whenever the light reached her, Maisey glowed like an angel. Rob's gaze traced the tender curve of her lips. He wished he could caress them with his own. He'd stolen the privilege last night. Yes, she'd invited him, but that didn't matter. He would do well to remember what she had gone through. Maisey was in no mental state to make wise choices. Rob glanced away in an attempt to dispel his yearning. He'd taken advantage of her by marrying her, and he shouldn't compound his error.

A movement outside the window drew his eye. Shane was already awake and no doubt preparing for their departure. He should go and help his cousin. Rob hoped Maisey would stand up well to the journey. She looked so vulnerable while sleeping.

Rob found Shane in the barn, pitching hay into Archibald's feeding trough. Shane stabbed the pitchfork into the hay in his wheelbarrow but paused in his task. He nodded to Rob. "Good morning. Did you sleep well?"

Rob shrugged. "Well enough."

Shane lifted an eyebrow. "Is that so?"

Rob had never been any good at keeping his troubles from his preacher cousin. Apparently, he wasn't going to start this morning. "I'm wondering something."

"Oh?"

"Maybe I should file for an annulment." Rob rushed out the words.

Shane studied him. "What brought this on?"

"Never mind."

"It's none of my business, I suppose." Shane went back to pitching hay.

Rob tried to picture Shane actually believing that. His preacher cousin tended to feel responsible for everyone and everything. It usually annoyed Rob, but this time he needed Shane's advice. "I wouldn't say that."

"No, no. Don't let me intrude." Shane tossed a forkful of hay into the stall beside the wheelbarrow.

"But you married us. Surely that gives you meddling rights." Rob could hardly believe that those words had come out of his mouth.

"Yes, well. I wouldn't have performed the ceremony if the pair of you hadn't convinced me so thoroughly that you love one another. I've wondered since if I owe you both an apology." He put a hand to the back of his neck. "Loving one another doesn't automatically mean a couple is ready for marriage."

"I don't want an apology." Rob grimaced. "Maisey should have one though, and not only from you. I married her for selfish reasons."

Shane nodded. "I doubt anyone enters into wedlock for completely pure motives."

"I knew it was the only chance I would get to court Maisey, so I took it." Rob shook his head. "I'm a wretched specimen of a man."

Shane grinned. "You're making progress."

Rob narrowed his eyes. "This isn't funny."

"No offense intended. When we examine ourselves, we all come up lacking. Only our Savior, Jesus Christ, ever qualified as holy." Shane sent another forkful into the stall. "All I meant is that admitting your own selfishness can help you move beyond it."

"That's what I'm trying to do by letting Maisey go." Rob drew in a breath.

Shane cocked an eyebrow. "What if she would rather stay with you?"

"I doubt she will. She didn't really want to marry me."

"So that's it." Shane picked up the wheelbarrow and moved to the next stall. A soft whicker greeted him. Shane rubbed Archibald's neck. "Have you considered taking her word for it? She was pretty convincing when she said her vows."

"I wish it was that simple." Rob shook his head. "Maisey only hoped to free me."

"That's not how it looked to me."

Rob ran a hand over his face. "This is all so confusing."

Shane laughed. "Welcome to wedded bliss."

Rob frowned. "I was hoping you'd have better advice for me."

"You promised to love her. Did you mean it?"

Rob stood taller. "I'm not in the habit of lying about such matters."

"Yes or no?"

"Yes."

"Well, then." Shane leaned on the pitchfork. "I suggest you give it time."

Emma woke with a start. What on earth was that racket? It sounded like the hooves of stampeding buffalo. She jumped out of bed, heart racing, and barely paused to tie on a wrapper before yanking open the cabin door.

Gideon was kneeling below her porch step, pounding a nail with a hammer.

"Goodness!" She placed a hand over her heart. "You scared me to death."

"Sorry about that." Gideon stood up and hung the hammer in his belt. "I knocked, but when no one answered, I thought you weren't home." He ran his gaze over her and ended by grinning.

Emma wished she had stopped at the mirror. With her hair cascading about her face in tangles, she must look a sight. She raised her chin. "I was napping."

"So early?" Gideon squinted toward the sky. "It's not yet noon."

"I'm still tired from being sick." Emma couldn't help feeling defensive. "So you're fixing my step, are you?"

"Fixed. I'm all done now." He smiled. "I did ask permission."

"Yes, I recall. How nice of you to fix it."

Gideon shrugged. "It didn't need much."

"I'm surprised you would trouble with your pa just home."

"Ma is keeping him busy for the moment, fussing over him."

"When do you suppose Mr. Walsh—and Reverend Hayes, of course, will come back with Mrs. Wilcox?"

"A day or so, according to Pa." He put a hand on the back

of his neck. "I should be going. My family will look for me soon."

"Yes, go to them." Emma smiled. "I appreciate your thinking of me."

"I'm glad to help." Gideon picked up his toolbox. "That board shouldn't give you any more trouble."

"Thanks for fixing it."

Gideon struck out for the path.

Emma glanced down at her attire. She would never have gone outside in her current state if she'd known he was there. Call it vanity, but she would rather look her best around Gideon.

Gideon had been awfully sweet to fix her porch step, and he'd given her all those apples. In fact, there were far more than she could eat all by herself. She'd thanked everyone else who had helped her while she was sick.

She ought to bake Gideon a pie. Yes, that's what she'd do.

Emma knocked on Felicity's door with one hand while balancing Gideon's apple pie in the other. The heady fragrance made her wish she'd baked another one for herself. She hadn't spared the time for that. After watching the Buckthorn wagon trundle off, she'd hurried to complete the task before Gideon returned.

The door opened, and Felicity looked out. "Emma! I wasn't expecting you." She smoothed the apron over her faded brown calico dress. "What do you have there?"

"It's for Gideon. I wanted to thank him properly for helping me while I was sick."

"Gideon wouldn't feel you needed to go to the trouble, but I'm sure he'll enjoy your pie. You've missed him, I'm afraid. He went to pick up a few items at the mercantile."

Emma murmured something vague. That was exactly what she had counted on. She wanted to thank Gideon, not necessarily to see him.

Felicity's face brightened. "Why don't you come in for a visit?"

Emma hesitated, torn between the desire to spend time with Felicity and an equally strong urge to avoid Gideon. She'd meant only to drop off his pie, and then hurry home before he returned. "I shouldn't intrude."

"You wouldn't." Felicity opened the door invitingly. "I'd love an excuse to stop cleaning."

Emma laughed. "Since you put it that way, I can stay a few minutes." Compared to conversing with Felicity, going back to her silent cabin held no appeal.

Felicity led Emma into the parlor, a comfortable room with blue wallpaper that boasted flocked birds perched on branches of gold. Felicity had given the room a feminine touch, even though the oversized rosewood furniture must suit her household full of men.

"Sit down wherever you like." Felicity hovered solicitously. "Can I bring you anything to eat or drink?"

"No, thank you." Emma sank into an oversized carved chair upholstered in brocade. "I'm content simply to talk with you."

Felicity smiled. "I feel the same about you. I don't find the chance for female companionship very often."

"Your parlor reminds me, in a way, of my grandmother's. She didn't have bird decorations like you do. Grandma Rose favored roses, for obvious reasons." Emma laughed. "She had them everywhere, even real ones in the garden."

"You speak of her fondly." Felicity occupied a chair that

matched Emma's.

"I loved her to pieces. She was one of those people who makes everyone smile."

"My mother was like that. When I was a little girl growing up, every so often she hosted a tea party for her lady friends." Felicity leaned forward, her eyes shining.

Emma smiled at her enthusiasm. "Those must have been special times."

"They were for everyone. We children were given cookies and cakes, but first we had to eat our vegetables." She laughed. "We never wanted to, but Mother was very strict. Afterwards, we played to our heart's content while our mothers lingered at the table."

"What wonderful memories you have."

"Here's an idea." Felicity gripped the arms of her chair. "What if I hosted a tea party for some of my friends in Liberty. Would you come?"

"Do you mean, just for your female friends?"

Felicity's smile widened. "No men allowed."

"That sounds perfect." Emma sighed. "I'm staying away from men, for the time being."

Felicity arched her eyebrows. "Why did you bake Gideon a pie, then?"

"For no other reason than the one I mentioned." Emma shrugged. "He fixed my porch step today, and it reminded me to show more gratitude."

"You can't blame me for wishing you had an ulterior motive." Felicity winked. "I like you, and I suspect Gideon may be sweet on you."

"Really? We get on one another's nerves a lot."

"That can be a sign."

Emma gave her a doubtful look. "I'm interested in a

mature man, someone like Rob Walsh who makes his own way in the world."

"I'm sure Mr. Walsh is admirable, but don't overlook men closer to your age."

Emma lifted a shoulder. "I find them awkward."

"Even Gideon?" Felicity shook her head. "I won't try to push my son on you, but I can't imagine that."

"Well, maybe not Gideon." Emma sagged against her seatback. "Truthfully, I don't know what to make of him. Just when I think I finally understand him, he does something I never expected."

Felicity's eyes gleamed. "How intriguing."

"How could this happen?" Rob kicked the wagon wheel but immediately regretted his decision.

Shane frowned while pulling tools from the jockey box on the side of the wagon. "Stop hopping about like a crow and lend a hand, will you?"

"Can I do anything to help?" Maisey called from the driving box, where she'd ridden as a passenger since departing Con's ranch that morning.

"You'll have to come down from there, I'm afraid." Rob reached upward, and she leaned down into his arms. Bearing her slight weight easily, he swung her to the ground. She lifted her head, and their eyes met. Rob swallowed. "I'd better go see what Shane needs."

Shane was hefting a wagon jack toward the broken wheel.

Rob hurried to him "Do you need help with that?"

"I can manage. It's more awkward than heavy, but I have it balanced."

Rob followed him around the wagon. "I sure hope Con

keeps a saw and spare spokes on hand."

"You're in luck on both counts." Shane glanced back at him. "Con is nothing if not thorough. We'll need the wrench to take this wheel off for repair. The saw would come in handy too. Spare spokes are stored beneath the wagon."

"I'll get them." Rob volunteered to save Shane the trouble of ordering him around. He retrieved the saw while the wagon jerked and tilted from Shane's efforts with the jack. By the time Rob returned to Shane, the wagon was propped on one side.

Rob gave Shane the saw and bent to the wheel. He applied the wrench to a bolt and turned it with an effort. Shane stepped in, and they traded off until the wheel was free.

Rob used his bandana to wipe sweat from his eyes.

Maisey brought them water in tin cups. "I wish we'd broken down in the shade."

Rob swept his gaze over her, noting the pinkness of her skin. "You might wait over there." He nodded toward a clump of ponderosa pines a small distance from them.

Her forehead creased. "That's so far away."

"I know." The idea of Maisey being out of reach didn't appeal to him, but neither did watching her burn to a crisp in the sun. "I'll walk over with you and make sure it's safe."

"Don't bother." She shook her head. "I'll be fine. I'd rather that you stay and help Shane so we can reach home sooner."

Rob would have objected, but the way she raised her chin alerted him. He stepped back, glad she'd decided to confront her fears. "I'll be within hailing distance."

Maisey walked away from Rob and Shane with a sinking sensation in her stomach. Maybe she should go back and ask Rob to come along after all. If she didn't need to overcome the fear that dragged at her, she might do so. This was ridiculous. The stand of pines wasn't far enough from the wagon that she should feel this discomfort. That was all the more reason to keep going.

The river writhed like a snake through the golden grasses that swayed on either side of the rutted road. The cloudless sky glowed, intensely blue. The sun beat down on her head. Maisey was grateful for hercanteen of water.

It was too bad about the wagon. Hopefully the mishap wouldn't prevent them from reaching Liberty today. She missed Phoebe, and the idea of sleeping outdoors made her breath quicken. She couldn't stop picturing Spukani following them. What if he'd bided his time while they were at the ranch, waiting for them to make a move? He might be even more angry than before because she had won favor with the chief and helped free Rob. It seemed certain that she'd embarrassed Spukani by revealing his ill-treatment of her. She doubted he would overlook those trespasses.

Glancing behind her quickened Maisey's heartbeat. How far she'd come. She turned around, determining to look only ahead. The scent of pines reached her, and she could see into the grove. Nothing appeared to be lurking there. The trees had the shagginess evergreens acquire in summer and were on the small side, but they would provide the relief she needed. Her skin prickled from the heat, and she was glad to reach shade.

Maisey crept beneath the tallest pine and drew up her knees. Although she strained her ears, she heard nothing but birds chittering throughout the grove. An unmistakable pecking soundednearby. Maisey searched the trees, soon rewarded by the colorful sight of a Lewis's woodpecker. It clung to a snag and periodically rammed its beak against the dead tree. She knew that the woodpecker was first discovered by the explorers Lewis and Clark, and that the bird had been named for Merriweather Lewis. It had no crest on its head like the eastern woodpeckers she'd seen while growing up in St. Louis. The iridescent green of the bird's back and wings made the feathered creature seem to wear a jacket. The pale gray ring around its neck resembled a gentleman's shirt collar. Maisey peered more closely. The bird's markings also included a pink belly and a dark red face. She smiled, considerably heartened, and searched for other feathered creatures to admire. How fortunate that the desire to conquer her fears had led her to such a delightful place.

Shane took the saw Rob held out and began to cut the broken spoke off the wheel. While they'd been moving about, the sun's heat hadn't been too terrible. Holding still made it odious. Rob retired to a patch of shade and waited in its dubious comfort for his own turn at the saw.

Shane took off his hat and ran his bandana over his glistening forehead. He blew out a breath. "This is going to take a while."

"It's a good thing we tied our horses behind the wagon." Rob shook his head. "Maybe we should ride the rest of the way to Liberty."

"I have to admit that I'm tempted. I don't like abandoning Con's wagon though, and we'd have to take his horses with us."

"We could send a wheelwright to repair the wagon, and the horses shouldn't be any trouble to lead."

Shane put his hat on and adjusted the brim. "I thought of that, but riding might not work out well for Maisey. She's pretty tired, although she doesn't let on."

Rob peered into the grove where Maisey had gone, glad to catch sight of her resting in the shade. Now that he thought about it, she'd looked a little droopy-eyed since mid-morning. "You have a point."

"Let's see how well we manage the repairs, shall we?" Shane turned back to the job at hand. "We must thank Con. At least we don't have to cut wood and shape new spokes."

Even so, the task proved more trouble than they'd expected. The wagon's shadow had extended into the grass across the road by the time Rob tightened the last bolt. He stood back. "That should do it."

Rob carried the jack this time.

Maisey returned from the clump of trees where she'd sheltered during the worst of the heat. She stood with her arms folded as they lowered the wagon to all four wheels. "We're not going to make it to Liberty today, are we?"

Rob went to stand beside her. "No, but we're near the camping spot beside the river that our family favors."

Shane joined them. "We should break for the night there."

Shane and Rob hitched Con's Morgans to the wagon and secured their own horses at the rear. Rob lifted Maisey to the wagon box to ride beside Shane and took his own position on several hay bales stacked behind them. The wagon rolled forward and soon passed the stand of ponderosa pines where Maisey had rested. They traveled for another mile before turning aside on a short side road. Shane pulled up in the shade cast by a group of willows beside the water.

"I'm not sure we should stop here." Maisey spoke quickly.

Rob looked down at her upturned face. "What's the matter with the idea?"

She bit her lip. "What if Spukani comes after us?"

"He won't." Rob spoke with confidence. "His chief told

him to leave us alone."

She clutched his arm. "Spukani doesn't always listen to his chief."

Rob covered her hand with his own. "I think he will this time. He only took you because he thought Chief Charlo would be pleased. When he wasn't, it must have embarrassed him before his followers. I doubt he would want to repeat the experience."

"Remember that he accepted horses in exchange for us." Shane called as they navigated a turn. "It's unlikely that he would double-cross his chief."

Maisey sighed. "I'm worrying for nothing."

"It's understandable." Rob recognized Maisey's need to recover from the ordeal she'd experienced. She'd given herself a good start by venturing out on her own today. He admired her for making the effort. His urge to protect her shook him. "Don't worry, Maisey. Spukani won't hurt you anymore." Rob kept his tone light, although he was making more of a promise than a statement.

Maisey breathed in the fresh night air but also caught a whiff of smoke. Burning wood crackled and flames shot upward in the stone ring within their camp. Firelight lit her companions' faces and climbed into the willows. The night wind shook the trees, and the leaves glistened as they swirled. The dark river beyond reflected the full moon and the tiny pinpoints of light clustered in the sky.

Maisey snuggled into the bed Rob had made for her in the wagon while Rob and Shane lingered around the campfire. Despite their assurances, she wasn't completely comfortable spending the night in the open. Their explanations for why

Spukani wouldn't come after them made sense. She supposed that if Spukani had followed them, he would have caught up before this. Emotions were not always logical, however.

With distance between them, she could think of her captor with more sympathy. He had lost a beloved child, and his way of life was changing. No wonder he'd lashed out like an animal in pain. Knowing this, she could summon the grace to hope for his peace of mind.

Tomorrow she would see her daughter. The bright thought pushed away the blackness that lurked in her mind.

A mourning dove sobbed through the willows as Maisey floated into a place of shadows. The lonely cry echoed through her dreams. She was running through the forest, sobbing, with a force of evil pursuing her.

Maisey gasped awake and opened her eyes in the moonlight. A dark figure rushed through the camp toward her. Her mouth went dry, and her pulse pounded in her ears.

"What's wrong?" Rob's whisper reached her as he stepped from the darkness into a patch of moonlight. "You moaned."

Relief coursed through Maisey like a tonic. She drew a steadying breath. "I had a dreadful nightmare."

"Oh?" He climbed into the wagon.

"A monster was chasing me through the woods."

"All the time you spent in those pines today must have brought the dream on." He pulled her into his arms.

She nestled against him without troubling to worry whether or not she should. "Deciding to go was so much harder than being there. I even enjoyed myself. I'd rather not have had to rest there alone, though."

"You didn't, Maisey. Do you think I wouldn't watch out for you the entire time?"

"Really?" She considered what that could mean, but her

weary mind traveled down too many paths to sort it out.

"Your dream couldn't possibly be true." Rob's voice rumbled beneath her ear.

"Oh?" Her eyelids were growing heavy. "Why not?"

He tightened his arms about her. "If a monster chased you, I'd be there defending you."

Maisey smiled. "You're just saying that."

"Allow me, Mrs. Walsh, to know whether I mean what I say. I can assure you that I do."

"Would you let a monster eat you instead of me?"

Rob chuckled. "Now you're taking advantage."

"Would you?" Maisey yawned.

"Yes, woman. I'd feed myself to the beast so you could walk free."

"That's good to know." Maisey's eyelids drifted shut. She frowned in concentration. "I wanted to ask you something. I wish I could remember."

Rob kissed her brow. "Go to sleep, darling. You can tell me tomorrow."

Maisey's lips curved softly. Tomorrow was such a hopeful word.

CHAPTER TWELVE

A FEATHERLIGHT TOUCH COAXED MAISEY INTO wakefulness. Wanting only to sleep, she burrowed into the arms that held her.

Arms were holding her?

Maisey jerked her eyes open. Rob's face was only inches from hers. His eyes were closed, and dark lashes curved above his cheeks. Rob's breath fanned her face, and Maisey recognized the touch that had summoned her from sleep. She shifted sideways, trying to extricate herself from his embrace.

Rob pulled her closer and sighed against her hair.

Maisey allowed herself the luxury of lying in her husband's embrace. She knew Rob's straight nose, full lips, and broad forehead by heart. Her fingers itched to run through the dark ginger hair springing above his brow.

As she gazed at Rob's face in sleep, a tide of yearning carried her on a swift current. Maisey caught her breath on a small gasp.

Rob stirred and opened his clear blue eyes. Maisey read in them his first shock of awareness at finding her in his arms, followed by deeply masculine interest. "Well, well. Good morning to you."

"And to you." She cleared the huskiness from her throat.

"Did you pass the night well?" He sat up, bringing her with him.

Maisey smiled. "You know how I slept."

A spark of humor lit his eyes. "Allow me, if you will, to

engage my wife in banter."

"Must you? I probably couldn't hold up my end. I've never been any good at small talk."

"There's no time like the present to learn." Rob kissed the tip of her nose. "And so, my darling, how did you spend the rest of the night?"

She laughed. "To the best of my recollection, quite well. It's hard to do otherwise while clasped so protectively."

"I suppose that's your way of telling me to let go." Frowning, Rob released her.

"That wasn't what I meant."

"If that's the case—" Rob pulled her back into his arms. "I'd just as soon hold onto you. I hope you will always allow me that privilege."

"Always is a long time, Mister Walsh." She spoke lightly to hide the emotions stirred by his remark. "Will your fervor last that long?"

"I'll stay as long as you want me." Rob's gaze swept her face, and then settled on her mouth. Desire kindled in his eyes. "Do you need proof, Mrs. Walsh?" He lowered his head toward hers.

Maisey waited breathlessly for the first touch of his lips.

"Are you two awake?" Shane called from the camp. "There are miles to go before we reach home."

Rob kissed her swiftly, then stood. "We'd better be on our way." He jumped down.

After the wagon stopped rocking from his departure, Maisey ran her fingers through her hair. Her fingers snagged in tangles. She went in search of the small satchel containing a comb and the other oddments Bry had given her. She wanted to look her best for Phoebe, a difficult task after a night spent outdoors.

The journey to Liberty occupied much of the morning. Shane drove, and Maisey sat beside him. Rob settled in the back of the wagon and occasionally whistled tuneful melodies. The road followed the Bitterroot River before reaching a crossroads crowded with serviceberry bushes. Shane turned the wagon eastward toward Liberty township.

Anticipating the reunion with her daughter lifted Maisey's spirits. However, wondering how Phoebe would take the news of her marriage dampened them. Maisey frowned. She'd given no thought to Phoebe's reaction before marrying Rob. In her own defense, the circumstances had been overwhelming.

She was probably worrying for nothing. All Phoebe had wanted for the longest time was for Rob to become her father. Would the reality captivate her as much as the dream? Before they told Phoebe anything, Maisey needed to know that Rob intended to remain in their marriage. The friendliness that had sprung up between them gave her hope. He'd said he would stay with her, but she needed clarification before they told Phoebe.

"Shane?" She spoke quietly. "I want to talk with Rob alone before I see Phoebe."

"Come over to my house when you're ready, but I hope it won't take long." He looked at her briefly before returning his attention to the horses. "Phoebe will be anxious to see you."

"Please let her know that I'll come for her soon."

"All right." Shane clucked to the horses, then smiled at Maisey. "We're almost there."

The mixed forest they were driving through thinned, and then broke right before the schoolhouse appeared. Maisey gazed at the two-story building where she had spent so much time. Questions crowded her mind. Chief Charlo hadn't been in favor of the school. Would the Salish continue to bring their children to her? After what had happened, did she want to continue teaching them?

Shane drove past the school and into the barn. The men jumped down. Shane went to the horses while Rob lifted Maisey from the wagon.

Rob lowered her gently. His hands lingered at her waist.

She glanced up at him. "I'd like to talk with you before we say anything to Phoebe."

Rob frowned, watching her face. "What's the matter?"

Shane didn't appear to be listening, but Maisey would still like to make sure their conversation was private. "Why don't we go to the cabin?"

Rob stood with his feet apart. "If you're going to send me packing, do it now."

She started. "Where did you get such an idea?"

Surprise swept over Rob's face. "All right, but I should lend a hand with the horses first. I can join you afterwards."

"No, I'll wait." Returning to her cabin alone didn't appeal to Maisey.

He glanced at her inquiringly, but then nodded. "It won't take long."

Maisey knew that to be a true statement. She'd seen Shane and Con hitch and unhitch horses many times, and they had it down to an art. She waited by the open barn door until they finished.

Rob walked beside her along the path toward the cabin, as he had on more than one occasion in the past. This time he would not leave Liberty to live elsewhere, or at least she hoped he wouldn't.

Cottonwoods closed about them, then the path led them into the clearing where the two schoolteacher cabins huddled. Maisey's windows stared out blankly. She paused with her foot on the lowest porch step. "Is it my imagination, or does the cabin seem to watch us?"

"It's an empty house, Maisey. They all do that."

Still she hung back. "The last time I was on this porch Spukani kidnapped me."

"That must be what's really bothering you. Here, I'll go in first." The door creaked open beneath Rob's hand. "I doubt I'll find anything wrong, but it's a good idea to check a place that has been standing empty."

Maisey waited on the porch while his boots thumped the floorboards. Unwelcome memories impressed themselves on her mind. She saw herself being pushed down the porch steps, forced onto the back of a pony, and sagging in utter defeat while she rode away from everything familiar.

Rob looked out from the doorway. "All's clear."

She followed him inside. Heavy silence lay over the cabin, and dust motes floated in the rays slanting through the kitchen window. She walked through the place, touching the walls to reassure herself that she was indeed home. In the front room, the copy of Godey's Lady's Book that she'd been reading sprawled face-down on the stand beside a wingback chair she favored. A quilt America had given her at Christmas covered her bed, a reminder of happier times. The rocking chair in Phoebe's bedroom brought memories of the countless hours she'd spent holding her daughter as a baby. She pictured Rob there also, cradling Phoebe and murmuring to her. Maisey touched the twining roses Rob had long ago carved into its backrest.

She returned to the kitchen, where Rob had slung himself into one of the ladderback chairs beside the table. He glanced up, his eyes intensely blue. "In case you wonder, I searched especially for monsters."

Maisey laughed. "How thoughtful of you." Some monsters invaded the mind, as she'd learned. Rob's presence helped her avoid them.

He sobered. "What's bothering you?"

Maisey slid into the chair opposite him. "What are your plans, Rob?"

He tilted his head. "I'm not sure I know what you're asking."

Maisey drew in a breath. This was harder than she'd expected. "Do you intend to remain here with us?"

Rob sat forward. "If you don't want me to—"

"That's not what I said." She twisted her hands in her lap. "What we tell Phoebe about us depends on whether you intend to stay married to me. Do you?" There, she'd said it.

"I see what you mean." Rob leaned back again. "I'm in favor of remaining married, if you're willing. Are you?"

"Yes." The word came out a little breathlessly. Maisey paused to collect herself. "Telling Phoebe will make our marriage more final. I'll abide by that, but I'm not sure I'm ready for—" Her face flamed. "At the ranch, I might have given you the impression--"

Rob smiled wryly. "I'll sleep in the loft."

America pegged the sheet in her handsto the clothesline then bent to pick up another wet bundle from the laundry basket. She paused to rub the ache in her lower back. Having carried two children to birth, she was no stranger to the discomforts of impending motherhood. Her pregnancies with Liberty and Seth had been easy compared to this one. The strain of raising two lively children while carrying a third might have something to do with it. Washday was hardest. Thank goodness Gideon had taken to coming by on Mondays to haul water for her. That, and Liberty watching her younger brother helped relieve the strain of doing laundry. America would never call boiling, scrubbing, and hanging the wash easy though.

Sometimes the children spent washday visiting Emma. America smiled. Emma took to her calling as a teacher quite well. She should make a wonderful mother one day. If only she would get over her interest in Rob, she might see the golden opportunity right in front of her. Gideon might not seem exciting compared to an adventurous man like Rob. However, there was a lot to be said for a steady, stable man. America was sure Maisey would agree. She'd gone through a great deal of turmoil over Rob. She hoped the two could set aside their differences. He'd gone after Maisey, and surely that must count for something.

America sighed. The sooner she applied herself to hanging the laundry, the sooner she could go inside. She shook out her blue gingham dress and pinned it on the line. It was one of Shane's favorites. Wearing it while he was away made her feel closer to him.

Thinking about her husband had her pausing again. She gazed into the grove of trees between her house and the cabins without really seeing them.

Where is Shane? Hopefully he'll return home soon.

Arms wound around her and pulled her backwards.

America yelped.

"It's only me." Shane laughed.

She spun around. "You scared me to death!"

"I could swear I made enough noise to alert you."

She shook her head. "I never heard you."

"Will you forgive me for startling you?" He turned the full

force of his very blue eyes on her.

She smiled. "It wasn't entirely your fault. I was lost in thought."

He kissed the bridge of her nose. "Were you dreaming of me, my darling?"

"If I answer that, I'm certain you'll struggle with pride."

Shane laughed. "Allow me to greet you properly this time." He pulled her into his arms.

America wound her arms about her husband's neck and tilted her lips toward his. "You're very good at saying hello."

The back door creaked, and small feet thumped on the porch behind them. Whoops and delighted cries rang out.

Shane grinned. "We're about to be interrupted." He bent to intercept Seth and Liberty as they hurtled toward him.

Phoebe came down the steps but held back while the other children greeted their father.

"Shane." America lifted her voice above their cries.

Her husband gave her an inquiring look.

"Where is Maisey?"

"She's settling into her cabin with Rob."

"Maisey is with Rob?" America puzzled over this piece of information.

Shane glanced at Phoebe. "I'll explain inside."

America turned her head in time to see Phoebe running beneath the trees on the path toward the cabins.

The cabin door thudded open. "Ma! You're home."

Maisey rose and turned. She gained the brief impression of springy blond curls and round blue eyes in an animated face, and then Phoebe flung herself into her arms. Maisey held her daughter tightly for the longest time, rocking her. She pulled away but kept hold of Phoebe's shoulders. "I was about to come and get you. How did you fare while I was gone?"

"I wasn't doing very well at first, but Mrs. Hayes helped me figure out some things. I felt better after learning that the Indians didn't hurt you."

"That's true, Phoebe."

Phoebe nodded. "I'm glad you're finally here. Once we found out you were at the ranch, it was hard to wait."

"I wanted to come sooner, but I was too worn out for the journey."

"It's good you rested, then. You still look tired. Let me do the dishes instead of you for a while."

Maisey smiled even while her eyes misted with tears. "I appreciate that, sweetheart."

Phoebe hugged her all over again, then broke away. She beamed at Rob, who was seated at the kitchen table, watching them steadily. "I'm glad you came back."

"Thank you, Phoebe. I am too." Rob stood up.

Phoebe smiled. "Are you going to live with us now?"

"Goodness." Maisey met Rob's glance, then turned back to her daughter. "Where did you hear that?"

"Reverend Hayes said so. I don't think he knew I was there at first."

Rob came around the table to stand beside Maisey. "Would you mind if I did?"

"Are you joking? I'd love it." Phoebe frowned at him sternly. "But you have to marry Ma first."

Rob cleared his throat. "Well, actually—"

"Otherwise it wouldn't be proper," Phoebe went on in a schoolmarm voice.

"That's true," Rob put his arm around Maisey.

"It's all settled then." Phoebe beamed, her dimples peeking

from her cheeks.

Rob grinned. "You'll be glad to know—"

Phoebe's eyes gleamed. "And of course, that will make you my Pa."

Emma stepped onto her front porch with the roosters crowing in the early morning. She'd been sleeping at odd hours lately, but it was time to return to her routine. She could find plenty to do at the school before summer's end. It felt good to stretch her legs on the path to the schoolhouse. Emma passed the silent hulk of Maisey's cabin, glad to know its occupants would come home soon.

She was organizing the desk she and Maisey shared in the schoolroom when her stomach growled. It was still quite early, but the prospect of breakfast beckoned. Emma finished her task quickly and struck out for home.

The birds were awake and singing at full throttle when she passed beneath the cottonwood trees. Emma strolled through dappled shade in the quickening light. The air felt cool as yet, but the day's burgeoning heat already infused it with the scents of sweet grass and musty soil.

Maisey's cabin stood silent as she passed. After breakfast, she would check the place. Ensuring that the cabin was ready for Maisey's return might not have occurred to America. Besides being with child, she kept busy caring for her children, and Phoebe besides.

Emma halted on the path, wondering if her eyes were playing tricks. Rob stood at the shared well located an equal distance between the cabins. Bare-headed, Rob was turning the handle that drew up the wooden bucket by its rope. Each turn stretched the blue plaid shirt he wore across his broad shoulders. A metal pail rested at his feet.

Emma smoothed a hand over her hair. She hadn't given it much attention before leaving her cabin, and it would be mussed by now. "What are you doing there?" she called.

Rob looked up and smiled. "That should be obvious, I would think."

Emma smiled back. "I meant, what are you doing here in Liberty? Last I heard, you were at your brother's ranch. When did you come back?"

"Yesterday afternoon."

"I'm glad you took no harm." She strolled toward him.

"Thanks for the sentiment." His gaze barely touched hers before sliding away.

Emma stepped closer. "Do you mean to stay a while?" She didn't bother to hide the invitation in her voice.

Rob lifted his head, his eyes reflecting his obvious surprise. "For the time being."

Emma moved nearer still, until they were almost touching. "Maybe we can go for a walk sometime. It would be nice to catch up with you." Her voice came out breathy. She was only too aware that her mother would not approve of such wanton behavior. A lady did not stand suggestively near a gentleman, nor did she invite him to walk with her. Emma didn't care. Those were stuffy old rules, and this was the West, where people enjoyed more freedom.

"Thanks for the offer." Rob touched her arm, his voice soft. "You'll forgive me if I don't accept. I'm rather occupied these days." He turned and took up the well bucket.

Not to be deterred, Emma sat down on the wooden well platform. Leaning on one arm, she looked over her shoulder at him with a brilliant smile. "I can be patient. I'm sure you'll find time eventually."

Rob gazed at her searchingly, then smiled. "You don't give up easily, do you? I hope someday you find a man who appreciates your tenacity." He poured water from the well bucket into his pail then straightened with a purposeful air. "It's not really a matter of being busy. You see—"

Phoebe burst out of the cabin. "There you are, Pa!" Her boots thumped across the porch and down the stairs. She hurried toward Rob with determined steps. "Do you need help carrying that water pail?"

Maisey backed away from her kitchen window. She hadn't meant to eavesdrop when she'd let in the cool air. Voices came in too. Emma's light tones carried far better than Rob's deeper voice. Even so, tantalizing scraps from their conversation wafted to her. It seemed clear that Rob enjoyed flirting with the young schoolteacher, and Emma made no secret of her interest in him. She'd never let on about that until today.

It was impossible not to feel betrayed. Maisey had poured out her heart to Emma over Rob. She'd shared confidences she would not have given if she'd known how Emma felt. What hurt worse, though, was Rob's inconstancy. When he'd said he wanted them to be a family, she'd believed it. Had that been a lie? She didn't want to believe he could be so fickle, but how could she avoid arriving at that conclusion? Everything she saw and heard convicted him.

What was she to do? If she separated from Rob, it would shatter Phoebe.

Phoebe burst from her room and looked out the. She didn't hesitate but ran out the door before Maisey knew what she'd planned. Maisey watched from the window as her daughter took the water pail from Rob. Emma followed the path toward her cabin while Rob and Phoebe started for home.

Footsteps on the porch announced their return before Maisey was ready to face either of them. Their shadows walked up to the door, which Phoebe had left ajar. Phoebe came in first, carrying the bucket without splashing as if it contained pure gold. At any other time, Maisey would have enjoyed her daughter's enthusiasm for a chore she normally spurned. This morning she couldn't find anything to smile about. Allowing Phoebe to become closer to Rob might be a mistake, and so could letting herself fall more deeply in love with him. Phoebe wasn't the only one with a heart that would break if Rob went away again.

Rob filled the doorway, and then he stood beside her. "I found a helper."

Maisey couldn't bring herself to reply.

He scanned her face, a crease between his brows. "Maisey?"

She hesitated in indecision. Should she mention what she had seen and overheard or let it go? The last thing she wanted was to upset Phoebe. Something told her that if she spoke of her suspicions, that would happen.

"I'll start breakfast." She reached for the wire basket holding the eggs America had brought by last night. She would make breakfast and leave Rob to his conscience. The pans might bang more than usual, but there was nothing she intended to do about that.

CHAPTER THIRTEEN

EMMA SHUT THE DOOR TO HER cabin and leaned against it, wishing she could vanish into the wooden panel. She would never, ever be able to face Rob Walsh again. Not ever. Why, oh why had she chosen this day out of all the ones she could have picked to let Rob know how she felt about him? Why had she gone on and on after he'd made it clear that he wanted nothing to do with her?

The old rules her mother had insisted that she abide by made a lot more sense after that awful encounter with Rob. If you didn't make overtures to a man, he couldn't reject you. She would never be guilty of such a miserable mistake again. Everyone knew that a woman should have the upper hand in matters of the heart. How had she forgotten that fact?

Emma pressed her hands over her heated cheeks. She'd made quite a mess of things, beginning with Gideon. Giving up on men altogether would make for a much more peaceful life. Yes, that's what she would do.

She detached herself from the door and rushed into her bedroom to fling herself across the bed. If only climbing back in and pulling the covers over her head could erase what she'd done.

Her friendship with Maisey was over, assuming that Rob had told his wife all about their encounter. Emma might never know whether he had. The only course of action that made sense was to avoid Maisey. Emma groaned. She'd never wanted to hurt her friend. Her noblest emotion had been simple joy when Maisey finally married the man she loved. Emma meant Maisey well, which was why she'd kept her feelings for Rob to herself all this time. She'd only slipped up and betrayed them this once. What had she been thinking? Coming upon Rob unexpectedly after days of worrying about him must have gone to her head. If she had known he was married, it wouldn't have happened at all.

Phoebe's excuse for interrupting them at the well had been completely transparent. Emma's face heated all over again. She would have to teach Phoebe in school after the all-too-fleeting days of summer came to an end. She propped herself on her elbows. It might be time to consider applying for a position elsewhere. Living next door to Rob, Maisey, and Phoebe could only make the situation unbearable. Leaving town seemed the only way to spare them all embarrassment.

The sooner Emma removed herself from Liberty, the better.

Gideon's knock shook the front door.

Emma buried her face in her arms. *"No, no, no, no, no."* She wouldn't answer it.

She groaned. He would probably come back later, and that might be worse. Riding on heightened emotion might lend her the strength to dispatch the problem of Gideon.

Emma jumped to her feet. She frowned at her reflection in the washstand mirror. Given her decision to always look her best around Gideon, this would never do. Emma splashed water on her cheeks to cool them. She hauled in air and let out her breath slowly in an attempt to calm her wild emotions. Only after smoothing her hair did she answer the door.

Gideon stood with his back to her, looking out over the wildlands that bordered her cabin. He spun about when she opened the door. "I was beginning to think you weren't home."

"I am not always able to answer the instant you knock."

"What's the matter?" He peered at her. "You look feverish."

"I am not unwell." She spoke with dignity.

Gideon gave her a baffled look. "Why are you talking that way?"

"What way?"

"Like someone who's stuck up."

She arched an eyebrow. "Was there something you wanted?"

"Only to thank you for the pie you baked for me. I shared it with my family, and we all enjoyed it."

"You're welcome." Emma felt herself thaw alarmingly. This conversation was making it hard to keep her distance.

Gideon smiled, looking annoyingly handsome. "I'm about to head for town. I wondered if you'd like to go along since you're feeling better?"

"Thank you for the invitation, but I am otherwise engaged."

Gideon peered into her face. "I seem to have caught you at a bad time. You do look a mite feverish."

"If you must know, I'm recovering from disconcerting news."

"Would you like to talk about whatever it is?"

That would be rich, explaining to Gideon exactly how she had embarrassed herself. Wouldn't he just smile over her humiliation? "No, thank you."

"If you change your mind, you know where to find me."

"Did you know that Rob and Maisey are married?" Emma jerked out the words, too upset to keep it to herself.

"So that's what's bothering you." Gideon shook his head. "How sad for you."

"I'm completely unaffected."

"That's plain as day."

Was he laughing at her? Emma gave him a suspicious glance. Instead of looking amused, as she'd thought he might, he watched her with a somber expression. If Gideon started pitying her, that would put an end to her composure. It was best to avoid the possibility. "I'd rather be alone, if you don't mind."

"Say no more." He left her abruptly, hurrying away with his shoulders slumped.

Annoyance shot through Emma. What did Gideon have to feel sad about? He had it good, with his family near.

She was the one who was all alone in the world.

Gideon turned a damp stone in his hand, letting the shiny bits of mica embedded in the dense white feldspar glint in the sun. Water swished through the creek that wended through the grass. A rainbow trout jumped in a pool below where he stood on the bank, its bright body glistening briefly before plopping into the water. Rings radiated over the surface. A dragonfly whirred above the creek on gossamer wings. Bees buzzed about, gathering nectar from the wildflowers strewn throughout the grass.

Gideon had sought solitude in wild places since his family moved to Liberty five years ago. He'd stopped telling his mother when he went scouting though, keeping it quiet for her sake as well as his own. She was never quite comfortable when her menfolk ventured into the wilderness. Pa understood the urge to explore their surroundings, for he felt it too.

Pa had regaled everyone in the family with the details of his search for Maisey. Gideon had listened curiously, but his father's frustration over his failures only served to magnify his own negative emotions. After Pa wound down, Gideon had slipped out quietly.

He wouldn't travel far this time, but he needed to put a little space between himself and Emma. If only he could so easily distance himself from the pain that gnawed at him whenever he thought of her. That was often, unfortunately. Gideon had a sneaking suspicion that he loved the vexing woman. If she would ever let him near, he might put his feelings for her to the test. Knowing whether he loved Emma was important, at least to him. She seemed to hold a different opinion on the matter.

He should be patient. Emma wouldn't shake off her unhappiness over Rob's marriage overnight. Gideon pulled back his arm and flung the stone across the creek. It skipped once, twice, three times, then sank. *Maybe she would never recover.*

Gideon shook his head at his own thoughts. They served no purpose but to depress him. The tenderness he felt for Emma was like a fragile flower just unfurling. Whether it thrived depended on how much care it received. He could water and feed it, but without the warmth of returned affections, it couldn't grow much.

"Gideon!" His brother's voice reached to him from a small distance. Jake took long strides across the grass, his brown tangles bouncing with each step. He followed the path their feet had forged over time, starting from behind the barn. That was also the direction from which Gideon had come. He'd assumed that Jake was visiting the Hayes household and not hanging about to overhear his conversation with Emma. Call it pride, but he wouldn't like his brother to witness how thoroughly she had spurned him.

Gideon waved and waited for Jake to reach him.

"I saw you on my way home." Jake puffed a little with the exertion of catching up to him.

"Did you keep out from underfoot, like Ma told you? Reverend Hayes is newly arrived, same as Pa."

"Yes, but I didn't have to. Reverend Hayes likes me around. He told me so. I keep Seth out of trouble, he says. Liberty plays tag with me when she and Phoebe aren't doing stupid girl things." Jake plopped down near Gideon and squinted upward. "I saw you talking to the teacher."

"Did you hear what we were discussing?" Gideon kept his voice unconcerned.

"Nah." Jake picked a blade of grass and nibbled its end. "It didn't look like you were having fun."

Gideon tousled his brother's unruly mop. "You're observant for one so young."

"Hey! I'm eight, remember? I had a birthday."

Gideon concealed his amusement. "How could I have forgotten?"

Jake tossed aside the blade he'd chewed. "You should forget about the teacher."

"I wish it was that simple." Gideon skipped another rock, but it sank straightaway. He dropped down beside his brother. "One day you'll understand."

Jake shook his head. "I already do."

Gideon examined his brother's face. The baby fat had melted into leaner lines that revealed the man he would become. "You can't say something like that without explaining."

Jake sighed elaborately. "I like Liberty, but she doesn't like me back."

"Ah." It occurred to Gideon that his young brother had

exactly stated his own woes. His problems were as simple and complicated as an eight-year-old's. "Will you try to change her mind?"

Jake sat cross-legged. "I've thought about it a lot."

"I can well imagine." In fact, Gideon could completely sympathize.

"The way I see it, there are only two choices."

"I'd love to know what they are." Gideon smiled wryly.

Jake pulled a handful of grass and scattered it to the wind. "I can try really hard to make her like me too, but what's the use of that? She either does or she doesn't."

"Wise man. What's the other choice?"

"Give up on love." Jake blew out a soft breath. "I think it's the best thing to do."

"You're sort of right, but there's a problem with your logic." A tiny hummingbird hovered above a willow on the opposite bank. It was a male, he could tell by the green vest beneath its gray breast and the magenta feathers fanning out in rays below the black beak. "Has it occurred to you that we wouldn't be here if Ma and Pa had done that?"

"They seem happy," Jake admitted.

"If you want my advice, don't be in such a hurry. You have years yet to sort out your feelings."

"I hate it when people tell me to wait until I'm grown," Jake growled. "I'm the same person now that I'll be then."

"Yes, but you'll know a bit more about life." Gideon shrugged. "Who knows? You and Liberty might wind up together one day. Or maybe not. I know it's hard to imagine, but there could be someone else for both of you. You won't know until you find out."

For spur-of-the-moment advice, it wasn't bad. Gideon decided to take it himself.

Rob paused in the cabin doorway and glanced over his shoulder at Maisey. "I don't suppose you want to walk with Phoebe and me."

Not after that halfhearted invitation, she didn't. Maisey worked off her feelings by putting a little more elbow grease into scrubbing the table.

"Please come, Ma." Phoebe turned pleading eyes on her. "It won't be the same without you."

Maisey wrestled with the desire to please her daughter. She wished that spending time with Phoebe didn't also mean spending time with Rob. She touched her temple, which throbbed. "I'd better stay here."

"Are you sure?" Rob scanned her face. "Fresh air might do you good."

She kept scrubbing. "I'll step out onto the porch for a bit."

"Suit yourself." Rob went out the door.

"Ma, you're ruining everything!" Phoebe rounded on her.

"Please stop shouting."

Phoebe folded her arms, glaring at her. "You could come if you wanted to."

Maisey sighed. "I have a headache."

"I notice that it's not so bad that you have to stop working."

Maisey scrubbed harder. "Stop trying to convince me."

"I give up." Phoebe flounced out the doorway. The cabin shuddered from the slamming of the door.

Maisey sat in one of the dining chairs and put her head in her hands. They couldn't go on like this. For all their sakes, she needed to get along with Rob somehow. It had been several days since she'd seen him with Emma, and during that time the feeling of betrayal had not faded. Rob was withdrawing from her, but she couldn't move past her feelings to change that.

How Maisey longed to go back to the happy years she'd spent with Avery. They shone in her memory like polished gems, tarnished only by the way they'd ended. She rose from her chair, pushing her thoughts away. What was the use of dwelling on the past? It was high time to busy herself with the present. She warmed water for mopping the floor in a pot on the stove. There was nothing like a little hard work to drive away sorrows. After scrubbing the floors until they gleamed, she sagged into a chair in the front room.

The day wore on, and still Rob and Phoebe didn't return. She kept listening for footsteps on the porch, but none came. She was frying bacon to go in the beans for supper when they returned at last. While Phoebe chattered throughout supper about the birds they had seen on their walk, Rob watched Maisey off and on without adding much to the conversation. He wore a pensive expression, as if lost in thought. He retired to the loft after the meal, leaving Maisey and Phoebe to finish the dishes in the kitchen. Exhausted from the emotions of the day, Maisey sought her own bed early.

The next morning, she turned from scrambling eggs in the cast-iron skillet to discover Rob standing, barefooted and unshaven, behind her in the kitchen.

Maisey started. She couldn't get used to Rob's presence in her house. "I didn't hear you."

"Sorry to startle you." Rob smiled. "Good morning."

Maisey narrowed her eyes in suspicion. Why should he smile at her so warmly? "Breakfast will be ready soon. The potatoes are almost done."

"I don't care about food." He slid his arms around her and nuzzled her neck.

Maisey caught her breath. Ambushing her like this wasn't fair. She had few defenses against the man, as she discovered anew when he claimed her lips. She surrendered for a brief moment of bliss, but then pushed him away. "Phoebe will see us."

Rob grinned. "What if she does? This was her idea."

"She suggested that you kiss me?"

"Well, not exactly that." He laughed. "I doubt she'd disapprove, though. Phoebe gave me an earful on our walk, and I must say it set me thinking. She wants us to be together."

So did Maisey, but if wishes were horses, she'd have a stable full. She backed out of his arms. "Breakfast will burn."

He scowled. "Is that all you have to say?"

"What else do you want from me?" The cry wrenched from her. He hadn't mentioned Emma, but Maisey couldn't pretend that his flirting with another woman didn't matter.

Rob stared at her. "Nothing, I guess." He strode to the door. "You can keep your breakfast." He didn't slam the door but shut it firmly behind him. That was somehow worse.

Maisey wrapped her arms around herself. What was she going to do?

"He'll be back." Phoebe came into the kitchen, her face fresh from sleep.

"I'm not so sure." Maisey shook her head. "I'm sorry, sweetheart, but this may not work out."

"Ma, you can't give up." Tears glistened on Phoebe's cheeks. "You have to keep trying."

"I wish I knew how." The stench of burning drew Maisey's attention to the stove.

"I'm going to Liberty's house." Phoebe banged the cabin

door behind her.

After removing the burnt food from the stove, Maisey followed Phoebe outside, ready to call her to account for taking off without permission. She caught sight of her daughter going around the bend in the path where it split and vanishing into the cottonwood stand. Maisey sank onto the top step. Phoebe was always welcome at the Hayes house, and Maisey was too upset to rush over to correct her daughter. She would speak to Phoebe a little later, after she calmed down. Right now, Maisey needed to take a moment for herself.

The cottonwoods hissed in the wind but stood strong. The birds continued singing in the trees, undeterred. The sun broke from behind clouds, shedding beams of light. Maisey shut her eyes and pulled in a deep breath. Had she been fair to Rob this morning? Maybe not. It must have been hard for him to approach her with so much to overcome between them. *What if he hadn't been flirting with Emma?* The question buzzed in her head like a pesky fly. It had sure seemed like it, but appearances could deceive. It would be terrible if she was holding her husband to account for something he hadn't done.

Maisey cradled her face in her hands. She didn't want to think these thoughts. It was far easier to be offended.

The well rasped and creaked.

Maisey lifted her head.

Emma was drawing water.

Maisey rose and went down the steps. This might be the best chance she would have to find out what was going on.

Emma looked up as she neared. Was it Maisey's imagination, or did she look guilty? "Hello, Emma." She spoke mildly, despite her inner turmoil.

"Hello, Maisey." Emma turned the well bucket and splashed water into the pail at her feet. Her aim was off, and water splashed the hem of her skirt. She straightened. "I was glad to learn of your safety."

"Thank you. I understand that you saw what happened and sounded the alarm."

"Your welfare means a great deal to me." Emma lowered the wooden bucket tied to a rope into the well. A faint splash reached Maisey's ears.

"Does it, Emma?" Emotion shook her voice.

Emma gave her a startled glance. "Why wouldn't it?"

"I saw you with Rob the other day, and I heard what you said to him."

Emma's face flamed. "I made a mistake."

"Is that all it was?"

"Yes, of course. I didn't know he was married."

"You knew how I felt about him. I told you everything." Maisey shook her head. "How could you, Emma? Do you care nothing about my feelings?"

"That's not the least bit fair." Emma picked up her pail, which she'd only partially filled. "What about *my* feelings? I tried to smother them for your sake, but they refused to die. I'm sorry I couldn't manage my emotions better, but it wasn't for lack of trying."

Maisey didn't know what to think. It would have been easier to picture Emma as scheming rather than trying to rise above a bad situation.

She warmed the water she'd drawn after Emma left her and rolled up her sleeves. There was nothing like a little hard work to drive away sorrows, and the walls were in need of washing.

She scrubbed the walls and started on the windows. Through the wet panes, she could see America's wavery image climb the porch steps. Glad to interrupt the unhappy thoughts that kept returning to her, Maisey went to open the door. "I hope you didn't mind Phoebe coming over this morning. She needed a little time away from home."

"Of course not. She's keeping Liberty occupied." America held out a covered porcelain dish with a handle that resembled an ear of corn. Maisey recognized it as America's best casserole dish. "I thought you might like some of my jerky stew for supper."

Touched by her friend's kindness, Maisey accepted the casserole dish. "Thank you, but you shouldn't trouble yourself in your condition."

"Don't be silly." America's smile relieved the weary look on her face. "I'm not so fragile a flower as everyone thinks."

"I'll try to resist the temptation to shield you." Maisey smiled. She opened the door wider and stepped back to allow her friend inside. "I only meant that with a baby on the way, plus your other children's care, not to mention your husband newly home, you have a lot to do already."

America followed her into the kitchen. "I don't mind sacrificing for a friend."

"I appreciate it, believe me." Maisey gave her a hug.

"You've been through an ordeal and gotten married besides. Carrying on with everyday life isn't easy after one disrupting event, let alone two."

Maisey smiled. "Sit down and I'll put on the kettle."

"That sounds wonderful." America sank into a dining chair. "I should go back soon and relieve Shane from the children's care, but taking the weight off my feet for a moment feels good."

"I promise to stop by more often and give you lots of chances to rest."

America accepted the cup Maisey extended to her. "Taking

tea with you reminds me that Felicity Buckthorn is hosting a tea party tomorrow afternoon. She asked me to invite you."

"How fun. I should be able to come." Maisey would welcome the chance to get out of the house and away from the recent tensions.

America studied her. "Is something the matter?"

She should have known that America wouldn't be fooled by her light tone. "I'm not sure Rob plans to stay with us."

A crease formed between America's brows. "Taking his vows should indicate that he does."

"Maybe he had other reasons."

"How will you know unless you ask?"

America was so practical, it put Maisey to shame. "What if he doesn't tell me the truth?"

"Maisey." America shook her head but also smiled. "Sooner or later you'll have to decide whether to trust the man you married."

Leave it to America to pinpoint her problem. Maisey hadn't considered that she lacked faith in Rob, only that he might betray her trust. What if she hadn't given it to him in the first place? That meant that the solution to her problem lay in her own hands.

Maisey moved about the cabin quietly after America's visit, pondering her friend's words. The visit had done her good. Her mood had improved, and her headache was gone.

Phoebe came home before supper. She sat sideways on one of the kitchen chairs. "Ma, I'm sorry about getting mad and running off earlier. I shouldn't have gone without permission."

Maisey looked up from stirring a batch of cornbread. "I'm glad you can see that."

"I won't do it again."

Maisey nodded. "That would be best."

Phoebe jumped up and encompassed her in a light hug. "I love you, Ma."

Tears pricked Maisey's eyes. "I love you, too."

Maisey was about to blow out her candle and go to sleep when boots thumped on the porch. Through the window she could see Rob's outline on the porch. She pulled a wrap over herself, aware of its flimsiness, but it was the best she could do at the moment.

She flung the front door open, and he strode into the cabin. Pride kept her from asking him where he'd been.

His gaze burned into her. "Sorry to wake you."

She gave no response, not wanting to betray that she'd waited up, listening for him.

He nodded, then stepped past her and climbed the ladder into the loft without satisfying her curiosity.

Maisey's candle sent a circle of light ahead of her as she retreated to her bedroom. The door closed with a soft click. Maisey leaned her forehead against the wooden panel.

Please Lord, help us find our way to one another.

CHAPTER FOURTEEN

MAISEY JERKED THE CABIN DOOR OPEN before America could knock. "I saw you from the window. You look beautiful."

"Thank you." America spun about in her best gown, which Maisey had helped her sew from blue figured-silk. The brown and white flower sprays woven into the fabric were perfect for a tea party. White linen lined the dress, making it more comfortable to wear in warm weather. The wide skirt hid her blossoming figure and gathered at the back into draperies accented by a small bustle.

She surveyed Maisey. "Why aren't you ready?"

"Please make my excuses to Felicity."

"You have to come." America smiled at her firmly.

Maisey groaned inwardly. Why had she accepted Felicity's invitation in the first place? She ought to have realized that attending a party so soon after arriving home would be a strain. "I really don't feel up to it." After her spat with Rob, that was the simple truth.

"You will once you're there."

Maisey fingered the skirt of her green calico dress. "I'll never be ready on time."

"You look lovely as you stand. Besides, it's just Felicity and us."

"Rob's gone, and I can't leave Phoebe here by herself." Maisey didn't elaborate on where Rob might be because she didn't know. Nor did she mention wanting to be close to home in case Rob failed to come home. Phoebe might need comforting.

America gave her a puzzled look. "She was at my house most of the morning, and the girls had a great time playing together. There's no reason Phoebe couldn't also spend the afternoon with Liberty."

"Can I, Ma?" Phoebe called from the front room, where she'd been idly flipping through Godey's Lady's Book. The fashion images bored her, and she thought some of the advice funny, but she begged Maisey to cook most of the recipes and pored over the short stories and biographical articles. Reading came naturally to Phoebe, and she'd advanced to a level far above her age. She cast the magazine aside. "Please, Ma. Liberty said I could braid her hair."

Maisey smiled. "You wouldn't want to miss out on that." She couldn't fight America and Phoebe both. Besides, visiting with friends would be better than sitting at home listening for Rob's boots on the porch. "All right, I'll go."

"Good!" America beamed. "Felicity would be disappointed if you'd begged off."

Felicity was so delighted to receive them that Maisey felt guilty at her earlier reluctance. In the face of her hostess's enthusiasm, it was hard to remain churlish. The warmth of Felicity's hospitality put Maisey to shame. By contrast, Maisey realized that she had been focusing mainly on herself. That might be a natural consequence brought on by troubles, but she didn't have to continue. Phoebe had asked her to try harder this morning. After experiencing Felicity's selfless kindness, Maisey thought she better understood her daughter's request. Maybe, if she'd realized all of this earlier, she and Rob wouldn't have fought so much. She couldn't accept the blame for all that had gone wrong between them. Rob was partly responsible. But then, so was she.

Felicity led them into the dining room, where wildflowers adorned a linen-covered table laden with delicacies. It took no effort to lose herself in the moment. Felicity plied her guests with steaming cups of Earl Grey tea, cucumber sandwiches with the crusts cut off, and savory beef pies. She passed plates laden with stuffed eggs and sliced tomatoes grown in the Buckthorn garden. The meal finished with carrot cake and the tinned lemon cookies Felicity had been keeping back for a special occasion. Maisey ate her fill but saved a cookie for Phoebe.

"This is such a pleasure, I wonder why I've never done it before." Felicity beamed at them as if they'd done something remarkable. "I know. Maisey, why don't we throw a wedding reception for you and your new husband?"

"Oh, no." Maisey shook her head. "I couldn't ask you to do that."

"Nonsense." America's face lit. "That's such a good idea. I don't know why it escaped me."

"I think perhaps..." Felicity smiled at her. "You've been rather occupied."

America blushed, although Felicity had not directly referred to her delicate condition.

"Really, a reception is not necessary." Maisey tried again. "Thanks all the same."

"Of course, it is." America turned a firm smile on her. It occurred to Maisey, all at once, that America and Felicity were equally matched in strength of mind.

"I wish Emma had come today." Felicity frowned. "She so needs companionship that it's especially disappointing. I imagine she'll want to help with the reception, though."

"Emma was supposed to be here?" Maisey's voice betrayed her emotion.

America studied her quietly.

"Yes, but she made her excuses." Felicity poured another round of tea. "Something about getting ready for the start of school."

"I imagine that keeps her busy." Maisey's teaspoon clinked as she stirred. She refused to feel guilty over Emma's choices.

"Did you know that she's skilled at folding napkins? It's amazing, really." Felicity brightened. "She'll have to show off her skill at the reception."

Maisey's objections appeared not to have registered at all. She would voice them more firmly, but during a party's afterglow was probably not the time to contradict your hostess. Maisey might be able to call upon America's formidable persuasiveness to rescue her. That meant confiding in her and possibly receiving uncomfortable advice.

Waiting a day or two before bringing up the matter would do no harm.

Emma strolled past grassy fields glistening in the sun. Now that she had mailed her letters applying for employment elsewhere, she could linger on the way home from town. There had been no mail for her in the tiny post office, but then she hadn't expected any. Her family would never again write to her. She'd withdrawn after their deaths and had kept her address in Liberty to herself. Emma missed her friends but corresponding with them could never be the same now that her family was gone. She didn't know if she would ever gain the emotional stamina to seek her friends out again.

With the sun warming the top of her head and a flock of Canada geese arrowing across the blue sky, being alone in the world didn't seem so bad. Pa had been right when he'd told her to depend on no one but herself. Letting others help had landed her in complications with Gideon and forged a bond with his mother she would be sorry to break.

She'd escaped from her cabin today out of fear that Felicity would summon her to the tea party. That would have been impossible. She was glad Felicity had told her Maisey planned to attend or the situation would have been awkward in the extreme. Maisey had made it quite clear that their friendship was over.

The trouble with caring about people was how badly it hurt to lose them. Leaving would be an unavoidable wrench. Emma would better protect herself from growing close to other people in her future dealings.

She'd never really belonged here, although she'd come to feel she did. The Hayes family had included her in their family events, but that had always felt like pity. She didn't want to be cast as a needy person. Moving would allow her to avoid that happening.

The road bent through a stand of larch trees. She'd gone partway into the grove when something rustled in the underbrush. Emma halted at once. She might have brought Pa's rifle, but the walk to and from town had seemed safe. That could only be an illusion, since the road traversed wild areas like this one.

Emma stood poised in indecision. She could either go forward or retreat, but she must decide what to do quickly.

It wasn't the right time of day to catch deer grazing. They usually appeared later than this or in the early morning. Perhaps it was only an injured bird, maybe a heron that nested around the creek. Then again, it could easily be a bear. Emma stopped herself from turning back. She'd only have to return this way later, at a more favorable time for nocturnal creatures to prowl about, hunting for prey. She stood poised in indecision, refusing to go back but unable to nerve herself to press forward.

A bear cub waddled out of the shadows ahead. Its mother was nowhere in sight, but Emma knew better than to engage with it. She skirted around the cub, but the piteous creature followed her, bawling.

An answering cry, deep-throated and utterly terrifying, set Emma's teeth on edge. A grown bear rambled toward them, taking long strides that ate up the ground. Emma backed away from the cub, her heart pounding. She didn't see the fallen log until after it tripped her. Lying in a heap with a horrid throbbing in her foot, she contemplated her fate. With the wind knocked from her chest, she couldn't rise. What did it feel like to be mauled by a bear? She'd hoped never to find out.

CHAPTER FIFTEEN

A GUNSHOT CRACKED. THE MOTHER bear roared louder, and her baby screamed.

Emma sucked air into her lungs just as blackness closed in. She gasped in a deeper breath, thankful when her vision cleared, and the world stopped spinning. She chanced lifting her head. The mother bear was loping through the buffalo grass toward the creek. The baby kept pace with her, wailing. Emma closed her eyes and lay still.

"Are you all right?" Strong arms lifted her.

She opened her eyes. Surely, Rob couldn't be her rescuer, and yet his face floated above her.

Rob peered down, a crease between his brows. "I thought for a moment that you were gone."

"I could have been if not for you." She gazed at him in admiration. He had saved her from destruction, and she owed him her life.

Rob shifted his hold on her. "Can you stand?"

"I'm not sure." Emma sat up with his help. "I twisted my ankle."

He lifted her to her feet.

The first attempt to put weight on her foot ended with her yelping in pain. She bit her lip to still its trembling. "How will I ever get home?"

Rob steadied her. "Lean on me."

Emma gritted her teeth and tried not to sag against him. The situation was already compromising without making it worse by leaning on Rob overmuch. She was keenly conscious of how Maisey would feel if she could see them.

Emma walked as far as she could before she had to rest. Rob guided her to a sun-warmed boulder near the road. Emma rubbed her ankle and peered down the road. They still had a long way to go. Why on earth had she decided to walk so far? "This is going to take a while."

He smiled. "Don't worry. I'll see you home."

"We'd better keep going." Emma levered to her feet.

Life wasn't fair, she decided as Rob slid his arm around her. Here she was with the man of her dreams, only he was married to someone else.

Maisey kept pace beside America on the path toward the Hayes house, enjoying the contented mood in the aftermath of the tea party. Maisey was glad her friend had persuaded her to go, after all. She would have moped around the cabin rather than enjoying herself among people she cared about.

America studied her. "Do you want to tell me what's troubling you?"

Maisey shook her head. "I'm sure that I don't."

"I suppose I'll have to accept your answer." America plucked a dandelion from the grass.

Maisey wrestled with her conscience. She shouldn't shut out a friend who onlywanted to help. "It has to do with Emma."

"I suspected as much." America twirled the yellow flower. "Have you fallen out with her in some way?"

"I wish it were only that." Maisey pulled in a breath and let the dreaded words out. "Emma seems interested in my husband."

America's face did not register surprise. "Go on."

Maisey drew another breath. "I'm not sure Rob doesn't return her affections."

The dandelion in America's fingers stopped twirling. "Have you spoken to Rob about this?"

"Not directly."

A crease formed between America's brows. "Then I assume you are guessing at his feelings."

Maisey felt the need to defend her suspicions. "I saw him flirting with her at the well."

"Are you sure?"

"Well, no. Not entirely."

America tossed the dandelion away. "And this is what has you tied up in knots?"

"Can you blame me?"

America halted on the path. "You could be right about Rob and Emma, but I doubt it from what I've seen."

"Why do you think that?"

"Rob shows every sign of being in love with you. Yes, temptation can enter, but it usually doesn't find a foothold unless there is already trouble within a marriage."

"Rob and I started on the wrong foot."

"Oh?" America adopted a carefully neutral tone, her face expressionless.

"Is there nothing Shane doesn't tell you?"

"I am his wife, and he needed to talk about what happened." America smiled gently. "I suspect you are learning the hard way that telling a falsehood comes at a cost."

America's accurate description of the root cause of Maisey's difficulties explained so much. "If I hadn't claimed that Rob was my fiancé, he'd be Spukani's slave."

"Unless God planned another way to free him."

America's statement was unanswerable. Maisey shook her head. "I couldn't have abandoned Rob in his need."

America smiled. "It's normal, even desirable, to want to protect those you love. However, losing your integrity in the process isn't what God intends."

"It's too late to fix what I did."

"You can't, anyway." America laughed. "Another thing common to us all is the desire to do God's work for Him."

"I can imagine how well that would turn out if I could."

"It's not too late for God to repair your marriage, Maisey. All you have to do is trust Him."

"I'll try."

America hugged her. "I hope your every dream comes true."

They continued to America's back door and into the kitchen. Shane came through from the hallway, and the excited clamor of children at play followed him from elsewhere in the house. "And so, you return." He greeted his wife with a kiss. "I suppose you are full of tea."

America smiled. "Indeed we are, Reverend Hayes."

He offered Maisey a smile. "It's good to see you so relaxed."

Maisey smiled. "Mrs. Buckthorn is an excellent hostess."

America's eyes shone. "We should all learn from her example."

"Liberty has been pestering me to invite Phoebe to spend the night." Shane tilted his head inquiringly. "What do you ladies think of the idea?"

"She's always welcome here." America spoke without hesitation.

Maisey felt more reluctant. It could mean spending the night alone in the cabin, but she didn't want to spoil the girls' fun. "That's fine."

Shane turned his attention to Maisey. "I need to ask whether you want to continue teaching the Salish children."

America moved nearer to Shane, and his arm encircled her. "We wouldn't blame you if you don't."

Maisey lifted her head. "I've given this some thought, and I'm willing. I can't fault the entire tribe for one man's misbehavior."

"Well stated." Shane grinned. "Are you up to teaching on Saturday? If not, we can always send the students away until you're ready."

"Don't do that." Maisey would like very much to take a little time off, but today she'd learned something about giving to others. "I'll teach."

"I'll help you." America glanced at Shane. "That is, if I can call upon my husband to watch the children."

"I can manage alone." Maisey softened her refusal with a smile. "Although I appreciate your eagerness to help."

America puckered her brow. "Are you sure? That's a lot to take on alone so soon—after—everything."

Maisey would very much like help, but she didn't want to impose on America to receive it. "I'll be all right." She extended a hand, which America took. "Thanks for persuading me to go today."

America's lips curved softly. "I'm glad I could."

"Surely you jest." Maisey grinned. "When you and Phoebe join forces, it would take a strong will indeed to resist you."

Shane chortled. "They both know their own minds and possess the kind-hearted desire to assist others to make up theirs."

America gave him an arch look. "Are you calling me a meddling woman?"

Maisey laughed. "I'll leave you two to sort that out. I'd better walk home before it grows dark."

"Would you like me to go with you?" Shane asked at once.

Yes, she would, but she didn't want to remove Shane from his family, especially not to ease fears she needed to master. "It's still daylight. I'll be all right but thank you."

A thumping sound carried to them amid joyful squeals. Shane hurried from the kitchen. Maisey started to follow.

"Let Shane deal with it." America called her back in an amused voice. "He's quite capable. It doesn't sound serious, and I doubt Phoebe's responsible."

Maisey wasn't so sure, knowing her daughter's lively nature, but she didn't dispute the point. She preferred to hold onto her relaxed mood, if she could.

America stepped onto the porch with her. "Let us know if you need anything at all."

Maisey turned back at the head of the stairs. "I'll bring clothes for Phoebe."

"Don't bother." America waved a hand dismissively. "I'm sure we can find something for her to wear. We still have a lot of her belongings from when she stayed with us while you were gone."

"Kiss her goodnight for me."

America's eyes softened. "I will."

Maisey started for home as the sky deepened above the stand of cottonwoods. The day was winding down while all nature held its breath in anticipation of slumber. Her feet made little sound on the path worn into the grass. It carried her toward Emma's cabin before splitting off toward hers.

America had suggested that Maisey should give her husband the benefit of the doubt about Emma. That made sense in hindsight. Only Rob and Emma could know the whole truth of what did or didn't lie between them. Maisey could only guess. Why then, had she chosen to assume her husband was faithless? Maisey knew the answer but hated to admit it, even to herself. She'd wanted to push Rob away by blaming him for Emma's overtures. How else could she protect herself from being hurt by him again?

Maisey emerged from the trees with her mind clearer. She'd learned so much about herself today, most of it uncomfortable. She should try to overcome her suspicions.

Emma must still be at the schoolhouse, for her cabin was dark. Although it was still light out, the inside of houses required a little illumination at this hour. If Emma was home, lantern light would spill from her windows. Maisey's cabin also lay in darkness, a state that answered her question about Rob. Wherever else her husband might be, he wasn't home.

A flicker of movement caught her eye.

She backed instinctively into shadow.

Along the path leading from the schoolhouse and the road beyond, two figures walked with an awkward gait caused by their embrace. Maisey peered at them with a sinking in her stomach. Rob had his arm around Emma, and she was clutching the front of his shirt.

Maisey pressed a hand to her mouth. Without betraying her presence, she watched them pass her cabinand turn aside on the path to Emma's place.

CHAPTER SIXTEEN

THE DOOR KNOB RATTLED UNDER ROB'S hand, but the door didn't budge. He frowned. Why should Maisey's cabin be locked and dark this early? It had taken him a while to fetch Doc Bailey to examine Emma's ankle, but it was barely past sunset. Even so, both Maisey and Phoebe must be sleeping. The trouble with that scenario was that he couldn't picture Phoebe going to bed at this hour on purpose.

He might have to intrude on Shane's household and explain that his wife had locked him out. That idea appealed less than a night in the barn with hay dust prickling the back of his neck and filling his lungs. Another option he liked better was to camp out on the front porch. It would be a rough night without a bedroll, plus Emma might see him from her window in the morning. He'd had enough trouble from that quarter without giving the impression that he and Maisey weren't getting along. Even if that was the case, he didn't want Emma to know it.

He'd have to wake Maisey.

That idea didn't appeal to him much either. They hadn't parted on the best of terms this morning. Rob could admit, after taking a walk to cool down, that he'd overreacted. Maisey needed patience, and he'd given her none. Worst, he'd pushed her to respond to him. Rob smiled ruefully. He'd gotten his wish, but not in the way he had hoped.

Rob sat down and leaned against the door's rough wood. The cottonwood leaves tossed in the cooling breeze. Darkness lay heavy over the wildlands beyond the trees. The creek winding through them sang more loudly at night. Stars riddled the sky, not even a scrap of cloud stopping their light.

Help me sort out the mess I've made of things. The prayer rose from him with the ease of breath.

A flicker of movement caught the corner of his eye. Rob turned his head toward the kitchen window. The pale curtain behind the panes still swayed. Maisey must have looked out. She might not have seen him sitting there, which would explain why she hadn't come to the door.

He stood up and knocked. The empty sound vibrated the air but did not summon Maisey.

He tried again. Nothing happened for so long that he was beginning to wonder if he'd only thought he'd seen the curtain move.

A light glowed in the cabin. A moment later, the bolt scraped and the door slid open. Maisey stood behind it as if holding a shield in front of her. She held a candle, her eyes wide. "I thought I heard someone, but when I looked..." She swung the door wider.

Rob stepped inside. "You went to bed early."

"I was worn out, I guess." Standing barefooted in a blue wrapper and with her hair in plaits, she struck Rob as desirable but vulnerable.

"Sorry I woke you." He pulled his eyes off her to bolt the door behind him. Rob turned around, surprising a sad expression on her face. He'd put it there, and it was up to him to remove it. "I have other regrets as well."

"Let's not talk tonight." Maisey's face went white. "I don't think I can bear it."

"I only want to tell you how sorry I am—"

"*Please!*" Maisey stared at him with stricken eyes. "I

already know that you're sorry you married me, and that you would rather be with Emma."

"What on earth are you talking about?" Rob glanced at the door to Phoebe's room and ended his question on a quieter note.

"Phoebe's not here. She's spending the night with Liberty."

That was just as well, if Maisey was going to continue saying outlandish things. Where had she gotten the idea that he wanted Emma instead of her? He'd repeatedly refused the schoolteacher's advances. She was attractive and intelligent, and he was sure she would find someone to love her. However, that person would not be him. "About Emma—I mean, about Miss Duncan—"

"I have eyes in my head. I saw how she put herself forward at the well. You didn't seem to mind at all."

"I'm innocent, I tell you." Rob struggled to take her complaint seriously, but it was ludicrous.

She narrowed her eyes. "Do you deny that you went to her cabin today?"

"You sound so happy to accuse me. I would think you'd want to be wrong."

She fell silent.

"If you'd listened to me, I would have explained." Rob slowly shook his head. "Now I don't want to." He started up the ladder to the loft.

"Leaving me again?" Maisey sniped.

Rob kept going. There was no point in talking when they were both upset.

The candlelight withdrew, and Maisey's door slammed.

Rob felt his way to his bed in darkness. Sleep didn't come easily, and it arrived with unwelcome visitors. He dreamed of battling Spukani and of being chased by a bear. Other nightmares left vaguer impressions. They warred with him, sometimes jerking him awake. Morning arrived none too soon. Rob sat up and pushed a hand through his hair.

He'd have done better to sleep on the porch.

Maisey groaned and clutched her pillow. She would rather remain asleep than wake to memories of the horrible fight with Rob last night. Her dream of marrying him had never resembled this painful existence.

How had it come to this?

She shouldn't have taken America's suggestion to confide her suspicions to Rob right after seeing him with Emma. She'd been too upset to bring the subject up rationally. America couldn't have meant that she should accuse her husband. Her advice wasn't at fault, only the way Maisey had applied it.

She dragged herself from bed and splashed water on her face at the washstand. The towel soothed her skin with its softness. Maisey contemplated her image. The woman in the mirror gazed at her with a somber expression. How different she appeared than before Rob's return. Her lips were pressed into a thin line, as if holding back bitter words. Pain darkened her brown eyes, erasing their usual warmth. A furrow marred the space between her brows. Only time could relieve her sorrow. Perhaps it would also restore the soft light of hope in her heart. That didn't seem possible in the present moment. Fresh tears choked her, and Maisey turned away from her reflection before they fell.

How could she and Rob ever bridge the gap between them? She would need to overcome her suspicions to even try. Rob was unlikely to make the effort. He always ran away from problems, didn't he? Last night he'd proven that all overagain by climbing into the loft to escape their conversation.

She sighed. Continuing to live together without resolving their problems would only cause fresh pain for themselves, and also for Phoebe. There seemed no good solution.

Maisey squeezed her eyes shut. Thinking about her troubles made her head throb.

Scraping sounds from elsewhere in the cabin reached her. What on earth was going on? She tiptoed to the door, not willing to warn Rob that she was awake.

She opened the door a crack and peeked out. The gap was too narrow to show her anything but the wall across the corridor. Wanting to peer sideways into the kitchen, Maisey pushed the door wider. The hinges creaked.

Rob stood up from the table. Unshaven and disheveled, he looked as rough as she felt. Their gazes clashed.

Maisey gave up cowering in her doorway and advanced into the kitchen. Sunlight streamed through the window, at odds with the darkness of her emotions. She picked out the saddlebags waiting beside the door.

Maisey gripped a chairback for support. "Are you going somewhere?"

He looked away from her. "I'm headed to the ranch."

"Are you coming back?" She wanted to shout the question but uttered it quietly instead.

He flinched slightly. "I don't know."

His face blurred behind tears. "Have you told Emma?" She couldn't resist asking, although common sense warned her not to pose it.

Rob jerked. "I'd just as soon not discuss Emma with you again."

"And what about Phoebe?" Maisey pushed the chair away

and thrust herself in front of him. "Maybe you could discuss your step-daughter with me. What do you plan to tell her? Or will you leave me to clean up the mess, like you did before?"

"Maisey—" Rob sounded infinitely weary. He strode to the door. "Tell her I've gone back to the ranch on personal business. It's not the whole truth but at least part of it."

"Personal business?" Maisey's anger drained away, leaving bewilderment in its place.

"I hope it works out." Rob took his hat from its peg.

He didn't name what he wished would work out, but it was beyond Maisey to ask.

Rob picked up his saddlebags and reached for the doorknob. He stood poised in the open doorway. "I'm sorry, Maisey. I didn't want it to be like this."

She nodded, unable to form words. Her gaze clung to his.

Rob's expression softened, and his eyes glistened with what looked suspiciously like tears. He thrust through the doorway, and his boots pounded down the steps.

Maisey rushed out behind him. She leaned against the porch rail and curled her hands around the rough wood. Dappled shade fell over her husband as he walked away from her and out of sight behind the trees.

CHAPTER SEVENTEEN

MAISEY DRAGGED HERSELF FROM BED AND hurried into the kitchen with scant time to fix herself breakfast. Whether any students would show up for the Indian school remained unclear. The situation could only be awkward for them, as it was for her. She would rather not teach so soon after Rob's departure, but if anyone came, she wanted to be ready.

Phoebe had spent last night with Liberty. Maisey was proud of herself for sleeping alone in her cabin. Hanging onto her composure had been hard at times, especially during the wee hours of the night. She hadn't realized until Rob was absent how much security she'd drawn from his presence.

She ate a bowl of porridge boiled with dried apples and spiced with cinnamon. She didn't have time to linger over coffee but carried her cup into the bedroom to drink while she readied herself for the day. She unlatched the window and slid it open, letting in the cool air and the sweet gurgle of meadowlarks.

Maisey spotted the brindled songbirds flicking through tall grasses beneath the trees on the way to the schoolhouse. They hid from her in the undergrowth, but glimpses of their yellow chests rewarded her vigilance. Silence shrouded the building as Maisey let herself in the front door. She went into the schoolroom and walked down the central aisle. The draft that came in with her scattered dust balls into the corners. Motes swirled in the rays struggling through dirty windows. The place needed a thorough cleaning. Maisey sighed. She and

Emma had pitched in together in years past. America was usually happy to help also. The three of them had made the chore into a party of sorts.

Not this year. Maisey would do her part separately from Emma. America was always willing to help, but in her condition, it would be better not to call upon her.

Maisey ran a hand over the schoolteacher's desk. Sharing it with Emma had once been a pleasing arrangement. They'd left little notes for one another and shared a box or two of licorice. She frowned. That wouldn't happen anymore.

The clock ticked onward, nearing the start of school. Maisey sat in the chair behind her desk and waited.

Although Maisey taught the Indians year-round, Emma was free from obligation during the summer. That was when busy pioneer children tended crops and cared for livestock. The Indian children moved about more in summer while foraging with their families but came to the school when they could. Maisey saw more of them in the winter, when much of the tribe camped at the Burnt Creek fork near Fort Owen. They'd found a champion in John Owen, the Indian agent married to a Salish woman. The tribe also camped at St. Mary's Mission, where the Jesuit priests welcomed them.

The clock chimed nine strokes, signaling the start of school. No students appeared. Fifteen minutes passed, and then thirty. Maisey stood to go, vacillating between relief and disappointment. She wouldn't have to endure the strain of teaching today. However, the lack of students might foreshadow the Indian school's struggle to survive.

The door opened. Se'ułku, who had been Maisey's interpreter when she'd first begun teaching, appeared in the opening. She wore a fringed dress, shells at her ears, and beads in her braided hair. Beside her walked Bluebird, several years older than when she'd succumbed to measles. Unlike Rain, Bluebird had survived under Maisey's care. The maiden had grown into a sloe-eyed beauty who walked with womanly grace.

Se'uɫku ventured down the aisle, giving Maisey a tentative smile. "Teacher, I am glad to find you here but sorry you have no students."

Maisey lifted her head. "I hope they will return in time."

Se'ulku nodded. "Many kept their children away today, thinking you will not teach any longer."

"Please tell them that isn't true."

"You have done only good for my people and deserve kindness. I have come to say that I'm sorry for what my brother Spukani did."

Maisey started. "I'd forgotten that Spukani is your brother."

Se'ulku hung her head. "I am sad to say he is."

Maisey's heart went out to the woman. "Thank you, Se'ulku. I have forgiven your brother."

Se'ulku met her eyes. "Spukani wanted to find favor with our new chief when he brought you to teach him your language. He only disgraced himself and shamed the tribe."

"I hope Spukani learns that neither I, nor any of my people, are his enemy."

"That is my wish." Se'ulku nudged Bluebird forward. "Meanwhile, here is a student for you to teach."

Emma pulled her gaze from the window. She'd spent a pleasant interlude daydreaming about wandering through the meadow outside her door, gathering wildflowers. She examined her swollen foot, which allowed no such indulgences. The bruising had lessened, but it would be a while before she could walk without the assistance of a crutch. Doc Bailey had left her two of the accursed things. The tender skin under her arms was chafed from too much use of them.

The sunshine beckoned to her. How horrid to be cooped up in the house with an injury. Emma reached for her crutches. Going out on the porch for a little while might relieve her restlessness. Learning that Rob was married must surely have contributed to her angst. Needing to resign didn't help either.

Emma maneuvered herself outside, running into the wall only once. She lowered herself awkwardly to the top step. The sun beat down relentlessly, and she immediately wished for something to drink. She sighed. The kitchen seemed so far away. She weighed the effort it would take to lever herself there against her need for water.

She could wait a bit longer.

A hawk winged through the sky, flying toward the wildlands. Emma wished she could copy that bird. How freely it glided about. What joy it must be to explore the world from on high.

Emma was forced to navigate by humbler means. She had only two feet, one of them injured. Even so, she was determined to move away from Liberty as soon as possible. America and Reverend Hayes might miss her. Maybe the children she'd taught would think of her. Perhaps Gideon would pause and remember her. Certainly, Felicity would look for her when taking tea. If Rob and Maisey thought of her at all, it wouldn't be with kindness.

She flicked away a tear. Of them all, leaving Gideon hurt worst. She didn't want to investigate why that was true. If she did, she might decide to stay. The situation was hopeless, however.

When Emma could endure her thirst no longer, she went inside. After drinking several dippers of water, she picked up her copy of *Little Women*, a book she had enjoyed immensely when it came out. She'd been wanting to reread it. While stuck sitting around in her cabin, she had plenty of time.

Emma plowed through several pages before giving up. Her mind would not settle to the story. It insisted on conveying her straight to Gideon. How ridiculous to be obsessed with him in this manner. When the day cooled a bit, she would go out and try to spot him next door. He'd been quite attentive but then suddenly stopped. Why was he ignoring her?

Whatever the cause, not having him around felt strange.

Maybe she should do more than look for him from the porch. Why not? She wasn't afraid of a challenge. She could stop and rest whenever she needed to. It might take a while, but what else did she have to do with herself?

An hour or so later, she heard Gideon whistling as he worked in the Buckthorn garden. The time was right.

Emma reached the stand of cottonwood trees together with the conclusion that she must have lost her wits. Crossing the actual distance differed considerably from what she had imagined. She was already committed and would go on regardless. She could rest at the Buckthorns' place before attempting the return journey. Felicity might even offer her tea.

Rest wasn't a bad idea right now, either. Emma sat down in the shade and leaned against a tree trunk. Her dress would need cleaning, but she needed to take the weight off her good foot for a while. She closed her eyes and let the chirping of birds lull her. Gideon's whistle drifted to her from his barn. He seemed always about the place doing chores. Raising both livestock and vegetables called for a lot of effort. Emma remembered putting in long hours on her family's farm.

Sometimes she'd resented working so hard, but laboring alongside her family brought back the best memories of the life she'd known before.

Emma sighed. Thinking about the past often led to melancholy. She pushed away from the tree and set off.

She found Gideon in the barn stacking bales of hay alongside his younger brother Jake and older brother Ben. Jake's rumpled brown hair and gray eyes contrasted with Ben's fair hair and blue eyes.

"Emma, what are you doing here?" Gideon propped his pitchfork against a stall near the hay mow and started toward her.

Jake glanced from Emma to Gideon, then turned to Ben. "Come to the house with me, and I'll show you where I hid your knife."

Ben's eyes narrowed. "I knew you didn't lose it like you said."

"It was a joke, Ben. I wasn't going to steal it."

"Very funny. See if I loan it to you again."

Gideon's brothers moved off toward the house, quibbling without real heat.

"Go easy on Jake, Ben. He's only a kid." Gideon called after them. He took Emma in. "Don't tell me you walked here on crutches."

Emma tilted her chin. "It wasn't that far."

"Always so independent. Emma, you're injured and should take it easy. What did you do to yourself, anyway?"

"I sprained my ankle. It's a long story, involving a bear."

"A bear! Where were you?"

"On the road to Liberty."

Gideon frowned. "You would be wise to take someone along with you next time. How did you escape?"

"Rob Walsh happened along. He rescued me."

"I see." Gideon dragged out the words. "Was his wife present?"

Emma blinked. "I hope you're not suggesting that I would go out alone with a married man."

"Of course not." Gideon smiled. "I'm sure your morals are unimpeachable."

"Thank you."

Gideon shook his head. "First you're sick, and then you hurt yourself. I'm beginning to wonder if you need a keeper."

She opened her mouth to retort, but then realized he was joking and smiled. Pain must be making her testy.

He grinned. "Why did you go to all that trouble to come over?"

"I wanted to ask when you plan to go to town again. I'd like to go with you, if I may." Emma's face heated. Her mother would not approve of her inviting herself along in this outspoken manner.

"Sorry, but there probably won't be room in the wagon. Make a list, and I'll come by for it before I leave next time."

"I'd better help you home. May I?" Not waiting for her response, Gideon swept her into his arms.

Emma was about to protest when a sudden realization struck her.

Being carried by Gideon felt a lot like flying.

Gideon had to admit that he enjoyed carrying Emma. She didn't weigh much, especially not for someone accustomed to lifting bales of hay. She'd endured a lot of trials lately, and it felt nice to make one thing easy for her. He had no illusions as to why she'd sought him out. Her reasons were piteously transparent. Confined to her cabin by her injury, she was starved for company. Gideon didn't blame her for looking to him for relief and actually liked her feeling she could. He wouldn't take this as anything more than that, though. Gideon suspected that Emma didn't know what she wanted. He needed to do his best to protect them both. Emma was like a fledgling bird, learning to fly. Until she stabilized, she was bound to bring down anyone who strayed into her path.

Farm work taught a man to gauge the odds against him. Gideon knew better than to put himself in Emma's way. That would not be good for her, and it would break his heart. Unless she got over Rob Walsh, she was too much of a risk to pin his hopes on.

They passed into shade beneath the cottonwood boughs in the place where he had kissed her. The memory of that event arose to tempt him. After a brief inner battle, Gideon forced his mind into safer channels. He thought Emma might be remembering, too. That would explain why she'd leaned her head against his chest. Gideon didn't plan to repeat the same mistake. If and when he kissed Emma again, she would be free of Rob Walsh. Until then, he must resist the urge, not easy while holding her in his arms. Emma was no help at all, sighing so sweetly.

Gideon told himself he was glad to reach her porch. He would go back for her crutches, which were still in the barn, after he made sure she was settled with everything she needed on hand.

He deposited the woman in his arms into one of the chairs at her kitchen table. Emma didn't unwind her arms from around his neck. She gazed into his eyes, so close he could see dark rings around her blue irises.

She parted her lips. "Thank you."

"My pleasure." That was nothing short of the truth, he acknowledged ruefully.

Emma's arms fell away from his neck.

Gideon straightened and glanced about. "Do you need help with anything while I'm here?"

"I can manage, but thanks." She shook her head. The light from the kitchen window picked out golden lights in her hair, which swept back into smooth wings. She'd gathered the curls at the back of her head into a bright cascade.

"You're welcome." He turned to go, ignoring the desire to linger. There was no point hanging around certain trouble.

"Wait!"

Her call halted him at the door. "Did you think of something?"

"In a way." She tilted her head becomingly. "Would you like to stop by once in a while?"

"Thank you kindly for the invitation." Gideon smiled to soften the blow of what he would say. "I'm a mite busy."

The shine went out of Emma's eyes. "I understand."

Gideon wished he could take back his refusal. He hated seeing her shoulders sag as if she was no stranger to loneliness.

There was nothing for it but to harden his heart. Gideon wrenched open the door and made good his escape. Only it felt like he'd left part of himself behind.

Maisey slid her knife beneath the skin of another potato. She'd already prepared coleslaw, and baked beans with bacon waited in the stove's warming oven. Phoebe favored fried potatoes, so she'd decided to indulge her. They would go well with the rest of supper. Keeping her daughter's spirits up took extra effort, but Maisey was glad to do what she could. Staying positive herself was harder. She couldn't stop grappling with the fact that Rob had abandoned her, yet again. How could he do such a thing?

Hope shouldn't hurt, but in this case it did. If he came back, she wasn't sure she should take him in. How could she ever trust him again? If he returned it could open her to more heartache. She needed to know that their marriage things would be better after this.

Phoebe sat at the table, cutting out paper dolls. She lifted her head. "When did Pa say he was coming home?"

Maisey set a peeled potato onto the cutting board where several others nestled. "He didn't know, exactly." What else could she say? Phoebe wouldn't want to hear that Rob might not come back or might not be allowed in if he did. Sooner or later, Phoebe would have to know, but Maisey couldn't face telling her while dealing with her own grief.

She reached for another potato, but her mind wasn't on her task. She seemed incapable of thinking of anything else besides Rob. Whatever he was doing, was he thinking of her? She hoped he missed her the way she did him, and that he would want to wipe the slate clean and start over together.

Maisey frowned. Too much had happened to make that likely. It might be better to admit that she and Rob were living a lie and end it. If they did, she and Phoebe might have to move. Even if Rob didn't settle in the area, how could she continue to stay on his cousin's property? It would be too hard.

The dream she'd cherished of having a complete family was crumbling. Memories rose to haunt her, bringing back the time before Rob rode off to Virginia City to mine gold. Could she have been more reserved, more thoughtful, kinder?

This is nonsense.

Maisey banished her punishing thoughts. She shouldn't lay the blame for anyone else's behavior on herself. Rob was completely responsible for what he did, the same as her. The hard truth was that it took two people to end a marriage, or to save one.

CHAPTER EIGHTEEN

"WHAT DID YOU SAY?" EMMA STARED in confusion at Gideon, standing outside her door, hat in hand.

"I've come for your list." He raised his voice, as if her hearing rather than her ability to understand him was at fault.

"List?" Emma gathered her scattered wits. "I don't know what you're talking about."

"Remember? The items you wanted me to purchase for you in town." Gideon spoke politely, but with a tinge of impatience.

"Oh, yes. One moment." Leaving him waiting on the porch, she scribbled furiously with her fountain pen. She blew on the page to dry the ink, and then hurried back to Gideon. "I only want a few things."

"It's no bother." He studied the sheet, and then her. "How is your ankle?"

Emma looked down at her foot wrapped in adhesive plaster bandages. "It's improving. I can walk without crutches, but not far."

A movement in his wagon, parked where the path split between the two schoolteacher cabins, caught her eye. "You have two of your brothers with you today."

Gideon nodded. "Jake and Ben wanted to ride along."

The two young Buckthorn brothers waved at Emma, and she returned the friendly gesture with a touch of wistfulness. The weather was pleasant and the birds were singing. Going on an outing sounded much better than hobbling about her cabin all day.

Jake cupped his hands to his mouth. "Why not bring Miss Duncan along, if she wants to go?"

"I second that idea." Ben grinned, showing obvious admiration.

Emma smiled. "It's nice to feel welcome, but I'd be in the way." She didn't want to impose on Gideon. He had, after all, refused to take her when she'd asked him before.

"Would you care to go?" Gideon asked quietly, between them.

"I'm not sure." Emma looked from his brothers to him. "Do you want me to come?"

"It's up to you." Gideon shrugged. "If you don't mind putting up with the likes of us, you're welcome to do so."

She laughed. "I'll just get my reticule."

Emma emerged a few minutes later, holding her bag over one arm. She'd taken the time to put on a straw bonnet. Tied beneath her chin with wide ribbons so the wind couldn't blow it off, the hat would protect her from the sun. It wasn't hot this morning, but the day would warm before long.

"That hat is becoming on you." Gideon guided her down the steps by her elbow before she could recover from her surprise at his compliment.

"Really, I can walk." She resisted him but smiled to remove any sting from her words.

He released her. "I only meant to help, not to decry your capabilities."

Gideon's response was so mild that Emma felt chastened for objecting. "I'm sorry to be so touchy."

He turned a surprised face toward her. "You've had to look after yourself for so long that it must be hard to change your thinking."

"That's part of it." Emma wasn't sure she was going to make it to the wagon before she had to lean on him. "My parents taught me to look after myself, plus I think it's in my nature."

"That's apparent." Gideon chuckled.

Emma glanced at him with suspicion. "Are you laughing at me?"

He grinned. "Perish the thought, Miss Duncan."

They reached the wagon before she could reply.

Ben and Jake took off their hats as she neared. "Good morning, Miss Duncan," they chimed.

"Good morning, Misters Buckthorn." Emma smiled back at them. The three handsome males, when viewed close together, made quite an impact.

Jake stood. "I'll help you up."

"No, you won't." Ben collared his brother and gave Emma a blinding smile. "If I may?"

"Never mind, the both of you." Gideon's hand tightened on Emma's elbow. "I will assist Miss Duncan."

Emma opened her mouth to say that she could climb in on her own. It might be awkward and painful, but she felt the need to assert herself. Before she could speak, Gideon grasped her waist and hoisted her upward. Ben, already in the wagon, reached to help her. Jake steadied her as she balanced on one leg.

She could always uphold her independence later.

Emma sat beside Gideon on the driving box while his matched Morgan horses ate up the distance to town. The temperature warmed, and Emma was glad she'd worn her straw bonnet. Birds opened their throats in every bush and tree and gave voice from the fields. After escaping the confinement of her cabin, Emma felt like singing along with the feathered creatures. The wagon rattled constantly, forming a steady background against the jingling lines and clopping hooves. She couldn't hear whatever Ben and Jake were talking about in the back, but their voices sounded happy. Gideon sent her shining glances but didn't try to converse as he handled the lines with practiced moves.

They reached town in no time.

Gideon pulled up in front of the mercantile. He climbed out of the wagon and secured their horses to the hitching rail.

Ben jumped down and hurried to Emma. Besides being a year older than Gideon, Ben also topped him in height. He gave her a beatific smile. "May I assist you, Miss Duncan?"

Emma discovered that she didn't feel the same urge to object with Ben. Besides, Gideon was busy with the horses. "Thank you." She leaned down to him.

He lifted her and set her feet on the ground, his blue eyes dancing. "You're light as a feather."

Before Emma could reprimand him for making so personal a remark, Gideon joined them. Emma's desire to speak vanished for several reasons, the most important being that she didn't want to pit two brothers against one another. If she mentioned Ben's most personal comment about her weight, Gideon would take her side against his brother. There was already plenty of conflict between the two. Their rivalry had been good-natured so far, but she didn't know how long that would last. Nor was she sure trouble wouldn't brew with Gideon narrowing his eyes at Ben. Level-headed Jake, who might be counted on to intervene, had disappeared into the store.

"Why don't we go inside?" Emma rushed her words out a little breathlessly.

"What's your hurry?" Gideon caught up to her on the

boardwalk.

"Maybe she's trying to get away from your frowning face." Ben came up on Emma's other side.

Emma smiled sweetly. "I simply want out of the direct sun."

Each brother stepped forward to open one of the twin glass doors in front of her. Emma offered them both as gracious a smile as she could summon, under the circumstances. The floorboards inside the mercantile creaked with every step. Tall shelves closed about her, displaying all manner of merchandise. She noticed cast iron cookware, bolts of fabric, remedies, sacks of grain, and a pickle barrel.

The brothers left their rivalry outside the doors, thankfully. Emma spent a blissful hour exploring the general store. The clerk, noticing her interest in a whirligig behind the counter, set the contraption into motion. Emma smiled in delight as the figure of a man began to chop wood.

Gideon joined her in watching the whirligig. "He's quite busy."

Emma turned to him, laughing. Her movement brought them closer than she'd anticipated. She caught her breath, and Gideon gazed at her intently. Emma stepped back in a hurry. "I've finished my shopping."

Gideon's eyes gleamed. "That's just as well because it's time to go."

She made her purchases, and Ben collected most of the items. Gideon hefted the sack of oats she'd bought.

Jake appeared at her side on the boardwalk. He pointed ahead. "Careful of that loose board, Miss Duncan."

"I will, thanks." If Gideon had said such a thing, she would have responded quite differently. In the privacy of her own thoughts, Emma could admit that she treated Gideon's brothers better than she did him. It was a revelation to realize that she wasn't always kind to Gideon. Emma thought she knew the reason for that, and it scared her more than the bear she'd faced.

They deposited their purchases in the wagon and continued down the boardwalk to the weathered frame building that served as the post office.

Gideon allowed Emma to precede him to the counter.

"There's something for you." The clerk sounded surprised, and no wonder. Emma never got mail.

"Thank you." Emma snatched up the letter the clerk slid to her. A peek revealed that the return address was the one she'd hoped to see.

Gideon glanced at her curiously. "Anything important?"

"I'm not certain." Keeping her voice casual, Emma slipped the envelope into her reticule. She would read the letter in private.

Emma lowered herself to the chair by the window in the front room of her cabin. She never grew tired of gazing at the familiar scene beyond the pane. A meadow gave way to underbrush and tangled branches in the forest beyond. The creek carved a winding path through the grass before parting the foliage beneath the timber. Distant mountains seemed to hang in the sky.

She let the quiet of the moment seep in before giving her attention to the letter in her hand. The response to her inquiry had arrived quickly. Emma scanned the brief lines and picked out the most important information.

We have reviewed your qualifications and find you suitable to teach the children of Rushing River, Wyoming. Please reply at your earliest convenience if you want to accept the position in our one-room schoolhouse.

Emma's ankle would not yet support her all the way to town. She felt reluctant to ask Reverend Hayes and America for a ride. They might ask why she needed to go to town, and she would have to invent a reason. Lying to a preacher and his wife didn't sit well on her conscience. She dreaded telling them she was resigning, but she would have to, regardless. The sooner she confessed, the better. She wasn't leaving them much time to hire another schoolteacher.

Maybe she should wait and walk to town. It might only be a couple of days before her ankle would take her weight, and a few more before she could cover the distance.

Emma lowered the letter, closed her eyes, and leaned her head against the chair rest. It was what she had wanted. Why then, was she stalling?

The citizens of Liberty grew on a person over time. That must be why the thought of leaving them was so wrenching. The first year after moving here, Emma had kept to herself while grieving her father's death. She'd attended Sunday Meeting but had slipped home before the potluck. America must have noticed, for afterwards she'd gently included Emma. A little at a time, Emma had overcome the need to withdraw. She'd begun to reach out to others, beginning with the parents of her students.

If only she didn't have to leave, but what else could she do after making a complete and utter fool of herself?

Emma tried to picture a life in which she never again saw Gideon's face. She gave up the effort as impossible. How it had happened, she couldn't say, but he had become necessary to her.

The letter slipped from her fingers and fluttered to the

floor. Emma searched for it but couldn't see past the tears that blurred her vision and dampened her cheeks. She brushed them away with an impatient hand. How ridiculous to fall in love with Gideon.

That was all the more reason she should go.

America closed *The Woman in White* and set the book on the small table beside her chair in the parlor. The clock on the mantle tripped mercilessly onward. It was long past her bedtime, but it had been worth staying awake a little longer to read a couple more pages. She yawned and stretched. Her eyelids refused to cooperate with her desire to keep them open.

She didn't often find a chance to read, but tonight Shane had put the children to bed without calling upon her help. It was Friday, and Phoebe was staying over with Liberty again. That way Maisey could get ready to teach in the Indian school without having to make sure Phoebe was ready on time. Tagging along with Maisey wasn't usually a hardship for Phoebe. She enjoyed people and had played with the Salish children from an early age. Sometimes she got bored at the school though. That was never a problem when Phoebe and Liberty spent time together.

America had repressed the urge to encourage Shane to bring back his cousin. Asking her husband any such thing would be meddling and unworthy. Still, she wondered if Shane would arrive at that solution on his own. He was sleeping peacefully in their bedroom, having spent much of the day presiding over a wedding at a nearby ranch. She was acquainted with the family and might have gone with the children for the companionship of the other women and their families. Feeling that she should stay near Maisey and Phoebe, she had remained at home. She wasn't sorry. She would go into labor in three month's time. With the child in her womb rounding her figure more thoroughly, travel was uncomfortable.

America frowned. Hopefully, Rob would sort himself out at Con's ranch and return to his new family. She didn't like the ghost of herself Maisey had become, and Phoebe smiled less often these days. Maisey hadn't spoken of the disagreement that had separated her from Rob. Phoebe, on the other hand, was full of information. How much was accurate, America didn't know.

She stretched and stood up. It was high time to retire for the night. Otherwise, the new day would find her too soon.

"I can't sleep." Phoebe spoke from the doorway.

"My goodness you're up late. You should be asleep."

"Do you have any more chocolate?" Phoebe asked wistfully.

America smiled. Phoebe had enjoyed the hot chocolate America had given the children with their popcorn as a special treat. "We're all out, I'm afraid."

Phoebe advanced into the room. "I keep thinking of Pa."

"It must be disappointing that he went away so soon after becoming your pa, but I'm sure he'll be back soon."

"I sure wish he and Ma got along better."

America had the same hope. "Sometimes it takes a married couple a while to become used to one another. That can be tough on newly-marrieds, but it doesn't mean they love each other any less."

"I know they love each other." Phoebe shrugged. "I just wish *they* knew it better."

Gideon moved his arm in a circular motion as he cleaned Lady Gray's saddle. The lantern hissed and sputtered, sending shadows skittering across him. He glanced up. The wick would need trimming soon. He saved simple tasks that didn't tax his strength for the quiet of the evening. Pa had worked alongside him most of the day, but he preferred hearth and home at this hour. Maybe one day if Gideon found a wife, he would feel the same. For now, he was content to keep his own company. He'd often drawn away to be alone ever since he could remember. His family accepted his habit, although they weren't shy about letting him know when his presence was needed among them. He smiled to himself. Their expectations were good for him, and he usually didn't mind.

The door from outside opened, and another light raced over the floor. Gideon squinted to see past the flame held by a figure in the doorway.

His mother advanced into the tack room, carrying a candle lantern. "It's late. Why don't you come in? Lady's saddle can wait."

"Let's see, how does the saying go? A stitch in time saves nine. Yes, that's it."

"That depends on what you're sewing. Refusing to give yourself rest, for example, could unravel your health."

He grinned at her quick wit but didn't back down. "I'll come in as soon as I finish."

She sighed. "The shine on that saddle is of less concern to me than my son's well-being. There's no need to push yourself. I won't have time to ride for a while."

He shrugged. "I don't like to leave a job undone."

"You're like your pa about that." She moved closer to him.

"The Good Lord gave us labor to satisfy us, but He never intended it as an escape from life."

Gideon dipped his rag in the tin of saddle soap while considering her remark. "True, but it can distract a person from troubles. I've known it to act like salve on a wound."

She frowned. "I heard you and Emma arguing in the barn the other day."

"Oh, that. It was only—" He broke off, not quite sure how to define his spats with Emma. They weren't friendly, but neither were they completely hostile. At least, they weren't for him. He was never quite sure what Emma felt. He suspected that she enjoyed sharpening her claws on him. His mother seemed to think he was working late to forget a fight with her, but he'd stated the simple truth. Whenever he started a chore, he liked to see it through. "Don't worry about Emma and me. We're getting along fine. I took her to town with us yesterday, and she seemed to have fun."

"Why are you frowning, then?"

"Am I? It must be because, when I said that, I remembered something odd. After Emma got a letter from the post office, she started acting secretively. I wonder why."

"Maybe you should ask her."

He could well imagine how Emma would respond if he did. "I don't think she'd tell me, and to be fair, it's none of my business."

"Is that so?" His mother gave him a mysterious look.

"Yes," he replied firmly.

She smiled. "I'll go in now. Jake and Ben were making popcorn, and who knows what state the kitchen will be in?"

"Make them clean up after themselves."

She nodded. "I plan to."

Rob matched his stride to Con's as they went over the Meadows ranch. A brook lined by willows tumbled through grasslands. The meadows gave way to ranks of trees that marched to the feet of the mountains. A red barn lazed in the sun, ready to house livestock. Rob could picture smoke curling from the ranch house built from hewn logs.

Could Maisey be happy here? It was far enough from Emma to allow them peace of mind. The ranch seemed a world apart, much like Con's place did. Maybe that's what he and Maisey needed. Isolating her from others would avoid her jealous tendencies. He'd never known Maisey to display that particular flaw. Marriage must have sparked the fault in her. Circumstances had certainly fanned the flames of suspicion. Unless Maisey overcame her mistrustfulness, it was doubtful they could live in harmony.

Even so, he couldn't leave her. He should never have implied that he might. He'd given in to anger at the time and said senseless things he didn't mean. An apology was in order, and he would give it, assuming Maisey cared to hear it. There was always the possibility that she'd had enough of him. He couldn't blame her, if that was the case.

Con turned to him with excitement on his face. "What do you think? You'd be within driving distance of my spread."

"This is definitely a possibility." Rob nodded approval, but his heart wasn't in the search for a home. If he lost Maisey, remaining near her could only be painful. Rob twisted his lips into a wry smile. That would be the height of irony—having the inclination and opportunity to move near his family only to learn that his best interests lay far from them.

"You might say that with a little more enthusiasm." Con

studied him. "Is something troubling you?"

Rob could hardly hide his emotions from his eagle-eyed brother. "I'm not sure whether I can settle here, after all. I'd like to, but it depends on Maisey and me."

Con lifted an eyebrow. "I wondered why you hurried back to my place. Trouble so soon?"

Rob caught sight of a deer bounding across the meadow, no doubt startled by their presence. "I love her, but I'm not sure that's enough."

Con clapped him on the back. "Whatever is wrong, don't let it trouble you overmuch. Newly-marrieds usually butt heads. It takes time to become comfortable with one another."

"This is more than that, I'm afraid." Rob started toward their horses.

Con matched his pace. "I'm sure every newly-married would say that to you. Troubles seem biggest up close. Give them the distance of time, and I'll bet they shrink."

They reached the horses, and Rob stepped into the saddle. "Maisey has taken the notion that I'm interested in someone else."

Con winced while gathering his reins. "I'm well aware how misunderstandings can crop up in a marriage."

"I don't know how Maisey can believe what she does about me. I haven't done anything. She trusts me very little, if at all."

"As I recall, you once broke her heart."

Rob peered at his brother. "What does that have to do with this?"

Con adjusted his hat brim to the sun. "In case you wondered, you can't leave a woman behind for three years and expect her not to react."

"You have a point." Con had a way of putting a matter

that rivaled Shane's. Eloquence seemed a family trait, one that had passed Rob by. That was too bad, since he could use such a gift when he threw himself on Maisey's mercy.

Con grinned. "Who knows why women think the way they do?"

"It's nothing to smile about, let me tell you."

"No." Con sobered obediently, but mirth lit his eyes.

"Thank you."

"Now what have I done?"

"You helped me put my problems in perspective."

Rob and Con turned their horses onto the wide trail and rode abreast. They reached the main road that mostly followed the Bitterroot River and picked up speed. Con seemed anxious to return home. Who could blame him, with a sweet wife and child waiting? If Rob hadn't given in to his temper, he could look forward to a similar welcome when he returned to Liberty.

Con was right, especially about what he very tactfully hadn't said. Rob had been impatient and unreasonable with Maisey, and he was ready to make amends.

The road laid out vistas at every turn. Rob caught glimpses of the river glimmering between its banks, grasslands strewn with flowers, and thick groves that shut out the light. Although stunning, the scenery barely registered for Rob. An image of Maisey, her eyes gleaming with love as she took her wedding vows, rose before him.

By the time they reached the ranch, the matter was settled in Rob's mind. Tomorrow he would head home to Maisey.

CHAPTER NINETEEN

"I HOPE YOU DON'T MIND MY intruding on you like this." Felicity slid a hot cup of the tea she'd brewed in front of Emma, then sat across from her at the table in the cabin.

"I never mind a chance to visit with you." Emma almost completely meant that. She'd been sunk in thought ever since receiving the letter, a fact that made it hard to focus on socializing.

Felicity picked up her cup and took a sip. "How's your ankle?"

"It's improving."

"I'm glad. There's nothing worse than hobbling about, barely able to manage everyday tasks."

"I do my best. How was your tea party? I'm so sorry I couldn't attend."

Felicity beamed. "We had such a good time. I do wish you could have made it. Maybe next time it will work out."

Emma said nothing in reply. By the time Felicity held another tea party, she would be gone. Her ankle should be strong enough for a walk to town tomorrow.

Felicity took a sip of the tea she'd poured for herself. "I hope you'll want to help with the wedding reception."

"Wedding reception?" Emma stared at her. "Is someone getting married?"

Felicity's face lit. "I'm throwing a party for Maisey and her new husband."

Emma busied herself stirring sugar into her tea. "That's

nice of you."

"America plans to help, and I thought you might be interested in decorating the table." She smiled. "It would give you a chance to demonstrate your napkin-folding ability."

Emma continued stirring, although every granule must have already dissolved. "That would be fun." She stated the simple truth but didn't add that she would be far away. Thank goodness, because working on a reception for the two people she most wanted to avoid sounded like an utter nightmare.

Felicity sipped her tea without speaking, and a small silence grew between them.

That wasn't how Emma had expected her to react. She stole a glance at Felicity and surprised a thoughtful expression on the older woman's face. Felicity clinked her cup into its saucer. "May I ask how you and Gideon are getting along? I thought I heard you arguing in the barn."

"Gideon can be maddening." Emma halted, discomfited to have criticized him in front of his mother. Felicity was so easy to talk to that she'd rushed into speech without taking time to consider her words.

Felicity laughed. "Thank you for such an honest reaction. I will say that sometimes my son gets on my nerves too. Gideon can be quite logical. He gets it from his father, whom I also love very much."

Emma smiled. "Please don't misunderstand. Gideon baffles me at times, but I care about him."

"Do you? I'm glad to hear it. Gideon is thoughtful, intelligent, and a hard worker. Those traits will see him far in life. I expect that he has a bright future ahead." She picked up her cup. "That's all any mother wants for her child."

Emma thought of her brother, who had drowned in the river, and her mother's wrenching sobs afterwards. Yes, a future for her son was all a mother could wish. "I hope your expectations for Gideon come true."

Felicity waved a hand. "Enough of that. I'm a doting mother who is overly proud of her son."

"You have a right to be." Emma realized that she'd truly meant what she'd said. Although annoying, Gideon was wholly admirable.

"I hope you don't mind my bringing up your argument. I didn't hear anything either of you said, but your raised voices made me wonder if you'd had a serious falling out."

Emma fiddled with her teaspoon and argued with herself. She should *definitely not* confide in Felicity. Who else could she tell, though? She drew a shaky breath. "It's worse than that. I think I'm in love him."

Felicity's eyes lit, but her face remained serious. "How troubling."

Emma nodded. "It's most annoying."

"Never mind, my dear. I'm sure you and Gideon will sort yourselves out eventually. Now, tell me. Did you have fun in town the other day?"

"We all did." Emma smiled, warming to the subject. "Your sons are very charming."

Felicity poured another round of tea. "Gideon said you received a letter."

Oh, he did, did he? Emma sighed. Was nothing that happened to her ever private?

America swept the hairbrush through Liberty's wet locks in a rhythmic motion that failed to soothe her tender-headed daughter. America did try. The clock in the hallway chimed six. Good. There was still time for her own bath. After she emerged from the washtub hidden behind a screen in the corner of the kitchen, Shane would take his own bath. America had already dealt with Liam and Seth, who were squealing happily while Shane entertained them in the other room.

Every Saturday, Shane hauled in the washtub and large pots of water to warm on the stove. In the winter, the kitchen window steamed up, and in summer the kitchen heated uncomfortably. Shane would empty the pots into the washtub. They all took baths, beginning with Liam, the youngest. America insisted on her children laying out their clothing for Sunday before they went to bed. Shane always went to the schoolroom early to pray before morning service, which left America to hurry their three children out the door for church on time.

During the town's beginning stages, they'd held Sunday Meeting once a month. That interval had suited those who traveled distances to join in. Now that the town of Liberty was more established, Shane preached every Sunday morning, although not everyone came all the time. Some, especially those who traveled, continued to arrive for Sunday Meeting once a month. Held during the late afternoon, it was always followed by a potluck.

"Ow! You're pulling my hair out." Liberty snatched at her hands.

"Please stop." America pulled the hairbrush out of reach. "I'm being as gentle as possible." Liberty's waves snarled easily, and that was unfortunate for both of them. America held onto her patience, remembering her own childhood. She'd protested in a similar fashion while her grandmother brushed her hair. Her lips curved at the memory. Dear Gramma had never been less than kind to her.

Shane looked in from the doorway. "I wish you would

stop torturing that child."

America met his gleaming eyes and smiled. "You're next for a trimming."

Shane made a face and tactfully retreated.

America grinned to herself. Shane's reluctance to let her cut his hair was a standing joke between them. As he'd told her, he enjoyed her fingers running through his hair, and he'd complimented her on the results.

She finished with Liberty by wrapping her hair around rags which she tied about her daughter's head. After the cloths came out in the morning, Liberty's hair would curl into ringlets.

"Ma?" Liberty spoke in a much calmer voice. "How do you know when you're in love?"

America paused while winding hair. "Is this about someone in particular?"

"It could be," Liberty answered mysteriously.

America wasn't ready for her six-year-old daughter to grow up quite so fast. "You have years to figure that out, pumpkin."

Liberty fell silent for so long America thought she'd dropped the subject. Liberty turned her head, causing America to lose her grip on the strand she was wrapping. Liberty looked up, her forehead furrowing. "I think it might be when a boy pulls your hair and chases you, but you like it."

America did her best not to laugh out loud. "That about sums it up. Now turn around and let me finish."

Liberty sighed but obeyed. "Do you think Jake is handsome?"

"All people have good qualities." America managed to summon the neutral statement despite her surprise. So that was how the land lay. Come to think of it, Jake had been coming over more than usual lately. He'd acted a little strange around Liberty too. She tied the last rag curl and covered Liberty's hair with a scarf. "All right, Missy. You're done."

Shane looked in at the door again. "I was going through the secretary desk and I found this." He held up a monogrammed envelope. "It's addressed to Maisey."

America gasped. "Oh, no! I completely forgot about that letter. It came while Maisey was away, and I put it there for safekeeping." She glanced longingly toward the screen with the washtub behind it. "Would you mind taking it over to her right away? I hope it was nothing urgent."

Maisey closed *Mrs. Overtheway's Remembrances* and laid the volume aside. "That's the end of the book."

Phoebe sighed. "Can we start it again tomorrow?"

"I'm certain we can." Maisey could understand why Phoebe so loved this book. Its beautiful descriptive passages and shifting stories connected by a common narrator must appeal to her daughter's vivid nature. As a mother, Maisey liked that the stories instructed without lecturing. It was pleasant to sit with Phoebe and recapture some of the peace she'd felt before Rob's return. She had known sadness during the years he'd lived in Virginia City, but not the emotional turmoil she'd experienced since his return.

She kissed the top of Phoebe's head, still damp from her bath. "Get ready for bed, but you don't need to climb in yet. I'll pop corn if you want some."

Phoebe's eyes lit. "Thanks, Ma." She pressed her head against Maisey's shoulder briefly, then flung herself from the chair. Smiling at the way her daughter propelled herself through life, Maisey padded into the kitchen on slippered feet.

She lowered the canister of popcorn from one of the shelves. After pouring oil and popcorn into a copper pan, Maisey clamped on the lid and slid the vessel onto the stovetop. She'd left the cookfire burning in the firebox, and the oil sizzled almost at once. The pinging of the corn against metal soon began. The popping grew more frequent, and then died down. Maisey filled two bowls, buttered the corn, and called for Phoebe.

"Thanks, Ma." Phoebe carried her bowl into her room.

"Take a napkin with you," Maisey called after her.

Phoebe returned, and with a sheepish grin, snatched a gingham napkin from the counter.

A tap came at the door. Maisey recognized it as belonging to Shane. It was late for a visit. Concerned that something was wrong with America, Maisey hurried to open the door. She hesitated at the last minute and took the precaution of looking out. Her experiences had taught her caution. Shane stood alone on the porch. Behind him the trees creaked and rubbed their branches in a windstorm and the sky glowed with colors so deep they reminded her of gemstones.

"You're out late." Remembering her manners, Maisey opened the door wider. "Come in."

"Good evening, Maisey." Shane's boots rang on the kitchen floorboards. He held up an envelope. "I've come to deliver this along with my wife's apology for forgetting about it."

Maisey stared at the letter, then at Shane. "I don't know who would write to me…" She took the envelope he gave her and turned it over. A familiar scrawl addressed the letter to her. The initials engraved on the letter belonged to her brother, Marcus Joseph Denniston.

Maisey's knees went weak, and she had to sit down on one

of the kitchen chairs.

"What's wrong?" Shane's voice reached her from far away.

Maisey took a moment to catch her breath. "It's from my brother in St. Louis."

"Your brother? I thought you weren't close." Shane studied her with a concerned expression.

"We're not." Maisey examined the letter. She wished she could know what it said before taking the risk of reading it. "I suspect it's bad news. Why else would he write to me?"

"Would you like me to keep you company while you read it?"

Maisey should let him return to his family. "I'd appreciate that, if you don't mind."

"Not at all." Shane shook his head. "I'm happy to stay."

Maisey broke the seal with trembling fingers. She lifted the letter from the envelope A piece of paper fluttered to the table. Maisey picked it up and found herself staring at the tidy sum inked into a bank draft. She glanced up at Shane, and he smiled encouragingly. Maisey unfolded the letter.

A moment later, she inserted the bank draft and the sheet of formal stationery bearing her brother's initials into the envelope. She placed the letter on the table in front of her and put her head in her hands.

"I can't help being curious, but if it's a private matter—" Shane's voice recalled her from her thoughts.

"I don't mind telling you." Maisey drew a deep breath. "My mother was seriously ill when my brother wrote. Marcus says that she asked for me. He included enough money for me to travel to St. Louis and visit her in the hospital."

CHAPTER TWENTY

THE MONOGRAMMED ENVELOPE APPEARED RATHER PRESUMPTUOUS on Maisey's scarred table. She let it remain as proof that Marcus really had invited her to St. Louis. She could hardly register the fact. From his angry accusations during their last encounter, she'd never have thought it possible.

Shane sank down in the chair across from her. "Will you go?"

"I don't know." She picked up the envelope. "I've dreamed of receiving a letter like this for so long. If it had come sooner, I'd have been eager to leave. It didn't, though. I wish I knew what to do in this situation."

"I think I can understand."

Maisey laid the letter on the tabletop. "What would *you* do?"

Shane sat motionless while a variety of emotions chased acrosshis face. Stirring at last, he folded his arms on the table. "It's not often that I speak of my Uncle Seamus, but for most of my childhood he attempted to raise me. He might have succeeded, but drink got in the way."

"I'm so sorry."

"That was a long time ago." Shane shrugged. "Living with my uncle was never easy, but then it became impossible. He turned his back on the entire family, including me."

"How sad." Maisey knew from her family's estrangement that there was a lot Shane hadn't said.

"Yes, it was. That kind of heartache stays with a person.

My uncle wasn't perfect, but I loved him. I still feel the loss of him, but it's more a lingering sorrow than sharp grief."

"I experienced something similar after giving up on ever reconciling with my family." Maisey crossed her arms. "It was easier than hoping for what didn't seem likely to happen. I wasn't prepared for an opportunity to crop up like this."

"Sometimes a family parts, but I'm convinced that's not God's first choice. Trying to resolve matters might hurt, but I hope you won't let the chance pass you by. I never received one. I located my uncle once and tried to intervene, but he refused to see reason." Shane shook his head sadly. "He went to the grave without relenting."

"What a tragedy." Maisey had known little more than that Shane and Rob had escaped Manhattan's slums. Shane seemed so composed that she would never have guessed he'd gone through so much.

He nodded "I recognized some things that freed me from the pain."

"I'd like to know them."

Shane's smile softened. "I realized that my uncle was not the enemy. He *had* an enemy whom he allowed to steal his life away."

Maisey gazed at him in sympathy. "I can't imagine your going through all that so young."

"It was painful, but it did drive me to seek God. I didn't mean to make you sad. I only brought up my story because I want you to weigh your decision carefully. I was angry at my uncle, and so I didn't try to contact him again. Months later, I found out by accident that he'd hanged himself." Shane lowered his voice and glanced toward Phoebe's door, which was closed. "I've often wondered if continuing to reach out to my uncle could have changed that."

"You can't blame yourself for someone else's decisions."

"I don't. Only for mine. When my uncle abandoned me, I failed to grasp that I didn't need to abandon him in return. Deciding to hold on to your hurt comes at a price." Shane stood up. "I'd better be going."

"Thanks for staying."

"Of course." Shane smiled, but then sobered. "Make a choice you can live with."

"I will." Maisey saw him to the door.

He turned back with the night behind him. "America and I will pray."

"Thank you." After he turned down the steps, Maisey closed the door and shot the bolt. The letter waited for her on the table. She lifted it, testing its weight in her hands. Shane had given her a lot to consider, and not only about her family in St. Louis.

Phoebe skipped beside Maisey on the path through the cottonwood stand. "Are we really going to ride the stagecoach?"

Maisey smiled at her daughter but couldn't echo her joy. Even under better circumstances, it was too early for such liveliness. The morning mists had yet to lift, roosters were still crowing in the day, and dew dampened the hem of her skirt.

America would be awake, Maisey had little doubt. She and Shane always rose with the sparrows. America would be kneading bread, starting soup, or engaging in some other domestic activity before the children interrupted.

Maisey had lain in wakefulness much of the night, her mind occupied with the decision she needed to make. If only she could have asked Rob his opinion, but he'd left her to sort out her life without him. That was no different than before they'd married, but she couldn't say it didn't trouble her.

"Good morning." America welcomed them at her back door with a quick smile. They followed her into the kitchen, where the day's bread was already rising. America took up a wooden spoon and stirred a bowl of batter. "I'm making sourdough pancakes. You will stay for breakfast, won't you? There's plenty."

"Yes, thank you, but let me help." Maisey had been too rushed packing to prepare much breakfast.

"You can make coffee."

"This is the *best* day," Phoebe chirped. "Did you know that Ma and I are going to ride on a stagecoach?"

"That will be fun." America's wooden spoon clunked the side of the batter bowl. "Liberty is in her room, Phoebe. I heard her making noise, so I'm sure she's awake."

"Oh, good. I can't wait to tell her." Phoebe hurried from the room with an air of purpose.

America wiped her hands on a dishtowel. "Shane said you were considering leaving for St. Louis."

"I've made up my mind to go." Maisey took the coffee grinder down from its shelf. "My brother sent a bank draft, but it will only pay my way. Fortunately, I have a little money laid by and can afford to cover Phoebe's expenses."

"Shane and I talked, and we don't mind keeping her here with us, if that works better for you."

"That's a kind offer, but she would be crushed if I left her behind. I don't know if taking Phoebe is wise or foolish, but this might be her only chance to meet her grandmother. I can't deny my daughter that." Maisey busied herself turning the handle on top of the box-shaped mill. The rasp of the beans grinding and the fragrance of freshly-ground coffee rewarded her efforts.

America lifted a cast iron griddle from its hook and laid it on the stove. "For what it's worth, I think you're making a wise choice."

Maisey smiled shakily. "I'm glad that you do. The trip could go completely wrong. Phoebe and I might wind up in the midst of chaos in St. Louis."

America turned to her. "You're a wonderful mother, but you can't protect Phoebe from everything that happens."

Maisey swallowed against the thickness in her throat. "I feel like a small child trying to find my way in a maze."

America embraced her. "You'll survive this, I'm sure of it."

"I'm sorry that I won't be able to teach for a while."

"Don't worry about the school or anything else." America carried the batter bowl to the stove. "We'll manage without you, and Shane will send word to Rob."

"I don't know if Rob will care." Maisey spoke her thoughts out loud.

"Why do you doubt it?" America poured circles of batter onto the griddle. They immediately began to sizzle. The aroma of sourdough pancakes filled the air.

"My leaving might make life more convenient for Emma and him."

America flicked a glance at her. "Don't let your imagination run away with you. There could be a perfectly innocent explanation for what you saw at the well." America took hold of a spatula and hovered beside the griddle.

"Oh?" Maisey couldn't think of a single one.

"Since it was right after you arrived, have you considered that Emma wasn't yet aware Rob was married." America flipped a row of pancakes.

"That could be true, but it wasn't the only time I saw them

together. The other day, I discovered Rob walking Emma home with his arm around her."

America's eyes widened. "That would trouble me too."

Maisey's conscience reminded her that her own behavior might have driven Rob from the cabin that day, but she didn't want to mention that.

"I don't know the answer to your question, but Rob does. Did you ask him at all?"

"He claimed it was a coincidence."

America removed the pancakes to a plate that she placed in the warming oven. Batter hissed onto the griddle, and a small cloud of steam arose. "Do you have proof otherwise?"

She considered carefully. "No."

"Maisey, can't you see that your husband may have done nothing wrong?"

"It's possible I overreacted."

"From what you've told me, that sounds likely. I can see why Rob felt the need to remove himself to the ranch, but that doesn't mean he should have done so." She shook her head. "A little time for thought might do you both good."

Emma hobbled toward Gideon behind the barn and watched him drive his axe into the stump he was using as a chopping block. He seemed lost in thought as he bent to retrieve the kindling he'd split and toss it into a bucket. He must have heard her approach, for he lifted his head.

Gideon straightened. "Good morning, Emma."

"Good morning."

He scanned her face. "What brings you around so early?"

"I heard you whistling when I stepped onto my porch to enjoy the cool air."

Gideon's eyes glowed. "I'm glad your ankle is improved."

His gaze had an unfortunate effect on Emma's composure. "Thank you."

Emma heaved a breath and decided to get it over with. "I came over to ask you to please stop meddling in my life." She smiled to soften her words.

Gideon sent her a baffled look. "Am I supposed to know what you're talking about?"

"You should have asked me what was in my letter rather than sending your mother to find out for you."

Gideon's amusement vanished. "I did no such thing."

Heat rose into her face. "I'm sorry. I thought—"

Gideon sighed. "I wish I knew why you mistrust others so much, even those who mean you good."

"People always let you down."

Gideon shook his head. "I won't deny that others can disappoint you, but most folks mean well. I hope you'll discover that for yourself some day."

Gideon watched with mixed feelings as Emma walk haltingly away from him. He ought to go after her and help her home. He turned around and finished picking up kindling. Emma was walking all right, if slowly. He'd better not push matters. She was apt to lean on him, and that would prove tempting.

On impulse, he followed the trail he and his brothers had trampled in the grass into the wild area beyond his family's holdings. It was time to do some serious thinking, plus he needed to stretch his legs.

He jumped the creek in a narrow spot, passed the snag where owls liked to roost, and kept going until he'd climbed to a defile. The narrow canyon led into the hidden valley where he sheltered during the worst of life's troubles. He sat cross-legged on a granite boulder and watched the play of light in the waterfall that flowed down the rocky side of a bluff. It splashed into a pool that boiled over, spilling into the first of a series of cascades. He'd discovered this sheltered place by following the cataracts that flowed from the headwater into the valley.

Gideon pulled in a deep breath. Being out here never failed to remind him of what mattered most. Emma might reject him, but God never would.

He needed to put a stop to the irritating encounters with Emma. He didn't know if she intended to annoy him or did it on accident. Either way, she seemed to have no clue of her impact on him. He'd mostly returned patience for her high-spirited behavior, but there was a limit to his patience. Emma seemed to base her actions on emotion, but logic was the very backbone of his life. It wouldn't be fair to expect her to change to suit him. It was probably best to leave her alone.

Emma might have the excuse of her inexperience, and she'd picked up strange ideas from her father. He could understand her wish to honor his memory. Until she eased up on her excessive need for independence though, she wouldn't be ready for courtship. He had to be honest with himself. That might never happen.

It was up to him to protect his peace of mind.

A couple of deer stepped into the open. They lifted their heads and froze upon spotting him. He'd been sitting so quietly that the deer must have thought they were alone. He waited without moving a muscle, wondering what they would do. Time stood still as he gazed at the wild creatures, and they returned his regard.

One doe lowered her head and nibbled at the grass. The

other continued to stare, but then afforded him the same compliment. Gideon had seen this reaction many times in the wild. Closer to the settlement, it didn't happen.

Gideon smiled. He learned so much from the natural world. The instinctive trust the deer gave him was not unlike what he wanted from a woman. He was willing to wait for it, even if it took a lifetime. If Emma became capable of such a vast departure, well, that would take a miracle.

Gideon had littered this valley with many prayers throughout the years. Today he would add to that number.

CHAPTER TWENTY-ONE

"WATCH THAT FIRST STEP." THE GRIZZLED stagecoach driver grinned, baring tobacco-stained teeth, and reached out with a gloved hand.

Maisey accepted his help into the stagecoach. Phoebe, already aboard, had claimed a seat by the window. Maisey settled between her and a matronly woman wearing a solid lavender gown that indicated she was in half-mourning. She would soon emerge from the obligations of grief. The woman's hair swept back in graying waves but was otherwise dark. Lines in her face told a story of impending age.

Across from her, a man wearing a leather vest, a blue shirt, and brown trousers swept the bowler hat from his head. "Good morning, ladies." Although he addressed them all, his gaze lingered on Maisey. She smiled at him but did not return his greeting. He seemed to be single, traveling alone, and she didn't want to encourage his masculine interest. Maisey wore nothing that might signal her marital status. She had no real wedding ring, only a thin cord. That had gone into a keepsake box when she'd reached the cabin. She'd looked at it once in a while, remembering. Since Rob had walked away from her, she hadn't opened the box. Maisey's lips curved at the irony that a flimsy cord accurately represented her marriage.

Phoebe leaned out and looked across Maisey at the matronly woman. "We're going to St. Louis."

"Don't be forward." Maisey whispered. She might have known that her outgoing daughter would strike up a conversation with a stranger.

"Please allow me to introduce myself." The woman spoke with polished grace. "I am Emily Darrington. I'm on my way home to Wyoming after a visit with my sister and her family in Liberty."

"I'm Maisey Walsh, and this is my daughter Phoebe. If I may ask, what is your sister's name?"

Emily's smile lent her face a certain youthfulness. "Nellie Haig. Do you know her?"

"Most folks in Liberty have met." Maisey laughed. "I see your sister at Sunday Meeting, but she keeps to herself, mostly."

"That doesn't surprise me." Emily frowned. "Nellie has become withdrawn. She's never recovered from our brother's passing. That happened more than five years ago, but her sorrow is still fresh. She can't seem to move beyond it."

"How sad." Maisey didn't know what else to say.

"I'm sorry, my dear. I forgot myself and shared more than I should have with a new acquaintance."

Maisey smiled with genuine warmth. "I don't mind."

Emily glanced at Phoebe. "Did your daughter say you were on the way to St. Louis?"

"Yes, and we get to take a train." Phoebe's eyes gleamed.

Emily exchanged a smile with Maisey. "That will be a grand event."

Maisey did not share Phoebe's enthusiasm. The idea of being confined to a great, mechanical monster that belched smoke made her shudder. The train would deliver them to St. Louis far more quickly than the wagon that had carried them westward. It seemed unnatural to her that people should travel so fast.

The driver called to the horses, and the stagecoach lurched

into motion. The horses clopped down the road and picked up speed once the town fell away behind them. The rattling of the stagecoach grew louder as the scenery rolled by more quickly. This morning they could ride with the windows open. A light shower in the night had settled the dust without creating mud. As the day progressed and the ground dried, they might need to lower the leather curtains.

They passed through green shadow beneath leafy boughs that formed a tunnel. Phoebe chattered happily. Maisey determined that their fellow-passengers were enjoying her daughter, so she didn't intervene. The stagecoach broke free of the trees and cut across grasslands on a path toward distant mountains. In the wide sky, cloud piled upon cloud, climbing to the heavens.

Phoebe's voice quieted, then faded altogether. She leaned her head against Maisey's shoulder, and her breathing rasped steadily. Maisey shifted to make her daughter more comfortable. The other passengers also slept, taking advantage of the smoothness of the road. She knew very little about stagecoach travel, but Elsa described it as uncomfortable in the extreme. Maisey wished she could drift off too, but her mind insisted on carrying her to Rob or else racing ahead to St. Louis.

Phoebe was excited by the journey, but Maisey felt hesitant about what they would find at its end. Would Marcus still be belligerent? She could hope that her mother no longer remained in the hospital but had recovered. Maisey didn't want to accept that her mother might lie in a bed beneath the sod, but that was also possible. That her parents could die without her ever knowing was the most heartbreaking aspect of their estrangement.

She'd felt powerless to change the situation, but after speaking with Shane, Maisey wondered if she'd used helplessness as an excuse not to try. Might she have done more to repair the break? Shane's advice not to abandon her family in return had come too late. She'd already made that mistake. Forsaking them had spared her the pain of further rejection but had also cut her off from the possibility of a reunion.

Maisey sighed and leaned her head against the leather button upholstery. She didn't know why, given all that had happened, but God must have thought she belonged within her family. Why else would He have brought her into it in the first place?

Another force, that of darkness, was to blame for breaking the ties God had forged. Marcus had always been favored as the first-born. In childhood, he'd accused her of the misdeeds he himself had committed. Her parents had often believed his lies over her protestations of innocence. By the time she'd reached adulthood, Marcus's influence over her parents had grown to an insufferable level. Both her mother and father had adopted Marcus's views to a frightening degree. Marcus saw Avery, who came from a less well-established family, as a poor suitor for his sister. Avery was not quite good enough for the daughter of affluent parents, her brother had argued, and must be rejected.

Maisey closed her eyes, as if that might dispel the memories. They came anyway. Numerous accusations returned to shame her. The torment of being torn between the man she loved and duty to her parents gripped her once more. She'd agreed to see Avery, thinking for the sake of honor and peace in her household that she needed to give him up. That meeting had not gone as she'd intended. After following her, Marcus had threatened and belittled Avery. That had been the last straw for Maisey. She could see a future in which Marcus controlled her thinking also. How close she'd come to allowing that terrified her.

She'd run away with Avery. It wasn't an honorable choice, but God eventually redeemed it. Avery was a good man, and they were happy together. They'd tried to make peace with her parents. The horrible scene following that attempt still haunted her.

Maisey drew a sharp breath and opened her eyes. What was the use of dwelling on the past? The pain of it could never be resolved. All she would dare to hope for was the ability to forget what had gone before and seek a better future.

Phoebe stirred against her shoulder, murmuring in her sleep. Maisey suspected that her tension had communicated itself to her daughter. Maisey drew a deep breath and exhaled slowly. Counting her blessings always restored her equilibrium.

Avery had left her too soon, but part of him remained in the beautiful child sleeping beside her. Their life together was a bright memory riddled with the darkness of sorrow. Her happiness with Avery had come at the cost of her family. Maisey wished it all could have happened differently, but there was no taking back the past. Whatever happened in the future, the joy of being Phoebe's mother would remain.

At the crossroads, Rob turned his horse toward Liberty. He passed through tree shadows that stretched long across the road in the softening light. He'd ridden out early, wanting to waste no time in reaching Maisey and Phoebe. His reasons for leaving them seemed less important than the desire to return to his family. He shouldn't have given in to the hurt caused by Maisey's lack of trust in him. Even now, if he let his mind dwell on their last fight, he could summon the same feelings of indignation, but to what purpose? It was better to forgive.

His saddle creaked with his horse's gentle swaying. The scents of oiled leather and horseflesh mingled with the sweetness of grass and the musty taste of dust. Trees closed in on either side like old women, ready to gossip. Their leaves hissed in the breeze. Birds hopped between branches, chattering.

A bright stream burbled on its course through the woods. It wended close to the road, and then farther away. When it returned, he stopped to water his horse. Rob dismounted and bent to the water, letting it cool his mouth and soothe his parched throat. He lifted handfuls to bathe his face and neck. Retiring to a rock in the shade, he watched his horse tear at the grassy bank.

Only a little farther, and he would reach the outskirts of Liberty. He was well aware that Maisey might not greet him with enthusiasm. Maybe she would let him apologize before she rejected him. Rob tossed a stone into the water simply to hear it plunk. He watched the surface break into ripples, his mind turning to his arrival in Liberty. In a little while he would know the battle he must fight. However hard it was, he wouldn't retreat again. If he hadn't understood before, he surely did now. There was no going back to a single life for him. Whether Maisey wanted him or not, he would remain her faithful husband. Hopefully, that would matter to her. It would if God was willing to show him any kindness.

Rob hauled himself to his feet. He'd needed a moment to prepare himself mentally for his return, but now he was ready. He pressed his horse to travel the last leg of the journey, anxious to have it over and done with. The trees thinned and the schoolhouse appeared. Shane's barn stood beyond it. Although Rob yearned to rush home, he restrained his impatience and turned aside to the barn. His horse had carried him a long distance and deserved to be treated kindly.

Rob saw to his horse, and then headed for the cabin. He tried to figure out what to say to Maisey and Phoebe, but his mind tangled worse than the ball of yarn Bry's daughter, Katie had gotten hold of the other day.

His steps slowed as he neared the cabin, and a sinking feeling discomfited his stomach. He squared his shoulders. No matter what happened, he needed to go home to Maisey. Pushing himself forward, Rob climbed the steps to the cabin door. He paused, listening. No sounds carried from within. The doorknob turned beneath his hand. Rob stood in the doorway, gazing about the silent cabin.

"Maisey?" he called without hope.

No one answered.

He would probably find his family at Shane and America's house. Rob's feet followed his thoughts, and he set off. It might be better to approach his wife in the company of others, and he couldn't think of a more neutral place than Shane and America's house.

America came in answer to his knock. Surprise registered on her face, and then relief. "Thank goodness you're here."

The first stirrings of alarm jarred him. "What's wrong?"

"Why don't you come in?" America stepped back and allowed him entry. "Shane isn't here at the moment. He took the children on a walking adventure."

Why was she going on about Shane not being home? "I went to the cabin but Maisey and Phoebe weren't there. I hoped they were with you."

She shook her head. "Shane should be home any moment."

The muscles at the back of Rob's neck tightened. Why

would she say that unless something was terribly wrong? His fear refused to wait for Shane. "Are Maisey and Phoebe all right?"

"They're not injured, if that's what you're wondering." The frown on America's face cleared. "Here's Shane now."

Light footsteps clattered on the porch alongside the thump of boots. Rob strode to the door and yanked it open. "Come in, man, and tell me where my family is."

"Hello, Rob. I see you've remembered where you live." Shane came into the kitchen behind his children, who immediately tackled their uncle's legs. "You'll want to feed these ravenous creatures, America. They're begging for a slice of bread and jam."

"They will have to let go of their uncle first." America gently extricated her children.

"Come with me." Shane led Rob through the door to the hallway and into the parlor. He gestured toward one of the overstuffed chairs. "Sit down."

Rob remained standing. "Just tell me."

"All right, then. Maisey received a letter while you were away. Her mother is in the hospital. She's gone to St. Louis."

Rob stared at him, trying to corral his thoughts. That hadn't been among the things he'd anticipated Shane saying.

"There was no time to contact you, I'm afraid. Maisey's brother sent a bank draft that paid her travel costs. She took Phoebe and went by stage this morning."

"I see." Rob gripped the back of his neck. "Do you have an address?"

Shane nodded. "Maisey gave me the name of the hospital and also her brother's address from the letter she received. Unless her plans change, she'll be staying in the Portman Hotel."

"Did my wife say whether she planned to come back?"

"I can't imagine that she won't." Shane's gaze pierced him. "Is there some reason you can?"

Rob lowered himself into one of the chairs. "We had words before I went to the ranch. I said some things that I didn't mean."

Shane sat squarely facing him. "What was the subject of your discussion, if you don't mind my asking?"

Rob dragged his hand across his face. "She thought I was flirting with Emma."

"And were you?"

"Of course not." Rob looked at his cousin askance. "Emma's a baby compared to a grown woman like Maisey. How can you even ask me that when you know how I feel about my wife?"

Shane lifted an eyebrow. "I thought I did, but you seem to have a penchant for abandoning her."

Rob took the criticism like a punch on the jaw. "I lost my temper."

"And your patience with it, apparently."

"You will admit it's frustrating not to be believed." Rob jumped up and strode to the window.

"It's also troubling to wonder. On what grounds did Maisey entertain her suspicions?"

"She saw me helping Emma home after she hurt her ankle." Rob paced about the room.

"Did you tell Maisey about that?"

"I tried to, but she wouldn't listen." Rob's conscience smote him. That wasn't quite accurate, as he suddenly recalled. He'd lost his temper and stormed up the ladder to the loft, refusing to explain himself.

Shane pinned him with a glance. "How much of an effort

did you make?"

"What does that matter?" Rob glared at Shane. "I shouldn't have had to make any."

"I agree that a wife should be able to trust her husband."

Rob glanced at his cousin suspiciously. "What do you expect from me?"

"Sit down and I'll tell you. Keeping up with your pacing is giving me whiplash."

"Sorry." Rob returned to his chair. "Please, tell me how to fix this. I'll do anything."

Shane shifted forward in his chair. "Stop acting like a fool, if you want the plain truth."

"What's that supposed to mean?" Rob knew he shouldn't let his cousin goad him, especially when he was so good at it.

"It's painfully clear you haven't settled relations between you." Shane shook his head. "If you tell me you don't desire Maisey, I'll know you for a liar. So, why are you allowing distance to grow between you?"

"I want her so badly it hurts," Rob answered curtly. "But I need to know for certain that she really wanted to marry me."

"We've been over this before." Shane shook his head. "When will you decide you are worthy of Maisey's love? Con freed you from the slum, but you seem to have brought it with you."

Rob lifted his head and met Shane's gaze. After a moment, he nodded. "Point taken. I've had a conversation with God about that in recent days."

"Now you're making progress." Shane smiled "You can only overcome your past once you recognize the need to do so."

Rob pushed a hand through his hair. "I once promised to tell you why I'd become so jaded."

"Ah, yes. While we were tracking Maisey's captors, as I recall."

Rob smiled sadly. "It was because of Daphne."

"I'm listening."

"She was an upstairs girl I hired when I believed I could forget about Maisey." Rob shook his head. "I should have saved us both the trouble. I couldn't bring myself to betray Maisey, not even in so shallow a way."

"That's comforting to know."

"I paid Daphne and sent her away. She begged me before she left to purchase a ticket for her to leave town. I refused, thinking she would cash it in afterwards for the money. I was certain she would spend it on wild living." Rob ran one hand over his face. "I was wrong."

Shane's face held compassion. "What happened?"

"She killed herself." Rob dragged in air. "Although I'd denied her the help she desperately needed, I did pray for her to escape the trap she'd fallen into. She'd impressed her unhappiness on me to that extent."

"You couldn't have known what she would do."

"No, but when it comes to helping a woman in need, I failed miserably."

"I'm sorry, Rob. I wish I could take back what happened, but I can't."

"I've thought something similar, time and again. I wish I'd had the sensitivity to guess what was coming. Daphne would be alive today and thanking me." Rob grimaced. "I had only myself to blame, but at the time I didn't know that the way I do today. After I found out about Daphne, I decided God was responsible."

"It may surprise you to learn that neither you nor God was responsible for the evil that wrested that poor woman from life." Shane steepled his hands. "It's easy to forget that there is an enemy of our souls who delights in destroying lives."

Rob drew in a breath. "Yes, I can see that. I don't intend to let my marriage fall prey."

"Well, Cousin, you'll have an easier time of it if you keep one thing in mind."

Rob smiled wryly. "I can't believe it takes only one."

"Listen to me carefully, Cousin." Shane gazed at him intently. "A man does well to remember his woman's need to feel stable in his love."

"Meaning a man such as me?"

"Any man, really. It took time for me to build America's trust in me. I started with a similar disadvantage as you. My wife had lost faith in herself and also in God's love for her. My job was to help America understand her own worth. That's a struggle I suspect Maisey copes with as well."

"Why are we talking about Maisey's value?" Rob tilted his head. "She's worth all the gold in Alder Gulch, and then some."

"Make sure she has no doubt you think that, and you'll be off to a better start."

"Assuming I'm given the opportunity."

Shane lifted an eyebrow. "Sometimes we have to make our chances."

CHAPTER TWENTY-TWO

Emma paused with her fist in the air, listening intently. About to knock on the Hayeses front door, she'd stopped when voices drifted through the open parlor window. Gideon's remarks from their encounter this morning had pestered her all day. She'd taken a short walk to escape them, but the dratted pests continued to follow her about. Between that intrusion and dithering over whether she should move to Wyoming, she'd spent a most unsettling morning.

Emma had stopped by the Hayes house in order to ask America's advice before she resigned. After overhearing Rob call her a baby, she had no further doubts that her future lay elsewhere. Now that she knew what Rob really thought of her, she never wanted to encounter him again. The only way of accomplishing that was to remove herself from his vicinity. She liked the idea of returning to Wyoming Territory, where she'd grown up. It might feel a little like going home.

She lowered her hand and turned away from the door. If she tiptoed around the back of the house and remained undetected, she might gain the safety of her cabin. Tears blurred her vision, but she held herself back from weeping. Gideon had wanted to know why she didn't easily trust others. This situation perfectly illustrated her reasoning. People always let you down. Pa had taught her that caring too deeply about others was a mistake that made you vulnerable. He ought to know, since his closest friend had cheated him in business. He'd recovered from that betrayal financially, but it had marked him. Emma would rather not wind up bitter like her pa. It was better to avoid deep attachments to prevent that from ever happening.

Rob was mad at her over the trouble between Maisey and him, but that wasn't altogether her fault. She'd only approached Rob in the first place because she'd believed he was unattached. If she had known that he and Maisey were married, she would never have made overtures to him. Her cheeks burned. She'd behaved so childishly. The creeping suspicion that Rob was partially right about her didn't make his criticism any easier to bear.

Dashing away the tears that dropped to her cheeks, Emma turned the corner of the house. Something rolled under her foot. throwing her off-balance. She cried out and went down.

Please, God, don't let anyone have heard.

Voices coming through the open kitchen window above her and the scuffling of footsteps dashed Emma's hopes. She rolled into a sitting position. The back door creaked open, and America rushed onto the porch with her children spilling around her. "Are you all right?"

"Yes." Emma picked up the carved Noah's Ark that had tripped her. "I don't think it's broken." Small animals were scattered about her, but by some miracle had escaped harm.

"Good grief! I'm terribly sorry." America hurried down her steps. "Seth, I told you not to leave your toys lying around outside. Come and pick them up."

"No harm done." Emma shifted in order to rise without entangling herself in her petticoat. America held out her hand, and she levered onto her feet. Her brown poplin skirt would hide any grass stains, thankfully. Shane and Rob were still talking and didn't appear. That seemed strange until she realized that the parlor window looked out the other direction.

The men must not have heard anything above their own voices.

America helped Emma brush off her skirt. "Why were you in the yard?"

Emma took a breath. "I have something to tell you."

"Let's go inside. You can sit down and recover."

Emma shook her head. "Thank you, but I'd as soon say it out here."

"All right." America tilted her head. "I'm listening."

"Very well." Emma moved a little apart from the children, who were picking up pairs of animals and storing them in the ark. At least, Seth and Liberty were doing that. Liam was taking the carved animals back out and strewing them in the grass with gleeful abandon.

When Emma judged they were out of the children's earshot, she turned to America. "I've decided to resign from my teaching position."

"How disappointing." A crease formed between America's eyes. "Are you unhappy with your work?"

"It's not that." What should she say? That she'd embarrassed herself over Rob and wanted to escape? Maybe not. "I'd like a change of scenery." Yes, that was best, although as a reason to quit a job, it was piteous.

America studied her a moment before speaking. "May I ask why you've decided on so drastic a step? You could always take a trip instead."

"That wouldn't be long enough. I want a more sustained adventure. There's nothing like exploring a new location." Aware that she sounded like a flibbertigibbet, Emma forced herself to stop babbling.

"I hope you'll reconsider." America hesitated. "Independence is not always freedom."

"My pa wouldn't agree with you."

America smiled. "I don't mean to gainsay your father's beliefs. I fear, however, that shifting about will isolate you from the best parts of life. I'm sure your pa wouldn't want that to happen. It would be hard to see you go, and not only for Shane and me. You've become a part of the community."

Emma glanced away. "They like me because I teach their children, not for anything else."

"That's not true. You're liked for your many skills, but also for yourself."

Emma cast a doubtful look toward America but didn't argue the point.

The children raced past them and pounded up the steps.

"I'd better go in." America touched her arm. "Promise me you'll consider what I've said before you write your resignation letter."

Emma nodded, but her decision wasn't likely to change.

Maisey smiled at her daughter's excited cries. After several long days of travel, the allure had begun to wear off for Phoebe, but boarding the train had revived it. The train whistle pealed, and the passenger car jerked as the engine pulled away from the station. Smoke billowed past the window behind Phoebe. Maisey drew a breath, steadying her nerves as the world sped by. The other passengers in the car appeared unconcerned at their rate of travel, so she assumed it was normal.

Maisey leaned against the brown leather seatback and did her best to pay attention to Phoebe's remarks, a difficult task in her nervous state. Phoebe's chatter gave her something else to think about than the possibility of a train crash. It also distracted her mind from thoughts of Rob or her family in St. Louis.

As the miles chugged by, Phoebe's enthusiasm faded into lethargy. She lifted sleepy eyes toward Maisey. "How much longer will it be before we arrive?"

"We haven't left Wyoming yet." Maisey kissed the top of her daughter's head. "Try to sleep."

Phoebe pulled away and sat tall.

Maisey repressed a smile. For a moment she'd forgotten her daughter's wish to appear grown-up.

Maisey sank into her seat, lulled by the rhythmic motion of the train. She was becoming used to the vistas that rolled past the window in a never-ending display. Prairies dotted with antelope and buffalo yielded ground to mountainous terrain, lakes, and geysers. The sky shone, vast and blue, above it all.

It would be a mistake to hope for too much. Her brother might have only sent for her at the request of their mother. He might not have changed, and Phoebe was so young. She hoped Marcus wouldn't prove a bad influence on his niece.

A stray thought whispered into her mind and would not be banished. If the reunion with her family went well, she and Phoebe should remain in St. Louis. She would have to give up teaching at the Indian school, but she was willing to make that sacrifice so Phoebe could spend time with her grandparents. Surely, she could find other work in such a large city. If she took care of herself and Phoebe, Rob could live the separate life he seemed to want. They could qualify for an annulment, if it came to that. Maybe it was best that they'd never consummated their marriage.

She blinked away tears. Letting go of Rob would break her heart, but she loved him enough to set him free.

CHAPTER TWENTY-THREE

MAISEY CARRIED HER SLEEPING DAUGHTER DOWN the paneled hallway in the Portman Hotel. The green carpet at her feet was patterned in beige and brown medallions, and crystal oil-lamp chandeliers hung from the ceiling. The porter followed with their trunks, which he deposited in the hotel room. His face wreathed in smiles, the gray-uniformed man nodded toward Phoebe. "Your little miss is all tuckered out."

Maisey smiled tiredly. "She's traveled quite a way."

She put her daughter down on one side of the double bed and covered her. Phoebe sighed and nestled into her pillow. Maisey flexed her arms, which ached from lifting her child. Phoebe was growing up. She would soon be too heavy to lift.

After the porter left, Maisey washed her face and laid herself on the bed alongside her daughter but couldn't fall asleep as easily.

Tomorrow, she would discover if her mother still lived. Memories of the last time she'd seen her parents arose to torment her, complete with the emotions she'd felt. Marcus's shouted accusations and her father's condemning silence still haunted her. Maisey pushed the troubling thoughts away. She shouldn't dwell on such things. Mother must have moved beyond them, or she wouldn't have sent for her.

Maisey should do the same. No good came of holding onto past hurts, as she could testify. Doing so had never brought her anything but pain. Whatever tomorrow held, God had led her to a point of decision tonight. It was up to her to respond.

Maisey released her parents and brother in forgiveness. Soon afterwards, exhaustion tugged her into sleep.

Phoebe woke her at midmorning. "Are you going to sleep all day? I'm hungry."

"What time is it?" Maisey sat up in confusion. She pushed the hair out of her eyes and leaned against the padded headboard while she gathered her wits. She turned her head to check the clock on the bedside table. "It's nine o'clock. You should have woken me sooner."

"I haven't been up very long, either." Sitting at the desk, Phoebe propped her chin on one hand. "There's a menu for the hotel dining room."

"Let me see that." Maisey scanned the card Phoebe handed her. "We'd better hurry if we want to be served breakfast."

Phoebe plopped onto the bed. "Will I meet my grandmother today?"

"I hope so, darling." Maisey pushed aside the covers and lowered her feet to the floor. "I sure hope so."

Linen-covered tables and cushioned rosewood chairs awaited them in the hotel dining room. More crystal chandeliers hung here, and wainscoting in a dark wood lined up against the walls. The true beauty of the room, however, was the stained-glass window embedded in the outer wall. Arched at the top, it depicted leaves and open flowers in shades of blue, green, and white.

Phoebe exclaimed over the window, and her enthusiasm proved infectious. Maisey had shed a heavy burden in the night. While gazing at her daughter's delighted face, more of her tension sloughed away.

After breakfast, Maisey hailed a hansom cab. She settled beside Phoebe in the carriage and called out the hospital's address through a trap door in the roof. The driver sat in a sprung seat situated above and behind them. From this perch, he guided the draft horse that pulled the cab through the broad city streets.

Mercy Hospital, a private facility, reposed well back from the road in a wealthy part of St. Louis. The brick three-story building overlooked a circular drive. The trap door opened above Maisey, and she handed up her payment and a tip to the driver. "Please wait for us," she instructed him. "I'm not certain we're staying."

Through the hatch, she saw the driver thump dust out of his top hat. He replaced it on his head before answering. "I'll stand by for a few minutes only." He reached for a latch, and the folding wooden doors opened, allowing Maisey and Phoebe to exit the conveyance.

Not wanting to be stranded without a cab, Maisey took the driver's warning to heart. She hurried Phoebe into the hospital lobby, which was paneled by a beautifully grained wood that looked as expensive as the golden chandelier suspended from the high ceiling.

A woman wearing a nurse's cap gazed at them suspiciously as they entered. "May I help you?" Her tone suggested that she might not want to do a thing for them.

Maisey had made sure that she and Phoebe wore their best garments, but the quality wouldn't pass muster in an elite hospital like this one.

Phoebe pressed against her side, abandoning her usual chattiness.

Maisey summoned the will to meet the woman's gaze squarely. "I'm here at my mother's request."

The nurse's demeaner shifted subtly, becoming less hostile. "What is her name?"

"Mrs. Edward Denniston. Is she still here? The message

my brother sent was delayed in reaching me." Maisey waited tensely for the answer.

The nurse sent her a puzzled glance. Maisey could see why. If relations with her family were normal, she wouldn't have had to ask.

"Yes, she's here, but you'll have to find the room on your own. I can't spare anyone to guide you."

Maisey released her breath. Her mother was still alive. On the heels of her relief came sorrow. Her mother was still in the hospital.

The desk nurse's scant directions led Maisey, with Phoebe beside her, to the third floor of the utilitarian building. She inquired of a second nurse, who paused from wheeling a laundry cart to direct her. Maisey passed a small waiting room, featuring stiff upholstered chairs in an unattractive shade of olive green, before she arrived at the correct door. She found it slightly ajar. Heart pounding, Maisey placed her palm on the wooden panel. A small push would remove the final barrier to her reunion with her mother.

She lowered her hand. She couldn't go in, not yet. Her nerves were in a jumble, and Phoebe looked subdued. Also, she wasn't sure whether they would be barging in. Perhaps someone was with her mother, like her father or Marcus. Was she really ready to face either of them again? Maisey backed away and ducked into the waiting room.

"What's wrong?" Phoebe touched her arm. "Don't you want to go in, Ma?"

"Yes, but in a minute." Maisey waited for her breathing to steady.

Phoebe embraced her. "Don't worry, Ma. I'll be right there with you."

Maisey gave her daughter a squeeze. "And I'll be with

you."

They returned to her mother's door. She didn't know the correct hospital protocol when a door was closed. Did a person knock or simply go in? Maisey decided to err on the side of caution.

She drew a deep breath and knocked.

The door opened and a man emerged. He pulled the door to behind him.

Maisey stepped backward. Recognizing Marcus, she restrained her gasp. The years had not treated him favorably. His watery eyes and paunch betrayed a life of excess. The hair that had once been a rich chestnut brown was dull and threaded by gray, and yet he was only a few years older than her.

He peered at her. "And so you arrive at long last. You took your sweet time."

Maisey summoned her voice. "How is she?"

"The doctor doesn't expect her to survive, if that's what you want to know." He looked Phoebe up and down. "I suppose this is your child."

Phoebe pressed more closely against her.

"This is Phoebe." Maisey did not prompt her daughter to acknowledge her uncle. The way Marcus was behaving, she didn't trust him to return a civil greeting.

He nodded toward the door. "You can go in. She wanted to see you, although she may not know you anymore."

Maisey braced herself to enter the room where her mother lay on her deathbed. She wished she could spare Phoebe this experience, but it was too late for that. What else could she have done? If she'd left her daughter behind, Phoebe would never have met her grandmother at all.

Regret flooded Maisey. Phoebe should have had time with

her grandmother. They'd lived too far apart for frequent visits, but something could have been arranged. At the very least, there should have been letters, maybe even packages. Phoebe hadn't deserved the cold silence she'd received.

The door yielded beneath her hand, swinging inward.

The figure in the bed bore little resemblance to the mother Maisey remembered. This woman was shrunken by the passage of years and the ailment that sapped her life away. Waxy eyelids lay across her sunken eyes like a thin film. Her skin held a yellowish sheen. Her chest rose so faintly with her breathing that she almost appeared to have already passed from this world.

Maisey and Phoebe tiptoed to the bed. Her mother might not wake. However, if she did, Maisey hoped that discovering them there would be more a surprise than a shock.

The filmy eyelids trembled and slid upward. Pale blue eyes focused on Maisey. The ghost of a smile traced the pale lips. The eyes closed again, as if leaving them open was too hard a task. "My daughter, you're finally here."

Maisey could have wept. "Hello, Mother. I'm sorry to find you so ill."

"Who is that with you?"

"This is Phoebe. I've brought your granddaughter to meet you."

Her mother opened her eyes. "Come here, child." She spoke in a stronger voice than she'd used before.

Maisey touched Phoebe's back gently but didn't push her forward. The decision needed to come from her.

Phoebe stepped forward. "Hello, Grandmother."

Mother's lips tilted in a gentle smile. "What a beauty you are. You look like your grandfather, may he rest in peace."

Maisey caught her breath. "What do you mean? Is Father

dead?" The questions wrenched from her. Marcus hadn't warned her, and she'd assumed her father wasn't present for some other reason.

"Didn't Marcus tell you? He died six months ago when his carriage overturned." Mother closed her eyes. "My poor darling Edward."

Maisey tried to dam up her tears, but they fell anyway. She gave them no sound, in case they might upset her mother.

"I'm sorry, Maisey. I should have told you after the accident." Mother's chest rose and fell, a sign of her distress. "Can you forgive me for that and also for all the time I wasted?"

"Please don't upset yourself. I do forgive you, and Father too."

"Thank you," she whispered.

"I love you so much. I'm sorry for not trying harder to reconcile."

"Don't let that trouble you, Maisey. I love you, my daughter." Her voice faded, and she lay still.

Maisey leaned forward. Her mother's eyes were glazed, and her chest didn't seem to be moving. Maisey rushed to the door. "Nurse!"

Hurrying footsteps echoed from down the hall. Marcus emerged from the waiting room and started toward Maisey. "What's the matter?"

"I think she's gone." Maisey choked on the bitter words.

"Then there's no more need to put up with you." Her brother pushed past her into the room.

Phoebe had remained at her grandmother's bedside. She flinched as Marcus neared.

"Please, you're frightening my child." Maisey hurried to Phoebe and held her close.

"Then leave. No one is keeping you." Marcus leaned over their mother. "Goodbye, Mother." He kissed her forehead and closed her eyes.

Maisey wanted to leave, but she stood, rooted to the spot. Her tears flowed for what might have been.

Her brother straightened. "If it was up to me alone, you wouldn't be here. I wouldn't cross the street for you, but my mother wanted to see you before she died. Otherwise, I wouldn't have written. When Father went, you couldn't even be bothered."

"I didn't know." Maisey gasped out what he must already understand.

"You should have kept in touch."

"They wouldn't let me."

"That's an excuse." He shook his head "You're a pitiful excuse for a person, and I want nothing to do with you ever again."

Maisey must have slept at some point, for she woke with aching eyes and the weight of grief on her chest. The feeble light that found its way around the hotel curtains picked out Phoebe, still slumbering beside her. She looked vulnerable and far too young to be exposed to death.

Maisey had waited for Phoebe to fall asleep before releasing her grief in a quiet storm. In the dark of night, she'd faced a harsh truth. All these years, she'd hidden her longing for a reunion with her family from herself. Laying claim to her dream had been too risky. If only she had understood sooner, she might have overcome her reluctance to reach out to her family.

Maisey had no more chances with her parents, and she

doubted Marcus would ever reconcile. She wasn't even sure she wanted to seek him out again. It would take a while to fully forgive him for his hateful remarks. They had made their mother's death much harder for Phoebe and her.

A wave of grief washed over her. Maisey stifled her sobs in her pillow.

Phoebe sat up beside her. "Ma, don't take on so."

Maisey tried to compose herself. "I didn't want to cry in front of you."

"Why not?" Phoebe patted her back. "You should if you need to."

Maisey released a shuddering breath. "I've lost my family all over again."

"But you haven't, Ma. I'm right here."

Maisey smiled, despite her sorrow. "Yes, you are, sweetheart."

"There's Pa, too."

Maisey gave no response. She couldn't pretend that everything would be all right between her and Rob. Neither would she burden Phoebe with the suggestion that Rob might not come home to them. She gave her daughter the only possible response—silence.

The reminder of Rob only made it harder for Maisey to maintain her composure. She closed her eyes, trying to forget her last argument with him.

"When the Indians captured you, I cried a lot too," Phoebe confided.

"I'm sorry you went through so much, sweetheart." Maisey pulled her daughter into her arms.

Phoebe rested her head on Maisey's shoulder. "I learned something from it, though."

"What was that?" Maisey stroked her hair.

"It happened when the sky made me sad."

Maisey couldn't begin to guess why Phoebe would say such a thing. "What do you mean?"

"The sky is so big that it seems to go on forever."

Maisey frowned, still trying to understand. "That's why you were sad?"

Phoebe nodded. "I felt too small to matter."

Maisey pulled in a breath. "I know what you mean."

"Troubles are like the sky. They make you feel like your prayers don't count."

Maisey nodded. That's how her problems with Rob seemed.

"Liberty's ma helped me see that my prayers aren't small because God cares about them, and He's bigger than the sky."

CHAPTER TWENTY-FOUR

PHOEBE SAT SWINGING HER LEGS FROM the side of the bed in their hotel room. "Do they have chicken pot pie in the restaurant?"

"I believe so." Smiling came more easily to Maisey today.

"That's what I'm going to order." Phoebe's eyes gleamed. "What will you have, Ma?"

"I'm partial to chicken and mashed potatoes with gravy." The thought of eating did not appeal to Maisey much, but she needed to make the attempt. They would board the train tomorrow on a homeward journey, and that would require strength.

Staying an extra day in the hotel had not been a luxury but a necessity. Yesterday, she'd splurged on room service to avoid venturing out with swollen eyes. With Phoebe's natural joy lifting Maisey's spirits, she felt capable of dining in the hotel restaurant today.

Coming back to St. Louis had reopened old hurts, like when a scab rips off an unhealed wound. She would be glad to leave the city of her birth behind. It had once belonged to her, but not anymore. She belonged in the West.

A knock pounded the door. Maisey started. What was Rob doing here? But no, it wouldn't be him. The porter's knock must sound similar.

Phoebe's face brightened. Before Maisey could react, her daughter yanked open the door. Rob stepped in from the hallway, looking the worse for travel. He must have come straight to their hotel. Stubble shadowed his chin, and his clothing was rumpled. He seemed leaner, and his face wore a weary expression.

Phoebe flung herself at him, and he embraced her. Rob met Maisey's eyes above Phoebe's head. "Hello, Maisey."

It wasn't fair that the sound of his voice had the power to make Maisey's knees go weak. She couldn't pull her gaze away from his. "I didn't expect to see you here."

Rob smiled slightly. "Did you think I wouldn't come after my family?"

"To be honest, I didn't know what to believe."

"It's been brought to my attention recently that I need to make you more sure of me."

That would be a start, but she would rather he had arrived at that conclusion himself. Maisey couldn't quite trust that the change in him was real. "Why did you come?"

"I wanted to be with you and Phoebe. How is your mother?"

Tears pricked her eyes. "She's dead."

"I'm so sorry."

Maisey nodded, accepting his sympathy. She could tell that much was genuine.

Phoebe stepped away from Rob. "Ma's brother yelled at her."

His jaw tightened. "What happened?"

"Marcus needs to learn better manners, that's all." Maisey preferred not to rehash the conversation with her brother in front of Phoebe.

"Was your father welcoming?"

Maisey swallowed hard. "He died six months ago."

"I'm sorry, Maisey. I wish I'd been there when you found out." Rob shook his head. "I'm kicking myself for the fool that I am."

She cut back the reproachful remark she could have made. Rob regretted his absence from her life, and that was more than she'd expected to hear from him. "It would have been nice to have you with me, but it might have made things worse with Marcus."

"I can't bring myself to care about that, except where it touches you." His gaze traveled over her. "How are you doing?"

She shook her head, unable to speak as tears gathered anew. A sob escaped Maisey, and Rob pulled her into his embrace. She laid her head against his chest, and his arms tightened about her. Time slipped away.

"I lost so many years with my mother," Maisey murmured when her tears stopped flowing. She shook her head. "It was such a waste."

Rob stroked her hair. "We all have regrets in life."

"I always had this hope in the back of my mind that things would work out between us somehow, but I didn't really try to fix what was wrong." She drew a shuddering breath. "I don't know how to go on without hope."

Rob kissed her forehead. "Start by forgiving yourself and sort the rest out from there."

"I'll try."

"Come home with me?" His blue eyes pleaded with her.

Maisey decided against asking him about Emma. The subject would have to come up between them, but not today. She couldn't handle the strife it would introduce. Rob wanted them to be together, and that was what Phoebe needed. It remained to be seen whether it was the best thing for Maisey, but she was willing to find out. "All right."

"Thank you." He spoke so humbly that she glanced at him

in puzzlement. She had seen this humility in him once before, on their wedding night. She couldn't interpret it now any more than she had then.

"You're just in time to go to dinner with us." Phoebe slipped her hand into Rob's. "What do you want to order, Pa?"

Rob grinned. "I have a hankering for a good steak."

They were in the middle of ordering supper in the restaurant when a man carrying a briefcase approached their table, his gaze intent on Maisey.

The waiter lifted his eyebrows. "May I help you, sir?"

"Pardon me, but I've come on a private matter with this young woman."

Rob looked the man over. "State your business."

"Before her death, Mrs. Denniston retained me as her lawyer to rewrite her will."

Maisey caught her breath. What had her mother done?

"Is there a private room where we can talk?" Rob directed the question to the waiter.

"Yes, of course." The waiter led them to a quiet section of the restaurant that was not in use.

Rob seated Maisey and Phoebe before sitting down himself.

"I'm glad to catch you still in town." The lawyer sank into the chair opposite Maisey. He opened his briefcase and spread a sheaf of papers on the table. "According to your mother's will, the bulk of her estate went to your brother, Marcus." He glanced over the top of his glasses. "She did set aside a tidy sum for you."

Maisey clasped her hands in her lap. "I wasn't expecting anything."

"Yes," he cleared his throat. "I appreciate that. Nevertheless, you will receive a small inheritance." He named a generous sum.

Tears started to Maisey's eyes. The money didn't matter, only that her mother hadn't forgotten her. That was beyond price.

Maisey woke to the rattling of the stagecoach. She lifted her head from Rob's shoulder, where it had rested. His gaze caressed hers, and she felt herself drowning in his nearness. Maisey straightened away from him, not ready for such an intimate moment. She needed to feel safe with Rob before she could let herself fully love him. Phoebe's yearning for a close-knit family matched the one she herself had long held. She couldn't pretend they had one yet, not even for Phoebe's sake. It would take time to recover, if they could, from the circumstances that had torn them apart.

Trees sped by outside the window, and the horse's hooves beat the dirt road in a steady rhythm. The sky shone copper around the setting sun and deeply blue above that. A gibbous moon shone faintly in the sky, waiting to come into its own.

Maisey's lips curved in a soft smile. Phoebe was sleeping with her arms clamped around Rob. The picture they made could heal Maisey's heart—or break it afresh.

"We're almost home." Rob kept his voice low.

"I can't wait." She planned to light the fire in the stove and heat water for a bath. A good soak followed by a night in her own bed would go a long way to ease the discomforts of travel.

Phoebe stirred and opened her eyes. "I'm hungry."

Maisey added another task to her mental list. Fixing food for Phoebe would be harder than usual. There weren't many supplies in the pantry at home. None of this would be a problem if Phoebe had eaten her dinner at the stagecoach station. Maisey couldn't blame her. Heavy-lidded, she'd picked at her stew and had fallen asleep as soon as the stage pulled out.

Porridge would be easy to make and might be best for Phoebe's stomach after the journey.

"There will be a slight problem when we reach Liberty." Rob removed his arm from around Phoebe, allowing her to sit up. "We'll either have to beg a ride or walk, I'm afraid. Shane dropped me at the stagecoach, as I'm sure he did you. That was convenient for the outset, but by journey's end it creates a problem. I'm sorry I didn't think things through better. I should have sent a telegram to let Shane know when we'd arrive home."

"Arrival times are hard to gauge accurately. It might not have helped." Maisey glanced out the window at the deepening sky. "I can't imagine that anyone will be driving to the edge of town this late in the day. Unless someone is willing to take us home out of kindness, we may have to walk." The bath she'd contemplated might have to wait until very late indeed, assuming she had any energy remaining when she arrived home.

"We'll find someone to help us," Phoebe asserted. "Liberty is full of kind people."

Rob inquired in the mercantile, and the owner declared himself ready to hitch up his wagon and transport them home.

"You were right, as usual." Rob grinned at Phoebe.

"Told you so." She beamed at him, and he chucked her under the chin.

Maisey's breath caught in her throat to see them acting so much like a father and daughter.Phoebe had been too young when Avery died to remember him. Rob was the only man she'd ever thought of as a father.

Whatever the future held, one thing was clear to Maisey. She had better work things out with Rob. Just how she would accomplish that remained to be discovered.

Maisey settled between Rob and Phoebe in a pew carved of oak. It was the first time they'd attended Sunday Meeting as a family. Around them in the schoolhouse meeting room, citizens of Liberty township and outlying areas waited for the service to begin. She should have expected the glances that came her way. It was only natural for their neighbors to be curious, but so much attention focused on her made Maisey want to hide.

Phoebe leaned close. "Can I sit with Liberty?"

"*May* I *please* sit with Liberty." Maisey shook her head. "You've been over at her house a lot lately. It's time to stay with us." She could understand Phoebe's desire. Maisey would have let her have her way, but America's hands were full minding her own children. The preacher's family sat in the front row during the service. Any misbehavior the children engaged in would come to the entire congregation's notice. After finding herself under scrutiny today, Maisey felt much more sympathetic to her friend's plight. People in Liberty were more relaxed about formalities, but they were still capable of placing expectations on a preacher's family that they couldn't meet themselves.

Behind the pulpit, Shane cleared his throat. "Today I will preach on a subject near to me. To do so, I must refer to an experience I recently endured."

Maisey went still, and Rob stiffened beside her. She could guess the event Shane referred to, and Rob must too.

"Speaking of forgiveness is easy." Shane's gaze rested

lightly on Maisey and Rob before moving elsewhere. "Actually, forgiving someone who has wronged you is harder."

Maisey had discovered as much. She struggled daily to forgive Marcus, and also Rob.

Shane stepped from the dais and started down the center aisle. "Most of you know that I recently underwent captivity at the hands of Indians. I would be within my rights to hold guilty those who restrained me against my will. I might even feel virtuous to be a victim." He raised the Bible in his hand. "Joseph's story, recorded in the Old Testament, tells how he forgave his brothers after they, out of jealousy, sold him into slavery. If Joseph hadn't forgiven his brothers, they'd have been lost to him." Shane scanned the congregation. "Wallowing in the offenses against us comes at a high price."

Maisey had a feeling that this sermon would remain with her. She made sure to keep her gaze fixed on Shane and away from Rob.

Shane returned up the center aisle, preaching as he walked. "The father of the prodigal son couldn't embrace his child until he forgave him. He might have chosen instead to hold onto his anger at the thoughtless way his son had left his home and wasted his inheritance. I probably don't need to mention what that would have meant for his relationship with his son. The father forgave every hurt inflicted on him and afterwards rejoiced that his son was restored to him."

Shane's words chimed within Maisey, convicting her for attitudes she would rather ignore. They spoke to something hidden deep within her soul too painful to examine.

"Take our Savior, Jesus Christ. In the midst of agony on the cross, He chose to forgive those who placed Him there. If He had refused, the world would have lost the chance of eternal life His death provides." Shane paused for several minutes. "I have no excuse for holding anyone else's feet to the fire when He did not."

After the service, Maisey moved with most everyone else into the gathering room where the congregation enjoyed a potluck. She spotted America in the kitchen, the center of activity. Maisey navigated through the bustling crowd to reach her. She had to raise her voice to be heard above the general chatter. "What can I do?"

"Whatever you find." America flashed a smile before turning her head to answer a question from one of the other women.

Maisey envied America the relaxed perspective that saw her through the many hurdles of a preacher's wife. She would do well to take a leaf from America's book.

The array of food was remarkable. Maisey noticed fried chicken, ribs, and beans plus numerous salads, breads, and desserts. She uncovered the bacon stew she'd brought and went about adding serving spoons where they were needed.

Maisey stepped back, about to turn. She had the brief impression of a yellow gingham sleeve and red hair shot with silver as a sharp heel ground against her boot. The other person let out a gasp. Maisey reached out and caught the person she'd run into. Arms clasped her, preventing her from falling. They tottered together in a clumsy embrace. Maisey regained her balance and pulled away. She smiled. Of all the people in the gathering room, she had run into Nellie Haig. She kept a hand on Nellie's upper arm until the woman had regained her balance. "Are you all right?"

Nellie nodded. "I'm terribly sorry. I didn't see you."

"No harm done." Maisey laughed. "In this crowded room, it was bound to happen sooner or later."

Nellie smiled. "I should get out of the way." She turned

toward the door.

Bry traipsed into the kitchen, having arrived with other family members from the ranch the previous day. Maisey set off toward her, but paused and looked over her shoulder at Nellie. She caught up to Nellie in a couple of steps. "I met your sister on the stagecoach. She weathered the journey well and arrived safely home."

Nellie's face brightened. "Thank you for telling me. That's good to know."

Maisey wasn't sure what else to say, but she ought to reach out. "She asked me if I knew you, and I answered that I did, but not nearly well enough." She blurted out the first thought that crossed her mind. "I'd like to change that."

Nellie's eyes glowed. "You're always welcome to visit us on a Sunday afternoon."

Maisey smiled. "Thank you, and the same to you."

It was amazing how much lighter Maisey felt after the overture she'd made. Nellie was the quiet kind of person others overlooked, but then so was she. That they each struggled to leave behind the deepest sorrow of grief would surely allow them to benefit one another.

Bry reached Maisey and embraced her. "You look wonderful. Marriage must agree with you."

Maisey almost laughed. She found marriage to Rob stressful, but she hoped that in time, Bry's statement would prove true.

It wasn't very long since she'd left the ranch, but it was wonderful to see Bry again so soon. She and Elsa had always pitched in to prepare for Sunday Meeting. They helped feed and shelter the families who traveled long distances to attend. Some arrived a day in advance and waited until Monday morning to go home.

Rob seemed to have vanished, along with several of the other men. She spotted him a little later setting up extra tables for the burgeoning crowd. He joined her afterwards, and they went through the food line together. Maisey had learned to spoon lesser amounts of the items she chose onto her plate. Otherwise, she would go home, groaning. Despite her efforts, she carried a plate laden with beans, fried chicken, cornpone, and several types of salad to Shane and America's table.

Phoebe was already there, having received her wish to sit with Liberty during the meal. Maisey smiled softly when she saw their blonde heads bent together. The girls got along well. Phoebe was blessed to have a playmate so near. On these special Sundays, Phoebe enjoyed the companionship of a wider group of children also. Maisey knew a moment of gladness that she had not moved away from this place as she had once planned.

America caught her eye from across the table. "Did any students show up for Indian school yesterday?"

"No." Sadly, even Bluebird had stopped coming.

Shane exchanged a glance with America. "We haven't decided anything yet, but we've been thinking and praying about the school."

"Me too." Maisey hated to see everything she'd built with Shane and America come to nothing, but she also didn't want to try to prop up the school if she should let go of it.

"We're wondering if the time for it is past. St. Mary's Mission is nurturing more and more of the Salish. The Indian camp is so close that reaching the mission doesn't require a journey. It's easy to see why that's more appealing."

"I've had the same thought." Maisey nodded. "I'm open to whatever decision you make."

"It will all work out for the best." Rob laid his arm across the back of Maisey's chair. Maisey turned her head to smile her thanks for his support and found herself enmeshed in his gaze.

Maisey trusted Shane and America to make a wise choice about the school. Even so, the possibility of change was unsettling. She'd given six years of her life to teaching the Salish children. To have the school she had sacrificed to establish vanish was hard to contemplate. Maisey sighed. She had meant what she'd said. Whatever God deemed best was what she wanted.

Maisey owned that she'd stayed in Liberty partly for the parents who had entreated her to continue teaching their children. She would never forget that event, for she'd recognized in it God's handiwork.

She prayed He would look after her now.

Emma slipped away from the gathering room a little early and let herself into her silent cabin, happy to escape the crowd. She would go back after the potluck and retrieve her grandmother's covered casserole dish. Spending time in the community she planned to leave was hard, but that wasn't why she'd felt the need to be alone. Reverend Hayes was to blame, due to the sermon he'd preached. She sank into the chair by the window, then leaned against the seatback and closed her eyes.

Hard telling what would come of it, but she needed to apologize to Rob. She'd ignored all propriety and thrown herself at the man, blind to the fact that he wanted nothing to do with her. If she'd had any doubt of that whatsoever, he'd made his feelings clear in his conversation with Shane.

She should also ask forgiveness from Gideon, although it galled her to contemplate the idea. She shouldn't have blamed him for mentioning her letter to his mother. Most definitely, she'd been wrong to suggest that he'd persuaded his mother to spy on her. She didn't really believe Felicity would spy on her, nor that Gideon would ask her to.

It was time to make amends.

Come to think of it, she might need to apologize to more people. Should she include Felicity? What about Maisey?

Emma blew out a breath. She needed to think about this. Maybe apologizing to so many people wasn't really necessary. It would be much more comfortable to ignore the prompting. After she left town, though, she'd like to be remembered kindly. That couldn't happen by refusing to make amends. There was another reason. She felt badly about what she'd done. Emma deeply regretted upsetting Rob and accidentally driving a wedge between him and Maisey. What had gotten into her lately? She'd let her emotions guide her actions far too often. Emma winced. This could get out of hand.

When it came to Felicity, it would be better to let sleeping dogs lie. She had no doubt that Gideon wouldn't tell his mother what Emma had said. Revealing it might cause her needless pain, and he would never do that. Emma wasn't positive she should approach Maisey since she hadn't intentionally wronged her. She needed to give more thought to the idea.

Emma folded her hands in her lap and sat quietly without lighting the lantern. The shadows lengthened outside the window, dancing as the trees swayed in the breeze. Peace seeped into her from the natural world, in keeping with her newly ordered thoughts. Everything else in her life might be in chaos, but about this one thing, she knew exactly what she needed to do.

Leaving Gideon was another matter altogether. No matter

how much she tried to persuade herself that she was doing the right thing, a part of her felt differently. She needed to make peace with herself. For the sake of her sanity, the sooner she did so, the better.

"Ma?" Phoebe sounded contented and perhaps a little sleepy as she walked beside Maisey on the path from the schoolhouse. Rob had remained behind to help the other men break down tables.

"What sweetheart?" Maisey bent her head toward Phoebe.

"You should forgive Pa."

Phoebe's simple statement matched Maisey's own suspicions. They had cropped up during Shane's sermon, and now they wouldn't leave her alone. She tried to divert Phoebe from her mission. "Haven't you noticed that we've been getting along since St. Louis?"

"Yes, but aren't you still mad about what happened a long time ago?" Phoebe turned an earnest face toward Maisey. "You know, when Pa went away."

Maisey drew a deep breath and released it slowly. For one so young, her daughter laid claim to a lot of wisdom. "I'll consider whether I need to do that."

"I hope you do. Nothing matters more than that you and Pa love each other."

Not even my pride.

They reached the cabin, and Phoebe promptly put herself to bed.

Maisey brewed a cup of chamomile tea and drank it at the kitchen table. As she sipped the warm drink, a realization crept over her, soft as the mists that descended into the valley. Phoebe was absolutely right. Maisey had been blaming Rob for going to Virginia City. She should have accepted his choice, but driven by her desire for a family, she had placed unfair expectations on him.

Rob had explained his need to seek his fortune, if she'd been willing to listen. She ought to have supported his decision, right or wrong. Instead, she'd taken his leaving as a rejection. What if it hadn't been one?

She was long overdue to forgive Rob and free herself from the pain she'd nurtured with such tender care. She glanced out the window at the fading light. Rob shouldn't be much longer, but the urge to find him and unburden herself sooner pulled at her.

Maisey looked in on Phoebe, who was snoring lightly. She doubted that anything would wake her sleeping daughter, but Maisey didn't know how long she might be gone. She decided not to risk it. She'd wait on the porch. Rob should be home any moment, and they could talk outside, away from any possibility of being overheard by Phoebe. Her daughter knew far more about their marriage than a child should be privy to.

Twilight, that uneasy passage between night and day, had fallen quickly. Maisey hadn't lit a lantern yet, and her cabin windows stared out darkly. She settled on the porch step to wait for Rob. A bird flew out from a branch across the path. Maisey started, but then sighed. It had only been a harmless dove winging across the sky. Would she ever stop being jumpy? She had nothing to worry about with so many people either hurrying toward the schoolhouse or walking away from it. The fear that had haunted her since she'd been kidnapped continued to intrude on her well-being, but it had lessened over time. She was thankful for that.

The crowd had thinned out by the time Rob strode toward her from the direction of the schoolhouse. Maisey drew in a breath to call to him.

"Wait up!" Emma stepped onto the path behind him.

Rob turned to her. "It's getting dark, time to be indoors."

"I'm glad to find you out and about." Emma's voice sounded breathy. She must have hurried to catch up to him.

"What's on your mind?"

"I have something to tell you." Emma leaned closer to Rob. "Something personal." She spoke in a rush, but more softly than before. Maisey couldn't hear what she said.

Rob murmured in deeper tones and took one of her hands.

Emma stepped closer, and he leaned down to her.

She tilted her face upward and murmured near his ear. She dashed away a tear, and Rob's arms slid around her.

Maisey stood up before they could break apart and look her way. The door clicked shut behind her. Her fingers trembled as they grasped the cold metal of the bolt.

She let out a shuddering sigh and rested her forehead against the door. She couldn't quite bring herself to lock Rob out of the cabin or out of her heart.

Maybe there was a logical explanation for Rob taking Emma into his arms. It seemed impossible, but she couldn't stop the hope that fluttered within her. Rob had gone all the way to St. Louis after her and Phoebe. Why would he do that if he wanted someone else?

He only went to appease his guilty conscience. The thought whispered through her mind. Maisey lifted her head away from the wooden panel before her. Of course! That had to be it. Tears slipped down her cheeks as she slid the bolt home.

CHAPTER TWENTY-FIVE

ROB PUT EMMA GENTLY FROM HIM. What had gotten into her, throwing herself into his arms like that? She'd offered a heartfelt apology, and he didn't think she was after him anymore. Embracing him must have been nothing more than a poor choice on her part. He could sympathize with her awkwardness, but he would rather that she found someone else to afflict it upon. A glance toward the cabin he shared with Maisey quickened his heartbeat. Had he seen a shift in the shadows as the door shut?

He appreciated Emma's desire to seek forgiveness, but she couldn't have chosen a more inopportune moment to bare her soul. He and Maisey had started to work through their differences, and he would hate for anything to jeopardize that process. If Maisey looked out the kitchen window she would see them together, which might be enough to create problems. Hopefully, that hadn't already happened. It was horrible to be accused. It made him feel guilty when he wasn't.

He would rather hurry home to Maisey than deal with Emma, but he couldn't in good conscience abandon a woman alone at the edge of a wilderness as night fell. "I'll see you home."

"Thank you." Emma spoke in a demure voice. In some respects, confessing seemed to have done her good.

"May I carry your dish for you?" It would be ungallant not to offer.

"No, thank you." She pulled it closer, as if he'd been about to wrest it from her. "It belonged to my grandmother. If anyone should break it accidentally, it had better be me."

"I hope you won't. It's generous to take an item so precious to a potluck." He wondered why she'd done so, but then she had no other family to share it with.

"It's a treasure. I'll never have my grandmother back again."

"Cherish your memories of her. No one can break those."

"She was a wise woman. If I'd listened to my grandmother's advice, I wouldn't have had to say I'm sorry."

Rob grinned. Emma was young yet, a fact that must account for her foolishness. She'd had a good upbringing, from the sound of it, and should turn out all right. "About what you said—we all do things we regret. Don't give it any more thought."

"I suppose you love Maisey very much?"

"I love her with all my heart."

She sighed. "I'm happy for you both."

They reached her cabin, but he stopped below the porch. For a variety of reasons, he wouldn't walk her to the door. However, he did want to wait while she went inside. After she waved from the window, he backtracked home.

On his own porch, he turned the doorknob. It rattled but didn't open. *Not again!*

The cabin was dark, but he knocked lightly. Nothing stirred. Rob repeated his action, with the same results. He swallowed his pride and tapped on Maisey's bedroom window. The only sound that answered was the lonely call of a mourning dove.

Maisey wasn't that sound a sleeper.

Anger flashed through Rob. His boots rang out as he paced the porch. There were other women who might welcome his interest. Accuse a man of infidelity, and he'd feel the urge to prove you right.

A man does well to remember a woman's need to feel stable in his love. Shane's voice intruded in Rob's memory like a pesky fly he would rather brush away.

Rob waged a battle with himself. The painful truth stared him in the face. He would rather be offended than accept the part he'd played in his wife's mistrust. The fight went out of him, and he sank onto the porch. Who was he kidding? Maisey was the only woman he wanted. His attempt to forget her with Daphne had proven that to him. He should never have given in to the temptation to hire a dance hall girl for the night. What a disaster that had been.

Rob sank onto the porch, prepared to camp out as long as necessary. Sooner or later Maisey would have to open the door.

When she did, he'd be waiting.

"What are you doing there?" A familiar voice roused Rob from fitful slumber. He lifted his head and opened bleary eyes. Shane swam into focus in the light slanting through the cottonwood trees. Rob levered into a sitting position. "I'm following your advice, if you must know. Why are you about so early?"

"It's my habit to start the day with prayer and to study the Bible. Since my home is overrun with guests, the meeting room affords me more privacy." Shane tilted his head. "What specific advice of mine do you believe you're following? I'm fairly certain I never suggested that you sleep on your porch."

"Ah, but you did. Maybe not in those exact words, but this is entirely your fault."

"I'm glad to hear it." Shane's eyes gleamed. "I'll lift you

and Maisey in prayer."

"Thanks, Preacher. I'm sure the Almighty is more inclined to listen to you than a sinner like me."

Shane lifted an eyebrow. "God hears every earnest person." Continuing on his journey, he broke out whistling. The cheery sound grated on Rob's nerves, considering his present circumstances. Despite what Shane had said, Rob wasn't all that sure God wanted to listen to him. He'd prayed earnestly for Daphne's well-being but it hadn't saved her. Maybe it was time to accept that God could only have done His part in the matter, not Daphne's.

Shane passed in and out of shadow on the path before moving out of sight.

Footsteps scuffled behind the cabin door, and Rob scrambled to his feet.

The door cracked open, and Phoebe peeked out at him. "You woke me up talking to Reverend Hayes, but Ma's still asleep. Did she lock you out?"

Rob ran a hand over his face. "It's a long story."

Phoebe stepped onto the porch in her blue-checked wrapper. With her hair plaited, she looked rested and fresh. "She's mad at you again, isn't she?"

Rob smiled wryly. "You could say that."

She plopped down on the top step. "I've been meaning to have a talk with you."

"Is that so?" After taking in her serious expression, Rob hid his amusement. He lowered himself to sit beside her. "Is there something on your mind?"

"I have an idea. Why don't you and Ma marry each other all over again, only this time for real?"

Rob knew people repeated their vows, but usually after years of marriage. Still, the idea held merit, assuming Maisey ever talked to him again. "Thanks for the suggestion."

"I hope you will. That way you can both know you mean it."

"You're amazing," Rob said when he recovered his voice. "Let me think about it."

"Good." Phoebe sprang to her feet. "You should come inside."

"In a moment." He stood up. "There's something I need to do first."

Phoebe glanced back at him from the doorway. "Don't take too long."

He nodded, understanding her meaning. A child of eight was an odd co-conspirator to have, not that Rob was complaining. He needed all the help he could get to win Maisey. Toward that end, it was past time to ask for help from another direction.

Rob gripped the porch rail and closed his eyes. *God, I'm sorry for being so bullheaded and insensitive with Maisey. I'll rely on You to help me show her how much I love her.*

Emma felt much better after making her peace with Rob. Today she would tackle Gideon. She slipped from her cabin in the early morning, knowing she would find him up and about his chores. With any luck, she would catch him alone. Apologizing to Gideon would be quite enough to go through without one of his brothers witnessing her humiliation.

She passed through the cottonwood grove, her feet making little sound on the damp path. The air, smelling of rain, touched her face with moisture. Songbirds rippled melodies in the branches overhead, greeting the day with enthusiasm. Perhaps, after she spoke with Gideon, she would share their exuberance. She doubted, somehow, that she would want to sing.

Emma walked slowly, going over the speech she'd memorized. She needed her wits about her when going up against Gideon. Why did she always wind up blurting out things she'd never meant to speak? Maybe committing to memory what she wanted to say might help her avoid that this time.

She couldn't quite come up with the words to tell Gideon she was leaving. Nothing seemed appropriate, but then neither did going without telling him first.

Emma turned aside onto a path worn into the grass. The barn where she would find Gideon tending his chores rose before her. It was painted red and built-in the western style with a peak roof over the hayloft to allow hay bales to be raised by a pulley. Gideon's voice came from within the large building. Emma hesitated. Who was he talking to? She could detect no other but a hoof thudding and a horse's snort.

Emma slipped into the barn through the open doorway. The morning chill receded, and the scents of warm animals and sweet hay carried her backward in time. Her brother's teasing banter made her laugh, although she pretended to be annoyed at his outlandish remarks. It had all been in good fun. Days later, he would be dead.

Gideon glanced up from the stall where he'd been talking to one of the horses. Was it her imagination or did he check briefly, as if bracing himself to face her? That would be most unflattering. A discomfiting notion turned up like an unwelcome neighbor. What if she'd earned such a reaction?

"Good morning, Emma." Gideon faced her fully.

Emma let a smile suffice. She might have answered him, but the power of speech had abandoned her. Clean-shaven and bright-eyed, he made quite an impact on a woman.

"You're up early." The statement sounded more like a question.

She couldn't blame him for being cautious. The last time she'd sought him out had been to accuse him. Emma looked away from the wariness in his eyes and cleared her husky throat. "I wanted to talk to you." She paused, waiting for his reaction.

"Oh? You'll have to hurry, I'm afraid. You've caught me about to leave town."

"You're going somewhere?" Emma pictured him taking a trip to a nearby town. Surely that was all he meant.

His eyes gleamed. "I've hired on with Con Walsh, Reverend Hayes's cousin, for a cattle drive."

"That's quite a change for you." It took Emma's breath away. Gideon would be gone when she left, so this would be their goodbye.

"I'm looking forward to it. I want to purchase my own land. I can't live with my parents forever."

"Will you settle nearby?" Emma wasn't sure why that mattered, since she herself would be gone, only that it did.

"I won't move far from my family." He gazed at her with quiet humor. "Now, tell me why you came over. What have I done this time?"

Emma flinched slightly. "Nothing." The surprise that crept over Gideon's face reproached her. "I'm the one to blame," she added before he could say anything more.

Really, must he stare at her with his mouth gaping open?

She took a moment to collect herself. Apologizing to Rob had been so much easier. "I accused you of sending your mother to spy on me. That was wrong of me when I knew it wasn't true." The words emerged formally, stilted almost, but they came out.

"I'll admit that made me angry. Thank you for taking it back." Gideon stepped away from the stall and walked toward her. "Why did you say it, that's what I want to know."

Emma stared at him mutely, not having rehearsed the answer to this particular question. "I was upset about leaving." She blurted out the truth.

"Don't tell me you're going away?"

Gideon sounded disappointed. Emma tried to read his expression, but it shifted as something behind her caught his attention.

"I thought I heard voices." Jake stood in the doorway. He smiled at Emma. "Good morning, Miss Duncan."

"We're having a private conversation," Gideon said before Emma could reply.

Jake's eyes widened. "Oh, sorry." He stepped out of the doorway.

Gideon's gaze returned to Emma. "Where are you heading?

"I've been offered a position in Wyoming."

"Is there something wrong with the one you have?"

Emma chose her words carefully. "I love teaching the children of Liberty, but it's time to move on."

"I can't understand the desire. Why don't you want to stay since you like it here?"

"I've been here several years already." Emma knew she was grasping at straws.

Gideon's eyes glinted. "I wasn't aware that there's a time limit for living in a place. Thanks for clarifying that for me."

"Don't be ridiculous. You must know that moving about is in everyone's blood these days."

"Not everyone's, Emma. Some of us are happy staying put.

It's a fact that plants without deep roots wither and die."

Explaining the real reasons for her decision would be far too embarrassing. Wretched tears sprang to her eyes. She looked down to hide them. "I need to be on my way, that's all." Her trembling voice betrayed her. Gideon lifted her chin, and his face swam behind her tears. She blinked them away.

He studied her, frowning. "Does this have anything to do with Rob Walsh?"

It was unfair of him to press her in a weak moment. Emma wanted more than anything for him to comfort her in his arms. That would never do. She might give away the feelings she was trying to stamp out. Caring for Gideon would give him the power to break her heart.

Emma saw a way out of her predicament, although it would hurt dreadfully. She dragged in air. "Yes."

Gideon released her. "I guess that says it all."

"I'll be back before you know it." Gideon embraced his mother. She'd been scrambling eggs in the kitchen and looking a little weepy-eyed while the family sat down to breakfast.

She waved a hand. "Don't worry about a foolish woman like me. I hope you enjoy yourself on the cattle drive."

He grinned. "There may be joy involved, but I imagine it will mostly involve hard work."

"You've never been shy about that." She dished eggs onto a plate beside strips of bacon and thick slices of fried toast. "Your pa sets a good example."

Gideon took the plate from his mother and carried it into the dining room. He laid it in front of his father at the head of the table. Jake and Ben, seated across from one another, were quibbling over who could run faster.

"Thanks, Son." Pa saluted Gideon with his coffee cup. "Are you all set for today's journey?"

"Ready and raring."

Pa smiled. "Oh, to be young again and setting out in the world."

"It's a little daunting," Gideon admitted.

"Sure, it is." Pa nodded. "That's how you know you're having an adventure."

"I'll remember that." Gideon grinned, but then sobered. "I hope I can measure up on the cattle drive."

Pa's eyes widened. "You can't be serious. Con Walsh hired himself a good worker. If he doesn't know it yet, he soon will. You'll do well, I have no doubt."

"Thanks, Pa."

Gideon returned to the kitchen, considerably bolstered.

Ma dished up more plates of food, which he brought to his brothers. Gideon went back to the kitchen to see if he could do anything else. He liked to ease Ma's chores, where he could. She didn't complain about how much work she did, but sometimes she looked tired.

"Did you tell Emma goodbye?" She pitched her voice low.

Gideon wished he could ignore her question. "Yes." He kept his answer short, hoping she would drop the subject.

Ma's face softened. "I guess it didn't go well between you."

"No."

"Maybe you two can work things out when you come back. Absence makes the heart grow fonder, as they say."

"I expect she'll have moved away by then," he ground out.

"What are you talking about?"

Gideon chided himself. "Sorry, I should have mentioned that more gently. I know you're fond of Emma. Sorry to say, but she's decided not to remain in Liberty."

"Did she explain why?"

"She suffers from a broken heart." Gideon lowered his voice. "Rob disappointed her when he married."

"That can't be true." Ma pursed her lips in the way she always did whenever she'd said too much.

He wasn't above prying. "Why do you believe that?"

"I shouldn't say anything, but—" Conflicting emotions chased across her face.

Gideon waited for her to speak.

She lifted her chin. "I wouldn't normally break a confidence, but I can't let this happen."

Gideon couldn't resist the urge to press her for more information. "What, Ma?"

"Emma thinks she's in love with you."

Gideon didn't quite snort, but nearly. "Are you certain?"

"She told me so."

He shook his head. "Emma sure has a funny way of showing it."

Ma smiled. "She has a little growing up to do."

He loved his mother's kind way of expressing a criticism. "I'm sure that neither she nor I are ready for declarations of love."

She watched him in that way of hers.

Gideon sighed. "I suppose it wouldn't hurt to ask her to stay."

Maisey couldn't remain in bed the whole day, although she found the thought tempting. She would rather avoid Rob to spare herself the unhappy task of confronting him. Last night, after the shock of seeing Emma in her husband's arms, she'd locked the door to prevent further upset. She'd fallen asleep long after Rob tapped on her window, her pillow dampened with tears. Pretending that their marriage hadn't ended before it truly began was deceiving herself. There was only one sane thing to do. That was what kept her lingering in bed, unwilling to broach the conversation that would end their sham of a marriage.

Rob's voice thrummed in the kitchen, overlaid by Phoebe's bright tones. She couldn't make out what they were saying, but the exchange brought up the troubling question without an answer that had long plagued her. How could she reject Rob when it would break her daughter's heart?

She should never have let Rob form a bond with Phoebe all those years ago. She'd told herself that her daughter needed a father figure, and that the tie between the two would enrich Phoebe's life. That was before her own relationship with Rob became complicated. Hindsight told her that encouraging a deeper association between her daughter and Rob had been unwise. She should have waited until she knew whether Rob wanted a family. When that proved not to be the case, he'd moved on. She'd been forced to live with the mistake they'd made together.

None of that changed where they stood today. Rob was the only father Phoebe had ever known, and Maisey was partly responsible for that. Tears clouded her vision. She loved her daughter too much to take Rob from her a second time.

She scrubbed at her cheeks with her hands. What other choice did she have? If she didn't send Rob away, he would probably leave on his own. It would be best to make a clean break. Allowing Phoebe to grow any closer to him would only increase her pain when he abandoned them. Did Maisey want to make the same mistake all over again? On that thought, she flipped back her covers and stood up.

Maisey groaned at her image in the washstand mirror. The rough night she'd spent showed in her swollen eyes, blotchy skin, and dull expression. The water in her pitcher wasn't warm, but it would have to do. She swirled it into the bowl and splashed her aching eyes. She groped for the towel and pressed its softness to her face.

She frowned at her reflection. Her puffy eyes weren't much improved, but then what did it matter? Concealing how much Rob had hurt her might salve her wounded pride. It might be better if he knew how his behavior affected her. She would ask Rob to take a walk with her to move their discussion beyond Phoebe's hearing.

Maisey dressed as quickly as her turbulent emotions allowed. She focused with difficulty and had to stop to bathe her face again. Maisey fumed at the interruption. Now that she'd made up her mind to deal with her failed marriage, she wanted nothing more than to discharge the burdensome task. Ready at last, she squared her shoulders and opened her bedroom door.

She blinked.

Wildflowers festooned the doorway, including several kinds she remembered holding during her wedding to Rob. She stared at the bright display, trying to piece together why they should hang there. Logic told her Rob was responsible but also that the flowers couldn't be from him. Her mind snagged on the riddle. Why would Rob court her if he wanted Emma?

Her husband stepped around the corner from the kitchen, clutching a handful of wildflowers in his hand. Above the riot of color, his blue eyes watched her unflinchingly. Rob pressed the bouquet into her hands and cupped them with his own. "I love you, Maisey, and only you."

Maisey stared at him, hoping against hope that this could be real. "What about—"

"Don't say it." He sealed her lips with a swift kiss.

Maisey recovered enough presence of mind to think of her daughter. "We should talk, but not around Phoebe."

"She's not here. Shane stopped by and invited her to spend the day with Liberty. She wanted to go, and I thought it would be best, under the circumstances."

Maisey nodded. Now that the moment to confront him was upon her, she felt reluctant to go through with it. Rob had ambushed her with flowers and attention, but that only confused the real issue. "I saw you with Emma last night."

"It wasn't how it looked."

She shook her head. "You embraced her."

Rob rubbed the side of his neck. "She hugged me after apologizing to me. What was I to do?"

Fighting her with logic wasn't fair. "You could have told her no."

"Possibly, but I don't think she meant it wrongly, and I didn't want to wound her. Didn't you notice that I stepped away quickly?"

Maisey frowned. "I wasn't going to wait around to find out."

He touched her damp cheek. "I'm so sorry, Maisey."

She heaved a shaky breath. "Why did Emma ask your forgiveness?"

"She was sorry for putting herself forward that day at the well. That was before she knew we were married, or she probably wouldn't have approached me."

"I saw what happened that day. It looked like you didn't want her to stop."

"Emma took me by surprise." Rob's face reddened. "I must confess that I know very little about how to deal with women."

She nodded. "I've noticed that in you."

Rob smiled wryly. "You might have protested a little, for the sake of my dignity."

Maisey resisted the answering smile that tugged at her lips. "What about the other time I saw you with Emma? You were walking with your arm around her, and she was leaning on you."

"You made your opinion quite clear at the time. I was helping Emma home after she hurt her ankle."

"Why were you together?" Maisey hated asking the question. It made her sound like such a jealous woman. However, posing it was the best way to clear the air between them.

"That was innocent, I promise. I went for a walk after our argument. It was fortunate for her that I did. She tangled with a bear, but I drove it off. Emma had fallen and was unable to walk alone. If I hadn't been there, she might have had to wait all night for someone traveling the road to find her. May I?" He took her flowers and laid them on the table.

Maisey wished for the bouquet back, which she had been holding before her like a shield.

Rob drew her into his arms. "I hope I have satisfied your suspicions, Mrs. Walsh. You should have asked me about these things sooner instead of letting them build up in your mind."

"I did that once, but I was upset at the time, and you took

what I said as an accusation."

"I have much to learn about being a husband." Rob kissed her forehead. "I hope you'll allow me that privilege."

She caught her breath on a sob. "I love you."

He nodded. "I suppose that's reason enough to cry."

She laughed and cried at the same time. When she could form words, she would tell him that she would suffer it all again, for the sorrow had carried her to this moment.

Rob kissed her eyelids. "I'll do my best to stop the tears." He touched his lips to hers in a soft caress. "Will you forgive me for being so impatient with you?"

She nodded. "I need to apologize, as well."

"Go ahead." His eyes smiled into hers.

"I can't think like this." She stepped out of his arms. "There, that's better."

"After a manner of speaking." He laughed, his eyes dancing. "Come back."

Maisey smiled but shook her head. "This is important."

"You sound like Phoebe about to deliver a lecture."

"Actually, she brought this to my notice—and Shane before her." Fresh tears prickled Maisey's eyes. "I've blamed you, all this time, for leaving to mine for gold. I shouldn't have, and I'm sorry."

"I knew, of course, but that means a lot. Thank you." Tension ebbed from Rob's face. "I suggest we leave the past behind us and go forward the wiser for having survived it. Do you agree?"

Maisey couldn't hold back her smile this time. "I do."

Rob grinned. "Those words are music to my ears. May you say them again soon." He pulled her back into his arms and claimed her lips.

Maisey pressed into her husband's arms. She had waited a long time for this moment of truth. His lips stroked hers, teaching her what it meant to be cherished. Maisey clasped her hands behind Rob's head, delighting in the crisp texture of his hair. He tugged her hair out of its pins and ran his fingers through the tresses he'd freed. Maisey let her hands stray down his neck to his shoulders, savoring the feel of firm muscles beneath supple skin. His mouth slanted over hers more purposefully. Maisey met his intensity, giving of herself to this man she loved above all others. As their lips communicated in perfect unity, every hurt that had separated them melted away.

CHAPTER TWENTY-SIX

GIDEON'S KNOCK SOUNDED MORE FORCEFUL THAN Emma remembered. The washstand mirror revealed the horrifying truth. Her eyes were swollen from crying. She bathed her face and afterwards pinched her cheeks in an attempt to revive their color. Emma sighed at her reflection. She would have to do.

Gideon stood on the porch, a pensive expression on his face. "I wondered if you were going to answer."

Emma clutched the door for support. "I thought you were already on the road."

Gideon studied her face. "A certain matter came up to delay my departure."

"Oh?"

"I have a favor to ask of you. Will you come out?"

"Of course." Emma stepped onto the porch.

Gideon swept his gaze over her and lingered on her eyes. "Were you crying, Emma?"

She repressed the childish urge to deny it. "Moving upsets a person."

He paced about. "Have you already resigned from your post?"

"Not formally." That wasn't a question she would have anticipated from him. "Why do you want to know?"

Gideon halted abruptly before her. "Can't you guess?"

Perhaps, but Emma wasn't ready to admit to that. "What are you talking about?"

"I don't want you to go." His eyes pleaded with her. "I

think I'm in love with you."

Emma grasped the porch rail. "This is unexpected."

"I did kiss you."

"Yes, but only once. It might have been a whim."

Gideon gave a brief shake of his head. "I don't kiss without meaning. I would hope you don't either."

"You never said anything about it afterwards," Emma pointed out.

"I wasn't sure I should."

"I suppose that's my fault." Tears touched her lashes. "I'm sorry."

He lifted her chin. "I can forgive you for your part in that, but I'd like to understand it better."

"Have you ever wanted something that didn't turn out to be good for you?"

He smiled. "Do you mean, like penny candy?"

"Being smitten with the wrong person can give you the same kind of stomach ache. That's the way it was for me with Rob. I was hurting so much I couldn't find my way to you."

"Are you over him?"

She drew a breath. "I held onto the dream of Rob, but I don't think I ever really loved him."

He lowered his head until their faces were only inches apart. "That's all I need to know."

Emma opened her mouth, ready to tell him how much he'd come to mean to her.

Gideon's lips covered hers, making speech impossible.

Maisey toted her bucket filled with cleaning supplies and rags toward the schoolhouse. This wasn't going to be easy by any means, but that didn't matter. Some responsibilities needed tending to, whether or not she felt inclined. Her reluctance couldn't be more evident in her slow pace. She'd been putting this off for days, but this morning the opportunity had presented itself.

The main schoolhouse door was already unlocked, which didn't surprise her. She turned the knob and went in. "It's me, Emma."

The tap of footsteps reached her from the classroom. Emma peered out from the schoolroom, and Maisey went forward to meet her. Emma put one hand over her heart. "My goodness you gave me a turn. I didn't think anyone would come in."

Maisey noticed that Emma didn't quite look at her as she spoke, which marked a change in her behavior. "Sorry. I did call out."

Emma nodded but said nothing further. A strained silence stretched between them.

"I saw you walk past my cabin with cleaning supplies." Maisey forged onward with difficulty. "May I join you?"

Emma's eyes widened. "Are you sure you want to?" Her face flamed, and she stared at the floor.

Maisey summoned the will to speak. "Last time we talked, I spoke in anger and made hurtful remarks."

Emma winced slightly. "I understood why you did."

"Even so, I need to ask your forgiveness."

"Of course, you may have it. I was more at fault than you." Tears swam in Emma's eyes. "I'm so sorry that I betrayed our friendship. It was a stupid thing to do. It upset Rob, hurt you, and I've had to pay for it ever since."

Maisey hadn't thought beyond her own apology. Receiving one in return gave her a lot to think about. Offering forgiveness was no easier than asking for it. In fact, it was harder. One lessened the weight of guilt, whereas the other required a burdensome decision.

Emma watched her out of frightened eyes. Maisey realized with a spurt of empathy that she half-expected to be rejected. All at once, Maisey could see what she should have known all along. Emma was both gauche and vulnerable. She needed friendships badly but tended to isolate herself. Her bond with Maisey, based on their similarities, had been an exception. They had both secluded themselves after being wounded by life. That they lived as neighbors and shared a schoolroom had allowed a special bond to grow between them. With sudden clarity, Maisey knew that she didn't want to break it, nor would she return evil for good. She took a breath. "I forgive you, Emma."

Emma's tears spilled over onto her cheeks even as she smiled.

Emma frowned. How vexing to be in this position. After knocking on America's back door, her carefully-rehearsed speech had instantly vanished from her head. Light footsteps echoed from within the house. It was too late to retreat. Emma squared her shoulders. She would get through this somehow.

The door opened and America peered out at her. "Emma. What a pleasant surprise. Come in."

Emma stepped into the kitchen.

America closed the door and followed her into the room. "You've chosen a good time for a visit. The younger children are down for naps, and Liberty is cutting out paper dolls in her room."

"That's fortunate."

Would you like tea or coffee?"

"No, thank you." That would take time, and the shorter Emma made this visit, the better.

A pucker appeared between America's brows. "Let's go into the parlor, shall we?" She led the way through the hallway and into the more formal room.

Emma sat in one of the overstuffed chairs. Birdsong drifted through the open window beside her. She had awakened with the desire to put this ordeal behind her. Now that the prospect was upon her, however, all she wanted to do was stall. "It's lovely weather we're having."

America sank into the chair that matched Emma's. "I wish summer could last, but the nights have been cooler of late."

"I've noticed that the willows are turning yellow. Their leaves show the change of seasons so early."

America sighed. "With autumn comes the start of school. Have you decided whether or not to stay on in your position?"

"That was what I wanted to talk with you about." Emma spoke hesitantly. It was humbling to ask for your job after declaring yourself ready to leave it.

"I hope you've decided to stay, after all."

Emma blessed America silently for making this easier for her. "I have."

"That's wonderful news." America beamed. "What caused you to change your mind?"

"Gideon persuaded me, but it wasn't only him." Emma cast about for words but came up short. "I guess what I'm saying is that I realized how much I belong here."

"You do, Emma. I'm so glad you've recognized that. You're certainly welcome to stay on as schoolteacher."

A feeling of peace descended over Emma, accompanied by the same deep sense of belonging she had known in her family. Emma released a soft breath, and all the tension that had plagued her sloughed away. She'd been searching all this time to find a home where she could belong, never recognizing that she had one already.

Maisey waited outside the schoolhouse meeting room for the wedding music to begin. She smoothed the skirt of the blue, white, and gold watered silk dress Elsa had given her. Bry's husband, Nick, stood beside her, looking elegant in a dark waistcoat and silk vest above tailored trousers. She placed her hand on his arm. "Thank you for stepping in like this."

"My pleasure."

Phoebe, ahead of Maisey in line, gazed at her from eyes the same shining blue as the ribbon that tied back her curls. Wearing a white taffeta dress that made her look like a fairytale princess, she carried a basket of wildflowers over her arm. "I'm glad you and Pa took my advice," she whispered.

Maisey embraced her daughter in a quick hug. "Me too."

Bry held a smaller version of Maisey's wildflower bouquet as she stood beside Con, Rob's best man. Her blue dress, the color of forget-me-nots, hid her swelling stomach. She glanced back at Phoebe and Maisey with a gleam in her eyes.

The processional began, and Bry and Con started off. Phoebe went before Maisey down the aisle, strewing flowers. Nick smiled at Maisey, and they began the last part of her journey to the man she loved.

Rob watched her from the front of the meeting room, breathtakingly handsome in his wedding jacket. Maisey passed Felicity, beaming beside her husband. The reception they would enjoy after repeating their vows was mainly due to her efforts. On Felicity's other side sat Emma. Maisey returned her smile, thankful that they'd made peace with one another.

America awarded Maisey a brilliant smile and finished by dabbing her eyes with a lacy handkerchief.

After that, Maisey gave all her attention to Rob, who came forward to receive her from Nick. Rob tucked her hand into the crook of his arm and brought her with him to stand before Shane and God. Rob took his position next to Con, and Maisey stood beside Bry.

Shane cleared his throat. "Welcome, and thank you for attending today. Every wedding is the celebration of a love story that culminates in a lifelong union. Today, we have gathered together in the sight of God and man to witness the joining of a very special couple. Mrs. Hayes, would you please come forward for the reading?"

America stood and went to the front. Shane stepped aside to allow her use of the pulpit. She gave Maisey a brilliant smile then consulted a Bible lying open on the stand.

"Charity suffereth long, and is kind; charity envieth not; charity vaunteth not itself, is not puffed up, doth not behave itself unseemly, seeketh not her own, is not easily provoked, thinketh no evil; rejoiceth not in iniquity, but rejoiceth in the truth; beareth all things, believeth all things, hopeth all things, endureth all things. Charity never faileth."

Shane announced that the time to speak their vows had arrived.

Rob met her eyes squarely. "I, Robert Devin Walsh, take thee, Maisey Lucille Wilcox, to be my wedded wife."

When it was her turn, Maisey put every ounce of love she felt for Rob into her vows.

Shane turned to Rob. "Do you have the ring?"

Rob looked to Con, and the gold circlet glinted between them. Rob took Maisey's hand and repeated the promises he'd made once before.

The ring glided onto her finger, a more substantial symbol of their love than the flimsy cord they had used before.

Maisey gazed at her husband with utter trust, certain beyond a single doubt that he meant every word.

Maisey turned the wedding ring in her hand and read the lettering—Maisey *and Rob Walsh, July 12th, 1870.* A smile tugged at her lips. How quaint it seemed to sum up their epic romance in the space of a few letters.

Rob rolled over in their bed. "What, are you looking at that ring again?" He grinned. "I'm beginning to think that you're more partial to it than to me."

Maisey smiled, rejoicing just a little that her husband could get jealous too.

She slipped the circlet onto her finger and held it up to gaze at it, yet again. It had been a week since they'd renewed their vows, and she still felt a thrill whenever she caught sight of the ring on her hand. Even with the curtains drawn in their bedroom, it gleamed with a golden luster. She would cherish her wedding ring all the more after having to forego wearing one. It was tangible proof that dreams could come true.

So many hopes had slipped from her grasp. She'd lost her marriage to Avery and the chance of a reconciliation to her family. Now that the Indian school was closing, another of her dreams lay broken at her feet. One bright hope remained however, and God in His kindness had granted that. She was truly Rob's wife, and he was the husband she'd yearned for.

Through it all, Maisey had learned to hold her dreams loosely but to hold tightly to God, the source of all hope.

Rob pulled her into his arms and kissed her neck. "I have a surprise for you and Phoebe." His eyes danced. "It requires a journey."

She smiled at his obvious excitement. "What can it be?"

"Pack for a couple of days." He kissed her swiftly then stepped out of bed.

Maisey felt keenly the loss of his arms about her but didn't call him back. Instead, she followed his lead. After dressing quickly, she roused Phoebe, then went to the kitchen to prepare a simple breakfast. Since they would travel today, she made porridge to soothe Phoebe's stomach in advance. She'd suffered travel sickness on the journey home from St. Louis. It would also provide enough stodge to carry them through to the next meal.

After eating and dealing with the dishes, she went into her bedroom to pack. Rob was closing his trunk. He glanced up and gave her a brilliant smile.

She rummaged in her wardrobe. "It would help me choose the right clothing if I knew where we were going."

He paused on his way out the door with his trunk. "You'll want to dress for the ranch."

Maisey frowned. It made no sense. Why was he acting so mysteriously if they were only going to his brother's ranch?

The front door closed, and his footsteps crunched outside the window. He must be going to the barn to hitch the wagon.

She finished packing and checked on Phoebe, who was nearly ready.

Maisey walked onto the porch to wait for Rob to drive up. The prospect of the trip lightened her step, and the bright rays of a beautiful day poured over her. Emma was at the well, drawing water. Maisey waved to her, and after a slight hesitation, Emma returned the salute.

With her hands on the railing, Maisey tilted her face to the sky. She breathed in the fresh air and thanked God for the many blessings in her life—every heartache she had endured had led her to them.

Hooves thumped, a wagon rattled, and harnesses jingled from the direction of the barn. Driving a wagon she had never seen before, Rob emerged from the tree shadows along the path. A pair of dapple greys with the arched necks and sturdy build of Percherons picked up their feet in unison. The tilt of Rob's head announced that he shared the draft horses' obvious zeal to travel down the road.

Maisey laughed for sheer joy.

The front door opened and Phoebe rushed out. "Are we going to ride in that wagon?"

"I imagine we will." Maisey started down the steps.

"Ho!" Rob called, and the wagon rolled to a stop. The horses tossed their manes and snorted, clearly eager to continue the journey.

Rob jumped down from the driving box and caught Maisey in his arms. "Do you like my surprise?"

She stepped back and gripped his arms. "How did you come by this wagon? And the horses?"

He grinned. "In the usual way, of course. I bought them. I figure that a family should have its own wagon, wouldn't you agree?"

"Most definitely." Maisey smiled.

"I must admit that it wasn't easy keeping it a secret. I'm not good at it, for one thing. I almost accidentally mentioned it to you a couple of times."

Having a husband who lacked the ability to deceive wasn't bad. Maisey ought to have realized it when she was breaking her own heart suspecting him of faithlessness. Her own insecurity had blinded her to the truth.

Rob glanced back at Phoebe. "Plus, I had to head our

daughter off whenever her love of horses carried her toward the barn, which was often."

"I wondered why you wanted to take so many walks." Phoebe came down the steps.

Rob chuckled. "My legs were fair falling off by the end."

Phoebe stopped before reaching the Percherons. "Can I pet them, Pa?"

"Yes, but look after yourself. They're gentle but weigh a good deal more than you."

"I'll be careful." Phoebe went forward with the confidence she always displayed around horses. Maisey envied her that, for she found the creatures mildly alarming.

Rob slipped his arm around Maisey's shoulders while they watched Phoebe introduce herself. Afterwards, he loaded their trunks, and they climbed into the wagon.

The sun warmed Maisey's skin, but she tied on a bonnet to shield her face. Phoebe didn't like the feel of a bonnet about her head, but Maisey insisted on her wearing one to prevent sunburn. Seated on hay bales stacked behind the driving box, Phoebe turned to engage them in happy chatter. "Can I drive, Pa?"

Maisey held back her laughter. "Why would a young girl want to do that?"

Rob smiled. "Maybe when you're older. At your age, these horses would pull your arms out of their sockets."

Phoebe subsided for a few moments, then cropped up again. "Are we going to Uncle Con's ranch?"

"Yes, if that's all right." Rob winked at Maisey.

"Oh, good. Playing with Fiona and Katie is fun."

Maisey's eyes moistened. Marcus had probably married and had children, but Phoebe would probably never meet those cousins. God had provided cousins for Phoebe despite that tragedy. She glanced at Rob to discover him watching her with a concerned expression. Maisey smiled at him. "Thank you for planning this trip."

"The best is yet to come." He broke into laughter. "Why the frown? I think you'll like what's coming. I hope you will, anyway. Leastways, you shouldn't hate it."

"I was only trying to figure out what you're talking about."

He gave her a gleaming glance. "Wait and see."

"All right." Maisey returned a tentative smile. If this episode indicated what Rob's behavior would be throughout their marriage, life would never be dull. She had seen this playful side before, but it had never shone more brightly. Loving and accepting her husband must have allowed him the freedom to reveal more of himself to her. If she had held back and remained in her hurt, she would never have known the happiness that brought.

Maisey sat beside Rob on the wagon box in the soft light of early morning. Last night, after sitting down to a feast with his family, he and Maisey had occupied the same room as before. This time, he'd forsaken the sofa in favor of his wife's arms.

Maisey gazed at him with a look he'd longed to see on her face. He leaned toward her and bestowed a gentle kiss on her lips. She smiled at him so sweetly, he yearned to draw her into his arms and express his love for her more thoroughly. With Phoebe behind them in the wagon, he restrained himself. They had a small drive to make before he could reveal his surprise.

Rob took up the lines and called to the horses. The wagon lurched into motion. Rob followed the same route he'd traveled once before. They rolled through shining grasslands and shadowy forests alike. The ever-present mountains lifted in the background, a mark of God's constancy. Maisey and Phoebe exclaimed over the views at every turn. Rob smiled to himself. The signs looked promising for a wonderful outcome.

They reached the Meadows Ranch, which was closer to Liberty than Con's place, by late afternoon. Rob drew up beside the ranch house. He'd gained a favorable impression of this place when he'd inspected it with Con, and he felt no differently today. The meadows and willow-lined creek were as sweet as he remembered them. Beyond that, trees crowded into a dense forest all the way to the foothills at the base of the mountains. The hip-roofed barn seemed to silently wait for its next occupants.

Maisey glanced at him questioningly.

Rob couldn't hold back his smile. He got out of the wagon and helped her down. "This place is for sale, and I think it might work well as a home for us."

Phoebe lowered herself down the side of the wagon. "I can't believe we could really live here."

Rob smiled. "Why not?"

Phoebe let out a whoop and ran toward the creek.

"Watch that you don't get your shoes wet," Maisey cautioned her. She looked up at the log structure rising two stories above them. "Can we see inside?"

Rob produced the key Con had obtained for him. Maisey called Phoebe from her explorations, and they went inside. The house was well-built, in good repair and fairly clean, considering it had been standing empty for a couple of months. Maisey and Phoebe went through the rooms, discussing the uses they could be put to. Rob followed them about indulgently. What mattered most to him was that Maisey liked it.

Maisey walked to the edge of the covered porch while Rob locked the house and Phoebe hurried toward the barn. Maisey swept a glance over the grounds. "The view is charming."

Rob came to stand beside her. "What do you think?"

She smiled at him. "It's a fine place to live."

"But do *you* want to live here?"

"That's a big house for three people."

Rob put his arms around her. "You never know. We might end up needing extra bedrooms."

Maisey turned to him, her eyes flying open. "What are you suggesting?"

Rob grinned. "Phoebe could use some siblings, don't you think?"

"I can't think about that yet." Maisey's cheeks went hot. "We've only just gotten married."

He laughed. "Sorry to rush you. I can wait, but a man has to plan ahead. This house would give us room to grow, if we've a mind to. If not, the extra rooms would come in handy when our family visits. But I don't want to offer for the place unless you like it too."

"I do." The house had impressed her, and the location was stunning. Maisey even liked the slight seclusion. Rob clearly loved this ranch, and that's what she cared most about.

"Those words still sound sweet on your lips, Mrs. Walsh. They make me want to replace them with my own." He pulled her into his arms and did just that.

EPILOGUE

MAISEY GRINNED AT ROB AS HE CLOSED Shane and America's back door. "It's a madhouse in there."

He laughed. "Our nieces and nephews are riled up, that's certain."

"It was quite a party." She started down the porch steps.

He followed and joined her on the worn path that cut through the grass. "Seth was so proud to be six, it was inspiring."

"I'm glad Phoebe is spending the night with Liberty. She's missed seeing her so often since we moved. We should invite Liberty for a visit once we've settled in a little better."

"That sounds like a fine plan. I'm glad Phoebe will sleep over with Liberty tonight for another reason." Rob grinned, his eyes gleaming. "Tonight we'll have our old cabin to ourselves."

With the Indian school closed, a second schoolteacher's cabin was no longer needed. Shane and America used Maisey's old home to shelter family members during their visits to Liberty.

"It's only been a couple of months since we left, but I already miss the place." Maisey sighed. "Life seemed simpler when we lived there."

Rob's eyes widened. "Surely you jest. There was nothing simple about our time at the cabin."

She smiled. "We lived at a slower pace back then. I agree that life was difficult, but we needed every moment of struggle."

Rob pulled her into his arms and landed a soft kiss on her forehead. "God works in mysterious ways, His wonders to perform. If you hadn't been kidnapped, I doubt we would ever have married."

"That would have been a tragedy for all three of us."

"I'm honored to be your husband and pleased that Phoebe wants me for her father. Claiming her as my daughter is a delight." Rob took her arm, and they continued along the path toward the cottonwood grove.

"I hope she isn't too lonely at the ranch. She's so enjoying Elsa's nieces and nephews."

"If they fail to improve their English, it won't be her fault."

Maisey pictured Phoebe teaching the German children to speak better English. "Helping them makes her happy, and she's picked up a smattering of German."

He laughed. "Do you think I haven't noticed that? I've dodged her efforts to instruct me. Keeping two languages straight in my head is enough."

"She's pestered me too."

He chuckled. "Better parents would be thankful for Phoebe's commitment to repairing their linguistic deficiencies."

"Her enthusiasm should fade once we move back to our own place. When will that be?" Maisey enjoyed the companionship at Con's ranch, but she yearned to spend more time in their new home. They had barely moved in when Con had called upon Rob's assistance to build cabins for Elsa's family. Agreeing to help had required a sacrifice. Their ranches were far enough apart that staying at Con's place until the cabins were built made sense. They returned to their own home whenever they could, but each time it was harder to leave it.

"We're almost finished."

"That's good."

"Yes, indeed. I'm anxious to take you and Phoebe home for good."

Home. The word wafted to Maisey like a sweet fragrance. Having such a beautiful ranch to call her own was wonderful, but she'd learned that home could be anywhere she could be with Rob. She shook her head. "I can't get used to thinking of the Indian school as closed. It was such a big part of my life."

"Time goes on, and none of us can stop it."

"I can still assist the Salish, but in a different way."

"St. Mary's Mission will be glad of your inheritance money."

"Thank you for understanding why I want to donate it."

"Do whatever you wish with your mother's money. I have enough to take care of us."

Rob had earned the privilege of saying those words by the sweat of his brow. Maisey admired him for that. She smiled, secure in the knowledge that her husband loved her.

Maisey's stomach churned with the nausea that had caused them to leave the party early. She would normally stay and help clear up. Supper had included forced-meat chicken, tidbits shaped into nuggets and dipped into batter before frying. Although delightful to the children, such rich fare didn't sit well with Maisey's digestion. She laid a hand on her stomach, concentrating on keeping down the meal.

Rob halted. "What's wrong?"

Maisey pulled in a deep breath of crisp autumn air. "I'll be all right."

He swept a glance over her. "You look green around the gills, if I may say so."

"You may not. That's an unattractive color to assign to a person, plus it's inaccurate. Fish gills are red."

"Which is probably how the expression came about. A green-gilled fish would be sick indeed."

Another wave of nausea swamped Maisey. She pushed all images of fish gills, green or otherwise, out of her head. "I'm sure it will pass. Let's keep going."

Rob's hand cupped her elbow. "You can put your feet up when we reach the cabin."

They stepped into the shadow of the cottonwood stand. Dark boughs met above their heads, weaving against the pewter sky. With the cold coming on, the leaves were stained orange. The breeze that cut through the grove hinted of winter's approach.

"Wait up!" Con's voice called from behind them.

Rob looked past her. "He sounds serious."

By mutual consent, they retraced their steps toward Rob's brother, who was hurrying toward them.

Rob slid an arm around Maisey. "Has something happened?"

Con stopped before them. "America's baby is coming."

"She seemed fine when we left." Rob shook his head. "How is she?"

"It's clear she's in pain."

"That fast?" Maisey drew her brows together. "I hope nothing is amiss."

"It may only be a short delivery, but I'm about to ride for the doctor. Bry and Shane are putting America to bed. Elsa is watching over the children in the parlor, but she has her hands full looking after so many. Will you come back?"

Rob sent Maisey an inquiring glance. "Are you up to returning?"

"I'm fine." She willed it to be so.

Rob scanned her face. "It wouldn't hurt to have Doc Bailey

examine you too."

Con left them at the back steps and strode around the corner of the house on the path to the barn. Dishes smeared with the remnants of chocolate cake were stacked on the kitchen counter, but the table was otherwise uncleared. Children's voices carried from the parlor but were soon hushed.

"I'll see if Shane needs anything." Rob passed through the doorway into the entrance corridor and out of sight.

Maisey surveyed the mess, then heaved a sigh and rolled up her sleeves. America often sacrificed for her. It was time to repay the favor.

Rob returned while she was scraping plates. "How are you faring?"

"The smell of chocolate is making me want to retch."

He guided her to a chair. "Sit there."

"Someone needs to clean the kitchen." She sank down anyway.

"I'm capable of pitching in when necessary." Rob rolled up his sleeves.

"I'll keep that in mind."

He grinned. "I have no doubt my words will come back to haunt me."

Rob had the kitchen in order by the time Doc Bailey arrived. He carried his bag down the hallway and turned aside as the door to Shane and America's bedroom opened. After an interval, Shane came into the kitchen. Bry followed behind him. Both of them looked the worse for wear. Shane wore a haggard look and a slightly bewildered expression. Bry was pale, and a crease had appeared between her brows.

Maisey bit back the inquiry she wanted to make. It was obvious from their faces that America was not doing well. She rushed to embrace Bry.

"She has to pull through." Shane sagged into a chair at the table.

Rob laid his hands on his cousin's shoulders. "Call upon that faith of yours, Preacher. I've seen it work wonders."

Con said nothing but lowered himself to the seat beside Shane.

Doc Bailey returned shortly. "It's a breach baby."

Bry sucked in an audible breath.

Maisey put her fist to her mouth.

Shane jumped to his feet. "Will my wife be all right?"

"She has every chance of pulling through. I think I can turn the baby." Doc Bailey laid a hand on Shane's shoulder. "Perhaps you would spend time in prayer."

Shane nodded.

Rob came to stand beside Shane. "I'll join you."

Con stood up. "Count me in."

Maisey nodded. She would pray also, in between helping Elsa put the children down for the night. She slipped from the room. The children were out of sorts, which was challenging but understandable. It was quite late before they were all in bed asleep.

Maisey and Elsa joined Rob with Shane and Con in the parlor. Bry was not present. After seeing her going in and out of America's bedroom tending to the doctor's requests, Maisey assumed Bry was assisting the doctor. The oil lamp above the bookcase cast a warm glow, but their faces were grim. "Any news?" Maisey whispered to Rob.

He shook his head.

She sank down on the sofa beside him. All Maisey wanted to do was sleep, but she sensed his need to support his cousin. She wouldn't ask to leave.

The clock's ticking filled the room, its repetition lulling her. Maisey leaned her head against the upholstery behind her and closed her eyes to ease their aching.

The chiming of the clock startled her awake. She sat upright. How long had she slept? The men sat in wakefulness, but Elsa slept in the chair beside Con.

Rob turned to Maisey. "I should take you home."

She shook her head. "No, let's stay."

"How are you feeling?"

The nausea had vanished. "Much better."

"I'm grateful for that."

An infant wailed from Shane and America's bedroom.

Shane sat taller. "Did you hear that?"

"I did indeed." Rob answered.

Maisey nodded, joy flooding her.

A while later the door opened, boots sounded in the hall, and Doc Bailey appeared in the doorway. Weariness etched his face but also a look of satisfaction.

Shane rose from his chair. "How are America and the baby?"

"Both are doing well and expected to recover. America is exhausted but happy. Go and greet your new daughter in her mother's arms."

A smile broke across Shane's face, and he rushed through the doorway.

Con rose. "My cousin has forgotten to thank you, Doc, but I'm sure he's grateful."

Elsa stirred at the sound of her husband's voice and opened her eyes.

Doc Bailey smiled. "I have no doubt of that."

Rob joined Con in the entrance with Doc Bailey. "Can we offer you a bed for the night? There's one going spare in our cabin."

"It's late, but I don't live far from here. I'd as soon make the journey home and sleep in my own bed. Thanks all the same."

After seeing Doc Bailey out, Rob returned to help Maisey to her feet. She rocked a little, taken by a bout of dizziness, and he caught her in his arms. "You said you were better, so I didn't ask the doctor to examine you."

"It's all right." Maisey smiled, having guessed what was wrong. It had been a long time since she'd carried Phoebe to birth. No wonder she'd forgotten the signs. She would see Doc Bailey to confirm her suspicions but wait until they returned to their own ranch to mention his potential fatherhood to Rob.

Author's Notes

Like the heroine of this book, I have experienced lost dreams and broken relationships. I had to give up my dream of writing the Montana Gold series after my agent queried publishers and came up empty-handed. God had a different plan, as I would learn. I am so thankful that He brought me together with Miralee Ferrell to bring these books to readers like you. My family has known the sorrow of estrangement but the reality of God's love. Much like Maisey, I have discovered that God gives beauty for ashes. If *The Forever Sky* delivers this truth to others, I am grateful.

Factual Historical Events in This Book

Chief Charlo and his wife, Margaret, actually existed. Chief Charlo took over leadership of the Salish tribe in 1870, after Chief Victor died. Like his father, Charlo prided himself on living in peace with the settlers. I included these words from Chief Charlo in this book: **"It was my father's boast that his hand had never in seventy years been bloodied with the white man's blood, and I am the son of my father."**

In later years, Chief Charlo's attitude shifted, and he expressed feelings of betrayal by the emigrants.

The diary of Major John Owens, proctor at Fort Owens, confirms the restlessness of the local tribe during Red Cloud's War.

In 1855, Chief Victor signed away his tribe's holdings in the Hell Gate Treaty. He had been led to believe that signing would limit encroachment and ensure his people's right to their ancestral lands.

The Salish tribe once gathered around St. Mary's Mission, which still stands today. Founded in 1841 by Jesuit priest Father De Smet, the mission was the first permanent settlement in Montana established by non-native people.

Join Janalyn Voigt's mailing list:
www.janalynvoigt.com/join-e-letter

Other places to connect:
Website: www.janalynvoigt.com
Facebook Author Page: www.facebook.com/JanalynVoigt

If you enjoyed this book, we'd love if you'd leave a review on any of the online sites that carry my books.

Book Club Questions

1. Could Rob have handled his decision to seek his fortune mining for gold differently to avoid hurting Maisey?

2. Have you ever felt small compared to a problem, as Phoebe did when she looked at the 'forever' sky?

3. Emma felt alone in the world even while isolating herself. How else could she have chosen to behave?

4. Rob learned that he couldn't find a way through life without God. In what ways have you learned the same lesson?

5. While America waited to hear that Shane and others she loved were safe, faith in God saw her through. Can you name a time when all you could do was pray?

6. Although Rob is admittedly clueless in his dealings with women, could he have tried harder to understand Maisey's feelings about his dealings with Emma?

7. Should Maisey have left for St. Louis without waiting for Rob?

8. Even as Maisey captured her dream of being reconciled to her family, it slipped from her grasp. God redeemed her desire in a way she didn't expect. Have you experienced something similar?

9. Emma felt she owed an apology to Felicity but decided it would do more harm than good. Can an apology be self-centered?

10. Which fears did Maisey have to work through, due to the traumatic experiences she had suffered?

Another Montana Story
from Janalyn Voigt!

Can't get enough Montana Gold? The next book is filled with surprises. The Montana Treasures series will follow the lives and loves of the Montana Gold children.

Upset with her parents after learning she is adopted, Liberty Hayes travels to St Louis searching for her biological father. What she discovers leaves her devastated.

Jake Buckthorn can't understand what's gotten into his childhood friend. Telling himself that his interest has nothing to do with his secret longing for Liberty, he rides off to bring her home.

Before Liberty can resolve her troubled relationships, she must reconcile with God. Only then can she open her heart to forgiveness and love.

Don't miss a single story. Join the Creative Worlds of Janalyn Voigt newsletter: http://janalynvoigt.com/author-newsletter